Other novels by Kris Lillyman

Thrillers

Bad Blood

World On Fire: Bad Blood Part II

Dance With The Devil

Perfect Day

Romantic Comedies

Jam Tops, The Fonz and The Pursuit of Cool

FINDERS KEEPERS

Kris Lillyman

For Netty, Scarlett and Dexter.

PROLOGUE

- 1 -

Berkshire, England 2003

By the time the party was over and the last of the stragglers had gone it was four in the morning but Peter Bearing, whose party it had been, was still clear-headed and focused. He, sipped a glass of ice cold Perrier as he wandered casually around his private gallery in his enormous home, trying to appreciate the great works that hung on the walls but, frankly, just not getting it. Peter was a refined, articulate and intelligent man but try as he might, art just didn't do it for him.

He was killing time as he waited for the staff to finish up and get off home before he went upstairs. Normally he would let them see themselves out but tonight, or this morning as it now was, he needed to be certain that the house was empty. For what he had planned, there could be no witnesses.

The gallery was sparsely decorated with just two very uncomfortable but extremely stylish black

1

leather sofas placed back to back on the polished, black marble floor in the centre of the large airy room. It had been designed to allow the ideal viewing experience, lots of open space in which to sit or stand and admire Peter's priceless collection.

It was comprised mainly of contemporary pieces, or 'modern art' as Peter rather disparagingly referred to it, by artists such as Pollock, Lichtenstein and Warhol. There was also a Matisse, which he thought was vile, a Monet, which was just about bearable, and a couple of extremely hideous Picasso's which Bearing just couldn't understand. There was a Lowry too which, in his considered opinion, might as well have been painted by a child. Hanging uncomfortably alongside these, and much to the chagrin of Peter's art advisor, he had a Rembrandt, a Vermeer and a Constable, which he thought of as 'proper art'. The advisor felt that even though these were masterworks, they did not sit well with the rest of the collection, giving it a haphazard appearance. Peter disagreed, if Rembrandt was considered 'haphazard' then the art world really was beyond his comprehension.

In truth, Peter didn't really care about any of the paintings or the names of the artists they were painted by for that matter. All he knew was that they were highly valuable, very sought after and, most importantly, his. And it pleased him very much to have things other people wanted.

Of course, no one from the party that night had been allowed into the gallery as this was reserved for only the most influential guests, those who could appreciate the value of the collection or those he was trying to impress. Mostly those he needed something from in return for his hospitality. Only one person fell loosely into that category tonight, but a look at Peter's paintings or indeed a weekend at his fabulous home wouldn't be enough to secure what he needed from that one. Other, more extreme methods were required for that. Bearing glanced at the shiny silver Breitling on his wrist and judged that by now, those methods should be well and truly underway.

The party had not been arranged for fun, not for Peter at least. It had been purely for business, the key part in a plot he'd been hatching for several years and tonight's entertainment had been for the sole purpose of achieving his goal. This was the moment when everything finally came to fruition.

He drank the remains of the glass of water, pressed his right palm against the small screen of the digital palm scanner by the door then, after hearing an approving 'beep', punched in his four digit security code. After that, he snapped off the light in the gallery and shut the thick metal door behind him as he entered the wide hallway that ran adjacent to it. He waited a second for the whir of the heavy-duty locking mechanism to kick in. A second 'beep' and three short red flashes of the tiny light above the handle told him the gallery was now completely secure.

The hallway was again very sparse with scrubbed wooden floors, plain white walls, conceptual leather seating and abstract sculptures. Very desirable pieces is how they had been described. Ugly monstrosities is how Peter saw them but again, they were highly valuable and greatly sought after, so he liked them.

The head of the catering company, who doubled as the head waiter for the evening, passed by and collected Peter's glass. "Nearly done now, sir," he said, "They're just finishing off in the drawing room and then we'll be off - shouldn't be long." Peter nodded his approval and the waiter went on his way.

Bearing gave the man and his team a little longer than had been estimated, just to be certain, but after ten minutes he took the stairs down to the kitchens to check that they had finished.

Years ago, the area 'below stairs' used to be the old staff quarters but only a couple of the small rooms had escaped the complete remodelling of the lower level when Peter took over the house. The huge kitchen had been entirely redesigned and modernised and now instead of staff quarters there was a full size swimming pool, a luxury spa and a private cinema that could seat over fifty people. The staff quarters, if ever any were required to stay, were now in the converted stable block at the back of the house. Modest accommodation but comfortable nonetheless.

However, Peter only hired staff by the event now, very few ever stayed the night, unless the occasion specifically required it and even then only those who were absolutely necessary such as maids and kitchen staff. However, Peter always hired the same people, from the same agency who had all been scrupulously checked out and who he paid very well to ensure their complete discretion.

The only permanent staff were the husband and wife team who stayed at the house whenever Peter wasn't using it, just to manage the day to day running of the place and the ten strong security force who had a permanent base in the grounds - even though the house itself had a state-of-the-art security system that made it as impregnable as Fort Knox.

"That's us done, sir. Goodnight!" Called the head waiter, who now had his white jacket off and his anorak on.

"Right. Thank you," said Bearing, "Goodnight."

"Goodnight, sir," hopefully see you next time." Said the waiter as Bearing locked the door after him.

Bearing's house was magnificent, built two centuries earlier in over three hundred acres of beautiful Berkshire countryside. Its landscaped gardens and lakes were breathtaking with a mile long driveway that meandered its way leisurely through the estate from the grand gated entrance to the grandly designed eighteenth century residence that stood regally at its end. On the outside the house was very much of its period, rich and exquisitely ornate, but on the inside it was a hi-tech, ultra modern palace with every luxury money could buy. No expense had been spared in creating the chic clinical lines and smoothly elegant curves that were a running theme throughout the highly contemporary inner space which made it an utterly breathtaking vision of style, design and elegance. The perfect advert for success, power and wealth that Bearing intended it to be.

The house had become Peter's after his father, Teddy, passed away seven years earlier. Back then, the place had been just another drab stately pile; an antique-filled throwback to the Georgian era it was built in. But, as soon as Teddy's funeral was over with, Peter brought in an architect who gutted and completely redesigned the place. The future was what Peter was concerned with, not the past.

But the house was not Peter's home. He actually lived in a fabulous townhouse in Mayfair that overlooked Hyde Park, with his young, soon to be ex-wife and their three pampered children who very rarely visited the house in Berkshire. Although most of the time Peter, himself, stayed a short distance away at his spectacular apartment in The City, either on his own or with one of a stream of mistresses.

The Berkshire house was primarily reserved for events, such as hunting, shooting and fishing weekends. It was where he entertained business associates, corporate fat cats and visiting leaders from various foreign states who could indulge themselves to their hearts content.

Peter's Palace, as the house had become known was a discreet place to play and Bearing laid everything on that his guests could ever need. It was not just the facilities or the fabulous food and drink that was on offer, but also women, or men too, if that was their preference - in fact whatever they desired.

But this particular weekend was for just one business associate by the name of Jonathan Wallace. Wallace had become a supremely irritating hurdle that stood in the way of Peter's meteoric rise to power and Bearing didn't like things getting in his way one little bit.

The party guests had been chosen purposely to complement Jonathan, there were none who would outshine him and none he would feel inferior to. The girls had been hand picked by Peter to cater specifically to Wallace's tastes and one in particular, who Bearing knew Jonathan could not resist, had been primed and paid to deliver exactly what was required. All of which Jonathan Wallace was completely ignorant of. He just assumed he was being wined and dined by a friend and colleague. A few drinks, a bit of relaxation and a nice party - ending the weekend on a high before returning to The City on Monday.

Back upstairs, in the main house, Peter now

made his way up the grand marble staircase to the first floor. He was thirty-five, good looking in an intellectual kind of way with brown hair and slate blue eyes. Tanned and fit, Bearing took good care of himself, he didn't drink excessively, didn't smoke, apart from the occasional cigar and was the product of an excellent education. He had a beautiful family and enough money for several lifetimes but for Peter none of that was enough. He wanted more. Much more.

At the top of the staircase, Peter paused for a moment to listen for the sound of any stray guests that may have escaped his watchful eye but there was only silence. He glanced out of the window, just to double check that the driveway was completely empty and the last of the revellers had indeed gone. The only cars still remaining were a Renault Clio and an Aston Martin Vanquish. The Clio belonged to the girl on Peter's payroll, the Aston to Jonathan Wallace, her companion for the evening.

Peter then carried on up to the second floor and walked along the wide landing to the farthest bedroom. Outside the door he listened again but once more heard nothing. He knocked softly and waited. A moment later the door opened and a striking blonde wearing very expensive, very sexy, green satin lingerie with stockings and garters ushered him in.

On the bed, next to her discarded Vera Wang

cocktail dress, lay Jonathan Wallace. He was completely naked, his flaccid penis as limp and lifeless as the rest of him.

"I trust he's just sleeping?" Bearing said.

"Like a baby," said the girl, her voice prim, very English public school. "He'll be out for hours darling - you could drop the atom bomb and he still wouldn't wake up."

Bearing made no reaction. "It all went to plan? No problems?" He asked.

"No, it was easy-peasie. I slipped the liquid you gave me into his whisky when he went to the loo and ten minutes later he was dead to the world."

"Not before—" Peter began.

"Oh, no. He managed that, darling - just - but I seriously doubt he'll have any memory of it. I certainly won't let's put it like that. He collapsed half way through so I just rolled him off and left him where he is."

"Good."

"Do we really need to carry on with the rest of it?" The girl asked quietly, "I mean, I've done my bit - he won't remember anything and I know what to say if anyone ever asks."

"Yes, we do" Bearing replied firmly. "He'll need to be totally convinced. To have no doubt about what he's done. He'll need to see evidence. You already know that and you've been paid very well."

"Well, yes, I suppose. It's just a bit frightening,

you know. You will be careful won't you? Like you promised - you won't hit me too hard - I mean, my face, well it's the first thing men see - it's my living darling, my fortune." She was clearly scared but knew she had entered into a wicked bargain for a very lucrative reward and there was no going back now.

Bearing looked at her. He understood exactly what Jonathan Wallace had seen in her; early twenties, fabulous figure, stunning looks and very upmarket in a really sexy kind of way. When she arrived at the party she could have easily passed for the nubile young daughter of a duke and duchess. Wallace would have had no idea that she was, in reality, a high priced whore. Peter had paid her enough to keep her in designer lingerie for years. But now she was going to earn it.

Bearing smiled, then picked up Jonathan Wallace's trousers, which had been discarded on the floor, and slid the soft leather belt from the loops before throwing the trousers back on the ground. He held the belt tightly with his hands about eighteen inches apart and tugged it twice to test its strength, hearing a rewarding whip-like crack in response. It would do very nicely indeed.

Still holding the belt, he walked over to the door and closed it as the girl looked on aghast. "Of course I'll be careful," he said, a wicked smile spreading across his face.

* * *

Forty-five minutes later, Bearing, breathing heavily and standing spent and sweaty above the girl, zipped his fly and re-buttoned his trousers. Then, being careful to leave as much blood on Jonathan's belt as possible, laid it down beside him on the bed.

Only then did Peter move away from the girl, who was trembling and terrified. "Stand up!" He demanded gruffly. But she made no movement and no reply. "Stand up," he said again, "Or I'll make you stand up. It's your choice."

The girl roused slightly, but still did not move. She felt weak, concussed, battered.

Bearing stepped angrily towards her but quickly she held her hands up, "No, please, I'll stand, I'll stand, I promise - just don't hurt me any more, please!" She implored. Her words were thick and slurred, her swollen lips were split and dripping blood.

Slowly she climbed to her feet and stood shakily in front of him, terrified. Her bra was torn, her knickers completely ripped off and her stockings severely laddered. There were strap marks on her legs, buttocks and arms along with large blue bruises.

"Come and stand under the light," he ordered and like a foal walking for the first time she staggered into the centre of the room.

Bearing went to the chest of drawers and pulled out an expensive Nikon SLR Camera, then turned and began taking photos of the girl, as if he were David Bailey at a fashion shoot.

He made sure he got close-ups of every bruise, whip mark, blemish and cut. He photographed all the blood and all the semen. The semen was his own but no-one would know that other than the girl. Certainly not Wallace who would have no desire to have it DNA tested.

With the camera whirring, Bearing made the girl bend over and touch her toes and then forced her to sit in a chair with her legs wide apart to ensure that he photographed all the lacerations on her private parts and the bite marks on her inner thighs made by his own teeth. Finally he photographed the girl's ripped and bloodied knickers which he draped over Jonathan Wallace's arm for dramatic effect.

As the dawn arrived, Peter finished his work and the girl grew stronger. With her strength a little glimmer of courage returned. "You're a bastard! You know that?" She said hoarsely.

"It has been said more than once," Bearing replied with a wry smile as he scrolled through the photographs in the camera's digital view finder, mentally making a note of the most compelling shots.

"I didn't agree to that. A couple of bruises is what we said. A light slap or two. Not that - definitely not that. Look at me!" Her lip started to quiver and her eyes flooded with tears but she held them back. "You've destroyed me. My nose is broken, one of my front teeth feels loose, I can hardly walk - I'm a wreck, for Christ's sake - everything hurts. How can I work? How can I earn money? Who'll want me now?"

"We had an agreement and you've been paid. That's all." Bearing didn't look at her as he spoke, she was inconsequential and their business was done.

"No!" She said. "That's not all and not what we agreed. That was over and above what we agreed by a very, very long way. I want more money. Another ten thousand, otherwise I'll go to the police and tell them exactly what you've done. And I'll have the money in cash, today, before I leave." The words were said with force but there was no real conviction behind them, no real intent and it was obvious.

Suddenly she had Bearing's full attention and his eyes fastened on hers in an intensely threatening manner. "Now, listen, my dear," he said, with cold steel in his steady, soft voice. "Listen very carefully. We had a deal for which you have been handsomely paid. You will not receive another pound, not another penny. If you ever - and I mean ever - mention my name or what has transpired here tonight or any part of our deal to the police or anyone then I'm afraid I will not be responsible for what is bound to happen to you. You see, whilst I am just an honest businessman I have associates who are far less gentle and far less understanding than me. In fact, the gentlemen I refer to are hardened mercenaries who kill for fun and would like nothing more than to track you down and silence you for good. It would be sport to them, nothing more. All I need to do is pick up the phone and ask, do you understand?"

What remaining colour the girl had in her face drained as she slowly nodded. She had no doubt whatsoever that he meant what he said and was more than capable of what he threatened.

"Are you sure?" Bearing asked, as I would hate for anything unfortunate to happen to you."

The girl nodded again. "Good," said Peter, "Then let's say nothing more about it."

"Alright," the girl said meekly.

"Now, with our business concluded, please feel free to use the shower. You must then get dressed and leave. After that I trust there will be no need for us to ever see each other again."

She nodded one last time, snatched up her dress and hurriedly hobbled off to the en-suite bathroom. A moment later Peter heard the shower running. He could also hear her sobbing deeply. Ten minutes after that the girl reappeared washed, dressed and with her hair brushed although she still looked as if she'd been in a car wreck, the bruises on her face were now in full bloom and her lips and nose were badly swollen. She was walking very stiffly, with a wide gait, the wounds between her legs and the welt marks on her buttocks caused by his belt had been made sore and angry by the hot water. But she had made herself clean, although she doubted she would feel properly clean ever again.

Bearing sat in an armchair by the window, the curtains open and the bright new morning shining in. She stopped short as she saw him, Jonathan Wallace was still out for the count on the bed and a trickle of remorse seeped into her brain. If Bearing could do what he had to her, what on earth had he in store for that poor soul she thought.

"All done?" Peter said brightly.

"Yes. Thanks," she said timidly.

"Good, then that's us done. Off you go - and remember, not a word."

"I'll remember. I promise." She said. Then after a pause she limped to the door and slipped silently out.

Peter watched from the window as several minutes later the girl climbed into her little Renault Clio and raced away from the house up the long driveway towards the main gates. He picked up the phone and buzzed security. "Open the gates, would you?" He said to the guard who answered, "A guest of mine is leaving and she's in rather a rush, so please do not detain her."

"Of course, sir," said the guard as Bearing replaced the handset.

He then turned his attention to Jonathan Wallace who was ridiculously oblivious to all that had transpired whilst he was sleeping and how very different his life was going to be when he eventually awoke.

Bearing smiled.

* * *

It was midday by the time Jonathan finally awoke. Very slowly he opened his eyes and almost immediately became aware of the pounding headache. "Christ," he thought, "How much did I bloody drink last night?" He was not usually a big drinker, the odd glass of wine with a meal perhaps, a couple of whiskies if he was out with friends, but not much as whisky made him bad tempered and irritable. He was not a good drunk which is why he rarely partook. But he must have downed a few last night because this headache was something else.

He lay there for a few minutes more before attempting to move and when he did the pain intensified. "Jesus!" He groaned aloud. "What the hell was I drinking?"

Still lying flat, Jonathan glanced slowly about him, trying to ascertain where he was. He was thirty-four but looked quite a bit younger. The strawberry blonde hair and fresh face giving him a boyish appearance and his good nature and friendly personality making him seem even more youthful. He was sharp and intelligent although not particularly worldly, but people generally liked him which greatly helped his acceptance within The Firm. At least with all but one of the board members.

Jonathan blinked, trying to focus, the room he was in was big and modern with large windows and decorated in the minimalist style. Then he remembered. He was at Peter's Palace. He was there for the weekend, to try and build bridges with his associate whose attitude towards him of late had been somewhat prickly.

Last night there was a party. But did he attend? Yes, yes, he did, it was slowly coming back. It was a good party from what he remembered, although it was all very fuzzy. There was a girl, he thought. Yes, that's right, very attractive, blonde, very striking and just my type. But what had happened to her? Then it came back, or at least flashes of it did. They were chatting he remembered, she had a lovely smile and a really infectious laugh. They kissed, he was sure of it. They were upstairs in this bedroom, kissing. She took off her dress. He recalled that she was wearing green satin underwear and stockings with garters, very sexy. He could then picture her on top of him, but the image was blurry. He was sure that they had made love, certain of it, yet he couldn't actually remember it. 'Dammit!' he thought, 'Why can't I remember anything else!' Then it occurred to him that she might still be there, maybe she was in the bathroom or downstairs having breakfast. He hoped so as he would really like to see her again.

'Ah, breakfast,' he thought, 'I'd better force myself to get up, Peter's going to think I'm a terrible house guest." He lifted his hand to rub the sleep from his eyes and a piece of cloth that had been lying on his arm slipped onto his face. He lifted it up and held it away from him to see what it was and saw immediately that it was a pair of green satin and lace knickers, identical to those that his elusive lady friend had been wearing last night. They had clearly been ripped off and discarded. 'Wow!' Thought Jonathan, 'did I do that?' He smiled. 'It must have been a good night." However, he then noticed what looked like a spattering of blood on the material and his smile was replaced by a curious expression.

Jonathan slowly sat up, his head banging like a drum, but the headache was soon forgotten as he looked down at himself, immediately seeing he was actually covered in blood spatters as if he had measles. Dried evidence of the sex he had with the girl was caked and matted in his pubic hair, confirming that they had, in fact, made love. Then he looked around him and saw that the bed was also stained with blood and speckled with dried semen.

Then he saw the belt. It was thick and gooey with partially dried blood. The buckle too was covered with it. Gingerly he picked it up and it left a thin red stripe on the bedclothes, like a long smear of paint and Jonathan, horrified, dropped it again quickly.

What the hell had happened? What in God's name had he done?

Clutching desperately at straws he thought that maybe the blood was his, perhaps he had been injured in some way, or something inside him had ruptured or burst but after hurriedly checking himself he could find nothing and apart from the banging in his head he felt no pain.

Then his eyes fell on the empty whisky glass and he remembered the girl. He thought of how he got when he drank too much whisky; irritable, morose, angry even but never aggressive. At least not previously. But had the drink made him aggressive last night? Had it made him violent? Had he somehow harmed that poor girl?

His heart started beating faster as the panic he was already feeling threatened to overwhelm him. And then the bedroom door opened and Peter Bearing strode confidently into the room.

"Ah, Jonathan, old man, I see you're awake. We're in a spot of bother, I'm afraid, as you've probably realised from your appearance."

"Oh, Christ, Peter, please tell me what I've done," Jonathan blurted, tears filling his eyes, "I haven't hurt anyone have I? That young girl I was with, the pretty one, she's alright isn't she? Tell me, Peter, please - for God's sake tell me everything's okay."

Bearing smiled inwardly, this was going to be even easier than he had hoped.

- 2 -

San Francisco, California, 2003

Elizabeth slowly raised her head from her pillow, the mascara from last night's tears still staining her pale cheeks and the argument with Roger still ringing in her ears. The small cut above her left eye where the wedding ring had struck her - which he had flung at her - was sore and stinging. But the gesture itself had hurt more.

Her head ached as she gently touched the tiny strip of broken skin, about a centimetre long, just above her carefully sculpted eyebrow. She winced, "Ouch!" she exclaimed, "Goddamit." It was going to scar for sure. That son of a bitch.

She was in their bedroom, fully dressed, wearing the blouse and skirt from the night before, having cried herself to sleep after their huge fight. The most violent and vitriolic so far.

Roger had stormed out. He had driven off into the night, drunk, high and angry, the stench of another woman's perfume still lingering on his clothes. Elizabeth had no clue as to where he was now - probably waking up in a bar or in jail or in the arms of one of his nubile young groupies, she did not know and she no longer cared.

The marriage was not yet a year old but already it was in tatters. Roger's womanising, his drug and alcohol abuse had fractured it beyond repair and whilst Elizabeth had tried desperately to make it work he had not.

Their romance had been quick, the attraction instant. He was twenty-five with looks to die for, the lead guitarist in an up-coming indie band which was starting to get noticed and she was a twenty-three year old knockout studying fashion and working as a part-time model. A matched couple, at least on paper.

But there had never been true love Elizabeth realised now. Lust and infatuation perhaps but not love. Roger was too self centred, too selfish to commit to anyone and she was too dedicated to her studies and her family to follow him from gig to gig and from party to party. She also realised, much too late, that her family's money had been a big attraction for him. The upscale apartment they now lived in and the classic Ferrari Daytona he now drove were paid for by her. So was the antique Gibson he now played, which he had begged her for in return for a few more nights at home. But he had welshed on the deal and she had ended up seeing him even less.

It was over. Last night was the final straw. Not least because of the thrown ring which had struck her hard on the temple and the complete lack of remorse shown afterwards. But also because he had not even tried to deny sleeping with other women. Furthermore, his drinking and drug-taking were spiralling out of control. He was living the rock star life style on her allowance and she had finally had enough. Her father and brother had warned her but she had refused to listen. Her foster brother had also tried to talk some sense into her but again she had ignored the advice.

Soon enough she was going to have to call her father's attorney and instruct him to begin divorce proceedings but not yet. She did not want to burden her father with anything else for the time being as he had already had a terrible week with the resignation of her brother, Jonathan, from the family firm.

Jonathan had been caught up in a horrible scandal involving a young woman whom he had supposedly raped and beaten. The incident had allegedly occurred at the country home of another partner of the firm, Peter Bearing. Bearing had apparently paid off the girl, buying her silence. He had then promised not to mention the matter again on the understanding that Jonathan resign from The Company. Even though Bearing supposedly had extremely incriminating photographs that supported the allegations, Elizabeth didn't believe a word of it. Her brother was undoubtedly being set up, if not why would Bearing have taken photographs? Besides, Jonathan was gentle, kind and wouldn't hurt anyone.

Elizabeth's father, Wendel Wallace, also suspected Bearing of orchestrating the whole thing, utterly convinced that it was all a sham, a complete fabrication. Bearing was a snake who had long wanted rid of both Jonathan and him and would stop at very little to make it happen. However, Jonathan was unable to prove his innocence and the mud would stick unless he did the honourable thing for the good of the firm. It was a despicable manoeuvre on the part of Bearing but Jonathan and her father had been powerless to prevent it and now her brother was out in the cold. Shamed, slandered and broken. Her father, still reeling from the hostility shown by Bearing and under an enormous amount of stress brought on by the whole situation, also knew that his head was next on the block.

Elizabeth had been desperately worried about both her father and brother all week and Roger had been less than sympathetic. In fact he couldn't have cared less. Rather than give her comfort and support he had gone out on a three day bender and had only come home late last night, completely wasted and stinking of perfume. She had then challenged him about the other women and he had admitted his infidelity, telling her to 'lighten up' and saying it was 'no big deal', which was how the fight started.

She had little doubt that he would be back at some stage as he relied too much on her money and when he did she would make an attempt to talk to him about a separation. This would possibly spark another fight but they could not go on like this as it was slowly driving them both insane.

However, her immediate plan was to take a long shower, put on a nice dress and go visit her mother, like she did every other Sunday. No matter what had happened in the last twenty four hours or indeed the last week, nothing would keep her from her weekly trip. She got up and walked to the bathroom and was shocked by the image she saw staring back at her in the large mirror over the basin. She looked dreadful, like she had gone a couple of rounds with Mike Tyson. She had a black-eye, with dark purple bruising around the socket and a trickle of dried blood drawing an unsteady red line from the cut above her eyebrow to halfway down her cheek. Her long, silky brown hair was a wild mess and her normally healthy tanned complexion was pale and sallow, the worry of the last week etched into her drawn features. Real Rocky-Horror she thought.

Elizabeth turned on the shower before stripping off her clothes, her young body, firm and toned, with long graceful legs, flat, tight stomach and firm, shapely breasts that most women would kill for. Briefly she looked at herself in the mirror, trying to avoid looking at her bruised and cut face. She was not blind, she knew she was attractive as scores of men had told her so since she was just a girl, but she had only succumbed to the charms of one. She knew she was desirable, sexy even, yet that clearly wasn't enough for Roger. She had so desperately hoped that it would be, that he would see the error of his ways, quit the womanising, the drugs and the partying - Christ, she had given him enough chances but now she had to face facts. It was over. Screw him. Time to move on.

She put a hand in the stream of water, it was getting nice and hot, the steam starting to fill the large glass enclosure, almost ready to wash last night's troubles away. Then, on impulse, before stepping in, she picked up the phone which hung on the Italian wall tiles beside the entrance, sat down on the toilet seat and punched in Ronny's number. It rang several times before her foster brother picked up. "Hello?" he said groggily.

"Oh, Christ, Ronny, I'm so sorry, I completely forgot it was the middle of the night in England - did I wake you?"

"Hi, Elizabeth, not quite the middle of the night but, yeah, it's early. Really early. Thanks for the wake up call."

"Sorry, Ronny, I'll let you get back to sleep."

"No, no. Don't worry about it, I'm awake now. You alright? Everything okay?"

"Yeah, sorry. I didn't realise the time. Just checking in. Worrying about Jonny I guess. Is he okay?"

"Truth is I don't know," said Ronny, yawning, "I'm pretty worried myself. He's really down, Elizabeth, this has really hit him hard. That bastard has just ripped poor Jonathan's life away, all his self-esteem. I wish to God I knew what to do. I was with him until late last night, he can't get over it, can't think about anything else.

I'm more certain than ever that Bearing is behind everything and that none of it was Jonathan's fault and I know, given time, I can prove it, but he won't listen. It's like he's broken and nothing I say can fix it.

I offered to stay over but he insisted that I came home. I'm going round this morning again though to check on him."

"That's good, Ronny," said Elizabeth, "I wish I was there with you. I'm sure Jonny could do with us both right now. Dad too. How's he?"

"I'm sorry to say that he's not good either. Worried sick about Jonathan, concerned for his own position at the firm - convinced that Bearing's trying to get rid of him too."

"You think he is?" Elizabeth asked.

"I'm sure he is. Peter Bearing is a cold, calculating bastard. He's got rid of Jonathan and now his sights are well and truly set on Dad. It's only a matter of time, Elizabeth, I tell you. Bearing's devious. Nothing will stand in his way not even Wendel Wallace. Dad needs to be really careful."

"Jesus, Ronny. What a mess. How can one man cause all this heartache?"

"He won't get away with it, Elizabeth. I promise you. One day, some how, he'll pay for what he's doing to our family."

"I hope so," replied Elizabeth. "I really do."

"Anyway, enough about all that," said her foster brother, "How about you - are you alright - and Roger?"

"Yeah, well, not really I guess, but I'll tell you about it some other time - you've got enough on your plate, Ronny, without me adding to it."

"Hey, don't worry about it. I've got a big plate, I can handle it. Now what's up? That spoilt rock star not treating you right?"

"Just a fight. I'm fine. Honest. I'll tell you about it some other time, promise."

"Sure? I can come over there and kick his backside you know, if that's what you want - just say the word and I'll be there."

"I know, Ronny, thanks. You're a good brother."

"Yeah, well, that's what big brothers are for you know."

"I know," said Elizabeth, wishing she could tell him about last night, desperate for his strength and advice, but no matter what he said, he really did have enough on his plate and he couldn't be her rock at the moment because others needed him more. "You just take good care of Jonny."

"I will. I promise."

"I know, Ronny. Goodnight.

"Hey," replied her foster brother, "That's not my name you know. I'm grown up now and no one calls me that anymore."

"I know," said Elizabeth with a smile, "But I like it."

"Yeah. Me too," he laughed. "Goodnight, baby sis."

"Night." The line clicked and he was gone. Elizabeth suddenly realised that the room was full of steam and the shower was still running. She stood up, hung up the phone and stepped into the hot, cleansing water.

* * *

The drive up to Napa was cathartic, the beautiful scenery helping to ease the turmoil in Elizabeth's mind. She had the top down on her Mercedes and the wind was rushing through her long dark hair, blowing away the painful memories of the previous night. The sun was warm and revitalising on her face, the cut on her temple concealed by make-up and a pair of huge Dior sunglasses.

She thought that maybe a trip to England to be with her father and brother in their time of crisis might help. Jonathan had been dreadfully upset by what had happened, his life now in ruins and his reputation seriously damaged. Her father, too, was not the man he once was and had taken Jonathan's forced resignation very badly. The company that he had helped build, that he had hoped to pass down to his son had all but destroyed him. Or, more accurately, the man who had so carefully stage-managed Jonathan's downfall had.

A trip to England would not only give Elizabeth the opportunity to visit her much loved father, brother and foster brother but would also give her and Roger some breathing space and some much needed time apart. It made perfect sense.

By the time she reached Napa her mind was made up and as soon as she had finished here today she would pack a bag and get on the first available flight to London. But first she would visit her mother.

The Green Acre Care Home for Mental Wellbeing was just an hour out of San Francisco nestling in a shady valley circled by tall trees and pretty wild flowers. It was an idyllic spot for a care home; quiet, scenic and restful. If someone couldn't find peace there then it was unlikely they would find it anywhere. It also had the best facilities available and a staff of expertly trained doctors and nurses on hand twenty-four seven.

Elizabeth always came up here alone, she enjoyed the peace and quiet and the slower pace of life. Life with Roger was lived at full speed so the weekly slow-down did her good.

Ella Wallace was a beautiful woman in her early sixties. She was tall and elegant with fine, delicate features and long white hair that was plaited down her back in a thick braid. She had been diagnosed with dementia almost ten years earlier which had been an awful blow not just to her but to the whole family. Ella had been a doctor so she was well aware of the ramifications and had tried to prepare the then teenage Elizabeth. But in actuality, nothing could have prepared her for what she now witnessed every Sunday.

From the stoop of the terrace, Elizabeth saw her mother sitting in the shade of a large oak tree and from that distance she looked just like 'Mom'. But it was close up where the change was most apparent, the lack of recognition and the blank expression as every weekend Elizabeth re-introduced herself to the woman who knew her better than any other. It was a killer and ripped her heart in two every time but occasionally, just occasionally there was a spark of recognition and very briefly, in those wonderful moments, her Mom returned.

Strangely, whenever Elizabeth's father visited from England, which he tried to do as often as his work would allow, Ella always knew him, as if she had been waiting there especially for him. Their marriage had been good and their love strong but it was far from a conventional relationship.

Before the dementia took her, Ella worked at the UCSF Medical Center and was firmly based in San Francisco, whereas Elizabeth's father, Wendel, whilst a San Franciscan by birth, was based mostly in England where his company's head office was located. Ella kept Elizabeth with her whilst Jonathan and her foster brother both lived in England with Wendel.

It was strange and complicated to an outsider but for Ella and Wendel it somehow worked. As a child Elizabeth spent her summers in England and at regular intervals throughout the year her father and brothers visited her in California. To her it was the most natural thing in the world. Then her mother was diagnosed with dementia and all their lives slowly changed. The disease did not claim her instantly but gradually crept in over a period of time, stealing their mother away bit by bit until at last only fragments of the true Ella remained, only surfacing in all too fleeting vignettes.

Elizabeth realised now that her marriage to Roger had just been a method of avoiding what was happening with her mother. But it had not worked, it had not numbed the pain or the sorrow or deep feeling of loss, indeed, it had only heightened it.

With trepidation, Elizabeth made her way across the beautifully cut lawn to the bench under the oak tree upon which her mother, Ella, sat, dearly hoping that today was one of the good days, that she would be visiting Mom as opposed to just an elegant, rather confused old lady. But as Elizabeth approached, she knew it was a forlorn hope. Ella was just staring blankly at her as she neared, her daughter completely unfamiliar to her.

Elizabeth smiled as she arrived at the bench and warily sat down beside her. "Hi, Mom," she said brightly. Her mother, clearly horrified by the close proximity of this 'stranger,' gazed at her with fear-filled eyes. "How are you today?" Elizabeth continued, "You look really pretty."

Ella was rigid with fright, her eyes wide with absolute terror, then suddenly, quite unexpectedly, she lashed out with her fist and caught Elizabeth hard on her cheek bone, directly under the same eye as the cut. Then she lashed out again with her other fist, this time catching Elizabeth a glancing blow on the chin. "Fuck off, leave me alone you bitch - whoever you are, whoever you work for - I'm not coming with you, you can't take me. Fuck off, fuck off. FUCK OFF!" The use of foul language had became more frequent as the dementia took greater hold. Very rarely before her illness did Ella swear.

Every time Ella cursed she got louder and every time she struck out again. One blow had knocked the sunglasses that were perched on Elizabeth's head onto the ground and two others had hit her shoulders before she managed to grab Ella by the wrists to stop the barrage. But the moment she did so, her mother began to scream maniacally.

"It's okay, Mom, it's okay. Please, it's me, I'm your daughter. Please not today, I could really do with your help I need you." Pleaded Elizabeth but it was to no avail the screams just got louder and Ella became increasingly more hysterical.

"I don't have a fucking daughter you lying fucking bitch!" Her mother squealed as two orderlies came rushing over to help. "You're a liar, a goddamn lying whore!"

Elizabeth stood up, treading on her sunglasses and breaking them, utterly shaken by what had just happened as the orderlies tried to calm Ella. The swearing had happened before but the insults and the violence were all new and horrible to witness. Before today, her mother had never struck her, barely ever even raised her voice let alone a hand.

Elizabeth, forcing back the tears, kept trying to explain who she was. But Ella would not have it and eventually the orderlies had to take her back to the familiarity of her room to try and settle her.

Elizabeth remained on the bench alone, her heart full of sadness. With trembling hands she took out a cigarette and lit it, as the tears finally came. She coughed as the first drag of smoke hit the back of her throat. She was only an occasional smoker, but today she felt as if she needed the comfort of it. But it didn't help and as she coughed again she stubbed it out. "Dammit!" she said aloud. She missed her Mom so much.

How Elizabeth wished she could talk to her like she used to, to seek her wisdom and her counsel.

The old Ella would have known what to do about Roger. She would have taken one look at the cut on Elizabeth's temple and told her to leave him. Then she would probably have found her wayward son-in-law and given him a peace of her mind. She would also have known how to console Jonathan and reassure Wendel. Furthermore she would know how to deal with this unscrupulous and highly ambitious partner that was so hell bent on removing them from the firm. But sadly Ella could do none of these things as her mind was no longer her own.

Elizabeth sat on the bench for a while longer trying to compose herself. It had been an unpleasant end to an emotional week but eventually, feeling drained of energy, she climbed back into the Mercedes and reluctantly headed back to the city.

She had been on the road for less than ten minutes when a call came into her cell. She saw the caller ID and smiled, it was Ronny, the very man she needed. At last a friendly voice to comfort her. She flipped open the phone and said, "Hey, there, you. I'm so pleased you called. I've had a terrible day."

"Hi, Elizabeth," said Ronny, uncharacteristically solemn. "I'm afraid I'm not going to make it any better. I've got some very bad news."

"Oh, God, What?" Said Elizabeth, "That bastard

hasn't tried to get rid of Dad now has he?"

"I'm afraid it's worse than that."

"Don't say he's actually done it - that Dad's had to resign too?"

"No. He's not had to resign, Elizabeth. I'm afraid I don't know how else to say this but - I'm so, so sorry - he's dead. Dad's dead and–" the voice on the end of the line cracked with emotion, "And so is Jonathan."

Upon hearing the words, Elizabeth felt nauseous and her head began to swim, her vision blurred as darkness suddenly came over her. As she blacked out with shock, the Mercedes, travelling at over fifty miles an hour, careered off the road, bumping unchecked over the rough grassy verge and crashing through a mile marker and on through a fence into a field full of grape vines. The car eventually came to a halt about thirty feet in, stopped by a tangled mass of wrecked vines. Elizabeth was slumped over the wheel, the voice on the phone, which was now laying in the foot well, shouting to her over and over again, but she was oblivious.

* * *

In her hospital bed, two days later, Elizabeth was nursing a broken leg and some very bruised ribs, but that was all secondary to the pain she felt in her heart. She had spoken again to her extremely concerned foster brother who was relieved to hear her voice and after making certain that she was up to it, he told her in more detail what had happened.

Jonathan, shamed and ruined and unable to prove his innocence had taken his own life. He had been found hanging in his bathroom. Upon hearing the news of his beloved son's suicide, Wendel, Elizabeth's father, suffered a massive heart attack and had died in the ambulance on the way to the hospital.

The loss of both her father and brother on the same day, within hours of each other, was unbearable and as Elizabeth lay in her bed grieving, she knew the blame for their deaths lay squarely at the feet of that greedy, unscrupulous partner who had framed Jonathan. Peter Bearing.

PART ONE

Chapter 1

He had been asleep for only about an hour when the harsh beep, beep, beep of the alarm woke him. Groggily he threw out a hand and slammed it down on the LED clock, his fingers quickly finding the button to turn off the infernal din before his head burst.

Jake Sawyer had only slept sporadically throughout the night, half an hour here, ten minutes there but he certainly hadn't gotten a full night as he was too anxious to sleep. Today was too big a day, too important. His whole future was riding on it.

He hadn't really been tired during the night, as his mind was too active, mentally rehearsing what he was going to say and how he hoped it would all play out. But, of course, now he was tired. That last hour he must have fallen into a very deep sleep and the harsh beeping of the alarm had violently shaken him out of it.

Slowly he sat up and as he threw off the duvet the cold of the morning hit him immediately. It was freezing but he stood and pulled on his boxers and an old t-shirt, then grabbed up his towelling dressing gown and quickly slipped it on, wrapping it tightly around himself, shivering as he did so. He stuffed his feet into a decrepit pair of sheepskin slippers as he stumbled over to the window and pulled open the curtains. Momentarily he was blinded by the pure white of the morning. Where he had expected to see spiky brown trees, dull green grass and the row of drab grey houses opposite, he saw instead a winter wonderland. Everything that had been so ugly the night before had suddenly been beautified by a light dusting of snow. But flakes were still falling and the sky looked fit to burst with a lot more. "Shit!" said Jake aloud. "Just what I need."

Jake lived alone now in the cheap, rented flat. None of the furniture was his, not even the bed. The only things that belonged to him were the few clothes in the half empty wardrobe, a laptop, a mobile phone and a few photographs of his children which he had dotted around the place in mis-matched frames. Everything else had either been taken by his estranged wife or sold to keep his failing business afloat, including the family home and car.

But today, all that was going to change. Today was going to be his salvation, his and Angie's and Zack's and Poppy's. Today was the day when he was going to turn it round and when all their lives would reboot. Today the crushing, unrelenting weight of debt and worry would finally be lifted. The new contract was certain, in the bag, needing nothing more than Jake's artistic signature along the bottom before the first, desperately needed instalment was transferred into his business account, and then he could breath again. He'd even planned to take Angie and the kids out to Pizza Hut for a celebratory meal. Nothing fancy, just enough to prove to Angie that things had changed. That he was back on top. A success, just like before. When she loved him. He could show her, prove to her, that he finally had a way to get out of debt.

The two year contract, putting together a monthly magazine would not only give them a fresh start it would also give him the time he needed to rebuild his business, to win other contracts and new accounts. A vital shot in the arm.

Admittedly it was not the most creative work, but it was regular and it was for Plancom, one of the biggest companies in Europe. Not some small little company with no budget, but a huge corporation with massive resources. Which meant no problems getting paid and right now, that was all that mattered. A safe account with a safe income.

Jake had to pitch for the job. His company, Sawyer Design, was up against two others - both larger than his which was, essentially a one-man-band. But even so, Jake knew the contract was his. The creative director of the magazine, Bob Hart, was an old friend and ex-colleague of his and he had guaranteed, with a nudge and a wink over a pint the previous week, that Jake's would be the winning pitch.

The contract was being awarded today, in Manchester, and Jake's signature, he had been told, was just a formality.

All he had to do was get to Manchester, a two hour drive away in normal conditions, but with an inch of snow on the ground that could easily turn in to three or four.

It was now 7am. The meeting was at 4pm. That meant he had to be on the road by twelve at the latest. No problem, all he had to do was call in at the office to grab his portfolio and he could get off, just take a slow, steady drive up, no sense in risking anything as the meeting was far too important.

Bracing himself, Jake stripped and jumped into the tepid, spluttering shower in the small, dank bathroom of his one bedroom flat, wishing more than ever that it was the hot powerful stream in the spacious wet-room of his old family home and that Angie was downstairs waiting for him with a nice cup of tea and a couple of slices of toast. Just like she used to be before he went off to work.

"Soon," he said to himself as he scrubbed the grogginess away, "Let's just get today done and dusted and then everything will be fine." Jake's biggest hope was that he and Angie would set up home together again, in a nice area, with a nice school for the kids. He didn't ever let himself think, for fear of believing it, that she was, in fact, gone for good.

Jake was thirty-three but looked much older. His glasses were out-dated, newer, trendier ones were an unnecessary expense. His beard was bushy and his sandy hair long and unkempt, both were flecked with grey. Once he had been supremely fit, a school boxing champion - he even had a black-belt in karate somewhere. Now though he was pudgy and out of shape. Exercise was a thing of the past, something that happy people did in their spare time. Once he had girls queuing at the door, now they didn't even look twice. It was not hard to see why.

Jake could barely look at himself in the mirror as he brushed his unruly wavy hair. He should really have had it cut but twenty quid for a haircut - were they kidding? Hair-cutting was just one other thing that Angie used to do. He hadn't had to go to a barbers for years - the last time it cost him less than a fiver, which was sometime back in the nineties.

By the time he was dressed and ready to leave the snow was coming down harder but he didn't even own an overcoat any more. And he was wearing his one and only suit. A smart blue Armani which was about the only thing of value he had left in his wardrobe. That and the shiny black Paul Smith loafers he had on - which were only worn on very special occasions.

Jake looked at the skies and then at the icy driveway, not wishing to spoil his suit and shoes, but the car was only a few feet away so it shouldn't be too bad. The car was an old, second hand Mondeo badly in need of a service, but a car nonetheless and dry too, with a working heater.

He made a dash for the car and got to it without slipping over. Jumping quickly inside, he shut the door and thrust the key into the ignition, wanting to get the heater on as soon as possible as his hands were already like ice.

There was a horrible wheezing sound as the engine slowly turned over then nothing. "Bollocks!" Jake said. "Not today, please not today!"

He tried again and the same thing happened. Then again, but this time it just clicked. "Fuck!" Jake yelled. Then he composed himself, trying to remain calm. "Okay, okay," he said. "It's just cold. No need to panic. Give it a minute."

Half an hour later the car still wouldn't start. He'd tried then waited, tried then waited again, but still nothing. It was now 8.15am and the pressure was building.

Jake had no breakdown cover but he'd phoned several garages and recovery services anyway. They were all extremely busy due to the weather and could not get to him for at least several hours. No good, the clock was still ticking.

Jake decided that a hire car would be the answer. It would wipe him out financially but he had to get to Manchester whatever the cost.

He rang three before he found one that could help him. Everyone it seemed had the same problem. All he needed was his driving license, last month's unpaid electricity bill and his passport as proof of identity. After collecting all three, he set off as quickly as he could to the nearest bus stop a quarter of a mile away and stood there for fifteen minutes in his best suit and shoes until the shuttle bus turned up. By the time he sat down he was soaking wet and frozen to the bone.

The bus was slow and so was the traffic, the weather getting steadily worse as the morning went on. But he finally reached the car hire depot, after yet another long walk from where the bus dropped him off, by 10.15am.

Using the three forms of identity, he hired himself a BMW 4x4, paying the £300 rental fee by cheque, knowing full well that it would undoubtedly bounce if he was not awarded the contract. Fortunately he knew that wasn't going to happen.

The BMW was far too pricey but it was the only 4x4 they had and in this weather it was what he needed to guarantee his safe arrival in Manchester. It was worth it too because it carved through the snow without so much as a slip.

By now though, Jake was absolutely freezing. His suit was soaking and his shoes were ruined. He'd have to go back to the flat and change. Quickly. But the BMW was well up to the task and he arrived back in no time. He shot upstairs and changed into a pair of clean jeans, a denim shirt, his old corduroy sports jacket and a knitted brown tie. He changed into some fresh warm socks and slipped his feet into his trusty tan brogues. It was a much more casual look than he had originally intended but at least he was still reasonably smart and looked suitably 'arty' which many people expected from someone in his profession, so he could carry it off quite easily he felt.

It was 11.15am by the time he was back in the car and on the road. Still forty-five minutes ahead of schedule. Warm, dry and in a very nice, very reliable 4x4. After calling by his office to get his portfolio he was on his way at last. It was 11.30am.

However, by now there was over two inches on the ground and it was becoming pretty treacherous even on the main roads. The gritters were out but they were fighting a losing battle.

By the time he was on the motorway traffic was almost at a stand still with the roads getting ever more worse. Slowly he inched his way towards Manchester, the time ticking steadily away. It was absolute mayhem on the roads, broken down and abandoned vehicles littering the motorway and cars skidding and slipping about endlessly. Even the

BMW skidded a few times but in four-wheel drive there was never any danger of Jake getting stuck. It was the other cars holding him up, not his. But still the snow kept falling.

By 2.30pm he was still only a third of the way to Manchester and with hope giving way to desperation he knew, finally, that there was no chance of him making the four o'clock meeting.

There was nothing for it but to call Bob Hart and explain the situation.

But when Jake called Plancom and asked to speak to Bob, he was told that Bob Hart no longer worked for them. Bob Hart, it seemed, had been 'let go' along with his PA.

With a sense of rising panic, Jake called Bob on his mobile to find out what was going on.

"It's true, mate. The bastards fired me this morning." Said Bob. "Someone told 'em that me and Julie have been having an affair and they sacked us both there and then. Instant dismissal. I can't bloody believe it."

"But you're a director, Bob," Jake said, "Surely they can't just get rid of you as easy as that?"

"Director in name only I'm afraid, mate. It was just a fancy title to go with my fancy salary, but I had no shares. Still, I've got a bit put by so I think me and Julie might go away for a bit. Australia, Thailand - maybe Bhali, I've always fancied that, seeing a bit of the world. Julie's up for it so I reckon it'll be a laugh.

49

Every cloud, mate, as they say."

"Yeah, sure, Bob, that's good," Jake said, "But what about the contract? What do I do about that?"

"Not my job now, Jake, sorry. I 'spect bloody Tess will be in charge of it."

"Tess? Who's Tess - do I know her?" said Jake, trying to hide the desperation in his voice.

"Tess fuckin" Brennan, cold-hearted bitch. If you'd met her you'd certainly remember her. Bloody man hater - except for the bosses of course, and she crawls all up their arses whenever she can. I reckon she's the one who shopped Julie and me. Can't prove it though, but I'm pretty sure it was her."

"Do you think she'll still sign off on the contract?" Jake's heart was in his mouth as he waited anxiously for the answer.

"Can't honestly say mate, but I wouldn't count on it," Bob said. "Best thing you can do is get there as quick as you can and try to get on her good side - not that she's got one."

"Yeah, but Bob, do you think–" Jake began.

"Look, sorry, Jake, but it's been a bit of a traumatic day what with one thing and another," Bob interrupted, "And truthfully mate, I've really got to get going and I've just about had enough of Plancom for the rest of my life - so, good luck with everything and I'll speak to you when I get back from wherever, okay? I'll let you know if I hear anything but I'm persona non grata now, so I can't promise."

That was pretty much the extent of the call and as Jake hung up he could feel the panic wash over him. Tess Brennan. Cold-hearted bitch. Man hater. Jake had never met her but he had to call her, appeal to her better nature, explain that he was going to be unavoidably late because of the snow. Maybe she was not as bad as Bob had said. Surely he was just bitter.

Jake rang, but he couldn't get passed Tess's PA. "Ms Brennan is not available but if you'd like to leave a message...."

Of course, Jake did leave a message but it was with a growing sense of doom. Somehow he already knew the outcome of the day's events. He knew that he was only going through the motions. Defeat, failure, disappointment upon impending disaster were all too familiar to him now. No matter how hard he tried, no matter what he did, everything always seemed to turn to shit.

He used to be an optimist - confident, successful, happy. He was a talented designer - good at his job but also good with people and everything he touched seemed to turn to gold. He married Angie, had some great times, holidays, cars, a fantastic life. Then the kids came along. Zack first, then Poppy eighteen months later. Great kids. *Great kids.*

But then everything just seemed to go so terribly wrong. A business hiccup, a downturn in the economy for a while, a bad decision or two. Then the loss of a major client, then another - both victims of the first recession. But he struggled on for years, helped by bank loans and re-mortgaging.

Angie left after the second missed mortgage payment, taking the kids with her to her parents. She came back and left twice more after that but when the bailiff's came round and threatened to take the furniture, she finally left for good.

Jake was lost after that. As Angie found a job, a boyfriend and a new lease on life he found himself in a pit of despair.

The house was sold, the car re-possessed, but he battled on, he still had talent, a passion for design and, ironically, it was work that saved him, even though it had brought him to his knees, cost him his wife and family, it was also his salvation. Bob Hart had given him the chance to pitch on the Plancom contract. Lucrative, long-lasting and his for the taking and he grabbed the opportunity with both hands.

Today was the day that it was all supposed to change.

Jake eventually arrived in Manchester at five thirty and an hour and a half late for the meeting. The Plancom building was in darkness, all locked up. Everyone, including Tess Brennan, had gone home for the night. Ironically the snow was only light in Manchester with only a mild dusting on the ground, nothing like the kind of weather Jake had driven through to get there.

During that long, hard drive, Jake had tried to

call Tess Brennan many times but at no time was he able to get through to her directly.

It was over and Jake knew it. The email that came into his iPhone just as he was getting back into his car confirmed it. It was from Bob Hart.

"Sorry, Jake. Just heard from a friend at the office that the contract was awarded to Wade & Walker Associates - Tess Brennan's old firm.

Don't think it would have helped even if you got there on time from what I understand. Hope that cushions the blow a bit mate. Anyway, just thought you'd like to know. Speak to you when I return. All the best, Bob."

As Jake read it, he felt like he'd been punched in the stomach. He slumped into the car, bent his head over the wheel and felt despair wash over him. He had nothing more. There was no Plan B. There was just Plancom, Angie, the kids and a fresh start. That was it. Nothing else. And now that was gone.

An hour later he was still there in the car park, in the dark. It was freezing cold and the snow was coming down harder now. The cold roused Jake and he switched on the engine and began to drive, the heater warming him. But he was unaware of it. Subconsciously he was heading home, crawling along the snow clogged roads for hours, but his mind was lost in other thoughts.

The initial hysteria had passed along with the breathlessness of utter panic. These had been replaced by a weird sense of calm, an almost detached sense of rationality as he observed his predicament with a kind of out-of-body pragmatism. Jake was eminently aware that he had nowhere left to turn, nowhere else to go and, possibly the worst of all, no one he could call who could possibly help or understand. Certainly not Angie. That ship had sailed long ago, he now finally realised. She was never coming back, and neither were the kids, she would see to that. Would they had he got the contract? He doubted that too now. She was in a new relationship which Jake had long tried to deny, but she was happy and was not about to give it up for him. Reality had well and truly set in.

The business was finished. Bankruptcy a certainty. Thank God his parents were dead so they weren't around to witness this, his final failure.

As he thought of his parents, the tears finally came. He couldn't help it. They poured down his face as he wept uncontrollably. With his eyes so blurry he could barely see the road ahead, so Jake slammed on the brakes and skidded the car to an icy halt. The car behind, a Volvo, the only other vehicle on the road, very nearly crashed into him and the driver honked his horn violently and glared at Jake as he slid around the BMW, missing it by the narrowest of margins. "Wanker!" he shouted. But Jake was deaf to him.

Eventually the tears subsided and he was left with just a general feeling of sadness in knowing that his life was irreparably broken.

He dried his eyes and studied himself in the rear view mirror.

If Jake had had a razor blade or a piece of hosepipe, he'd have just sat there in the car and ended his stinking, miserable, useless life. But he didn't have those things, he didn't have anything apart from a portfolio and he doubted he could beat himself to death with that.

He turned on the windscreen wipers and swept away the thick coating of snow that had formed since he'd pulled over. It was dark now, although with all the snow, strangely still light. The country road he was on was completely deserted and through the curtain of heavy flakes he could just make out the shape up ahead of a bridge.

The idea occurred to him immediately, almost as if he was receiving a message from above. He didn't need a razor blade or a length of hose anymore because now he had a means to end his suffering.

The bridge was there for him. Just waiting for him on that deserted road offering him a way out. And he was more than ready to accept.

Chapter 2

The thick acrid cigar smoke curled upwards into the heavy white sky. Snow was coming, the clouds were full of it, and Charles Khan wondered if he would make it back to London before it really started coming down. He hated the snow, hated the winter but after all his years abroad it was good to finally be home again for longer than just a few days. But not here, not in Liverpool and certainly not at this God forsaken container terminal on the banks of the freezing cold Mersey.

Home for Charles now was a plush new apartment in London's Docklands; swanky, stylish, incredibly expensive and all his. Not that he had spent much time there since his recent return from Johannesburg but, now that he was retiring, there would soon be time enough. He had certainly earned it - fought long enough and hard enough for it and now, after all that fighting, he was going to take a well deserved, very wealthy, rest.

Charles had driven up the night before to oversee the container's arrival, a job which, in truth, he would not have trusted to anyone else as its contents were too valuable, both in worth and to his own future. But he had arrived in Liverpool earlier than anticipated and out of sheer boredom had gone out to find a bar and some female company for the evening. Needless to say it had turned into quite a heavy night and a rather late one.

Now, in the afternoon, after the night before, Charles felt particularly rough. Too much whiskey, not enough sleep and a horrendously early start this morning was the cause, but he could blame no one other than himself. He just wished they would hurry up and get his container off so he could begin the long drive home. It was still only early afternoon yet already his king-sized bed back in London was calling him.

Khan had the bearing of a soldier which was not surprising after all his years in one uniform or another. He was well built, wide at the shoulder, thick at the neck and beginning to thicken at the waist but he was still in good shape. His closely-cropped hair and strongly carved features gave him a hard appearance, which was an image he was happy to cultivate.

Although as Charles pulled up the collar on his cashmere overcoat, he laughed at how quickly he had become soft. For too many years he had lived a soldiers life of little sleep and early mornings having had nothing more for a bed than a sheet on the ground and the stars for a blanket. Drinking, smoking, playing cards with the enlisted men until the break of dawn and then marching God knows how many miles on a half-empty belly. Yet he had thrived. But after just a month back in the real world he was already whining like a little girl. He smiled at himself as he puffed noisily on a long King Edward cigar, his fifth of the day and only one of his many vices.

The ship had docked the night before and had started unloading at eight this morning. Charles had been there since seven, waiting, watching, itching to get his hands on the contents of one particular container. Anxious not to miss the moment when it was offloaded, eager to get inside it, recover his property and get home to London.

But it was taking forever. He looked at the sky again as the first flakes of snow glided down from the packed clouds. This was just the start of it, he knew, more was forecast. It had apparently been snowing hard down South since the early hours and was becoming extremely treacherous. On his car radio the police were advising those thinking about driving to stay at home unless the journey was absolutely necessary.

Charles's journey was. He wanted to get his precious cargo back to London as soon as possible no matter how bad the snow was. He had hated the snow and cold since his time in Chechnya when he never thought he'd feel warm again, but he had learned to cope with it having fought, marched and driven through weather the English could only imagine. So the drive back didn't faze him, especially not in his brand new Range Rover with heated seats and climate control. As for the road conditions, well they would be just child's play compared to Chechnya.

At last, in the late afternoon, as a light dusting of snow lay upon the dockside, the much anticipated container was offloaded. Charles lit up yet another King Edward as a large docker in filthy yellow oilskins approached him. "You'll be Mister Khan?" he enquired gruffly in a thick Glaswegian accent.

Charles surreptitiously checked the heavy bulge of the holstered gun underneath his overcoat as he replied. "I am. I take it you're Crowe?"

"Aye. You got my money?"

"All in good time. Open the container first." Replied Charles, puffing on his cigar.

"I don't think you heard me, old son. No money, no container. Understand?"

Charles understood all too well and smiled inwardly.

"Of course, I understand. My apologies," he said. He looked furtively around him, noticing several other dockers working nearby, although none were paying him or Crowe any mind. "But perhaps we should move out the gaze of prying eyes first, agreed?"

"Aye. Whatever, old son. Just as long as I get it or they'll be no container, know what I mean?" Crowe said gruffly.

"Yes, I know exactly what you mean," said Khan.

"You'd better follow me," Crowe said and as Charles followed, he led him from the parked Range Rover to the container a short distance away where it had been set down neatly by crane, in the middle of a long even row of others. After satisfying himself that they were not being watched, Crowe led Charles over to the far side of the container where they could complete their business without being seen. When they got there he said, "Right. No eyes. All nice and private. Now where's my fucking money?"

Charles smiled with the smoking cigar clamped between his teeth. "I have it here." He said and reached inside his heavy coat. Crowe shuffled, nervously as he eagerly awaited his pay off. But then suddenly, as quick as a flash, Khan seized him by the throat and pushed him hard against the cold metal side of the container. Then something else cold and metallic was shoved firmly up under his chin. Crowe knew instantly that it was a gun. "Jesus Christ!" he yelped,

"What are you doing?"

Charles Khan put his mouth an inch away from Crowe's ear and with smokey breath whispered, "What I am doing is getting you to open the fucking door of this container before I blow your ugly fucking jaw through the top of your ugly bloody head, understand old son?"

Crowe nodded meekly. "Sure, sure, no problem - just don't shoot me, alright?"

"Just do as I say and you get to keep your good looks. Now open the door!" Khan growled as he shoved Crowe towards the front of the container, transferring the barrel of the shiny chrome-plated gun from the man's jaw to the small of his back. "Move!" he demanded.

Crowe staggered forward, fumbling hurriedly in the greasy pocket of his oilskin jacket, eventually pulling out a large set of keys. As Crowe stood at the door of the container, Khan kept to the side of it, puffing on the cigar and aiming the gun at the docker's belly as he selected a key and hastily opened the padlock. He lifted the catch on the container's door and opened it ajar. "There, it's open, now please, put the gun away."

Charles smiled broadly. "See, that wasn't so difficult was it?" He pulled open his coat and pushed the big chrome gun back into its leather holster then reached into his inside pocket and pulled out a thick envelope which he thrust at Crowe. "There. Take your money and fuck off - and never let it be said I don't pay my debts."

Crowe began to stammer something but Charles fixed him with a hard stare. "Go!" he said and Crowe turned and shuffled quickly away, stuffing the envelope into the pocket of his filthy oilskin as he went.

Charles waited until Crowe was a good distance away, then finally opened the door to the container and stepped inside.

The large interior smelled of seawater and rust but was clean and dry. The forty foot container held a variety of cargo; stacks of polystyrene packed washing machines, boxes of plasma TVs, two bright red Ducati motorcycles, an S-Class Mercedes and several large crates of South African Chardonnay.

Charles, knowing exactly where to look, headed for one of the crates which had the initials *P.B.* scratched on it, then took a pen-knife from his pocket and prized it open.

He removed two layers of packed straw and a layer of expensive vintage wine before, at last, finding what he, himself, had placed in the crate over a month before in Johannesburg; a large black, leather-bound briefcase. He smiled greedily and briefly clutched the case to his chest as he would have a lost child that had been found safe.

Then he replaced the wine and the straw and, after re-locking the container, took the briefcase and stowed it behind the passenger seat of the Range Rover. Charles then took out his Blackberry and sent a text message to his brother.

"Got it. Should be back by eight. You supply the

champagne, I'll supply the ice!" it said.

He started the car, flicked on the wipers to clear away the layer of powdery snow and slid the heater control up to max. He also put on the heated seat for added warmth. No point in being chilly on this hellishly cold evening. Then, putting the Range Rover into gear, he began the long drive home, leaving two wet tyre tracks in his wake as the big 4x4 cut a trail through the snow covered terminal.

Driving conditions were not too bad for the first forty miles of his Southbound journey, sporadic snow flurries and powdery roads but nothing too worrying. But then, suddenly, the light smattering quickly turned into a blizzard and the powdery roads turned into a thick carpet of hazardous snow and slush.

It was slow going, what should have taken maybe half an hour to get to where he was had taken an hour and a half and he still had the major part of the journey to do. Furthermore, he was desperately tired, his activities of the previous night seriously beginning to catch up with him. Also, he was having to concentrate hard on the road ahead and that, too, was adding to his fatigue.

Charles was warm now. So with the Range Rover veering dangerously about the road he shrugged out of his heavy coat, allowing a brief glimpse of the big chrome gun concealed beneath the jacket he was wearing under his top coat.

With the coat removed Charles once again focused on the road ahead, staring into the relentless, mesmerising blizzard.

A hundred miles later, driving at a snail's pace along a clogged, slippery and extremely treacherous M1, Charles was beginning to fall asleep at the wheel. Abandoned vehicles lined the motorway, snow ploughs were out but fighting a losing battle and Charles' journey was getting longer and longer. He was tired, desperate for sleep and wanted nothing more than to get home to bed. He had tried several times to phone his brother, Arthur, to let him know he would be arriving late but the conditions were messing with the signal. And now his phone was dead. It had been on since the crack of dawn and the battery had finally gone.

On the outskirts of Northampton he hit a detour, due to an accident up ahead, which sent him off the motorway and onto the back roads. They were deserted and his was the only car on the road. It was late now, with the snow deep on the ground, but Charles, even though extremely drowsy was still keen to get home, and as the 4x4 was coping so easily in the icy conditions, he saw this as an opportunity to make up some time. He pressed down on the accelerator and the Range Rover immediately responded. Charles had over seventy miles still to go but with these back roads clear of stranded vehicles he could probably make it back in under two hours, if he pushed it.

However, before long, Charles began to nod. He didn't even realize he had been asleep until he opened his eyes and saw the corner approaching much too fast. He span the wheel and the car slid into the bend. For a moment he thought he was going to make it but then he saw the BMW parked awkwardly at the exit of the corner, half covered in a thick layer of snow and Charles had to quickly spin the wheel again to avoid smashing straight into it.

The Range Rover, snaked wildly as he lost control of the back end and as the wheels on the passenger side lifted off the ground, as the whole car began to roll Charles Khan knew that he would not be getting back to London that night.

Chapter 3

Disappointment and despair had clouded Jake's mind and eroded his rationality and he was teetering on the edge of sanity as he stared, almost euphoric, at the bridge. His life for the last few years had been awful and just for the briefest time, thanks to Bob Hart and the Plancom deal, he thought he had a way of making it so much better but now those hopes had been utterly dashed and he could not bear to face life as it was now bound to be.

He had lost everything; his wife, his children, his house and now his business. His parents were long dead and whatever friends he may have had in the past had all moved on. He was completely alone. He knew his children would miss him, but what life could he offer them now. How would they feel, growing up, having a total failure for a father? No, they were better off with Angie and the whole world would get by just fine without him.

Suicide was the obvious answer. It would not be

sad, it would be a happy release and finally put an end to the relentless disappointment of living. How could death be any worse?

Jake climbed out of the hire car and was struck immediately by the biting cold. The snow was deep and he had to tread carefully in his smooth soled brogues so as not to slip. Hugging his corduroy sports jacket tightly around him he made his way slowly but surely to the bridge. It was hard going and seemed to take forever in the extreme conditions. The snow was like a blizzard now, thick flakes whipping round in a wild frenzy but finally he reached the large metal structure.

The bridge was the kind that stretched over a motorway but Jake neither knew or cared which one. Whichever it was there was no traffic noise and no lighting from below, just a dark void flecked haphazardly with the unrelenting snow.

Slowly, perilously, Jake climbed over the railings, his brogues slipping like skates on the icy metal, his jacket and tie flapping like flags atop the mast of a ship navigating Cape Horn. The wind slapped at his raw face like a woman betrayed as it howled around, livid, in the freezing night. His soaked shoes offering no grip as he clung perilously to the cold handrails of the bridge, trying not to think of the black void beneath him, or the hard tarmac that he knew lay in wait, unseen, thirty feet below. Snow danced around him, frenzied and angry, as it fell slanted from the swollen clouds above. The flaps of his jacket now desperate to take flight, his tie doing the same as it whipped wildly around his face and pulled like a noose at his neck.

On the other side of the railings, Jake closed his eyes and said a silent apology to his children. He was not a religious man but now, at the last, he said a prayer, to ask God to keep Zack and Poppy safe.

He was now ready. Standing there, freezing, he prepared himself to jump. His heart thumping in his chest as he relaxed his grip on the railings and braced himself to plummet into the black unknown.

Then he heard the sound of the car and instinctively his fingers tightened once more onto the frozen railing.

He turned, seeing the headlights first and then watched helplessly as the out of control vehicle burst into view.

The Range Rover rounded the corner behind the parked BMW travelling far too fast. It slewed wildly to avoid collision with Jake's hire car then skidded across the road where it bounced off a tree and somersaulted, airborne, towards the bridge.

Jake could do nothing as the large, heavy car flew through the air heading straight for him. He ducked, but clung on vice-like as the big, weighty Range Rover struck the thick upright beam on the opposite side of the rail with an almighty clang sending vibrations up the whole length of Jake's body.

The vehicle then bounced violently off and rolled end-over-end several times into the middle of the road where it crashed down onto its roof and spun like a top for several seconds before finally creaking to a very slow, metallic halt.

Momentarily Jake was stunned, not quite believing what he had just witnessed. Strangely the snow had now stopped and the wind had died. Everything was suddenly silent and white and calm. After a couple of seconds Jake's brain popped into gear and he leaped over the railings and rushed, slipping and sliding, to the wreck to see if could help whoever was inside.

As he wrenched open the dented driver's door, he immediately saw the blood which began spreading like a nosebleed onto a giant white handkerchief of snow. A middle-aged man with greying hair and a big, burly frame was hanging upside down lifelessly behind the wheel, still strapped into the luxury leather of the vehicle by his seatbelt. His face was crushed. Completely smashed in. The airbag had deployed but it was not enough to save him and now it billowed like a collapsed parachute around a portion of the man's brain which lay on the bloodied roof lining.

Jake gagged but felt for a pulse, although it was obvious the man was dead.

Then something caught Jake's eye, in the back of the car, also on the roof lining, which now doubled as the floor, sitting among a carpet of glass fragments.

It was a gun. A big chrome-plated pistol and the sight of it surprised him.

Jake didn't know anything about guns but this one looked expensive, all blinged and shiny like the sort of thing some gangsta rapper might own. He knew enough to know that it certainly wasn't police issue. Whoever this man was, he was definitely no policeman.

Jake was shocked. More by the dead body than the gun, although he'd never seen either before. He'd been too young to see his parents after they had died, and he tried to block an image of how their faces might look after their car accident. God he hoped they didn't look anything like this poor soul.

But then his mind came back to the gun. Who would own a gun like that?

His next thought was to call the police and he pulled out his phone and punched in 999. Before it started to ring Jake hung up as another thought flashed into his mind.

If he called the police it was going to interfere with his own plans. His suicide. He leant back on the Range Rover, considering what to do, his feet crunching on more fragments of glass. The glass mingling with the ice on ground, all glistening prettily in the silent night amongst the carnage and self-loathing.

He didn't think it fair for the police to find his

body here too, either on the motorway below or, now that he had a gun at his disposal, with his brains shot out in the middle of the road. But if he waited around for the police his chance would be gone and he just couldn't face another day of living, knowing what living had in store.

Near freezing as he mulled this over, he gingerly made his way around to the passenger side of the car, to see if he could find a coat to put on. Crunching on more glass as he went, Jake noticed how well the Range Rover had stood up to the huge crash. It had very few dents, the passenger door and the tailgate had burst open on impact but neither looked overly battered. Obviously the vehicle as a whole had taken some damage but nothing that looked too major. Even the windows remained intact. Cracked yes, but none broken.

Jake leaned into the open passenger door and found a large cashmere overcoat heaped over an upturned open briefcase. Both covered in small fragments of glass. Quickly he pulled the coat over him and immediately felt the warmth.

Then something suddenly struck him. Why was there so much broken glass when all the windows of the Range Rover were intact?

He bent down, turned over the briefcase and from a small open compartment, which was only one among many others, he scooped out a handful of what he had at first presumed to be glass. He studied it closely. Then he studied the other fragments on the floor.

Just to be absolutely certain that he wasn't seeing things, he rushed around to the other side of the Range Rover, nearly slipping onto his backside as he did so, to check the fragments there too.

Then, after a few seconds of utter disbelief, he looked up to the snow filled clouds above and in a hushed, awestruck voice said, "Oh, my God. They're diamonds!"

Chapter 4

Arthur Khan had spent most of the day at his club, The Connaught, in Chelsea. He had read the papers, had a marvellous lunch and then enjoyed a cigar and a whiskey by the fireside in the afternoon.

Previously, he had not been in England long enough to enjoy the club's simple pleasures but since his return home he had made full use of it. The club was specifically for ex-military and Arthur found that he fitted in rather well even though his own military career had not been spent solely in the service of Her Majesty and was rather more chequered than most of The Connaught's other members.

Today the club was a wonderful retreat as it was a cold, brisk day in London, the sky threatening snow and the forecast confirming that it was on the way. The Midlands had already got it, The North was getting it later and by tonight London would have it too. Arthur thought of his younger brother, driving back from Liverpool, pleased that it was him out there and not the other way around as it so easily could have been. It had been a coin toss and Charles had won but he had been keen to go anyway. Charles was not good at trusting others.

Let him go, Arthur thought. Let him drive the four hundred mile round trip to collect the case. He was bringing it back to London anyway and Arthur would have his hands on it by tonight. He had absolutely nothing to lose by letting Charles collect it.

Arthur stayed at The Connaught, enjoying the warmth of the fire and the comfortable leather upholstery of his favourite wing back chair, allowing his lunch to fully digest, until mid afternoon, before finally making his way home at four.

By four fifteen he was back in the luxury of his mews house in Chelsea, just a short walk from his club. The text came in from Charles shortly afterwards and Arthur smiled as he read it.

"Got it. Should be back by eight. You supply the champagne, I'll supply the ice!"

It did indeed call for some champagne. A quick celebration of his own might also be in order. He pressed the speed dial on his Blackberry and ordered a girl from the agency he used whenever he was in town. A lot of expense for just an hour or so but, hey, he could afford it - especially now, so why not push the boat out?

Half an hour later the girl arrived who was just

his type; mahogany coloured skin, dark eyes and a tightly cropped afro - as was his taste, which had been acquired over many years in Africa. She looked like a Zulu princess, only instead of being dressed in feathers and animal skins she was dressed in tight fitting silk and killer heels.

Without a word passing between them, Arthur opened the door and ushered her in. She was tall and graceful with long, lean legs which looked almost polished in the lamplight. Arthur studied her, as if appraising cattle. She would do.

Silently he led her to the bedroom, then said just one word. "Strip," and she immediately did as instructed. She had been forewarned that this was his way. Arthur's specific requirements were well known now to her agency and she had been well briefed as to what to expect. Do not speak, do not look at him directly, do not make any pretence at enjoyment. This was about his enjoyment only.

By now, Arthur had changed out of his Prince of Wales cheque suit and was wearing a dark blue satin kimono with a fire breathing dragon motif emblazoned across the back. He slipped it off and stood before her naked, however, the girl's head was bowed and her eyes downcast. "Get on the bed on all fours. Face the headboard," he demanded and, without lifting her eyes, the girl silently obliged.

Khan marched backward and forward behind her, studying the girl, as if contemplating the best way to mount her, his manhood swelling with each step. His powerful, muscular body was covered in a carpet of thick black hair.

Taller than his brother at an inch over six feet, Arthur was more Egyptian in appearance with tanned skin, a hooked nose and strong masculine features. His curved moustache was dark grey and flecked liberally with white as was his neat crew cut. But it was Arthur's deep set eyes that were his most notable feature. They were dark, cold and cruel as they focused on the polished ebony behind of the young black girl.

At last, when he was firmly erect, he strode forward and thrust himself violently into her and began rutting like a crazed animal. There was no chit-chat, no tenderness and absolutely no concern for the girl, it was all about him and she was less than nothing. The girl screamed and groaned but they were not cries of pleasure.

Two hours later, Arthur was dining alone at Claridges in Mayfair. Roasted duck foie gras accompanied by their finest bottle of champagne. Perfect.

He was now dressed in a tailored navy blue three piece suit with a crisp white shirt and a canary yellow silk tie, looking very much the wealthy businessman, a role he was very keen to assume in the future. By looking at him, no one could have guessed the things he had done in the past or the things he was still very capable of. He exuded an air of sophistication and of breeding, which had been supplied to him by his parents, but for too long those things had taken a back seat to roughness, violence and brutality - three things in which he and his brother truly excelled. But tonight his new life began, a life of fine dining and extravagant luxury.

He dabbed his mouth with the corner of his clean white napkin as he chewed on the excellent foie gras, relishing the taste. This was definitely how life should be.

Tomorrow night, after viewing the merchandise, he would dine with Peter and Charles and share the celebration but tonight he wanted to just savour the moment alone. Just him and the knowledge that he was now set for life. No more soldiering, no more battles. No more relinquishing the spoils of somebody else's war. From now on he was going to benefit too - more than he could have ever thought possible.

At eight thirty Arthur gave Charles a call but could not get through to him and a niggle of irritation growled. Nevertheless, he ordered a dessert of rich chocolate gâteaux and sunk another two glasses of champagne. This was a celebration after all.

At nine he called Charles again but there was still no response and the niggle of irritation grew into a roaring indigestion. Where the hell was Charles?

He tried again every quarter of an hour thereafter

but each time there was no answer. By ten he was becoming quite concerned. Surely it was due to the weather, it was coming down hard now in London too. It was almost March and yet the country was experiencing the worst snow storms in years. Arthur did not mind, it could have been raining locusts for all he cared. All he wanted was those diamonds and to see his brother arriving with them.

Briefly it entered his head that Charles might have taken them for himself but he dismissed it almost immediately. Firstly, he trusted his brother more than anyone else alive, except maybe Peter. Secondly, both Charles and he needed Peter's contacts to sell the merchandise, his carefully cultivated connections that would ensure safe exchange of the stones and limit the risk of any unwanted attention from the police. It was Peter who had financed the whole operation, his brain that had conceived it and he who had most invested in it.

Arthur knew that he should really be phoning Peter to put him in the picture, knowing that his friend would be displeased if he failed to keep him in the loop. But Arthur was sure that Charles would phone at any moment so put off making the call until he had some good news to impart.

Eleven o'clock came and went and Arthur was now back at home in Chelsea trying to keep calm. But he was failing miserably. The meal he had just had sat heavily in his stomach and severe heartburn was adding to his growing concerns.

From the shoulder holster beneath his tailored suit jacket, Arthur took out his gun, the exact same model as his brother's, and began polishing it. Usually this simple ritual helped him relax but not tonight. Tonight he could think of nothing other than Charles and a case full of priceless diamonds.

At fifteen minutes after midnight Arthur finally picked up the phone and called Peter, his celebratory mood well and truly over.

Chapter 5

Jake slumped to the ground in disbelief, his back against the upturned Range Rover, just staring at the pile of gems in his frozen hands. On the ground surrounding him, around the whole vehicle, there were many more, shining, twinkling, dazzling. Inside the car and in the black leather bound case too, particularly in there, there were still more.

For a moment Jake thought he must be dreaming. Then he began to shiver and realised he was awake, fully conscious and this was really happening. In a stunned daze, he then leant into the car and pulled out the briefcase. It was compartmentalised, each compartment holding several velvet bags. Each bag containing a small amount of stones. Some of the bags and compartments had not been disturbed whereas others had, hence the amount of spillage.

Working on a kind of autopilot Jake quickly began gathering all the diamonds he could see and shoved them haphazardly back into the bags and, in turn, back into the compartments. He was putting them back in any order, his hands shaking, but guessed each bag had originally contained a similar weight or size of stone. He scrambled about in the snow around the car, his knees wet and icy, anxiously trying to find every single gem, which suddenly became a matter of utmost importance. Some had fallen several feet away, thrown out of the car as it span, no doubt. But, after several minutes and his hands now frozen with cold, Jake was sure he had got them all. Eventually he closed the briefcase, but then stood there, uncertain of what to do next, not even sure of why he had gathered up all the stones. Although sub-consciously he already knew.

Jake was in an extremely fragile state of mind, suffering from severe stress and deep depression, completely suicidal. Just minutes ago he was going to throw himself off a bridge to end his miserable stinking existence, but now he was standing there with a case full of incredibly valuable diamonds. The man who had them, clearly someone of questionable morality, was dead and Jake was alone, with no one else around. Just him and the case.

Then the fantasy started playing in his mind. He could take the stones, sell them, pay off his creditors, get himself out of debt, start a new life free of bank loans and mortgages and credit cards and bills. He could start anew. Angie, the kids, everything could be made right again - everything could be saved.

He would have to go abroad first, to sell the stones, it was too risky to try it in England, too much of a gamble particularly if the diamonds were stolen, which he suspected they were.

It was then that it hit him. That this was fate - the whole wretched day had been fated, right from the off, right from when his car refused to start. He had needed his passport at the hire company and he still had it with him - surely that was more than just good fortune. It meant he could leave tonight, right now, there was no need for him to go home. Nothing there for him except a stack of unpaid bills and once he sold the diamonds those would soon be settled in full.

He would drive to Dover, get on a ferry, head to France. He spoke French, or enough to get by at least. From there he was sure he could find a buyer for the stones. He was a designer, an ideas man, people paid him to be creative and he was sure he could make this plan work.

Then it dawned on Jake that he would need cash, at least until he had managed to sell a diamond or two, and he didn't have any.

He thought for a long moment, knowing what he had to do and seeing no other option, he bent down, crawled back inside the Range Rover and rifled through the dead man's pockets. He found the wallet in an inside jacket pocket, thick with notes and he took them all. He then returned the wallet to the pocket.

He should have felt ashamed for what he had just done. It was unforgivable. Despicable. But Jake was desperate and not himself. Now he had the fantasy in his head he had to make it real, whatever it took.

The actual reality was that Jake was not thinking at all. He had given no thought to the consequences of what he was about to do, no thought as to who might own the diamonds or what manner of person they might be. He was functioning out of pure despair, temporarily insane and completely caught up in the moment having been given a glimmer of hope at last. A final chance.

In the real world, Jake was an honest man and never would have considered for an instant stealing money from a dead man let alone absconding with a case full of diamonds. But after all that he had been through, all that he had lost, his judgement was seriously impaired. He was on the edge, out of control and ready to do anything that would make his life better.

It had stopped snowing but there was still a thick blanket on the ground and Jake carefully made his way back to the BMW, his hands numb with cold his legs wet and freezing from crawling around in all the snow. But he made it safely back to the car and stowed the briefcase securely behind the drivers seat.

The road was eerily quiet, completely deserted except for the crashed Range Rover and the rented

BMW. Jake started the engine and turned up the heater feeling immediate warmth from the still warm engine. He pushed the gear stick into four-wheel drive mode and pulled away from the icy verge, the tyres crunching on the snow beneath the wheels.

Jake intended to take it slowly. He had a long, treacherous drive ahead of him and if he was to make it to that early morning ferry in Dover he did not want to risk an accident.

Chapter 6

The London offices of Wallace Bearing occupied the top six floors of a large hexagonal tower on the North bank of the Thames, within spitting distance of St. Paul's, The Old Bailey and The Bank of England. The top floor apartment offered incredible views of the world below from each tall window, especially at night when that world was covered in snow and dotted with lights. It looked magical and Christmassy, even though it was nearly March.

Peter Bearing, grandson of property baron, Randolph Bearing and golden-boy son of retail and shipping magnate Edward 'Teddy' Bearing, was oblivious of the view as he sat in his plush leather recliner in the majestic opulence that was the beating heart of his business empire. It was more than just a spectacularly appointed apartment, it was also his main office which was totally state-of-the-art. It had a conference room complete with a panel of satellite communication screens which allowed him to speak face to face with multiple heads of department in any of his numerous offices around the world. It had two luxurious bedrooms, each with its own bathroom and giant wall mounted plasma TV, and a spacious, ultra-modern, private living room in which to entertain guests or just relax in peace. One flight below was a fabulous swimming pool which had the initials *P.B.* emblazoned across the bottom in tiny mosaic tiles. In addition to that there was a sauna and a superbly equipped gym and up on the roof of the building was a landing pad for his personal helicopter.

He had equally sumptuous offices in New York, Madrid, Paris, Rome, Sydney and Johannesburg with equally astounding views but London was his preferred capital and where he chose to be based. It was also where two of his ex-wives lived and three of his seven children.

In the space of just six years Peter had married and divorced twice. His second and third wives had both spawned him two offspring but he did not see, nor wish to see, any of them regularly. His first wife and his three children by her were living with him once more in Mayfair where they were attempting a life together again but it was not going well. Peter was already sick of the children's constant whining and the sex with his ex-model, ex-wife was much less thrilling than he remembered. Thankfully a string of mistresses prevented him from getting too bored but Peter realised years ago that it wasn't women or a happy family life that excited him but money, business and power.

Spread across Peter's giant glass desk, held down at one end by a crystal tumbler full of ten-year-old malt, were the second draft of architects drawings for an enormous construction project close to the site of the proposed Olympic village. 'The Bearing Building' would be a futuristically conceived glass tower offering both high-end office space and luxury living accommodation. Underneath would be a huge shopping mall and multi-level underground parking facilities. It was an ambitious project but nothing Peter couldn't handle and only one of many such ventures he was overseeing around the globe.

He had been poring over the plans for most of the afternoon, making notes and adding suggestions in red ink, drawing arrows to the areas he thought needed improving or highlighting in some way, scrawling directions to the architect in his messy, difficult to decipher handwriting. But now the red pen had been laid to rest and Peter's wire framed spectacles sat on the plans as he rubbed his temples gently with his fingers.

The Bearing Building was the last thing on his mind now as he spoke to Arthur Khan on speakerphone. The only thing of importance to Peter at the moment was the telephone conversation and the time on his solid silver Breitling.

His voice was quiet, well-educated. Devoid of

emotion as he spoke to the man on the other end of the phone. "It's after midnight, Arthur, and you say there's been no word from Charles. Yet, rather than call me the moment you suspect something's wrong, you choose to call me now, some three hours after the arranged meet. Your delay has served no other purpose than to anger me, Arthur. Nothing more."

"Listen, Peter," said Khan, "I'm sure everything's fine. It's snowing like hell up North, so I suspect it's just something to do with the weather - maybe he can't get a signal, who knows, but I'm sure everything's gone without a hitch. There's nothing to worry about —"

"Firstly, Arthur," Bearing broke in, "There is much to worry about. I have significantly more invested in this than you and I'll thank you not to forget it. Secondly, you may well be correct in your assumption that it is the weather that has caused the lack of information from Charles but I expect to be kept up to date immediately the moment something deviates from what has been previously arranged, not hours afterwards. Am I clear?"

"Quite clear, Peter, yes." Replied the other man, "And of course I understand your agitation, but these things happen —"

"Not to me, Arthur. Not to me. Now the moment you hear something from Charles, call me. I'm staying at the office tonight so you know where I am and my telephone most definitely does work.

Understand?"

"Yes, Peter."

"Good. Goodnight then, Arthur." Bearing punched the button on the speaker to end the call then picked up his glasses and slid them gently back on. He was greying at the temples but otherwise looked younger than his forty years. He was fit, tanned and as usual, dressed immaculately. Even though it was after midnight, his Windsor knot was still pushed all the way up to the buttoned neck of his Saville Row shirt.

In the enormous bedroom, which led off from the office, an ex-Miss Bulgaria lay naked in his silk sheets patiently awaiting his attentions. But Peter was in no hurry. He picked up the crystal tumbler and swilled the ice in the ten year old malt. He took a sip and savoured the burn as the fine whiskey warmed his throat and belly.

He enjoyed the trappings of wealth. He liked the best of everything, liked to be the best at everything and he had worked damned hard to reach the position he now held as the head of Wallace Bearing. During his meteoric rise to power his methods had been far from moral and he had resorted to many ruthless and unscrupulous tactics in his quest for dominance of The Company. But viewing those methods from where he was today, it had all been worth while. Peter was a winner, to him there was no such thing as second place, no such words as 'nearly' or 'almost'. He was out to win, no matter what the cost, no matter what he had to do. Defeat was not an option.

He now controlled a vast empire and had designs on expanding it beyond the bounds of conventional business. But in order to do that, he needed a little more on the bargaining table than just money.

Using the diamonds as currency, he could buy himself a great deal of influence around the globe amongst the less scrupulous regimes, bringing about changes in world power to suit his own ends. He already spent much of his wealth funding private wars and financing various military actions which resulted in shipping, trade, import and export all being directly influenced by his guiding hands. However, in order to further this, the diamonds could make a real difference. They were the ultimate negotiating tool amongst the tin-pot dictators, military junta and jumped-up generals of the world whose countries natural resources held the key to untold wealth and power.

So it was imperative that Charles Khan made contact and brought the diamonds safely back to him.

However, far from appearing irate or anxious, he exuded calm. A cool head was his trademark, he was known for it, respected for it. But inside he was angry.

Peter swilled the whiskey in the glass again,

contemplating these possibilities.

"Are you coming to bed now, baby?" Miss Bulgaria shouted in tired, heavily accented English from the bedroom but Peter ignored her as he took a sip from the glass.

"Baby? Are you coming?" The girl called again.

"Soon, Anya," Peter replied, mildly irritated at being hindered in his thoughts. Arthur had angered him but that was not why he was troubled. Both the Khan brothers were normally highly reliable and if Peter was being honest with himself, then they were his only true friends, they were certainly the men he had known longest and liked the best. But this was business and Charles was missing, as were the diamonds. So where were they?

As Peter considered this, Miss Bulgaria appeared in front of him. She had been drinking and was slightly tipsy and clearly bored of waiting for Bearing to go to her. She was used to being wanted and to men giving her the attention she desired. She was only twenty-three but her preference was for rich, older men. The richer and more powerful the better, they were the ones who could keep her in the style to which she had become extremely well accustomed. Bearing, at just forty, was a catch. Mega-rich, mega-powerful and still young enough to keep her amused in bed. If she played her cards right, kept him happy and satisfied sexually, she could easily become wife number four and whether the marriage was successful or not, she would be set for life.

She stood in front of him, tall and naked with long blonde hair that hung loosely above her small but perfectly formed breasts. She had a nipped in waist, a smooth, flat stomach with a small round diamond that twinkled shyly in her belly-button. Further down sat an inch wide strip of neatly trimmed hair that led enticingly down to her womanhood. Her legs were long, shapely and toned. She was the ultimate distraction but Peter was not yet of a mind to be distracted.

"What's the matter baby?" She said, squatting down between his legs.

"Nothing." Peter managed a smile. "Just tired. A long day."

"My poor baby," said the girl, reaching up and loosening his tie before expertly popping the top button. Peter felt the irritation prickle again but remained outwardly cool with a lop-sided smile on his face as the girl moved her hand down and began rubbing his crotch. Despite his irritation, Peter stiffened. "That's better, isn't it, baby?" Miss Bulgaria said as she felt him grow magically under her touch. "You like that, don't you?"

Her voice was whiny, her accent grating and Peter was already annoyed by the lack of news about the diamonds. Miss Bulgaria was making it worse, but he couldn't help himself react to her touch as she undid his belt and unzipped his fly.

Peter had not been properly satisfied sexually since that night at his Berkshire home five years earlier with the high-class whore in the green satin lingerie. He could still not get it out of his mind, the brutality of it, the powerful, all-conquering feeling that it gave him. He still remembered how the girl cowered under his touch and the raw, unbridled pleasure he derived from it. He had tried to put those memories to the back of his mind but every so often, during sex with one of his wives or girlfriends, when they were engaged in one mundane act or another, he would fantasize about the girl in green and what he did to her. Peter realised though that these fantasies were dangerous, particularly for a man in his position, and had resisted the urge to act on them for fear of where they might lead.

Yet this girl tonight, this Miss Bulgaria, with her whiny voice and annoying accent, was somehow causing those fantasies to flare up again and as she worked on him with her mouth, he suddenly became stiffer, more sexually charged than he had since that night with the girl in green.

Unable to stop himself, Bearing roughly grabbed a handful of hair at the back of Miss Bulgaria's head and pushed her head down hard into his crotch whilst repeatedly thrusting himself forcefully down her throat. Immediately the girl started to gag and choke but Peter did not stop even as her teeth bit down on him he just thrust harder. The act of choking was preventing her from biting him properly as she desperately tried to free herself to draw breath.

Peter, so highly aroused, climaxed quickly but Miss Bulgaria had already turned blue and her eyes had rolled upwards in their sockets, showing only the whites as she began to suffocate. But then it was over as Peter, fully spent, pushed her head away and she sprawled on the floor, choking, grasping deep lungfuls of air as she vomited repeatedly on the hard wooden floor, heaving until nothing came up but clear bile.

Bearing eyed her curiously, but without a care for her wellbeing.

His annoyance slowly subsiding, the years of sexual frustration slowly abating. He had confirmed how he must now achieve his release and he knew that it could perhaps lead to difficulties ahead. But that was a problem for a different day.

Miss Bulgaria had recovered enough to sit up. She wiped her mouth and looked directly at him, her expression unreadable. "So, you like to play rough," she said in a flat tone.

"So it would seem," said Peter, his voice equally steady. Again the girl regarded him for a long moment, evaluating him, her eyes never leaving his.

"Good," she finally replied. "Me too. Now, unless you intend to fuck me on this floor, I'm going to bed. Goodnight, baby." With that, she stood up, kissed him on the forehead and returned unhurriedly to the bedroom.

Peter couldn't help but smile. Maybe Miss Bulgaria was not so annoying after all.

He drained the remnants of his whiskey. The distraction had turned out to be a welcome one, but now his thoughts inevitably returned to Charles Khan and the diamonds. Something had happened, Peter felt sure of it in his gut. Charles would have called, found some way to get in touch even if the weather was terrible.

Bearing, normally so controlled, so confident, so famously calm, felt just the first stirrings of dread. His diamonds better turn up soon because they represented Peter's future and no one was going to steal that away from him. No one.

Chapter 7

Arthur Khan, sat in bed aimlessly flicking through channels on his big screen TV with his remote. There was nothing on that appealed to him - God knows how many channels there were now and all there was to watch were movies aimed at teenagers, chat shows hosted by gay comedians or reality TV shows featuring teenagers and gays getting drunk. What in the hell had happened to proper TV?

But Arthur wasn't really concerned about that tonight as his mind was elsewhere, still pondering the whereabouts of his brother. He was unsettled by the conversation with Peter, knowing that he was right. As usual.

Bearing was the boss, always had been, even though he had always been smaller, weedier than the two brothers it was Peter's brain that had always got them through. And brains meant power, particularly when money was involved.

Arthur and Charles were close, separated by

just eighteen months. They took care of each other, shared everything, watched each others backs. Fought together, played together, worked together. They owned matching black Range Rovers and matching chrome-plated pistols; Desert Eagle .357 Magnums, the most powerful handguns in the world.

The brothers came from good stock, Egyptian father, English mother, they were well-educated and always given what they wanted. But they were nothing more than thugs. The only person they ever backed down to was Peter Bearing, who held this mystical power over them. They respected him, loved him like they would a smarter brother who had done well for himself. And Bearing regularly exploited that.

Arthur and Charles Khan met Peter when they were all up at Oxford together. They had much in common; wealthy parents, privileged lifestyle, abundant ambition and a lust for power. They also shared a cruel streak and were a perfect match right from the start. But even though their friendship remained strong, destiny separated them.

Whereas Peter's glittering path led him from academic success to business triumph, culminating in his remarkable take-over of Wallace Bearing from his cancer ridden father at just twenty-eight, the Khan brothers' path led them in a totally different direction.

After being expelled from Oxford for possession

of drugs and subsequently being disinherited by their diplomat father, the brothers joined the army. After stints with the parachute regiment and then the SAS, the Khan's eventually branched out on their own as soldiers for hire. They fought together in Chechnya, Georgia, Mozambique, Somalia, Angola, Uganda and Sierra Leone using South Africa as their base. They dabbled in a variety of criminal activities but drugs and people trafficking soon became their businesses of choice. From that, after cultivating lucrative connections in Sierra Leone and South Africa, their path led them at last to the illegal diamond trade.

Conflict diamonds funded many military actions in Africa, particularly in the late nineties, and the Khan's were responsible for much of the bartering, smuggling and general slaughter involved in obtaining and trading these blood-soaked gems. It was dangerous, exhilarating and highly illegal work but the brothers not only survived but thrived on that. It was what they were born for. And Peter Bearing financed it all.

Arthur knew this particular shipment was important to Peter. It was important to him and Charles too as it was their last one. Their retirement plan.

For many years, on Bearing's orders, the Khan's had been hand-picking the best diamonds. The largest stones of the highest quality and value. Then using their own cutters, they had them transformed into gems of the finest cut, clarity, colour and weight. They represented the mother load. The best of the best. A horde worth tens of millions. The brothers had been saving these particular stones for years, keeping them for the right time when they would be of most use to them.

The Khans had put the briefcase full of diamonds in the container themselves, hidden inside the crate of Chardonnay marked *P.B.* and en-route to Peter Bearing. Then they had flown on ahead to

London for a reunion meal with their friend and business partner to toast this, their most lucrative venture.

Over a month later their ship had quite literally come in and Charles had driven up to Liverpool to collect the stones. The text message from Charles confirmed that he had collected them, but where was he now? He had been due back four hours ago but Charles had still not arrived.

Arthur was seriously worried now and becoming more convinced that Charles had had some kind of accident as it just wasn't like his brother not to call in. He thought about getting in the car and going out to look for him but the conditions were atrocious. Charles may have been forced to take an alternative route or to hold up somewhere for the night; a motorway services maybe or perhaps just a lay by. That would be the more likely of the two seeing that there had been no contact - and if

Charles' phone was dead then that would explain it. But Arthur had a niggling feeling, a brother's intuition. Something had happened, he felt almost sure of it and the consequences of that he just didn't want to contemplate.

Chapter 8

In Northamptonshire, the following morning, the snow had turned to heavy rain and the previously clogged, near impassable roads had turned to a sludgy but drivable icy mess.

The bridge was on a quiet country road crossing over a dual carriageway, which had been in darkness the night before due to scheduled repair work, although the blizzard had prevented that.

The upside down Range Rover had been discovered by a gritter truck driver in the early hours and was now surrounded by a whole gaggle of people and vehicles. Uniformed policemen, a forensics unit, accident inspectors, firemen and CID officers.

The body had already been removed and the car had been minutely inspected as had the surrounding area, even though the conditions were horrendous.

The dead man had been identified as Charles Khan, whose name popped up on the police database. It transpired that The Metropolitan Police had been keeping an eye on Charles for many years even though he was never in the country long enough for them to convict him of anything. Usually just a couple of days at a time, sometimes slightly longer. But, according to the database, he was a known mercenary, one of the top dogs, and London was where he and his brother apparently did much of their recruiting.

A weapon had been found at the scene, a .357 calibre. Large, powerful, showy and unlicensed.

Also, a diamond had been found. A big one. Not in the vehicle, but on the road several feet away from it. Close enough for it to be linked with Khan, perhaps, who, according to the records, was known to be based in South Africa - the source of many of the world's most valuable stones.

The Officer in Charge, Detective Inspector Jeff Grainy, was a tall but slender man with lank hair, a big nose and a perpetual cold but he was a good cop with good instincts. He was a Londoner who had started his career with The Metropolitan Police until family commitments forced him to move a little further North, first to Cambridge and then onto Northampton, where he had finally settled. Now as a father of three, he was glad of the less hectic pace but occasionally he got a pang to work on something bigger.

He had been at the scene since a little after eight that morning. Now, two hours later, he was wet, cold and desperate for the cup of coffee and bacon sandwich that his sergeant had just brought him back from Northampton.

DI Grainy had sent his sergeant into the town to get the diamond valued and the jeweller had given him a conservative estimate of at least thirty-thousand pounds.

The stone in Grainy's wife's engagement ring cost nearly five hundred pounds and he thought that was expensive but the diamond that had been found on the bridge was huge by comparison and the valuation staggering.

Grainy knew this was a potentially big case, that the diamond had probably been in Khan's possession and was most likely stolen, but he simply did not have the time, manpower or resources to investigate it fully. Besides, Khan was under investigation by Scotland Yard so by rights he knew it was their case. Grainy looked at the name on the case notes of The Met's Officer in Charge and smiled. It belonged to an old friend, another good cop. If anyone could get to the bottom of it, he could.

Grainy finished his bacon sarnie, drained his coffee, then took out his phone and gave his old friend a call. Today was one of those very rare days that he wished he had stayed at Scotland Yard.

Chapter 9

The ferry was not busy, just some holiday makers and a few truckers and, after changing the wad of stolen notes for just six hundred euros at the Bureau de Change, Jake managed to easily find a seat alone. He sat down in a comfortable faux leather armchair with a frothy latte looking out of the tall rain splashed windows onto the choppy, grey English Channel, still caught up in the euphoria of salvation.

There was no going back now, at least not for a while and strangely he felt exhilarated by this, liberated. For the moment he was still rapt up in the madness of the situation, he was excited by it and had still not given any real thought about the consequences. All he was focussing on was paying off his debts and trying to win Angie back, even though she was now with someone else. If he returned to England rich, debt free and with no more worries then maybe, just maybe he could get her to come back to him. However, had he been thinking rationally, he would have known that ship had sailed long ago. But, as his actions of the last few hours proved, he was far from rational at present.

The briefcase was stowed safely between his feet as he had not wished to leave it unattended in the rented BMW parked three decks below. He was tired now, after his long journey down to Dover. It had taken him five and a half hours to drive the hundred and fifty miles, much of it through heavy snow, blocked roads and extremely hazardous conditions. However, as night turned slowly to day, the snow turned to sleet and eventually to heavy rain which quickly began washing at least the main roads clean. By the time Jake hit the coast there were only a few snow patches left on the ground as rain swept in diagonal rods across the stark white cliffs.

Jake took a sip of the latte which was warm and comforting as he watched England slip further away and tried to organise his thoughts to formulate some sort of a plan.

He was thinking clearly enough to know that the dead man in the Range Rover was probably someone of dubious nature. The gun told him that much. He also knew that he did not want to be traced and for that many diamonds, someone was bound to come looking.

So that became Jake's immediate priority; to make himself as untraceable as possible. He took out his beloved iPhone, the only thing of non-necessity he had bought for himself in several years. Stored within its memory were all his contacts, his diary, his emails and pretty much his whole life. But now it was a possible liability. Jake was no expert in technology but he had seen enough movies to know that phones could be traced - whether that was hard fact or just Hollywood fiction he could not be certain, but he did not want to take that chance. So, after downing the last warming remnants of his latte, Jake left the comfort of the lounge and went outside onto the rain lashed deck, the briefcase gripped firmly in one hand, his iPhone held tightly in the other. He forced himself into the driving wind, staggering uneasily in the blustery conditions, the ferry rocking to and fro as he made his way precariously to the rail.

Once there, he stood for a second contemplating his next move. By ridding himself of the phone he would not only be limiting the ability of anyone to trace his whereabouts but also eliminating the possibility of his kids being able to call him whenever they wanted to. But he knew they were safe with Angie and he would be returning to them soon enough. When next he saw them he would be worry free, debt free and financially secure. He could be the father he so desperately wanted to be without all the baggage he had carried with him over the last few years. Surely that had to be worth it.

Next time he spoke to his kids and to Angie he wanted it to be as a new man, someone who they would all want to be with, a winner, and the thing he was about to do was the first step towards that goal. This was the beginning of his regeneration, the beginning of the new Jake.

In that instant of irrational, stress induced madness, that moment of false clarity, he threw the iPhone far out over the rail, watching it arc high up into the angry grey sky then slowly fall and plop insignificantly into a giant dark swell rising ominously out of the cold, unforgiving sea. Soon he'd be able to buy as many new iPhone's as he wanted.

Two hours later, Jake was feeling exhilarated, excited and ready for the adventure ahead as he drove off the ferry at Calais and headed inland.

Even though he had not slept now for over twenty-four hours, Jake drove for six straight hours. He had been tired on the ferry as a result of his snowy drive down to Dover but that had passed now and he felt almost refreshed as if in the grip of some euphoric trance that had him driving through a land where problems just melted away, his thoughts full of triumphant family reunions and a happy-ever-after future.

He stopped only twice to refuel, aiming west, by-passing Paris and taking the clear, congestion free toll road through Le Mans and Tours until finally, by late afternoon he reached Poitiers. Jake knew this area well as he and Angie had holidayed here several times in happier years.

Quickly finding a shopping centre on the outskirts of the city, he parked up and, with the briefcase still clutched tightly in his grip, went in search of the item he needed. Within half an hour, he was back in the car with a newly purchased backpack sitting on the seat next to him. Setting off again, Jake drove out of the city and into the beautiful surrounding countryside, the sun now setting on a lovely French evening, the rain having ceased about an hour out of Calais.

Jake drove around many narrow lanes trying to find somewhere suitable to park up for the night and shortly before dark found just what he was looking for. In a field, surrounded by woodland was an old, tumbledown barn, the entrance concealed from the road. Jake pulled over and quickly surveyed the building, finding it empty and apparently unused. It was perfect and he drove the BMW inside, hiding it completely from view.

It was only now that the tiredness finally hit him. Suddenly Jake felt utterly exhausted from his long journey and the events of the last twenty-four hours. His eyelids were leaden and he needed desperately to sleep.

Jake took off his glasses and placed them carefully on the dashboard, then reclined the seat and made himself comfortable as he pulled Charles Khan's warm cashmere overcoat over him. As the darkness closed in around him he fell almost immediately into a deep, dreamless sleep.

Tomorrow his new life would start in earnest.

Chapter 10

Detective Chief Inspector Roper Coyle had his head buried under the pillow and the duvet pulled up over the top of that but he could still hear the buzz of his mobile phone, which was switched to 'vibrate' in the hope that he would not be disturbed from his much needed slumber. He was wrong.

Coyle had closed a particularly taxing case just the day before and had been working long into the night finishing up the substantial amount of paperwork associated with it, so had not climbed into bed until four that morning.

He lived alone, having divorced his wife some years earlier after discovering her in bed with his former commanding officer. Yet now the dust had settled he bore her no ill will as they had both been too young when they got married and had simply grown apart.

He was now thirty-eight, unknowingly good looking and attractively dishevelled in a way that appealed greatly to women. There was no front with Coyle, what you saw was what you got and people responded well to him because of that. He was also tenacious to a fault, when he got his teeth stuck into a case he just would not let it go which earned him respect within the force. Sometimes though, this tenacity worked against him with his superiors as even when a case went completely cold, Roper refused to give up on it and had difficulty moving on to other more pressing ones.

However, he had closed a big case last night and now he was trying to sleep but his damn phone wouldn't stop buzzing. Exasperated, he threw out an arm and snatched up the phone. "Coyle!" he barked, "What is it?"

"Well now," said the voice on the other end of the phone, "that's not a very warm greeting."

Coyle opened an eye and saw the name on the phone's screen. "Jeff?" He said groggily, is that you?"

"Yeah, it's me Roper and I've got a very late Christmas present for you."

"Listen, Jeff, it's great to hear from you but I've just finished a really late one and I'm absolutely knackered," Coyle said, hoping to end the call quickly.

"Well I think when I tell you that Charles Khan was found dead in his car this morning and a diamond worth easily in excess of thirty-thousand pounds was found nearby you might want to wake up."

Grainy was right. Coyle immediately sat up and was instantly alert. "Khan's dead?" he said. "Tell me more."

Roper had spent much of his career chasing after the Khan brothers but every time he came close to catching them they had, for one reason or another, managed to slip through his fingers. Indeed, they had proven to be most elusive so it was with keen interest that he listened to everything Grainy had to say.

* * *

Roper showered, dressed and chugged down two cups of black coffee before receiving the case notes by email from Jeff. After reading them avidly, Coyle concurred with Grainy, who was not prone to exaggeration, that there was something more to this than a simple road accident. But what that was remained to be seen.

By 2.30pm, he and his lanky, young Detective Sergeant, Dave Eckhart, were standing in the doorway of Arthur Khan's mews house in Chelsea and had just broken the news to Arthur that his brother had been found dead.

Both detectives looked tired and world weary as Coyle said, "I'm very sorry for your loss, sir".

Arthur was stunned. "Charles is dead?" Somehow he already suspected this but to hear it said aloud made it seem all the more terrible.

"Yes, Mr. Khan. I'm very sorry."

"You're sure - absolutely sure it's him? There are

a lot of black Range Rovers about - maybe —"

"I'm sorry, sir, there is no doubt. Your brother's driving license was found in the car, as was his wallet containing his credit cards."

"Oh, my God." Arthur was clearly shaken. His worst fears had been realised, Charles was dead. His younger brother gone. It was like he'd been punched in the gut.

"I'm afraid I have some questions for you too, Mr. Khan. Some questions that I really must have an answer to if we could just take up a few moments of your time. I know it's an intrusion into your privacy at this extremely sad time, but like I said, it is quite important."

Arthur Khan looked up, straight into the piercing blue eyes of Roper Coyle. *Oh, Christ - the diamonds! They've got hold of the diamonds!*

"Um, look, this is all a bit of a shock, Arthur said, "Maybe you could come back later perhaps - or tomorrow—".

"Like I said, Mr. Khan, it's really quite important that we speak with you now. We won't take up too much of your time. Just a few minutes, I promise."

"Fine, fine. Come in then if you must. But please, I'm still trying to absorb what you've told me about Charles, so I'd be grateful if you would make it quick."

"Yes, of course. I quite understand" Roper said as he and Eckhart followed Khan into the modern, expensively decorated interior of the trendy mews house.

Once in the sitting room, Arthur collapsed onto a white leather settee and gestured for the detectives to sit in the two chairs opposite. Arthur was a big man. Burly, broad shouldered, his charcoal hair closely cropped. He sat with his forehead resting on his hand, the grief on his tanned face clearly etched. "So what is it you so desperately need to know, detective?" He said.

"Could you tell me what it is that you and your brother do for a living, Mr. Khan?" Coyle asked, knowing only too well.

"What we do for a living?" replied Arthur, slightly relieved, having half expected the first question to be about a briefcase full of priceless diamonds. "We're retired military, Detective Chief Inspector. Old soldiers. We dabble in a few matters of business - logistics, import, export and the like but nothing too serious. Mostly we do nothing. We play golf, enjoy a nice glass of wine, occasionally enjoy the company of a lady. You know the form, don't you? Two bachelors with too much money to spend - what would you do?"

"Quite," said Coyle. "You've only just recently moved back to the UK, I understand. From living abroad, I mean?"

"That's the life of a soldier, Detective Chief Inspector. Never at home for long. Listen, is this all you want to know because —"

"No, sir. It's not all, I'm afraid." Do you know if your brother owned a gun?"

"A gun?" Arthur exclaimed, feigning shock, "Of course he didn't."

"You're sure, Mr. Khan? You're sure your brother didn't own a chrome-plated Magnum?"

"Good lord, no! Why on earth would Charles own one of those cannons?" Arthur sincerely hoped that DCI Coyle did not check the coat rack on the way out because he would have found his own chrome-plated Magnum in its tooled leather shoulder holster hanging there.

"Because one was found in his car, Mr. Khan and because he was wearing a shoulder holster custom made to accomodate it."

"I'm sorry, I know nothing about that. If that's correct then I'm extremely surprised. Charles was an ex-soldier, as I have said. He knew guns very well. Maybe that's something to do with it, I don't know."

"Do you own a gun, Mr. Khan?"

Arthur looked up at the question, again staring into Coyle's inscrutable eyes. "No, Detective Chief Inspector, I most certainly do not. I am a respectable man and so was my brother." Any minute, Arthur thought, this policeman's going to ask about the diamonds and that's going to make Charles' possession of a gun a trifling matter.

"You say you were soldiers, Mr. Khan, until

you retired. Yet our records show that you and your brother both bought yourselves out of the army some years ago - which leaves quite a gap between your leaving the army and your return to the UK. What was it you did in the intervening years?"

"I said that we were soldiers, Detective Chief Inspector, I didn't say for who. I'm afraid Her Majesty doesn't pay her armed forces quite so well as some other organisations." Arthur was feeling irritated now. *Ask about the bloody diamonds and get it over with.*

"A mercenary, then?" Roper said.

"A soldier."

"Quite." When did you last see your brother, Mr. Khan?"

"Night before last. We had dinner together."

"And he was heading where? Do you know?"

"Sorry, Detective Inspector, I don't know."

"It must have been important don't you think, it's pretty treacherous out there. The coroner says the accident happened sometime last night, perhaps around ten."

"Like I said, I don't know. I'm not my brother's keeper."

"No, of course not. But to be travelling last night in all that weather - well, it must have been important, that's all.

"Yes. I suppose. Now, if you've finished I'd like to get on with grieving for my brother, if that's alright."

"Yes, of course. Thank you." Coyle and Eckhart stood up in unison. "My deepest condolences once again."

"Thank you - Mister...? I'm sorry I've forgotten your name." Arthur couldn't believe it, no mention of the diamonds. Nothing. *What the hell had happened, or was this guy just bluffing?*

"Coyle. Detective Chief Inspector Roper Coyle and Detective Sergeant Eckhart. We'll see ourselves out sir. Thank you for your time. We'll no doubt be in touch."

At that moment, Arthur Khan's mobile phone, which lay on the coffee table in front of them, sparked into life, the ringtone sharp and offensive in the solemn atmosphere. Coyle glanced down and saw the caller display. Peter Bearing. He made a mental note.

Khan snatched up the phone and quickly silenced it. "Sorry," he said. "Now if that's all —"

"Yes, of course."

"Er, sir," Eckhart said to Coyle, pushing his boyish blonde hair back with the palm of his hand, his acting rivalling that of Olivier's "There was just that other thing —"

"Oh, yes, that's right," Roper replied, looking up at his gangly sergeant and giving him just the very slightest of winks, his theatrical skills matching his partner's.

Here we go, thought Arthur. Here's where they

117

ask about the hundreds of diamonds they've found in Charles' briefcase.

"Do you know whether your brother had anything to do with diamonds?"

"Diamonds?" Arthur said, a little too casually, "No, why?"

"It's just that one was found at the scene, a few feet from the car. I'm told it's worth well over thirty-thousand pounds," Coyle said.

One! One solitary diamond! Not hundreds - but one. What the hell is he trying to pull?

"My God. No, I'm afraid I can't help you again, Detective Chief Inspector," replied Khan feigning innocence. "Maybe it was lost by somebody else. I'm sure I would have known if it belonged to Charles."

"Yes. I'm sure you would, Mr. Khan. Anyway, just thought I'd ask. Like I said, we'll see ourselves out."

And with that, Coyle and Eckhart departed. Leaving Arthur Khan in a state of complete and utter shock. And this time it had very little to do with the death of his brother.

* * *

An hour later Arthur Khan was sitting in Peter Bearing's enormous office. His big frame hunched miserably in a wide leather swivel chair that sat directly across from Bearing, the large expanse of his contemporary chrome and glass desk spanning the width between them. The floor to ceiling windows, with their spectacular views of The City looking out onto a grey, gloomy day that matched the sombre mood within.

Khan had lost a brother and Bearing a close friend. But they had more to worry about than Charles.

"One bloody diamond, Peter. Can you believe it?" Arthur said.

"I must admit I do find it extremely difficult to comprehend," replied Bearing. He exuded calm even under circumstances such as these but his concern was clear to see. "Either the police have them, in which case we must wait for the other shoe to drop, or —"

"Or what? You think they've been stolen?"

"I think it most likely don't you?"

"I don't know. I can't think straight, but yes, I suppose it's possible.

But by who? A passer-by? An opportunist thief who thinks he can get away with stealing millions of pounds worth of diamonds? I mean it's not petty stuff we're dealing with here. If it was one or two stones or maybe even a case full of money then yes, maybe. But that many diamonds - four, five hundred big rocks - I mean come on, how stupid have you gotta be?"

"I know," said Bearing, "I quite agree. But still the fact remains, the stones are missing and if the police don't have them, then who on earth does?"

The room was silent for many minutes as both men pondered the situation. Peter rose and walked over to a large glass cabinet and fixed Arthur another whisky. As he handed it to him he said, "Wherever the diamonds are, we've got to find them, agreed?"

"Agreed," said Khan.

"And whoever's got them needs to be dealt with."

"Agreed again. Especially if they had anything to do with Charles' death, I'll take great delight in killing them myself."

"Yes, I'm sure," said Bearing, who knew very well that his friend was more than capable of doing so. "So I propose we call in Sumpter."

"Aaron Sumpter? Why? I can handle this, Peter. I'll find the bastard who's got them and I'll deal with them in my own way."

"I know you could, Arthur. But I feel we need a subtle approach. You're too emotional at the moment, quite understandably so, but I'm not sure that's best for our present needs. If the person who took the diamonds was responsible for Charles' death then you will have your vengeance I promise you, but for now, let Sumpter take the lead."

"I don't trust him, Peter, you know that and I could —"

"No, Arthur. Aaron Sumpter has been with me a long time and with my father before that. He is trustworthy and what is more, he's a rottweiler, he'll gnaw away at this until he finds something. He'll stick at it through thick and thin until he finds us our diamonds."

"But, Peter —"

"My decision is final, Arthur. That's the way to play it, you mark my words. Sumpter will get us our diamonds back, you see if he doesn't.

* * *

DCI Roper Coyle sat at his desk back at the yard drinking a lukewarm coffee from a polystyrene cup. His short brown hair was stylishly messy, although quite unintentionally, and he had a five o'clock shadow darkening his square jaw which was down to a serious lack of sleep and an extremely heavy case load. He rubbed his sad blue eyes that every woman on the force had fallen in love with and thought about Charles and Arthur Khan. Something definitely wasn't right. Roper was a good detective but he didn't need to be Sherlock Holmes to work that one out.

Jeff Grainy had known it too. The two of them had worked together many years ago and had kept in touch ever since. Grainy was an old school detective who followed his instincts. Coyle was the same and everything about this case had his instincts screaming.

Firstly there was the gun, so much more than just a defensive weapon. Then there was the military background - mercenaries who made their fortune from illegal wars. And then there was the diamond.

Over thirty thousand pounds worth in just one big stone. Perfect cut, colour and clarity it said in the notes. This troubled Roper more than both the other two things put together.

Added to all these things was the name Peter Bearing, which had flashed up on Arthur Khan's phone. Of course it could have been just one of many Peter Bearings, not necessarily the Peter Bearing who was a big name in The City and who, along with the Khans, had also been on Scotland Yard's radar for some considerable time. But, and it was a fairly big but, if it was that Peter Bearing, then that, too, flagged up another interesting little twist.

This case certainly had many avenues to explore and Roper intended to search each one to the full. There was something bad happening here, he knew it, he felt it in his gut and as the cops always said on TV, his gut never lied.

Chapter 11

Jake was awoken early by the dawn chorus in the first faint light of morning. He was cold now and his limbs ached but he had slept well and felt surprisingly refreshed. He scratched his thick, sandy beard and rubbed his bleary eyes before putting on his glasses. Then he climbed out of the BMW and had a long, revitalising stretch before taking a much-needed leak behind the car.

The air smelt fresh and clean and the sound of birdsong and the gentle trickle of a nearby stream was all that could be heard in the tranquillity of the meadow. It was a new day and a new beginning for Jake.

He was shivering now in the chill of the early morning so returned to the car and pulled the heavy overcoat around him once more. Then he reached for the briefcase and snapped open the catches. It was the first time he had opened the case since taking it, the first time he had dared. Jake noticed now that there were twenty compartments inside, ten down each side and all with clip fastening plastic lids. He unclipped one of the compartment doors and slid out the velvet bag it contained, then slowly pulled the drawstring seal open and carefully poured the contents into his hand. Ten big diamonds fell into his palm and sparkled beguilingly up at him. They were dazzling. The only diamond Jake had seen up close before was the one in Angie's less than modest engagement ring, but the ones he was looking at now were huge in comparison. They were also much brighter and clearer and, he realised, significantly more valuable. Indeed, the contents of his hand would be worth an absolute fortune. He dropped the diamonds back into their velvet bag and returned it to its compartment. He then opened another compartment, then another and yet another. Each time finding diamonds of an equal or larger size than the first. It was staggering, utterly mind-blowing and he could not even begin to comprehend the enormous worth of what he possessed.

However, with the night's rest had come some semblance of rationality and Jake at last began to realise the enormity of what he had done. For the first time he also considered the consequences.

These diamonds would undoubtedly be missed. Whoever owned them would most definitely want them back. But Jake was certain that no one knew that he had taken them. The road had been deserted and he had left no trace of his presence there so there was nothing to tie him to the accident or the diamonds. But guilt had also crept in now along with regret. He had stolen from a dead man. Rifled through his clothing and taken his money. He should have just called the police told them what had happened and left the diamonds well alone. But no, he had absconded, taken the case, taken the money and left the country like a common criminal.

But it was almost too late to go back now. And back to what? He asked himself. Back to debt, to bankruptcy, to an empty house that would soon be repossessed? The kids were with Angie and she was with her new man. They all had a new life now and Jake was not a part of it.

For the moment at least, they were undoubtedly better off without him. Without the worry and the bills and the sleepless nights and the fear of the bailiff knocking on the door. And in that instant his mind was made up. What was done was done. Going back would solve nothing. He had been honest his whole life, squeaky clean, whiter than white and it had got him nowhere. But two nights ago, fortune had shined on him for the first time in a very long time and he was determined not to waste it.

His intention was to sell a few of the diamonds and set things right for Angie and the kids financially. As for him, well time would tell but to be debt free would be a very good start.

Jake put the diamonds back and closed the briefcase. He then opened the large, newly purchased backpack and pushed the case into it.

It was time to get going.

Jake got out of the BMW and closed the door, leaving the keys inside. He knew the car would be found eventually, hopefully later rather than sooner but, with luck, by then he would be long gone.

Then shrugging the backpack onto his shoulders he set off on the long walk back to the main road.

* * *

Two hours later, after picking up a lift with a jovial German truck driver, Jake was back in Poitiers. Once there, he bought some new clothes, a pair of jeans, some trainers, a couple of cheap shirts and a zip-up waterproof jacket. Then he went to the public toilets and changed, dumping his old clothes in a waste bin when he had finished.

After that he found an internet cafe, bought himself a croissant and a latte and sat down to do some research on diamonds.

Three hours later, feeling much more informed, he was on a train heading for Paris. From there he caught another one to Brussels. By the following evening he was in Amsterdam, holed up in the cheapest hotel he could find. The four hundred euros he had left in his pocket was dwindling fast but at least now he had a plan, a way forward. It was going to be extremely difficult and fraught with danger but, to make a better life for him and his family, Jake was ready for the challenge.

Chapter 12

Peter Bearing had called Aaron Sumpter a rottweiler but he looked more like a rat with his sharp pointed features and searching, inquisitive eyes. Bald-headed except for an inch wide line of red hair that ran in a semi-circle from ear to ear, making him appear older than his forty-two years, but his slim, wiry frame was tight with muscle and he was in excellent physical condition.

Arriving home after his meeting with Bearing and Khan, he snapped on the lights in the hallway of his neat, perfectly maintained semi in Hampstead.

The walls of the hallway were lined with memories. Photos of him with Wendel Wallace and Teddy Bearing and both their families. Pictures of Wendel with his son and daughter, taken when they were just little kids and pictures of Teddy and his various wives. There were also several photographs of Peter Bearing and the Khan brothers, pictured during their first year at Oxford.

These memories represented Sumpter's family. He had none of his own, no memory of his father and just the briefest recollection of his mother. With no brothers or sisters, his early years were spent in a series of foster homes and orphanages. Until the age of fifteen when he went to work for Wallace Bearing. That was when his life truly began and what he would always be eternally thankful for.

Aaron walked into the small kitchen and clicked on the kettle then crossed to the wall monitor to check the video feed from the three CCTV cameras discreetly mounted on the outside of the house. Zero intruders.

He took his cup of tea upstairs and flicked on the lights.

The biggest bedroom was used as a store room, filled with archived files, notebooks, diaries, boxes, envelopes and video cassettes all laboriously categorized and organized so that the information could be accessed in seconds. However, much of this hard copy had become obsolete, as all the data Sumpter had collected over the years could nowadays fit onto just one tiny storage device. But Aaron liked to keep back-ups. Just in case.

The second bedroom was Aaron's office which was where he spent most of his time. It was equipped with two thirty inch monitors, a super-powerful Macintosh tower, a stand alone database and a video editing suite. There was also a coffee machine and a teasmaid as Aaron liked his caffeine.

The third bedroom had been converted into a darkroom. In here, a cabinet housed his cameras and telescopes.

Finally, the small fourth bedroom was where Sumpter slept.

Aaron took out his phone and downloaded the data stored on it to his laptop, which he kept with him at all times.

Sumpter kept records of everything, including tape recordings of secret conversations, photocopies of illicit transactions and the financial mis-dealings of people that had been or could be useful to Peter Bearing.

Aaron had it all. Evidence, leverage, ransom. But that was his job.

That was what Peter Bearing paid him for. He was not a Rottweiler but bloodhound, a tracker and he was exceptionally good at it. Bearing used Sumpter's skills to ensure that whatever he wanted was made possible. The information he supplied was used to encourage people to bend to Peter's will. Whether they wanted to or not.

Business was for winners and Peter always won.

The brief he had given Aaron this time was simply to find the diamonds and whoever took them as quickly as possible.

However, Sumpter had advised Peter and Arthur that this particular task could take many months to complete as there seemed to be no obvious leads.

They agreed but were emphatic; find them no matter the cost, no matter how long it takes. Just find them.

* * *

Back in his office in Hampstead, Aaron Sumpter took a sip of his tea, flexed his fingers and pulled his keyboard closer. Then typed the words 'Northamptonshire Police' into his search bar. His first job was to hack into their files and find out exactly what they knew.

However, it was not long before Sumpter discovered that the bulk of the case had indeed been handed over to The Metropolitan Police, as Arthur Khan had already informed him. The detective in charge being a DCI Roper Coyle.

To gain proper access to the relevant files The Met's system would require a little more work than a simple hacking job. It meant knowing passwords, circumventing firewalls and working through many other security protocols and trap doors that Scotland Yard had in place.

Normally Aaron could do this with his eyes closed, but because he would be poking around in The Met's files for more than just a brief period of time, his presence would have to be as seamless as possible. Hackers could be traced and Aaron most definitely did not want that. It was safe enough to go in, have a quick look around and then get out again, but to maintain serious long-term surveillance was very risky and the ramifications should his prying be detected were not something he wished to contemplate. So more covert tactics were called for.

For this Aaron had to physically enter Scotland Yard posing as a member of the janitorial team who were contracted to clean the building at night. This was a much more straightforward task. He hacked into the files of the contractors, added an alias of himself to their list of employees, then forged an identity card, printed it out and laminated it. Then, for one night only, he reassigned the janitor who normally cleaned the particular floor he was interested in.

The following evening, wearing a disguise and kitted out in the appropriate attire, Aaron reported for work at Scotland Yard at ten o'clock. It was surprisingly easy to gain entrance to the building, the busy desk sergeant only giving his fake ID a cursory glance before admitting him inside. Within minutes Sumpter was on the relevant floor. Fifteen minutes after that he had fitted a tiny bug to Coyle's phone and attached a small device to his computer that would allow Aaron to see exactly what Coyle was seeing on his screen from the comfort of his home in Hampstead.

After the real purpose of his visit had been completed, Aaron gave the offices a thorough clean so as not to arouse suspicion.

By eight the next morning he was back in the office of his small semi-detached, showered, refreshed and sitting in front of his huge monitor screen. He had a nice cup of freshly ground coffee in his hand as he watched and listened to Roper Coyle going about his investigations, Sumpter's presence completely undetected.

Before long he would have all the information the police had on Charles Khan and the missing diamonds.

Chapter 13

Jake had spent two days and nights trawling the streets of Amsterdam, surreptitiously asking questions about where he might be able to sell some diamonds. He asked in cafe's and bars and, very tentatively, in backstreet, less reputable looking jewellery stores. He knew that Antwerp, not Amsterdam was the diamond capital of the world, but thought he had a better chance of making a sale here. He had visited Amsterdam before and it was a beautiful city but it also had many seedy clubs and bars where someone might easily find a buyer for illegal merchandise. But it was dangerous, street crime was common so for Jake to make it known that he had something of value in his possession was not the wisest move he could make. However he had no choice but to take the risk.

On his third day in Amsterdam, Jake was given the name of a man called Gerhardt who, he was told, would possibly be interested in what he was selling.

Gerhardt could apparently be found after midnight in a room he used in the Red-Light District behind a brothel. Jake, clutching a scrap of paper with the address written on it, felt slightly sordid as he passed the strip clubs and the peep shows and the naked girls sitting in their windows beckoning to him, their ever-present red-lights illuminating the otherwise picturesque canal at midnight. The streets were heaving, drunken men both young and old lining them, ogling the shameless delights on display, the faint whiff of alcohol and marijuana being carried on the cool night breeze. Jake navigated his way through the cobbled streets and dark alleyways trying to find the address he was given until he at last stood before the building he was looking for, the obligatory red-light and naked girl in the front window.

Nervously, he opened the door and went inside. The girl, completely nude except for stockings, suspenders and a pair of thigh high black PVC boots, closed the curtain in front of her and stepped out of the window to greet him with a fake smile. "You want fuck or suck?" she asked in heavily accented English.

"Er, neither, actually, thanks," Jake said with a guilty smile, "I'm looking for Gerhardt, I was told I could find him here?"

The girl's smile immediately dropped as she tutted and climbed back into the window. "Back there," she said, indicating with her thumb over her shoulder, "Last door. Knock first."

"Thanks," Jake said but the girl had already re-opened the curtain and was too busy positioning herself in a provocative pose to hear him.

Jake looked about the tiny room in which he was standing, there was a small bed with dirty ruffled sheets and a nightstand next to it with a lava lamp on it as well as a basket full of assorted condoms and a box of tissues. Across from the bed there was a small hand basin and next to that was a door concealed by a beaded curtain. Jake walked uncertainly over to it, pulled aside the beaded curtain and turned the handle to reveal a narrow corridor with several doors leading off from either side. He saw the door he needed at the far end of the passage and tentatively headed toward it. The sound of people having sex was emanating from behind several of the other doors making Jake feel slightly embarrassed and awkward. However, when he reached the door he wanted, he paused for a moment to compose himself then knocked twice. There was no response but Jake could hear movement, he felt anxious, suddenly fearful - this was not a world he was used to but it was too late to back out now because at that moment the door opened.

Jake was not sure what he was expecting, some burly thug perhaps, or a swarthy villainous looking type, but certainly not the person standing before him now. "I'm looking for Gerhardt," Jake said to the short, balding gentleman who looked very much like a university professor in his knitted bow tie and tweed jacket.

"I am he," Gerhardt said in perfect English. "How may I help you?"

"Er," Jake began, a little taken back, "I have, er, something you might be interested in - something of value, for sale."

Gerhardt gave Jake the once over, then said, "I see. In that case you had better come in."

Jake followed the little man into the room which was small and dingy with very little furniture except for a desk, a few chairs and a filing cabinet. The carpet was threadbare and the ancient curtains were closed but the glow of a red light could be seen clearly through them. The room itself was lit solely by a large angle-poise lamp on the desk.

"You will forgive my humble surroundings," Gerhardt said, taking a seat behind the desk and waving Jake to a chair on the other side, "But the rent is cheap, so I cannot complain."

"That's fine. I understand." Jake replied, sitting down.

"Now, my friend, you say you have something of value for sale? Please, enlighten me."

Jake hesitated for just a moment before reaching into the front pocket of his jeans and pulling out a carefully folded piece of tissue paper. He leant forward into the full glare of the angle-poise lamp and slowly unwrapped it, finally revealing a single diamond. He had purposely chosen one of the very smallest, not wishing to set any unnecessary jackpot alarms off in Gerhardt's head.

"Ah, I see," said Gerhardt, "may I examine it?"

"Yes, of course."

"Thank you." Gerhardt picked up the diamond which was about the same size as a small pea and held it to the light between his thumb and forefinger. "Very nice," he said. "Very pretty." He then reached into a drawer and pulled out an eyeglass and a pair of tweezers. Fixing the glass into his eye socket and now holding the diamond with the tweezers, he gave it a more thorough examination. "Yes, very pretty indeed. Excellent colour, excellent clarity, a nice size - I assume it is stolen?"

"Er, what?" Jake was suddenly caught off guard. "Er, no, I mean–"

"Please," Gerhardt interjected. "I am not a judge. I merely ask to protect myself. You are someone who I have never met before, you could tell me anything. But if the diamond is stolen, there are certain parties I can sell it to. If it is not, then there are other, more legitimate parties I can approach. However, if you say it is not stolen and then I find out it is, I could find myself severely compromised. In that instance I will have no hesitation in providing any interested parties with your description. On the other hand, if you are truthful with me from the outset I will take your identity to the grave."

"I see." Jake said. Then after a moment's contemplation, he added, "How do I know I can trust you?"

"You don't. All I can tell you is that this is my livelihood, I am respected within my field and to break a confidence, to reveal a source without an extremely good reason would be tantamount to both business and most possibly actual suicide. My word is my bond, that is how I operate. But betray me and that bond is broken."

Again, Jake thought for a moment. Regardless of his surroundings, Gerhardt did seem trustworthy. Honest, almost. "Yes, it is stolen," he said, "But not intentionally, it was more of an accident–"

"Please," Gerhardt interjected. "It is of no importance. But thank you for your honesty, it is appreciated. Now, this diamond - I assume you know its true value?"

"I do," Jake bluffed. After his research on the internet he estimated that the stone he had here was worth somewhere between maybe twenty and forty thousand euros but he had no real idea. It all depended on clarity and cut and colour and many other variables that could make one diamond much more valuable than another of similar size. He suspected that this was a good quality stone, that they all were, but how good was beyond his extremely limited knowledge.

"Good." Said Gerhardt, "You know also, of course, that I cannot pay you anywhere near that amount, not for a stolen stone and I would also like to make a small profit myself."

I bet you would, thought Jake. "Of course," he said.

"So, how much do you want for it?" Asked Gerhardt.

Jake had to gamble, knowing it could cost him the deal but he also needed to gauge the worth of the diamonds he possessed. The internet was good for research but nothing could beat an expert's opinion, no matter how sleazy they might seem. A dealer was a dealer and Jake couldn't be too choosy. With a straight face, he said rather hopefully, "Twenty-five thousand."

"A good and fair price for a stolen item such as this," Gerhardt said. "But sadly too rich for my blood. As you can see I am not a wealthy man. The best I could offer is ten."

Jake couldn't believe it. If Gerhardt had thought twenty-five thousand to be a fair price for a stolen diamond such as this then the actual value could be two or three times as much. He was momentarily staggered, but ten thousand was far better than he had actually hoped for. He could of course go elsewhere and maybe get a better deal but he was running out of money fast and finding another buyer could prove difficult to say the least. "Fifteen," he said. "That's the best I can do. Take it or leave it."

Now it was Gerhardt's turn for contemplation as he studied the diamond again. "Very well, fifteen thousand euros. We have a deal." He held out his hand and Jake shook it. Then Gerhardt reached into the drawer again and pulled out a wad of notes. He counted out fifteen thousand euros with the expertise of a bank teller and handed it to Jake. "Very nice to meet you," he said.

"Likewise," Jake said, then as a purely spontaneous afterthought he added, "Would you be interested in buying any more?" It was another gamble to reveal that he had more diamonds to sell but thought it was worth the risk. Besides he was desperate with few other options.

"Alas," said Gerhardt, "When I said I was not a wealthy man, I meant it. Fifteen thousand euros is as much as I can afford at present. However, for a small commission, I could put you in touch with someone who would be able to buy more from you. Perhaps many more, if you have them."

"When you say commission, what are we talking about?"

Gerhardt's eyes glinted with anticipation as he said, "Another stone, say? My contact is worth it, I assure you."

"I'm sure he is," Jake smiled, knowing he was being played but nevertheless finding himself trusting Gerhardt. He was a very strange little man who reminded him very much of the Donald Pleasance character in The Great Escape. An intellectual duck-out-of-water who has been forced to adapt to a life that was not necessarily of his own choosing. He guessed that Gerhardt was not a naturally dishonest man but circumstances, whatever they might have been, had forced him to become one. Jake felt strangely sorry for him - although for all he knew Gerhardt could quite easily be one of the greatest criminal masterminds of the twenty-first century, but somehow he doubted it.

"While we're at it," Jake continued, "I don't suppose you know anyone who could supply me with a passport, do you?"

"But of course," said Gerhardt, "As many as you need."

"And the cost?" Jake asked.

Now it was Gerhardt's turn to smile, "Shall we say another diamond?"

"Why not." Said Jake, knowing he had fallen right into that one.

Chapter 14

DCI Coyle had hit a brick wall. The investigation into the death of Charles Khan was going nowhere and he was snowed under with more pressing cases - some with leads that actually led somewhere. But he couldn't stop thinking about the Khan case. About the gun and the diamond, about Arthur Khan and Peter Bearing. And it irked him.

Coyle had been a detective for many years and he knew that there was a lot more to this than a simple car crash. And he knew that the big, expensive diamond found close to the scene was somehow linked but he just had nothing more to go on.

He looked across at Dave Eckhart, his Detective Sergeant who worked at the desk opposite; young, recently married, a baby on the way, but a natural copper with good instincts. "I'm going for a smoke, Dave, okay? Give me a shout if you need me."

"Okay, boss."

Coyle hated smoking but never seemed to have

the time to quit. Besides, it helped him to relax, or at least that was his excuse. He stood out on the fire escape and tapped out a cigarette from a half empty pack, bought only this morning but he'd need another one before night fall.

It was getting warmer now. Just a week after all that bloody snow and Spring finally felt as if it was on the way. Roper was pleased, he loved the outdoors but hated the cold. Police work was miserable enough without that too. For the first time in years he thought about his mother, she hated the cold, too. Hated most things in fact, including him, it turned out. She was the one responsible for giving him the name, 'Roper', her maiden name, and a Christian name which never failed to get him noticed at school. But it had made him tough, determined, dogged even. And he supposed he had her to thank for that. She left when he was ten. He still did not know why. Nor did his father but they had coped well enough without her.

Roper married his childhood sweetheart shortly after his father's passing. But after almost ten years of marriage, he was alone once more.

Even though his wife had been unfaithful, it was fair to say that he had not been the most attentive husband; his job being a significantly contributory factor, but it was a job he was good at and it was now all he had left.

And when something had him beaten it bugged him.

Coyle took a long last drag of his cigarette, then flicked the butt over the railings. As he turned to go back in, Eckhart's six foot two of blonde haired boyishness barged through the fire escape door. "Boss, I think we might finally have a lead," he said.

* * *

A man who had been driving along the same stretch of road shortly before Charles Khan's accident had come forward. He was the driver of a Volvo who had apparently had to swerve to miss a BMW 4x4 that had pulled up abruptly at the side of the road. The man recalled that the car was a rental as he distinctly remembered seeing a sticker on the back, but he couldn't quite remember which one, Hertz maybe or Eurofleet, possibly Avis. He was also foggy on the driver of the BMW, long hair and glasses he thought, but it was a week ago and he couldn't be sure.

Roper wondered if that same BMW, parked so badly, had been the cause of Charles Khan's accident and, if so, where was it and the driver now?

After speaking with the driver of the Volvo, it took Roper a further two weeks and dozens of phone calls to discover that the BMW had been hired by Easyrent to a Mr. Jake Sawyer.

The car, it turned out, had never been returned and Mr. Sawyer had been missing ever since the night of the crash.

When Coyle spoke to Mr. Sawyer's estranged

wife, Angela, on the phone, she was baffled by his disappearance and was concerned for his safety. She, and her two children, were now living with her lover, Mr. Richard Maddox and from what Coyle could ascertain, she had left Jake because he had been drowning in debt.

* * *

Aaron Sumpter had learned and logged all these things, monitoring the investigation from his home in Hampstead, thanks to the devices he had installed on Coyle's phone and computer.

He had also dutifully reported his findings to Peter Bearing and

Arthur Khan, once again stressing that it could be a long-winded investigation and not to expect immediate results.

Bearing acknowledged this, as did Khan, but Sumpter could tell that Arthur was already growing impatient and made a mental note to keep an eye on him. In Aaron's experience, hot-headedness often led to unnecessary complications.

Chapter 15

Gerhardt had been as good as his word and had given Jake the address of a diamond buyer in Antwerp. He had also phoned ahead and made the necessary introductions, smoothing the way for a meeting and offering his own personal guarantee that Jake was trustworthy.

Gerhardt had also introduced Jake to a forger who, for the cost of another diamond, had made up four new passports for him. Jake thought it prudent to have more than one, just in case he should need them. The workmanship was excellent and sitting next to the genuine one the counterfeit versions looked identical.

In possession of his new passports after an insufferable three week wait for them, Jake finally left Amsterdam taking the train to Antwerp where he had an appointment with Gerhardt's diamond buyer.

* * *

Jake had spent most of the previous three weeks

holed up in his hotel room awaiting word from both Gerhardt and the forger. Three weeks with nothing but guilt and regret for company but it was too late to go back now and he resolved to push on with his plan, convinced that ultimately it would be for the best.

However, as Jake stepped off the train at Antwerp Central station he felt a great burden of culpability upon his shoulders. Whatever else had happened in his past, he had always been honest. But now he was a thief with a criminal agenda. He knew not to whom the diamonds belonged but they were certainly not his and now he bitterly regretted taking them. But that was of very little relevance now.

He looked around at the magnificent architecture of the historical building but was immune to its beauty today. Glancing up at the metal and glass dome, where in a previous life, he would have been impressed by the sheer scale of design, he only saw dark clouds above and heavy rain lashing against the window panes. The weather matched his mood.

Outside, in the pouring rain, keeping his backpack close, he hailed a taxi and asked the driver to take him to a reasonably priced hotel somewhere near to the Diamond District, which he duly did.

The Rubens Antwerpen Continental was comfortable enough for an overnight stay and either a brisk walk or a short taxi ride away from where Jake was due to meet the buyer Gerhardt had laid on.

For the moment though, Jake was wet, tired and hungry. After a long shower, he sat on the bed in a towel and ordered a sandwich from room service, then raided the mini bar for a beer and a bag of nuts - pretty much the same diet he had lived on for the last three weeks. He clicked on the TV and watched a pay-per-view movie - 'The Shawshank Redemption' but turned it off halfway through as its depiction of prison life did little to ease Jake's guilt and conjured up images of what might happen to him should he ever be arrested for his crime. Jake opted for an early night as he had to be up bright and early for the meeting tomorrow but he only slept sporadically as guilt and nerves kept him from sleep. He really didn't know what to expect in the morning, only that the outcome of the meeting would determine what his plans might be afterwards. So far, he had been operating on a day to day basis, but depending on what the buyer offered him for the ten diamonds he intended to sell he may well be able to plan possibly weeks, maybe months ahead.

However, the thing of most importance was to send money back to Angie and the kids and to pay the debts that had piled up which had set him on this reckless path in the first place.

* * *

The meeting the next morning was not at all like the one Jake had with Gerhardt. On the contrary, this time he met with the buyer in broad daylight in a prestigious, very impressive building in the heart of the Antwerp Diamond District and the buyer was a much more well-heeled individual; tailored suit, Italian shoes and a Monte Carlo tan. He also had two extremely large bodyguards stationed outside the double smoked glass doors of his luxurious office.

Hugo van Elst was separated from Jake by a huge desk that appeared to be made entirely of glass. Van Elst reclined nonchalantly in an ultra-modern white leather chair, his legs crossed and his fingers casually entwined on his lap. He had snowy white hair with matching goatee and sitting there in his crisp suit and silk cravat it appeared that he and Gerhardt belonged to different planets let alone different trades. However they were in the same trade, just at opposite ends of the spectrum and it was clear to Jake that the pair had done business many times in the past, indeed, when Jake first entered his office, van Elst had enquired after Gerhardt's health and was obviously pleased to hear he was well.

The meeting reminded Jake of one he had had with his bank manager in the days when he was still worthy of his time - good natured yet financially motivated and, like in that meeting, he felt more than a little intimidated. But Gerhardt had been as good as his word and had laid the groundwork for him.

Van Elst knew why he was there, what he had to sell and that the merchandise in question was not of a legitimate nature and, even though his demeanour was pleasant enough, he was all business.

"You have the stones?" he asked.

"I do," Jake replied, pulling out a small velvet bag from the inside pocket of his jacket. "Is it okay to show you them here?" He asked, unsure of accepted protocol in the transaction of illicit merchandise.

"Please." Replied van Elst, waving a hand casually across the desk, clearly unperturbed by the thought of having the stolen stones scattered across it, confident in the knowledge that they would not be disturbed.

Jake opened the drawstring seal and poured ten diamonds, slightly larger than the ones he had given to Gerhardt, onto the desk in front of him.

"Ah, so beautiful, don't you think?" Remarked van Elst. "They never cease to delight me. You will permit me to take a closer look?"

"Please. Of course." Said Jake.

Just as Gerhardt had, van Elst produced an eyeglass and tweezers from a drawer then proceeded to make a thorough inspection of each of the diamonds, Jake looking on in silence as he did so. He knew the stones were good, the very fact that Gerhardt had given him fifteen thousand euros so readily for the first one told him that much, but he did not know how much this ten would be worth, maybe a hundred thousand euros, perhaps a bit more. Gerhardt had told him that stolen gems changed hands at a fraction of their actual worth.

"These are of remarkable quality. Truly excellent. Gerhardt was right to send you to me." Van Elst said at last, returning the eyeglass and tweezers to the drawer.

"Thank you."

"So, that just brings us to the price," continued van Elst.

"It does. Yes."

"I am not a man to haggle, I believe Gerhardt may have told you that."

"He did."

"But the price I give will always be fair. These stones are stolen, their quality ensures that they will not be forgotten and, if I were the original owner, I would most certainly want them back. All these things I must consider before making you an offer. Indeed, all these things you must consider before accepting my offer. If I possessed these stones, they would not be traced back to you, this I guarantee. Other buyers may offer you a better price but I cannot speak for their integrity. However, the choice is yours."

"I understand and appreciate your honesty."

"Very well. In that case, my offer is two hundred and fifty thousand euros. Cash. Take it or leave it.

Jake very nearly fell off his chair with surprise. He couldn't believe it, he knew the diamonds were of a good quality but two hundred and fifty thousand euros worth? What on earth would they be worth if they were not stolen? And that was just for ten of the smaller stones - the whole case would be worth millions.

"I see from your reaction that was a pleasant surprise," said van Elst, "I should have offered less, perhaps?"

"Maybe," said Jake honestly, still reeling.

"But as I said," continued van Elst, "The price I give will always be fair. My offer stands. Do you accept?"

"Yes. Yes I do, thank you," said Jake now smiling.

"Good. Then I will get you your money." Van Elst picked up the phone and immediately spoke to someone on the other end in Dutch. When he replaced the receiver he addressed Jake once more. "Will you permit me to offer you some advice?"

Jake nodded, uncertain of what he was about to hear.

"It is none of my business, I understand, but I get the sense that you are new to this - would I be correct?"

Jake smiled cautiously, "Is it so obvious?"

"I'm afraid so, yes. Forgive me for being so blunt."

"Of course."

"You strike me as a pleasant young man of good character and Gerhardt speaks well of you. But I must warn you, this is not a business to take lightly. You are fortunate to have met men such as myself and Gerhardt. We are men of integrity and honour but there are many others who are not so honourable and you risk much by seeking to sell stones such as these. Possibly your life. I do not know if you have any more in your possession but I suspect you do. If that is the case, my advice to you, for what it is worth, is to store them somewhere extremely safe. Ideally a bank vault. And then exercise extreme caution before discussing them with anyone. That is my advice. Take it, leave it, it makes no difference to me."

"Thank you," Jake said. "You're very kind. I didn't know what to expect but–"

"Please," van Elst interjected, "I am a businessman, my clients' wellbeing is of prime importance to me. Needless to say, if you ever wish to sell any more diamonds, you know where to find me."

"Yes. Thanks." Jake said.

At that moment there was a gentle knock on the office door and an assistant entered the room carrying a metal briefcase. He placed it on the table in front of Jake and opened it.

"Please," said van Elst, rising from his chair, "Take your time to count it. The case is yours, with my compliments. I will return in a few minutes." He and the assistant then slipped silently out of the room leaving Jake alone.

He opened the case and stared at the contents in wonder. Two hundred and fifty thousand euros.

More money than he had ever seen in his life in any currency. It was staggering and he was till trying to come to terms with it but van Elst's words of warning were also ringing in his head. He had to be careful. Very careful indeed and so far he had been anything but. He had been foolhardy and naive but fortunately very lucky although he knew his luck would not last forever.

At present, the remainder of the diamonds were in a hotel room down the road, in a backpack, unguarded, unsecured. A gift for any opportunist thief. It was incredibly stupid of him to leave them there like that but he did not know what else to do. The hotel safe deposit box was far too small and he did not want to invite any undue attention. But now he realised that he had to take much more care.

He had to stash the diamonds somewhere safe, somewhere no one could easily get at them. A bank vault, van Elst had recommended and in that moment Jake made the decision to travel onto Switzerland where he would find a bank and store the diamonds securely in its vault.

Ten minutes later van Elst returned to the office and Jake, satisfied that he had been paid the agreed amount, shook his hand, thanked him again for his advice and left the building a much wealthier man than when he had entered.

* * *

Two hours later, Jake was on a train headed for

Switzerland and by the following morning he was in Zurich.

Chapter 16

Six weeks after discovering that the car had been rented to Jake Sawyer, the BMW was found abandoned in France.

It had been dumped in an old run down barn near Poitiers and only discovered by the landowner who, quite by chance, was considering selling the derelict building to developers.

DCI Coyle arrived in Poitiers on a Ryanair flight from Stansted a day later. At the airport he took a cab to the local Gendarmerie to introduce himself. From there, the officer in charge escorted him to the barn where the BMW had been found. He spent an hour having a thorough look around but found nothing. He was then escorted to the depot where the abandoned vehicle had been taken, but it was empty, offering no clues as to where the driver might have gone. The French police could offer nothing new either. As far as they were concerned, this was just an abandoned vehicle of very little importance.

DCI Coyle then thanked the officer for his help and took a cab back to the airport to catch the evening flight home.

The next day the real DCI Coyle arrived in Poitiers only to discover that an impostor had been there the day before asking the exact same questions.

Roper couldn't believe it. Someone had been there, in France, posing as him, asking questions about what had previously appeared to be such a trifling matter as an abandoned car.

This, however, proved to Roper that his gut was right. There was more to this case. Much more. But where to go now? There were no further leads to pursue, no clues that the car had revealed and Jake Sawyer was still missing without trace. Vanished, it seemed, into the ether.

* * *

After a day posing as DCI Roper Coyle, Aaron Sumpter arrived back from France only slightly wiser than when he had left. Knowing only that the BMW was of no further use to him and that Jake Sawyer was now the person to find. But unlike the real Coyle, Sumpter had knowledge that could lead him further in the investigation, he knew of the diamonds, of how many there were, of their value and of the likely places someone might try to sell them. He also now knew, with near certainty, who it was who would no doubt be keen to find a buyer for them.

Chapter 17

Zeiss Schiller was a very old and established bank sitting in the Paradeplatz in downtown Zurich, a place synonymous with wealth and banking. The austere architecture of the square lent a certain weight to the surroundings and the bank itself with its grey columns, beautiful stonework and ornamental balconies was incredibly imposing as Jake, now dressed in a suit with his beard trimmed and hair tied back in a neat pony tail stepped into the oak panelled foyer. With him he carried the leather bound briefcase containing the diamonds and the metal one he had been given by Hugo van Elst which contained the money. Had he been mugged on the way to the bank his attacker would have been extremely fortuitous indeed. But thankfully he had not.

He walked up to the pleasant looking young lady at the reception desk and asked to speak with Otto Drescher with whom he had made an appointment the day before.

Drescher appeared within minutes, impeccably dressed and military in bearing but smiley and professional in his manner. He led Jake through to a vast private office, again all oak-panelled with a heavy antique desk in the centre and two comfortable leather bound office chairs either side. Drescher ushered Jake to one of them then sat down opposite. "You wish to open a numbered account, I understand, Mister Sloane, is that correct?"

"It is," Replied Jake, now using the name printed on one of his counterfeit passports. "If that is possible."

"Of course."

"I would also like a safe deposit box, if I may, to store a few items of value. Would that be okay?"

"Certainly, Mister Sloane. Whatever you require Zeiss Schiller will be more than happy to oblige."

"Good. I would also like to make several one off payments to various recipients and set up one regular payment on a monthly basis."

"Of course. I can certainly help you with that, it is very easy." Said Drescher.

"Thank you. And these payments would be anonymous?"

"Yes, Mister Sloane, that is the benefit of a numbered account. The bank will not reveal your identity to anyone. It will be kept entirely secret. The account will be authorized by a code word known only to you and me, thus ensuring your privacy and our complete discretion."

"That sounds ideal for my purposes, Mister Drescher. Thank you," said Jake.

"Not at all," said Drescher, "Once we have completed the paperwork I will lead you down to the vault where you will be able to access your safety deposit box in complete privacy."

* * *

Forty minutes later, Jake had deposited one-hundred thousand euros into his newly opened account and had made anonymous payments to all his creditors, settling his debts in full. He had also set up a regular monthly payment to Angie and the kids.

Now he was three floors below ground level in the pristine bank vault of Zeiss Schiller. The white polished floor and bright white lighting seeming very modern and clinical in contrast to the more traditional surroundings of Drescher's office. Drescher had escorted him down to the vault in the private elevator, leading him through two sets of thick iron gates each manned by a security guard and accessed via iris recognition. He had then been led into one of three large rooms within the vault, each one again with its own security guard. Down two of the walls were banks of white doored security boxes, all about eighteen inches square, all with two key slots and a small keypad on the front. At the far end of the room were four curtained booths each containing a small desk and a swivel chair.

Drescher guided Jake to box number 1301 and inserted his own guard key. He then instructed Jake on what to do next. When he was sure that Jake understood, he said, "I will be waiting for you outside. There is no rush. Please take as much time as you need." With that, he gave a curt nod of his head and walked away.

Jake watched him leave then turned his own access key in the slot, which was given to him upon opening his account. After that, he pressed *set* on the keypad, punched in his unique pass code and then hit *enter*. The door clicked open and he pulled out the large plastic box it contained and carried it over to the first booth, drawing the curtain closed behind him. He then set the box on the desk and placed the leather bound briefcase alongside it.

Jake snapped open the case and took one last look at what it contained, randomly picking out a bag or two and studying the contents. He had parted with fourteen diamonds in total but the case still housed hundreds more, however, Jake had sold as many as he needed to. He would not sell any more.

Sense and reason had at last caught up with him, the initial rush of adrenaline had passed and his previously fragile state of mind had been given enough time to recuperate. He had finally regained his sanity and his morality. And along with it his guilt.

However, the fact remained that he had stolen the diamonds. He could not alter that now, what was done was done. He had done what he needed to; paid off his debts and set up a fund to help Angie and the kids. But enough was now enough and the madness of the last few weeks had to stop. He would take some time, a few months maybe, just to get his head completely right - enjoy life without stress or worry for a while. Then, when the time was right, he would return home and face up to life again. Either with or without Angie.

Jake closed the case, placed it into the plastic box and returned it to the drawer. He then went to find Drescher who escorted him back upstairs. The receptionist gave Jake back the metal case of van Elst's, which he had left with her whilst he was down in the vault. He thanked her and Drescher then left the bank.

Back in the Paradeplatz, Jake flagged down a taxi. "Airport please," he said to the driver.

As the taxi moved into the flow of traffic leaving the bank and the diamonds far behind, Jake felt the burden of responsibility slip from his shoulders.

Chapter 18

Roper decided that he should visit Angie Sawyer in person, to see if she could think of anything, no matter how seemingly insignificant, that could help him find her missing husband. So he and Eckhart drove down to Northamptonshire to meet with her.

Angie Sawyer was a very attractive woman in her early thirties with long dark hair, deep brown eyes and a good figure that was disguised by a baggy jumper and comfy jeans. Her new partner, Richard Maddox sat next to her with a protective arm around her shoulders. As a couple they looked somehow mismatched as Maddox was not a particularly attractive man, blonde but balding, lanky but with a slight pot-belly. However, judging by the house and the Jag parked in the driveway he was clearly successful and obviously quite wealthy. Knowing a little about Mrs Sawyer and her estranged husband's previous circumstances Coyle guessed that the money was probably the attraction.

Roper spent some time with Mrs Sawyer asking her about her husband, about his work, his life, his financial situation, anything to see if she could shed any light on to why his rented BMW had been found abandoned in France and why he had gone missing. But she couldn't. Except to say that Jake was under enormous pressure and suffering from severe stress and possibly clinical depression.

However, what she did say had happened since they had last spoke, was that all hers and Jake's debts had been paid in full and two payments of £2,000 had been paid into her bank account from an unknown benefactor, once several weeks ago and once more just yesterday.

Again, Coyle was astonished. The money, it seemed, had been wired into Angie's account from an untraceable source. Why and by whom? Coyle had a good idea as to the whom but as to the why or, more importantly, the how, remained a mystery. Once again Roper's thoughts came back to the diamond found at the scene of Charles Khan's accident and the certainty that this, or possibly others like it, were the key to this case.

* * *

Again Sumpter reported his findings to Bearing and Khan and this time was left in no doubt of Arthur's impatience. Particularly when he revealed what he had just learned through Coyle's computer, of Angie and Jake Sawyer's debts being paid by a mysterious benefactor.

Sumpter had felt uneasy about revealing this information but Khan was pushing. He wanted results and Aaron felt that he had to placate him. He now wished he had not as Arthur Khan was likely to take matters into his own hands, which could possibly put the investigation back months.

Chapter 19

The anonymous call came in at 6.05pm, the caller asking specifically for Detective Chief Inspector Roper Coyle. The voice on the line was tinny, as if it was being synthesized or played through a computer.

"Who is this?" Coyle asked.

"Who I am is not important," said the metallic voice. "What I've got to say is."

"And that is?" said Coyle.

"Angela Sawyer and her family are not safe."

"Not safe? What do you mean?"

"I mean exactly that. She and her family are in danger."

"From whom?" Asked Coyle.

"I can say no more, except that you should take this warning seriously."

"How can I take it seriously when I don't even know who you are–"

"That's of no consequence to me," the metallic voice interrupted. "Believe what I say or don't believe it, but you have been warned."

"Now hold on a sec–" Coyle began, but the line had already gone dead.

* * *

Sergeant Janet Willow had not heard from her boyfriend, Colin, in four days. In fact, she was not sure if he was actually her boyfriend as they had only been out a few times, the last time to a country pub on the outskirts of Northampton. They had slept together that night and the following morning Colin had left before she awoke. He had texted later that morning to say thanks for a lovely time and that he would call her later in the week. But so far he had not and she was starting to feel anxious. She really liked him - she had actually fancied him for ages but she did not think he knew she existed. Then out of the blue he asked her out and now, just five dates later, she thought she loved him. But he had not called.

Janet was sitting at her desk daydreaming, doodling his name in biro on her desk pad, scrawling a heart shape around it with her name underneath. It was 6.20pm, she was finishing at six-thirty. She'd had quite enough of Northants Police for one day and was keen to get home to see if there were any messages from Colin. Just ten more minutes and she would be free.

Then the phone rang for her boss but he was out so she took the call.

"Could I speak to Jeff Grainy please? This is DCI

Coyle from The Met."

"Sorry, sir, but DI Grainy is not here at the moment, can I take a message?" Said Janet.

"Yes - but it's important that Grainy gets this as soon as possible - do you understand?"

"Yes, sir," said Janet, stifling a yawn, "of course."

"Good. Now listen, I've just had an anonymous tip-off saying Angela Sawyer and her family are in grave danger and I have every reason to believe that they are. They are going to need protection."

"Protection. Yes, sir."

"Tell Grainy to get a car over there tonight. Tell him it's important - got that?"

"Important. Got it, sir. I'll tell him." Janet said.

"Good," Coyle replied. "If he's got any questions ask him to give me a call, would you?"

At that moment, Janet's mobile phone began buzzing in her handbag and she reached down to grab it. "I'll be sure to tell him, sir," she said as she pulled out her phone and saw the caller ID. It was Colin. Janet's heart skipped a beat, she had to answer, she didn't want to miss him. "Thank you, sir," she said. "Goodbye." The moment she put the phone down to Coyle she hit the answer button on her mobile. "Hello, stranger?" she said. "I thought you'd forgotten about me."

"Now how could I forget about you - especially after what you did the other night - I still don't know how you did it–"

"Sssh, you naughty boy," Janet giggled. "I'm still at work and someone might hear. But if you're lucky, I might do it again."

"Sounds great. How about tonight - I could pick you up from work and we could go back to your place–"

"Oh, we could, could we?" Janet teased, all thoughts of her previous conversation washed from her brain as it flooded with ideas of seeing Colin in just a few minutes. "And do what, exactly?"

"Well, I thought perhaps you could do that thing again and then when I've reciprocated, we could take a shower and then maybe go out for dinner. How does that grab you?"

"It grabs me," she giggled again, "very much."

"What time do you get off?"

"Shortly I hope."

"Now who's being naughty? I meant what time shall I pick you up?"

"Can you be here in ten minutes?"

"I can be there in five."

"Good. I can't wait. See you outside."

Janet was over the moon as she switched off her computer and grabbed up her bag, already fantasising about what she and Colin were going to get up to in just a short while.

As she walked excitedly through the double doors on the way to the car park, she passed DI Jeff Grainy on the way back to his desk after an afternoon in the field. "Goodnight, sir," she said.

"Goodnight, Janet." Replied Grainy. "Have a good evening."

"Oh, I will," thought Janet as the door closed behind her. "I will."

Chapter 20

It was four in the morning when Arthur Khan parked the Range Rover in the small copse close to Richard Maddox's house. Parking it well out of sight, he chose to travel the rest of the way on foot, unseen, across the fields. Maddox's house was separated from the rest of the village by a short country lane and backed out onto open fields at the rear, the garden easily accessed over a low fence, which was absolutely perfect for Arthur's entry and exit.

Arthur was a little out of shape these days, but still fitter than most men in their forties and the short jog across the fields was easy to cope with. Just enough to get his heart rate going and his adrenaline pumping. He was in full commando gear with his face covered by a balaclava, his eyes the only visible feature. He felt good, exhilarated. Excited.

All in black, he had a skinning knife strapped to his ankle, a machete in his belt and his lovingly polished Desert Eagle .357 in the hand-tooled shoulder holster that was the duplicate of his dead brother's. Very apt as this mission was for Charles.

He also wore a lightweight backpack which contained certain tools which may be of use as the night wore on.

The outfit Arthur was wearing used to be his standard attire in Africa. In the Congo and in Mozambique and Somalia and all the other places Arthur and his brother had fought. But tonight he was in Northamptonshire alone, there would be no more battles fought together. But, if he didn't get the answers he wanted tonight, there would be blood spilled in Charles' name.

Arthur felt alive, completely in his element, his years of training instinctively kicking in. This was what he did. What he had done for more years than he cared to remember. And he was good at it.

The air was still and cool and the night smelt of dew and grass and blossom. It was the end of April now, over two months since Charles' passing and there had been very little word from Sumpter. Nothing whatsoever on the diamonds. Just one lead on someone who might know something. But he was missing and his family claimed not to know where he had gone. Arthur would see. Tonight he would find out for himself if they knew anything or not. If they had information, he would get it out of them.

For a big man he ran in near silence and he vaulted the fence almost as if it wasn't there. He landed on the other side with just the slightest thud. Then froze, listening, his breathing only a little more laboured than usual. Waiting and watching for any signs of life.

He checked his watch. Sixteen minutes after four. The house was in darkness, the inhabitants all tucked up in bed, unaware of what was about to unfold.

He was inside the house in less than a minute, again making no sound, the inadequate lock no problem for a man of his skills. They may as well have left the door open for him.

Once inside, he pulled a small torch from his backpack and shone it around to make sure there was no one downstairs. Then, after making certain it was clear, he made a leisurely inspection of the large, spacious lower level. He wandered through the lounge and dining room, pausing to look at photographs and paintings and even spent several minutes flicking through Maddox's CD collection; Elton John, Lionel Ritchie, George Michael, a bit of Queen. Nothing to his taste.

Eventually he found his way into the farm house style kitchen, completely at home in the darkness. By torchlight he admired the bespoke cabinets and the African slate floor. He opened the big American-style fridge and casually took a swig from a carton of fresh orange juice, quenching the slight thirst he had from his jog across the fields.

Leading off from the kitchen he noticed a bolted door. Immediately curious, Arthur went over to it, silently slipped the bolt and turned the handle. Behind the door he found a flight of concrete steps which fell away into blackness. Arthur tugged on the pull-cord light just beyond the door to illuminate the staircase then, being careful to mind his footing on the narrow treads, slowly eased down the steps. At the bottom he found a large, brick built cellar with low wooden roof beams. The space was empty except for an enormous chest freezer, an old settee, a couple of dusty dining chairs and a child's snooker table. An old threadbare rug had been thrown down on the cold concrete floor to make the room more cosy.

Arthur smiled. This would be ideal for his needs.

* * *

Minutes later, Arthur was climbing up the main staircase, his big, highly polished combat boots as quiet as an old man's slippers.

All the members of the household were up these stairs, right where he expected them to be.

The first room he came to belonged to the little boy, Zack. He was fast asleep. Nine years old and with the face of an angel. Just like many Arthur remembered. Children, just like this one, with equally angelic faces in circumstances that only the hardest hearted men could not be affected by. But in Africa, Arthur had been hardened. Atrocities were rife; torture, mutilation, rape, murder, they were all everyday occurrences. In many cases, he himself had given the order and, sometimes, he had performed the act. Out there, it was the way things were done. It was a job and Africa, well, it was a different world, a hell that he'd had to become immune to in order to survive. After years of witnessing and taking part in horror, it eventually became as nothing. And so it would be tonight, if needs be. But only as a very last resort. He had no desire to hurt a child unless absolutely necessary.

He quietly closed the door and moved onwards along the landing.

Next was the little girl's room. Poppy's room. She was seven. All wrapped up in a Barbie duvet and as cute as a button. Again he quietly closed the door and moved on.

At last, Arthur arrived at the master bedroom and carefully he slipped inside.

Angie Sawyer and her lover, Richard Maddox were spooning. It was sweet, really, but Arthur couldn't help but think how irritated he would be by it. Why did women always insist on cuddling in bed, why couldn't they just stay on their own side and sleep in their own designated space. But Maddox was still probably trying to impress, trying to make a good show of it. He'd even fallen asleep with his arms draped around her waist, still in mid-cuddle. Give him a year, Arthur thought, I bet things would be different then.

The woman was snoring slightly. Her breathing heavy and contented. But she was a looker. A stunner, Arthur imagined, with her hair done and make-up on. Good figure too from what he could see at least. Maddox wasn't up to much though. Balding, skinny. A safety net, Arthur surmised, probably with a bit of money and no financial worries, unlike the missing husband.

Thinking of whom, it was time to wake the happy couple to find out exactly where the errant Mr. Sawyer was.

Arthur silently withdrew the skinning knife from its sheath, the wide stainless steel blade shining murderously in the moonlight, the edge sharp enough to slice through a hair at the merest touch. Then he bent over the bed. It was time to get started.

Chapter 21

Arthur pushed the point of the skinning knife firmly under Maddox's chin, drawing blood, and simultaneously clamped a hand over Angie Sawyer's mouth causing both to wake with a tremendous shock. Their eyes wide, Maddox clearly in pain, as they each stared into the masked face of Arthur Khan as he lent closely in over them.

"Make a sound, either of you and you die," Khan hissed.

Angie made to scream but Arthur pushed the knife a little harder into Maddox's chin, causing him to whimper, his head forced backwards in a futile attempt to escape the pain.

"Ah, ah, ah." Arthur cautioned Angie, gesturing with his head to Richard. "Think about him. Think about your kids."

Angie's eyes filled with tears and nodded her compliance.

"I'm going to take my hand away," he said. "Now

no sudden moves, no screaming and you'll both make it through the rest of this night alive. Understand?"

Angie nodded again. Richard tried to but the point of the knife prevented it. "Good," said Khan, releasing his grip on Angie and pulling the knife away from Maddox. "Now get up. We're going down to the cellar - but quietly does it, you don't want to wake up those two beautiful children of yours."

Angie was weeping and shaking like a leaf but slowly got out of bed. She tried to cover her nakedness with one hand whilst reaching for her robe which lay on a chair beside the bed.

Arthur pulled the Magnum from its holster and pointed it at her. "No clothes," he said. "Let's have you just as God intended."

He gestured to Maddox, "You, too, lover boy. Quickly now, we haven't got all night." Khan then smiled. "Well, actually we have, but no sense in wasting time, eh?"

Richard Maddox looked terrified. Tears running down his face and a smear of blood on his chin where the knife had been. He climbed out of the bed, also naked, and Khan glanced at his shrivelled manhood. "You know, what, Angela?" he said, "He might have money but he hasn't got a whole lot else, has he? I think you've sold yourself a little short, my darling."

"Please, please don't hurt us," Angie pleaded, her voice a whisper. "Please don't hurt my children - I'll give you anything but please, don't hurt them."

179

"Oh, you'll give me what I need, alright," Arthur replied, casting an eye over her full breasts and very shapely figure, lingering over the thick black curls between her legs. She certainly didn't disappoint. "But I've got no interest in hurting children," Arthur replied, "Although I will if you don't get moving. So move. Get down to that cellar and not another sound."

Quickly but quietly, Angie and Richard led the way to the cellar, their white bodies almost glowing in the moonlight as they crossed the landing and hurried down the stairs. Khan was right behind them, his skinning knife in one hand his Magnum in the other. He felt powerful and masculine. He was also surprisingly aroused by the site of Angie Sawyer's nude helplessness. He had not expected her to be so attractive.

Moments later, Angie and Richard were rushing down the cellar stairs, their bare feet slapping on the cold concrete steps. Arthur, following, closed the door behind them to block any sound that may shortly emanate from the basement room, no sense in waking the whole household unless absolutely necessary.

In the cellar, Arthur slipped off his backpack and told Maddox to sit in one of the dining chairs. He then told Angie to open the backpack and take out a thick roll of duct tape. "Tape him to the chair," he said to her, "and make a good job of it because I'll

180

be watching."

"Please, don't hurt us." She said again.

"Look, I've got money - you can have it," Maddox begged, "All of it - I promise - but please, please don't–"

"Shut up!" Khan snapped. "I don't want your money. I don't care about it. Now tape him up," he said again to Angie, "before I kill him."

Angie hurried to Richard and did as she was told. Both of them were crying. Maddox seemed to have aged dramatically in just a few minutes, the terror etched on his face as Angie wound the tape around his wrists and ankles.

"Silence him, too." Khan instructed. "I don't want to hear another word out of him."

Angie looked apologetically into Richard's eyes as she fastened a thick sheet of tape over her lover's mouth. "I'm so sorry," she whispered.

When she had finished, she turned to face Khan, standing awkwardly as she tried in vain to conceal her nakedness, her hands covering her breasts and womanhood.

"Move your arms and come over here," Arthur beckoned. Tentatively, Angie let her arms drop, unwillingly showing him her shapely body. She had goose bumps and was acutely aware that her nipples were erect and hard with cold. For a second she did not move, paralysed with fear. "Come here, now." Khan said sharply and she forced herself forward.

"Put your hands behind your back and turn round," he said when she reached him. She did as instructed and Arthur admired her firm backside as he took the tape from her and bound her wrists.

Khan put his mouth next to her ear and whispered, "Where's your husband?"

"What?" Angie said with surprise.

"Where's your husband?" he asked again.

"I don't have a husband," she said, "I mean we're separated, not together. Richard and me are–"

"I know all that," Khan growled. "I know you're separated. But I want to know where your husband is - understand?"

"Yes, yes - I understand," said Angie, "But he's not here - he doesn't live here. This is Richard's house."

Arthur holstered his gun then grabbed a handful of her hair and pulled her head back, his lips, through the balaclava now on her ear as he spoke, "Stop being stupid and listen to me. Now where, in the world, is your husband?"

Suddenly the penny dropped and Angie at last realised what this was all about. "I don't know where Jake is - I already told the police–"

"Don't lie to me, Angela. So far, no one's been hurt - I can soon change that!" Arthur could feel the swell in his loins as her naked bottom brushed the front of his fatigues. This was not what he had intended for tonight. In Africa he had tortured and raped women but never a white woman. Never a woman such as this. But now he was here and she was in front of him, nude, desirable and helpless. He could feel a demon taking him over, just as it had many times before in the heat of battle and in the spoils of victory.

"I'm not lying. I promise," Angie cried.

"No?" Arthur sneered, "Well we'll soon see." With that, he dragged her backwards, behind the settee and forced her to bend over it, so her head was almost touching the seat cushion and her round backside was mooning up at him. With her wrists taped behind her she was powerless to resist him. "Will you tell me now?" He asked, kicking her legs apart.

"Please," Angie was sobbing, "I don't know. I don't. Please don't do this. Please let me go."

Richard Maddox was grunting madly with the tape over his mouth, writhing about in the chair trying desperately to free himself and stop what he knew was about to happen, unable to avert his eyes from the horror unfolding before him.

"Oh, I think you know, Angela. I think you know only too well and you will tell me," Khan said. Then, without another word, he tugged down his flies and unleashed himself, his penis thick and hard as he fumbled around between her legs before forcing her open and thrusting himself deeply into her.

Angie screamed, tears running in rivers from

her eyes, "Stop, please - please don't do this."

Khan ignored her pleas as he rammed violently into her again and again, one hand fastened on her hair the other still gripping the knife.

"You will tell me what you know, woman - by the end of this night you'll be begging to tell me. I promise."

By now the red mist had descended over Arthur's eyes and he could no longer hear Angie's cries or the sound of Maddox weeping as he watched, helplessly from just a few feet away.

* * *

Angie blacked out shortly after that and only came round again after Khan had finished. She was now sitting on the dining chair next to Richard's and Arthur was busily taping her ankles together. Maddox had slumped forward in his chair in utter despair and was crying softly. Mucus dripping from his nose onto the threadbare rug beneath his feet. Angie felt like she had been through hell. Her body ached, her intimate areas were sore and bleeding and she was shivering violently from the coldness of the cellar.

Arthur looked up at her to see that she had awoken. "Ah good, you're awake. You slipped away before you could tell me anything."

"But I don't know anything," Angie croaked, hoarse from all her screaming and feeling totally defeated. "I haven't seen Jake in weeks - I promise. I don't know what trouble he's got himself into but it's nothing to do with me or Richard, I swear."

"But of course it is, my darling," Khan said. "You are Sawyer's wife, those two children upstairs are his children. And you will tell me where he is."

"But I don't know. Please, believe me–"

"How can I believe you, my darling, when I know for a fact you are receiving money from him. Money that by rights belongs to me."

"What money?"

"Please, Angela. Don't insult my intelligence. I know very well that you have received two large payments into your bank account in the last two months and I know as well as you do who paid them. So I'll ask you again. Where is your husband? Tell me and this will all become a lot less painful."

"Look," Angie was exasperated, not knowing what more she could say, "I've already told you. I don't know anything. I don't know where Jake is, I don't know where the money came from - I can't help you - if I could, I promise I would."

"Fine," Arthur said, rising to his feet. "I sense you're bored and that you are determined not to tell me anything. Admirable. Very admirable indeed. So maybe it's time I tried a different approach."

Without any warning, Arthur lifted Richard Maddox's head up by his hair and stabbed him in the shoulder, burying the knife right up to the hilt before pulling it out again. Maddox squealed in muffled agony, his lips still fasted shut by tape as tears streamed from his eyes.

"Oh my God!" Angie cried, "No, stop it, stop!"

"Tell me, Angie. Tell me where Jake is," Khan said calmly.

"Please, I swear - I don't know–"

Khan stabbed the knife into Richard's other shoulder, again burying it to its full length. Richard writhed in agony, crying hysterically.

"Stop, please stop!" Angie yelled, seeing blood pumping from the gaping wounds in her lover's shoulders and flowing freely down his arms and chest.

"Tell me, Angie." Khan said again.

"I don't know, I don't know, I don't know!" Angie roared, her teeth gritted her face contorted with anguish and rage.

Khan shrugged, unaffected by her anger, then casually withdrew the machete from its sheath. Briefly he admired the shine of the polished stainless steel before placing it between Richard's legs, lifting up the sack of his testicles with the long flat blade. Maddox, already in an enormous amount of pain let out a muted wail; his mouth clamped shut.

"No!" Angie cried, "Please, no!"

"Tell me, then." Khan shrugged impassively.

"You monster! You fucking sick, deranged monster - can't you understand? Can't you get it through your thick fucking skull?" Angie yelled, "I don't fucking know!"

Then, from the back of the room, at the bottom of the cellar steps, another voice spoke. "Mummy?" Poppy Sawyer said. "Are you okay?"

Chapter 22

Arthur span round to see Poppy standing there in her Barbie nightie, holding a teddy bear almost as big as herself by the arm. Next to her, in his Buzz Lightyear pyjamas stood her brother Zack. Both looked confused by the scene that lay before them but it wasn't until Arthur turned to face them that they were able to see Richard Maddox and the fountains of blood pumping from the horrific gouges in his shoulders. They were also able to see Arthur in all his murderous glory; balaclava, skinning knife, a huge pistol holstered under his arm and a long, evil looking machete poised to castrate their step-father. If Freddy Kruger had a brother it was Arthur Khan, covered in blood and looking scarier than any nightmare they had experienced in their short lives.

Angie turned awkwardly, bound to the chair by duct tape, her eyes full of tears and terror. "Don't hurt them," she squealed at Khan, "Please don't hurt them!"

As she said it Poppy started to scream, a long, piercing unrelenting sound. Then Zack started too.

"Shut up!" Arthur barked. "Shut up that noise!"

Scared out of her wits, Poppy dropped her teddy bear and fled back up the cellar steps, screaming hysterically as she went.

Arthur dropped the machete and pulled out the shiny Desert Eagle and fired. The shot hit the wall just to the side of Poppy, blasting away a large chunk of breeze block. She squealed but carried on going, the sound of her mother's pleading sobbing in the background as she begged Arthur Khan to let her children live.

Poppy had nearly made it to the cellar door as Arthur took aim but as he fired Zack flung himself in the way to protect his little sister.

The boy did not stand a chance as he flew backwards onto the cold stone steps, his head exploding like a ripe melon.

Arthur did not skip a beat as he raced over to the stairs leapt over the dead child's body and up the stairs in pursuit of the girl who had now made it through the cellar door and was running, terrified, through the kitchen.

Angie Sawyer was manic as she wailed from the basement, deep, harrowing sobs as she fought to be free of the chair, wrestling to be near her son and willing her young daughter to freedom. But then, momentarily silencing her screams there was another loud shot from upstairs. A minute or so passed as Angie prayed - prayed that their attacker had missed and that little Poppy had escaped. But then her whole world collapsed as Khan re-appeared at the top of the cellar stairs with a small body flung over one shoulder, dressed in a bloody Barbie nightdress.

Arthur placed Poppy's body down gently on the settee, with the wound in her back facing away from Angie who was now almost paralysed with grief. Unable to speak, move or even think clearly. Her children were dead and she had been powerless to protect them.

Khan knew that it was over. The sound of the gunshots would travel in the silence of the dawn. Trouble would no doubt soon be on its way.

He holstered the Magnum and picked up the machete. Time to end it. He wandered over to Maddox who had long since passed out from pain and blood loss. His head hung limply and Arthur raised the machete and finished him.

He then walked back to Angie. "You didn't know anything after all, did you?" He said.

Angie raised her face to him, but she had no words, only sorrow and pain and loss. Arthur raised the machete again. "Sorry," he said, then swung it sharply downwards, sending her to meet her children in a safer place.

* * *

Arthur Khan got back to his Range Rover as the sun was rising. His clothes were covered in blood, as was his skinning knife and machete. Calmly, Arthur stripped off his clothes and bundled them into a plastic bin bag that he'd brought along for the purpose. Then he cleaned his knife and placed it, along with the machete and the Magnum, in a canvas bag in the boot, zipping it up securely afterwards. After changing into a sweatshirt, jogging trousers and a pristine pair of Nikes, he climbed into the Range Rover and headed back to the main road.

The fire engine passed him, going in the opposite direction, about a half mile later. Following, almost immediately, two police cars sped by.

Arthur checked the rear view mirror and in the growing daylight could just make out the glow of the fire and the clouds of black smoke billowing into the early morning sky. The Fire Brigade would have little hope of salvaging anything, the flames had taken hold quickly and were already licking the upstairs roof beams before Arthur had made it halfway back across the field.

The mission had failed. Firstly, he had found out nothing more than he already knew. Jake Sawyer had gone and his family definitely did not know where he was. Sumpter was unfortunately correct.

Secondly, Arthur's presence at the house had not been as clean as he would have liked. He had lost control. The red mist had descended and he now bitterly regretted the rape but he had not been able to stop himself. The same thing had happened in Africa. Arthur knew that it was a power thing - something about him being dominant and the woman being defenceless. But Angie Sawyer was an English woman, a civilized woman, not some worthless savage. It was obviously an issue that he was going to have to work on.

Then there was the children. He had hoped he would not have to harm them, but once they started screaming he had no choice but to use the Magnum. Quick and effective - although messier than he would have preferred.

Nonetheless, three loud shots had rung out. Someone in the village was bound to have heard and called the police.

Working quickly, Arthur had carried all the bodies up into the living room then set the house ablaze. He waited just long enough to make sure the flames took hold, then exited the same way as he entered.

Now, less than two hours after entering Maddox's house, he was on his way back to London, still no closer to finding the missing diamonds. The whole wasted trip had been for nothing.

* * *

Whether it was human error, or bad policing, or just a terrible mistake, Coyle didn't know, but his message was never logged, never actioned and never pursued. And it cost Angie Sawyer, Richard Maddox and two young children their lives.

* * *

Peter Bearing was incandescent with rage. For an emotionless man, the dam had well and truly burst.

"You bloody fool, Arthur," he shouted. "What on earth were you thinking?"

"I'm sorry, Peter," Khan replied, but I was trying to find out what they knew. Sumpter's taking too long–"

"I know he's taking a long time. He said it would didn't he? It's only been a few weeks Arthur for godsakes - what were you expecting, miracles?"

"But Sumpter–" Khan began, but Bearing cut him off again.

"Forget Sumpter, this has nothing to do with him. This is about you and what you have done. Not only have you quite literally burned a source of information that may well have proved exceptionally valuable in the weeks or months that possibly lay ahead of us in our search. But you've also given the police cause to jump to any number of conclusions. Why, for example, were Sawyer's family murdered for one? What made them so damned important? What did they know that was enough to get them killed? These are questions, Arthur, that the police might well be asking. And if I were any half decent detective I'd be pretty keen to find some answers."

"But the diamonds, Peter. We need to get them back," said Khan.

"Of course we do." Replied Bearing. "And we will. Mark my words. But we've got to give Sumpter time. If there's anyone out there trying to sell that many diamonds, Sumpter will find them. And if it is this Sawyer, and I'm almost certain it is, then Aaron will get him. Jake Sawyer is a graphic designer, an artist, not an expert in international espionage. What on earth does he know about selling black-market diamonds?

"What I suspect it is with you, Arthur, is vengeance. You want it for Charles and I quite understand. And you will have it, my friend, but you've got to be in it for the long haul. Unfortunately, I suspect all your nocturnal activities did last night was set us back some considerable time. We must now let the dust settle and wait for the police to lose interest. But behind the scenes, Sumpter will be working away. He'll turn something up, you'll see."

"You're right, Peter, of course, and I'm sorry", Khan said. "I shall just have to wait. I see that now. But I've said it before and I'll say it again, I don't trust Sumpter, I never have. The man's got his own agenda, I'm sure of it."

"We shall see, Arthur. Time will tell. At the moment, Aaron has my complete confidence, but if he gives me reason to doubt him, then we'll deal with him as necessary. But for now we wait. Agreed?

"Agreed," Khan said. "We'll wait. For now."

Chapter 23

Jake had been travelling for much of the last few weeks, trying to enjoy his new life without the stress and worry of before. He was free to do what he wanted now and even after paying off all his debts, which in reality only used up a very small proportion of the money Hugo van Elst had given him for the diamonds, he still had more than enough to live comfortably on for many years.

From Zurich he had taken a flight to Tokyo and from there he had flown to Sidney. He and Angie had always said they would like to travel and spent many hours during the happier times planning holidays that they may have at sometime in the future. However, now Jake could afford it, he was finding it hard to enjoy himself. It was not the same without Angie or the kids.

In his luxurious hotel room with views of the magnificent harbour and Sidney's famous opera house, Jake decided that it was time to go home. Back to England, back to his kids and, hopefully, back to Angie if she would have him, although he knew that would be a tough battle to win. But he would not give up, he would fight for her, try to earn her respect again, try to win back her love.

On his way home, he flew from Sidney to Los Angeles and from there onto New York where he intended to do some shopping, get Zack and Poppy a few souvenirs, maybe buy Angie some Jimmy Choos - he would have bought her a diamond but for the time being he had seen quite enough of them - besides, he had a whole case full locked safely in a vault in Zurich. She could have her pick.

But he was getting ahead of himself. Firstly he had to make himself a bit more presentable, take a bit more pride in his appearance, make himself look a bit more like the Jake she fell in love with.

He checked himself in to the Waldorf Astoria under the name of John Sinclair, the name on yet another of his passports. He laughed at himself for having had four made up. Talk about being over cautious, he thought. No one knew who he was or that it was he who had stolen the diamonds - he did not even have the diamonds with him anymore so there was nothing to tie them to him. He was safe and clear and as soon as he got back to England he could forget all this cloak and dagger business and become Jake Sawyer once again.

He stepped out of the shower and towelled off

his new buzz cut and cleanly shaven chin, courtesy of the hotel's barbershop. It took all of two seconds to dry and he couldn't think why he had not done it years ago. He studied himself in the mirror, short hair, no beard, newer, more stylish glasses. He certainly looked different, younger too.

As he walked out of the bathroom feeling clean and refreshed, there was a soft knock at the door and he immediately tensed. Being wary had recently become something of a habit.

"Who is it?" He called, his English accent immediately apparent.

"Room service, sir," came the reply.

"Just a minute," Jake said as he pulled on a complimentary hotel robe and strode over to the door.

He peered through the spy hole, then, satisfied, he opened the door and accepted the trolley, dropping the hotel waiter a twenty for his trouble.

"Thank you very much, sir," said the waiter.

"No problem, goodnight." Jake shut the door and pushed the trolley into the room. On it was a large silver plate cover that was keeping his double cheeseburger nice and toasty.

Jake was weary from travelling, sick of aeroplanes, he needed a good night's sleep and something to eat. The burger would do nicely. He lifted the cover off the plate and saw what he had been fantasising over for hours. New York's finest;

cheese, bacon and beef with a double portion of fries and a strawberry shake. Excellent.

He sat down on the bed and took a bite of the burger. It didn't disappoint.

His brand new laptop was open on the bed and he turned it to face him. He had stopped off at the Apple Store on Fifth Avenue on the way from the airport and treated himself to the very best one they had with the highest possible spec. Seventeen inch screen, dual core, eight gigs of memory, wifi, bluetooth, the works. He also bought himself a brand new iPhone to replace the one he had ditched several weeks ago in the English Channel. He bought the kids an iPod each too. What the hell.

He sparked up the web browser and navigated to the live streaming on the BBC News website to find out what was happening in the UK.

Jake took another bite of the burger, the juice running down his now cleanly shaven chin, but he did not care. He was starved. The news anchorman was talking away in the background about some horrific fire, saying that a whole family had been killed.

Jake was not really listening as he was more interested in the cheeseburger, but then he heard the word 'Northamptonshire' and his ears pricked up. He stared at the screen and listened more intently.

And that was when his whole world fell apart.

'Mrs Angela Sawyer, Mr Richard Maddox and

Mrs Sawyer's two young children, were all found dead at the scene.' The news anchor said. *'The two children, Zack aged nine and Poppy, just seven, are also thought to have been shot, although police have not yet confirmed this. However, they have confirmed that this is being treated as a murder enquiry. A spokesman said that because of their horrific injuries, the badly burned bodies were identified through dental records. As yet, there is no sign of the children's father, Mr Jake Sawyer, who, according to neighbours, has been missing for some weeks.'*

Jake suddenly felt like he had been kicked hard in the gut and he bent over and threw up the burger onto the carpet.

"Oh Christ, oh my bloody Christ, no. Please, please, no!" He wailed. Tears flooded his vision as he watched in utter despair.

It was his fault, he realised, with abject horror. They had all died because of him, because of what he had done. Because he had been so selfish, so weak, so unbelievably stupid. He even had the arrogance to think that he had got away with it, never once thinking that his family would be at risk. That they might be murdered.

Tears were now streaming down his cheeks, his body heaving as he sobbed uncontrollably, sickeningly aware that his reckless actions had caused this terrible thing to happen.

* * *

Two days later, after much grieving and crying and hard soul searching, Jake was still struggling to believe what had happened. He had neither eaten or slept in nearly forty-eight hours and now he just felt numb. Completely bereft.

The rolling news had been playing on the laptop constantly and each time the report came on it was equally as traumatic as the first time Jake heard it, but he needed to understand everything. There was a fire, but also a murder. Zack and Poppy had been shot. Angie and Maddox murdered too. Both decapitated is what the reporters were now saying. He could barely bring himself to think about what they had suffered.

But he knew, without question, that the murderer was looking for him and that was why they were killed.

Jake's initial thought was to end it all, just as he should have done all those weeks ago, up on that bridge. But that would have been the coward's way out. Nothing would bring Angie, Zack and Poppy back, certainly not jumping out of the window of the Waldorf Astoria.

Jake knew, beyond doubt, that he would feel guilt for their murders every day of his life. It would always be with him and he deserved it to be. And that would be his punishment. A self-imposed life sentence. But within that sentence he could try to make some restitution. He did not know who it was who had killed his family nor did he have the first clue about how to go about finding them but he did know that they were looking for him and that one day they would surely find him, no matter how many times he changed his name or switched location.

But he also knew that when that day came, he would be ready. They owed him a debt of four lives and they were going to pay for every single one.

Chapter 24

Roper Coyle pushed a hand through his messy hair and sighed with frustration. He glanced across at Eckhart's empty desk, the cards of congratulations still sitting on top of his computer monitor.

Dave's wife, Lucy, had given birth to their first child, a daughter called Gemma, two days ago and he was on paternity leave.

But it was of little importance where the case was concerned as every lead had gone cold, every snippet of information had dried up and they had nowhere left to go with it.

Northamptonshire Police were still busy with the murder hunt, trying to find the killer of Angie Sawyer and her family, but so far nothing had turned up that could lead to a suspect. At least not officially. But again, Roper's gut was telling him otherwise.

The only real evidence, which could possibly be argued against in a court of law, was the ballistics report from the forensic team. A bullet, very bent and misshapen and completely charred had been pulled from the cellar steps at Richard Maddox's burned out house, and was 'consistent' with having been fired from a .357 Magnum. It was also consistent with a hole found in Zack Sawyer's tiny skull.

Not much to go on in itself, but when coupled with the knowledge that Charles Khan was found with a Desert Eagle .357 Magnum, it started to raise one or two questions. Such as, did Arthur Khan own one too?

Of course, Roper had revisited Arthur Khan and asked him that exact question but naturally he denied it. Khan also denied any knowledge of Angie Sawyer or her husband Jake, but Roper didn't quite buy it. And so the suspicion remained.

Coyle was still furious with Northamptonshire Police for allowing this terrible crime to happen. No one needed to have died if they had only acted on his warning. But that was all in the past now. The woman he had spoken to had been reprimanded but that would not bring the Sawyers back.

He had tried to trace the call from the anonymous tip-off he had received about a possible threat to the Sawyer/Maddox family, but again, it turned up nothing. In fact Roper's list of unanswered questions almost filled a file all by them self. The whereabouts of Jake Sawyer, the .357, the incredibly expensive diamond, whether Arthur Khan and possibly Peter Bearing were somehow involved.

These mysteries all needed solving. As did the murders that took place a little over a month ago in that sleepy Northamptonshire village.

However, the murders were largely a case for the Northamptonshire Police and not for The Met. Roper had already spent far too much time on it and he was now receiving pressure from his superiors to let it go. He had a backlog of other cases that required his urgent attention and they needed to be cleared quickly.

Reluctantly, Coyle closed the file and placed it in the drawer of his desk. He would still monitor the case from afar and continue to revisit it once in a while in his spare time or in quieter moments - not that he had much of each. But for now, his full time involvement was at an end. His bosses had spoken and if he wanted to remain in his job he had to listen.

The murderer was out there somewhere and so, too, was Jake Sawyer and one day, Roper sincerely hoped to find both.

PART TWO

Chapter 25

Two years later. Nassau, The Bahamas.

Jake woke early, the silk sheets cool against his naked skin. The room was bright and airy and another beautiful day shone in through the open french windows. A large ceiling fan was whirring silently above the enormous bed, distributing the fresh morning air to all corners of the spacious bedroom. An easel was set up by the window, looking out to sea and a stack of various sized canvases leant against the white painted wattle and daub wall.

Jake sat up and stretched, glancing at the Barhamian beauty lying next to him still sleeping like a baby.

The latest in a long line.

At first there hadn't been any women. Not for a long time. But then, in an effort to feel something other than empty for even the briefest time, none soon became many. But they never stayed for long. Jake was too closed up, too withdrawn for that. Most wanted something deeper and he did not. But he did want to feel something.

The girl in the bed stirred. He would end it today and she would not mind. They had only been dating for a couple of weeks but already it was clear that it was not going anywhere. She wanted more than he was ready to give. Perhaps ever.

Jake was slim now and physically fit, more so than at any other time in his life. He had taken up boxing again and karate and worked out hard with his trainer every day at both. His body was firm and muscular with a six-pack that Brad Pitt would envy. He was quick, agile and sharp and as ready as he could be for whatever or whoever might be coming.

His looks had also changed dramatically with the long hair and bushy beard having been replaced by the neat buzz cut and a cleanly shaven face. The glasses had now gone too and his eyes had been lasered which, with his new slim physique made him look late twenties rather than mid-thirties. For the first time in years he looked as handsome as he used to be, before his life went to hell.

Jake got out of bed and pulled on a pair of linen beach pants with a drawstring waist, then strolled out onto the wide veranda, the sun warming his tanned, muscular torso as he admired the enormous expanse of deep blue ocean that greeted him every day.

His bungalow was just one of many dotted around the exclusive resort, traditionally built from mud and stone with an immaculately maintained thatched roof. Inside, however, they had all the luxuries that the upscale clientele would rightfully expect; fifty inch plasma, four-poster bed, hot-tub, wet room and a private veranda, complete with its own infinity pool and magnificent sea view. And it was this that Jake appreciated the most. He found it relaxing and sometimes, just for the shortest time, whilst he watched the waves rolling in and out, the horrendous events of his past faded briefly from memory.

Since the murder of Angie and the kids Jake had moved around quite a bit, sometimes staying in a place for several months and at other times just a few days. But the emptiness within him was a constant. As was the guilt.

In Nassau, however, on the paradise island of New Providence, he had at last made a home of sorts. Albeit in a rented bungalow at the Crystal Waters Resort. But he had been there for four months and, at present, had no immediate plans to move on. It was comfortable and peaceful and the service was excellent. Furthermore, the management left him alone and were happy for him to rent on a month to month basis. It also had an exclusive clientele who liked to keep themselves to themselves and that suited him just fine.

On the veranda, Jake went through his morning ritual, beginning with a few stretching exercises then a hundred sit-ups and a hundred push-ups to get his blood pumping, forcing himself to feel alive. It was a tough task though as since New York, Jake had felt dead inside.

Normally he would go for a run around the resort then down onto the sand for a brisk five miles. Fitness was important to him now, keeping his body in peak physical condition by taking regular exercise and eating a healthy diet. But the run would have to wait today, until the girl had gone.

When he had finished the push-ups, he stood up and again stared out at the ocean, taking some deep cleansing breaths of fresh morning air. Standing there, he noticed a small white sail boat drift into view, a fair distance out on the quiet, turquoise sea and Jake thought how beautiful it must be to be out there this morning, bobbing carefree on the calm Caribbean. He watched it for a little while before going back into the bungalow to take a shower.

The girl had awoken when he had finished and he sat down beside her and gently ended it. She was saddened but not sorry. As Jake had suspected, she was not happy either and knew the relationship was going nowhere. She was fond of Jake but said that he kept his emotions too tightly bottled and wondered, quite kindly, if he might be as well to see a therapist to help him release them. Jake nodded but suspected he had no more emotions to release. His ability to feel, to love, to even care about much at all had all but turned to dust along with the remains of his murdered family. Just getting through each day was all he could focus on and it was slowly getting easier but that just made the guilt worse.

A short time later, Jake came back from his run glistening with a light sheen of sweat. His breathing was only slightly laboured as he jogged up the short, narrow track that led from the beach to his veranda. Quickly he stripped out of his T-shirt and shorts and kicked off his Nikes then dived naked into the cool aquamarine water of the infinity pool. He completed a couple of lengths fully underwater before bursting through the surface and completing four more with an impressive front crawl. For the fifth and final length he broke into a leisurely breaststroke before climbing out onto the warm deck, dripping wet but feeling nicely refreshed. He patted himself down lightly with a towel, then slung it over his shoulder and headed inside. The maid had already been and the bungalow was once again immaculate. The bed was made, the wine bottle and glasses from last night had disappeared and there were fresh flowers everywhere. Jake walked over to the sleek open plan kitchen and pulled open the refrigerator. He found an open carton of juice and glugged down several mouthfuls of it straight from the carton. He shut the fridge and kept the juice with him as he switched on the coffee machine and headed off for his second shower of the morning.

Jake wandered barefoot back out onto the veranda a short time later dressed in a light pair of combat shorts and a fresh cotton shirt, untucked with the sleeves casually rolled up to the elbows and at least three of the top buttons undone. A pair of Ray-Ban Aviators were hooked in the opening. Carrying a gloriously aromatic ground coffee and a newly delivered newspaper he sat down in one of the big, wicker armchairs that made-up part of the luxurious deck furniture. He sipped the coffee and looked out again at the ocean, noticing that the sail boat was still there. It seemed not to have moved but Jake thought little of it as he opened the paper and began reading the stories of the day, unaware that from out at sea, he was being watched.

Chapter 26

Arthur Khan put Aaron Sumpter's investigation back months when he killed the Sawyer family. Sumpter had called the police anonymously to try to prevent the murders but for some reason they had failed to act and the Sawyers had all died anyway.

Aaron could not believe what Khan had done or the manner in which he had killed that poor family. Nor could he believe Arthur's utter lack of remorse or the blasé way in which he openly discussed the murders with Bearing.

Peter Bearing, however, had been absolutely furious with Khan and Sumpter had never seen him show so much unchecked emotion. But he realised it was not emotion for the deaths of four innocent people but for the delay their deaths would inevitably put on the hunt for the diamonds. Sumpter knew Bearing to be cold but even he was surprised by the complete lack of conscience and the callous way in which he dismissed the murders, finding them nothing more than an inconvenience in his pursuit of the stones. However, it was not Sumpter's job to judge, he was employed to find the diamonds and find the diamonds he most definitely would. Nevertheless, for a while after the murders things were far too hot for Aaron to go poking around asking lots of questions. He did not wish to raise suspicions so he had to wait, bide his time until things cooled down a bit.

Once they had, he set to work again, his remit unchanged.

However, it now seemed to Sumpter that he had been searching for Jake Sawyer forever. For a long time the man appeared to have vanished from the face of the earth and Aaron could find absolutely no trace of him. He had put out feelers all across Europe to all of the known diamond buyers trying to find some evidence of Sawyer's existence but they turned up nothing.

Eventually, in order to placate Bearing and Khan and to show he was actually doing something, he flew to Antwerp himself, the most logical place someone wishing to sell diamonds would head for, and sniffed around there for several weeks. Sumpter even went to see Hugo van Elst but he said he knew nothing of the man Aaron was looking for.

It was only on his last day in the city that a diamond broker told him of a man in Amsterdam called Gerhardt who bought and sold small quantities of stones - a strictly small time dealer but a lead worth following up nonetheless.

Aaron arrived in Amsterdam and visited the seedy little office in the back of the brothel, finding Gerhardt there, looking much like a down-on-his-luck professor. But Gerhardt apologised and said that he had not seen anyone matching Jake's description.

It was only after that, when Sumpter began asking around some of the backstreet jewellers in Amsterdam, purely out of desperation, that he found out that Gerhardt had been lying to him. One of these jewellers clearly remembered Jake and even recalled writing down Gerhardt's address for him.

When Sumpter revisited Gerhardt, the diamond buyer still denied all knowledge of Jake and it was not until Aaron threatened him with a visit from Arthur Khan that he finally, very reluctantly, admitted to knowing him. With a little more persuasion, Gerhardt gave Aaron the details of the forger who had made up Jake's fake passports.

Sumpter called on the forger next and for a relatively small amount of cash was given the names and the numbers on the four passports he had made up for Jake.

From that moment on Sumpter's task was slightly less challenging. Knowing the names and passport numbers Jake was travelling under made him much easier to track although he had covered his trail well and frequently varied the names and passports he used. Often he would use more than one identity in whatever place he happened to be and would vanish for weeks on end. He criss-crossed the globe staying in some places for just days and others for weeks and always Sumpter was just too late to find him.

But then, after a considerable amount of time and patience and one hell of a lot of detective work, he eventually tracked Jake to The Bahamas where he had been staying for several months at the Crystal Waters Resort in a rented bungalow.

He was watching him now, from a sail boat, out on the calm Caribbean ocean, taking photographs and spying on the bungalow through the long telephoto lens of his expensive Leica camera. He smiled as he watched Jake reading the newspaper and drinking his coffee, impressed by his new muscular physique and strikingly different appearance but in absolutely no doubt about who he actually was. "Hello, Mister Sawyer," he said.

After two and half years of searching, Aaron Sumpter had finally found his man.

Chapter 27

Her legs were aching now, her calf muscles tightening as she pounded along the sand. The music on her iPod, which was strapped to her arm in a little velcro pouch, was pumping its way into her brain, the rhythm spurring her onward for the last punishing mile of her usual six mile morning run.

Lizzie Barnes loved this time of day, when Malibu was at its quietest and the beach was as near to deserted as it ever got in the daytime. Just joggers, dog walkers, the odd early morning swimmers and her. Everyone else was either still in bed or heading out early to get a head start on what was sure to be another sweltering hot day in California.

She enjoyed the run and even with the loud music hammering her ears it gave her a little quiet time before her day began in earnest. A run and a swim, then breakfast with the papers before a shower and work.

Lizzie saw the house up ahead and she picked up

the pace a little. She was panting hard as she ran up the wide wooden steps and onto her pretty terrace at the back of the property - the best side of the house, which gave her uninterrupted views of the ocean. It was her own prime piece of Californian real estate and every day she was thankful that she had snapped it up when she had - bought with some of the money her mother had left her and somehow it made Lizzie feel as if she was still there with her.

She slipped off her trainers, ripped the velcro strap from her arm and tossed the iPod onto a padded lounger. She then stripped off her sweaty vest and shorts to reveal a dark blue one-piece swim suit that was cut high over her hips. Her body was tight and firm, her legs long and her breasts full - a true Malibu beach babe but with brains that easily matched up to her incredible body. She skipped down the steps and sprinted down the powdery white beach toward the sea, diving headlong into the surf as she reached the ocean.

For fifteen minutes she swam back and forth, never too far from the beach and always within clear sight of home. Backstroke, crawl, butterfly and then finally breaststroke as she made her way back to the shore, her workout for the day now over.

Now, refreshed but weary, she strolled lazily back to the house letting the early morning sunshine slowly dry her golden skin. Her long dark hair hanging sleek and wet down her back like the luxurious pelt of an otter.

Back on the veranda she pulled on a crisp white robe and towelled down her thick mane of hair. When it was less wet but still damp, she pushed it back off her face and gathered it into a long rope which she let fall loosely between her shoulder blades.

Cautiously she checked that no one was looking and then bent and retrieved a key from under a painted plant pot. She unlocked the glass patio door and slid it back its full length letting the fresh morning air into her home.

Twenty minutes later she was on her second glass of OJ with the morning papers spread out on the kitchen table. She was studying the financial pages with interest whilst eating a small bowl of Lucky Charms - a sugary vice that she categorically refused to kick. The little table was now bathed in sunlight that was streaming through the wide open patio doors and after chasing the very last Lucky Charm around the bowl with her spoon and slurping up the last remnants of pale blue stained milk, she folded the papers, grabbed what was left of her orange juice and headed upstairs.

Lizzie turned on the shower and peeled off her robe. She gulped down the remainder of her juice and was just about to step into the hot stream of water when her phone rang.

The name on the caller ID meant that it was important. She flipped open the phone. "Hi," she said. "Tell me you're calling with good news."

* * *

Now, less than two days since that call and as a direct result of it, Lizzie Barnes was climbing out the pool at the Crystal Waters Resort in Nassau in a white bikini looking like a goddess.

Jake had noticed her, as had every other man on the sun deck.

He was sitting on a stool at the pool bar at the Club House, having just taken delivery of a Crystal Club sandwich; a ham, turkey and Swiss cheese speciality prepared for him by Delroy, the barman. "Now that is paradise, right there, my brother," Delroy said in a deep Bahamian patois, noticing where Jake was looking.

Jake smiled but didn't answer, although Delroy was certainly not wrong.

The girl was a vision. Long dark hair, movie star looks, firm, full breasts and never ending legs. She also had a golden tan which, along with the striking white bikini, complimented the entire package to perfection.

Her dark, almond shaped eyes briefly met Jake's before she turned and walked away and, for the first time since New York, he felt his pulse quicken slightly with anticipation. Which caught him completely unawares.

He watched the girl surreptitiously as she returned to her sun lounger, peering over the top of his sunglasses as she quickly dried herself down. She pulled her long hair back and fixed it into a pony tail with a scrunchy then tied a brightly coloured floral sarong around her narrow waist. She then hoisted a huge straw beach bag onto her shoulder and slipped her feet into a pretty pair of white sandals before leaving the sun deck and vanishing from Jake's view.

Immediately he knew he had to see her again and was staggered by the strength of his reaction to her - as if something had, at last, awakened inside him that resembled emotion. Momentarily he felt silly, after all he had just set eyes on the woman, how on earth could he have that strong a reaction. But for the rest of that morning and all through the afternoon he could not stop thinking about her and hoping that he might see her again.

That evening, at dinner, Jake's hopes were rewarded as she sashayed past his table, being led by the maître d' on the way to be seated.

She had her hair tied back once more and was wearing a floral mini dress with a hipster belt and gladiator sandals. The outfit making the most of her long tanned legs and slim waist. Again their eyes met and Jake risked a half smile. She smiled politely back, but was gone almost immediately as a waiter led her to a table several rows away from Jake's.

She was seated at a small table for two on the terrace but she dined alone. Jake was relieved to see the seat opposite remained empty for the duration of dinner. He tried not to stare but could not help himself. When she ordered, she smiled delightfully at the waiter who was clearly not immune to her beauty and fawned sickeningly over her for the entire meal. But she seemed relaxed and carefree and once or twice Jake heard her laugh and he found the sound intoxicating.

But then the guilt returned. Even the possibility of being happy was something he knew he did not deserve - but even knowing that he couldn't stop himself from glancing over at the girl again. She was looking out over the balcony, out to see, a glass of white wine in her hand. Utterly breathtaking.

My God, Jake thought, what's happening to me. And he stood up in a rush, suddenly eager to be out of the restaurant, to clear his head and gather his thoughts. But in his rush he knocked over his empty wine glass and the sound as it smashed on the flagstone floor made heads turn. The girl's included.

"I'm sorry," Jake said to the waiter, as he hurried away, thrusting twenty dollars into the man's hand for his trouble.

The restaurant quickly returned to normal as the diners got on with their meals. All that is apart from one. Lizzie's eyes remained on the door which Jake had just left through, her expression mildly perturbed. The purpose of her visit to Nassau had just walked out.

* * *

An hour after dinner, Jake was at the open air bar with a long, cool beer in his hand and feeling fairly stupid. There was a slight breeze and he could hear the waves lapping at the shore over the sound of the calypso band that was playing somewhere off in the distance. It really was an idyllic spot and in another life it would have been paradise.

"Hi, anyone sitting here?" An American voice asked.

Jake turned to see the girl and smiled. Surprised at just how pleased he was to see her. "No. Please, sit down. May I get you a drink?"

"Um, yeah, sure. Why not. A mojito, if that's okay - thanks."

"No problem." Jake signalled to the barman and gave him the order, then turned back to the girl. "Hi, I'm Jake, by the way. Jake Sloane."

"Hi, Jake Sloane. I'm Lizzie Barnes, nice to meet you." She held her hand out and he shook it. It was soft, very feminine.

"Nice to meet you, too, Lizzie. Just in today?"

"Last night. Late." The barman placed the mojito in front of her and she took a drink. "Ah, that hits the spot. What about you - you been here long?"

"Yeah. A while. I'm kind of living here for the time being."

"Living here, huh? That's cool. Must be some kind of job you got that lets you live at the Crystal Waters Resort."

"No, not really," Jake said, "Just where I happened to end up."

"Hmm, sounds interesting, tell me more," Lizzie said, tucking a rogue strand of hair behind her ear and taking another sip of her mojito.

"It's just convenient for the moment, that's all." Jake said, a little uncomfortable with the line of questioning. "What about you - you're from the States?"

"Wow, smooth subject change." Lizzie smiled. "Keeping your cards close, I get it. But that's cool too. Yeah, I'm from the States. The original California girl. You're British, right?"

"Yeah, born and bred."

"A Limey, huh?" She teased.

Jake looked into her big brown eyes, she was absolutely stunning, high cheek bones, full lips and perfect white teeth that dazzled when she smiled. The only blemish he could see was the slightest little scar on her left temple but somehow that just seemed to add to her appeal.

"You got me." He replied, "And you're a Yank."

"Guess I am at that." She raised her glass in salute, her eyes looking playfully into his, "Thanks for the drink, Limey," she said, and took another sip.

"My pleasure, Yank." Jake returned her salute and took a gulp of beer.

They both laughed.

"So, what is it you do in California, Miss Yank?"

"Uh-uh. You're the one who wanted to be mysterious - two can play at that. Let's just say I'm a business woman."

"Okay, Business Woman," Jake chuckled, "Do I get to know whereabouts in California you're from or is that off limits too?"

"No, I guess that's okay. I'm from LA. Malibu."

"Very nice. So what brings a Californian beach babe all the way to New Providence, surely not the sun?"

"Beach babe, huh?"

Jake smiled and nodded.

"Change of scenery. That's all. I needed a vacation and the Caribbean is so beautiful, so I thought, you know, why not?"

"Why not indeed. It's definitely beautiful, alright." Although Jake wasn't talking just about the Caribbean.

"So, Mister Lime, whereabouts in the UK you from?"

"You know England well?"

"I know it's cold."

"You got that right. Well I'm from a small town to the south of London."

"Small town boy, huh?"

"That's me."

"And now an international man of mystery." Once more she was teasing him. The rogue strand had come loose and was again hanging freely, adding to her already considerable allure.

"Not exactly. Just wound up here sort of by accident."

"Nice accident."

"Yeah. So, are you here for long?"

"Again with the change of topic. You're really working that mystery man angle."

"Is it working?" Jake smiled.

"Maybe." Lizzie said. "I'll let you know."

"Okay. That's good. So, like I said, are you here for long?"

"A few days, perhaps. Maybe longer, it all depends."

"Depends on what?"

"On whether or not I decide to stay."

"Sounds like you've got an understanding boss."

"Who says I've of got a boss?"

"Ah, so you're the boss," Jake said, "Beauty as well as brains, I like it."

"Glad you approve," Lizzie grinned, taking another sip of her drink. "And what about you? How long are you going to stay?" She asked.

"It's like you said, it all depends."

"On your boss?"

"On circumstances."

"Sounds intriguing."

"Not really. Not worth boring you with."

"Who said I was bored?"

"No one. But it's a conversation for another

time, maybe."

"Now I really am intrigued."

"Don't be. I'm nowhere near as mysterious as you seem to think."

"No? Well I think I'll be the judge of that, Mister Lime." Lizzie smiled and finished her drink. "But I think, for now, my investigations are over for the evening. I'm whacked and about ready to hit the hay."

"Ah, so you were bored after all," Jake grinned.

"Not at all. Quite the opposite actually. I'm tired, that's all."

"Of course, I understand."

"Hey, but thanks for the drink."

"My pleasure."

Lizzie, stood up. "See you around, Limey."

"Sure. Goodnight, Lizzie. Nice to meet you."

Jake watched her as she walked away, then on impulse, he called after her. "Hey, Yank!"

She turned, smiling.

"How about dinner tomorrow night?" He asked.

She shrugged and said, "Sure, that'd be nice. Thanks."

Jake grinned. "Great, shall we meet here - say eight o'clock?"

"Sounds good, Mister Lime. Until tomorrow then." And with that she was gone.

* * *

Jake had felt strangely anxious all the following day. Excited too, which was a feeling he had not had in a long time. That night he wore a lightweight pale grey suit over a white cotton shirt, open at the neck and a pair of soft brown loafers and looked every inch like an affluent, eligible bachelor; handsome, stylish and sophisticated - a million miles from the scruffy, overweight image he used to present. Now he would not look out of place on the catwalks of Milan. However, on the inside he felt ugly, damaged and unworthy. But he fought against those feelings as he glanced at his Omega watch at a little after eight.

Lizzie arrived ten minutes late but he forgave her instantly. Tonight she was wearing her hair loose and it was thick, dark and lustrous as it fell down her back. She was a vision in a sky blue Dior dress that was just a few inches short of her knees. Around her neck she wore a simple string of pearls and on her feet white strappy sandals with a dangerously high heel. The outfit was finished with a tiny white clutch bag. The contrast of the sky blue against her tanned skin looked exquisite and Jake drank her in.

"Hi, there, Yank." He said. "Wow, you look beautiful."

"Why thank you kind sir, you don't look at all bad yourself," she grinned.

"You mean this old thing," he joked, making light of his clearly expensive suit, "Just something I found in the wardrobe."

She laughed and it was delightful. "Good find. You oughta think about going into salvage. Could work out pretty well for you."

"Now there's an idea," he said with a smile. "Can I get you a drink?"

"Yes, please. A Jack Daniels would be lovely."

"Ice?"

"Great."

Jake signalled the barman and ordered two Jack Daniels on the rocks. When they arrived, he gave her one of them and said, "Cheers."

"Cheers," she said and they both took a sip, their eyes locked on each other.

Jake surprised Lizzie. She really hadn't known what to expect, except for a guy in his mid thirties. She had thought he would be arrogant maybe or look a bit more 'criminal', whatever that meant. She knew he was a thief though, someone who had stolen millions of pounds worth of diamonds, so she thought he might be someone who was obviously dishonest or unlikeable. But she did like him, much against her better judgement. He wasn't like any of the stereotypes she had conjured up in her brain. He seemed genuinely nice. Quiet, reserved and intelligent. She also found him extremely attractive which had surprised her more than anything else and worried her slightly as even at this early stage she knew deep down that he was someone she could easily fall for. She would have to be careful that things didn't get out of hand. After all, this was a mission with a firm and unquestionable objective and Jake

Sawyer, or Jake Sloane as he was now calling himself, was just a small cog in a much bigger machine and she had to remember that.

"So, Jake Sloane." She said, unable to tear herself away from his eyes, "Snappy dresser and international man of mystery, what is it that you really do?"

Jake smiled, but couldn't hold her gaze any longer. He had anticipated the question and had an answer prepared. "Okay, you got me. I'm a spy. You've heard of James Bond, right? Well I'm his more sophisticated younger brother."

"Sorry," Lizzie chuckled, "I'm not buying it."

"It was the bit about being the younger brother wasn't it? Catches me out every time. M's going to kill me."

She laughed again. "So what do you do really?"

"Something a lot more boring and much less interesting, I'm afraid. I'm an artist. I'm out here working on pieces for a new show. Oil on canvas mainly - seascapes and tropical scenes, nothing very exciting but it pays the bills." Jake hadn't strayed too far from the truth. He did paint regularly and his bungalow was full of recently painted canvases. They were his escape, the way he unwound. They were pretty good too, probably with some fairly good value but Jake couldn't even contemplate anything like selling them or even exhibiting them for the moment.

"Wow! It must pay pretty good if it lets you stay

here," said Lizzie.

"Sometimes. I'm no Van Gogh, but I do okay."

"No, that's great. And it is very interesting. I'd love to see some of your work, sometime," she said and then she gasped. "God! That sounds really forward, doesn't it? What I meant was, I would like to see some of your work at some point in the future. I'm sure it must be very good." She was blushing.

Jake chuckled. "Sure, no problem, I'd like that."

They were both smiling now, a little embarrassed. Lizzie felt like a child on a first date and Jake couldn't get over just how much this girl was getting to him.

They each took a drink and for a moment it was quiet before Jake said, "So what is it that you do? Are you a model?" Then he checked himself, "Sorry, that sounded like a line, I didn't mean it to. It's just that you look like a model, that's all." Now he was the one who was blushing.

"I bet you've used that one before, right?" she teased.

"No. Honestly," he smiled. "That was the first time - and I think the last!"

She giggled. "Yeah, sure! But yeah, you were close. I did some modelling for a while among other things, now I'm a fashion writer. Freelance. Which I love. I work from my home in Malibu but my stuff goes out in New York, London, all over, so it's great.

"Sounds nice."

"Yeah, it is, kinda." Lizzie drained the last of her

drink. "I'm a lucky girl." She smiled at him, he really was cute and she would definitely have to focus on the task in hand.

"Hey, I'm starving. Are you hungry yet?" Jake asked.

"Famished," she replied. And suddenly she really was.

"Great!" he said. "Let's go eat."

* * *

At dinner, Jake learned that Lizzie was twenty-eight and divorced. Her parents were both dead and apart from a brother, she was pretty much alone.

She, in turn, learned very little about him as he managed to divert the conversation every time it looked like coming around to him. But she didn't appear to mind.

However, she did get around to asking if he was married. "Not anymore," was all Jake said in reply.

They had fun and got on exceptionally well with the chemistry between them fizzing nicely. Somehow, much later on, they got onto the topic of exercise and it turned out their fitness regimes were almost identical - a good, long run followed by a refreshing swim to cool off. "Well, I'll be out on the sand tomorrow morning if you're up for it?" Jake said.

Lizzie smiled and looked once again into his gentle, almost vulnerable eyes. She had been doing it all night and had taken to physically trying to stop herself but somehow they drew her like an irresistible force and she couldn't help herself.

"Is that a challenge?" She said.

"Maybe. I go at it quite hard - I don't know if you'll be up to it." He was teasing her now, suspecting quite rightly that her fitness levels were easily as high as his. "I don't want to have to leave you behind." He couldn't resist a smile, giving himself away.

"Well, I think that was the sound of a very heavy gauntlet being thrown down. I accept your challenge, Mister Lime, - but what do I get if it's me who leaves you behind?"

Jake grinned widely. "How about breakfast? Made with my own fair hands, of course."

"Fine. You're on. I hope you got some Lucky Charms cos they're my favourite."

"I'm not sure if I can manage those but I can do a great English fry-up - how's that sound?

"Sounds good," she said, "It's been a long time since I had one of those."

"Yeah? Said Jake. "Well you've gotta win first."

"Hmm," Lizzie smirked. "Don't you worry there, Limey - you'll be cooking alright!"

They both laughed, equally happy with the arrangement and the thought of seeing each other again so soon.

Shortly afterwards, Jake signed for the meal and the two of them left the restaurant. Outside, Jake asked if she would like a nightcap but Lizzie declined. "No thanks. It's the big race in the morning and I gotta prep."

"Haha!" Jake laughed, "How could I forget. Can I walk you back then?"

"No, thanks. I'll be fine - I'm just a short walk away."

"You sure?" Jake felt uneasy about leaving her alone but they were still within the very secure confines of the resort and there were lots of guests and staff members still milling about.

"Yeah, perfectly. But thanks for a great evening, I've really enjoyed myself - you're good company, Jake Sloane."

"Thanks. You too."

"Until the morning then?"

"Until then. How about we meet here at say seven-thirty - is that too early?"

"Didn't I say I was up to the challenge?" She grinned.

"You know, I believe you did."

"I can't go falling at the first hurdle then, can I?"

"No you can't."

"Until seven-thirty, then. Goodnight Jake." She leant over and gave him a quick peck on the cheek and he savoured the smell of her and the gentle touch of her lips on his face. But then she turned and walked away.

"Goodnight, Lizzie," he said after her and she threw up a hand and waved without looking back.

He watched her for a few moments longer, admiring the way she walked, swaying her hips confidently like the model she had once been. Then, when she was maybe forty feet away, she yelled, "Hey Jake! I like three sausages and plenty of bacon - I hope you got that!"

He couldn't help but laugh. "Yeah, I've got it! He yelled, already knowing he would lose the challenge and very much looking forward to defeat.

Chapter 28

The next morning, Jake arrived at the restaurant at seven-twenty to find Lizzie already there going through her warm-up routine.

"Hey there, Limey - wassup, you're alarm break?"

Jake laughed. "Yeah, something like that."

She looked great, even in the old Abercrombie T-shirt and frayed Daisy Dukes she was wearing. Her hair was pulled tightly off her face and held in place by a white towelling scrunchy. Her pony tail falling freely just like a real pony's tail. Her legs were long and golden and glistening with coconut oil which smelled deliciously tropical on this beautiful Caribbean morning. Lizzie's Nike's were high-end, custom-fitted and clearly well used and if he didn't already, Jake knew now that he had a race on his hands.

Jake wore a battered Quiksilver T-shirt and a pair of lightweight Billabong combats. His Nike's were off the shelf but equally well used. As he performed a few stretches Lizzie admired him out the corner of her eye. Even in his scruffs he was a sight to see.

"You ready?" Jake asked a moment later.

"Born ready," she smiled.

"Want a head start?"

"Not a chance."

"Thought not. Okay, once around the resort then down onto the beach until you see the trunk of a big palm tree lying half into the sea. Then turn and head back. I'll point out my place on the way - we'll finish there, okay?"

"Okay."

"Alright then, Lizzie. On your marks, set - go!"

The pair of them shot off as if their lives depended on it and were pretty much neck and neck as they headed down passed the Club House and around into the small village square which had a little supermarket, a deli and a Starbucks. Resort staff were out sweeping the walkways and tidying the lush gardens, the sprinklers were on soaking the rich green lawns and the water was running down onto the narrow road as Jake and Lizzie splashed by. It wasn't long before they were dashing past the small block of exclusive apartments which were owned by resort club members and then down onto the road that ran parallel with the beach which was dotted with the first hamlet of private bungalows. Minutes later they were running around the southern end of the golf course but soon left that behind as they headed up the cliff road into open countryside with breathtaking views of the sea. They had fallen into a rhythm by then, their legs perfectly in sync as their feet lightly slapped out a steady beat on the tarmac. Both of them were still breathing easily as they approached the next small hamlet of bungalows. Jake was starting to sweat a little now as they were going a little faster than he normally would. It wasn't anything he couldn't handle but he was glad when they were heading downhill again into an avenue of tall palm trees which offered them a welcome canopy of shade that shielded them briefly from the early morning sun.

Five minutes later they were adjacent to the little cluster of dwellings that belonged to Jake's neighbours and then on passed his own bungalow which was the last one in the row. He pointed it out to Lizzie who was at his shoulder, and said, "That's my place, right there. That's where we'll finish, okay?"

"You mean that's where you'll cook me my champion's breakfast?"

He laughed. "Maybe," he said, suddenly shifting it up a gear and leaving her behind.

"Oh, you wanna play it like that, huh?" She shouted after him, "Well okay then, that's fine by me!"

They were both enjoying themselves immensely as they bounded down the little track that led from

Jake's bungalow and onto the beach. Once they were on the sand Jake knew it was a straight two and half miles to the downed palm tree and then the same back. This was where the race would be won or lost, running on the sand was much tougher than on the road and it was a case of whose stamina was the better. Jake was still ahead but only marginally and he could hear Lizzie's footfalls right on his tail. The girl was fit there was no doubt about it but Jake felt he had it under control.

Jake was sweating hard as they approached the downed palm tree that marked the halfway point of this final section and Lizzie was right there with him. They were neck and neck as their feet simultaneously struck the tree trunk before turning and heading back.

Then, like an Olympic athlete, Lizzie suddenly kicked and found a new burst of speed which quickly left Jake floundering some way behind her. She laughed wickedly, "See you there, Limey! Mmm, I can already taste that bacon!"

"Hey! What are you, a ringer or something?" He called and heard her giggle.

Jake couldn't help but chuckle. Until now, he had been semi-toying with her and had always intended to let her win, just for the sheer pleasure of having breakfast with her. But now he really did have a race on his hands. She was quick and had already built up an impressive lead. The sun was now heating up nicely and Jake knew he would struggle to catch her. It was one thing to let her win, but to let her win by a considerable distance was more than his pride could stand. Instantly he put his head down and shifted it up a gear, determined now to make a proper race of it.

Jake did gain ground but no matter how he tried he just could not seem to get closer than a few feet away from her but then, with maybe less than a quarter of a mile to go, Lizzie suddenly seemed to flag. She was good and fast but she too had been running at a much quicker pace than she was used to and the sun which by now was climbing steadily into the clear, cloudless sky, was really starting to give off some heat and taking its toll on her stamina. With Jake's bungalow now looming large in the distance he suddenly appeared at her shoulder. But he was breathing heavily as he said, "Hey there, Yank - how's your cooking?"

Puffing hard but still smiling, she replied, "You're not going to find out today, Limey!" As soon as she said it, she magically got her second wind and once again put her foot on the accelerator. Jake was still hot on her tail, but try as he might, he couldn't fully catch her. She was going to win and there was nothing he could or wanted to do to stop her.

He was literally a couple of feet behind her as they both bounded up the little track from the beach and onto his veranda but by then it was over and she had deservedly won.

Lizzie threw her arms into the air and jumped up and down. "Haha! I win, I win!" She exclaimed like an excited child. "How'd you like that, Mister Lime!"

Jake couldn't help it as he started laughing at her. The sheer joy of seeing how pleased she was warmed his heart and made him happier than he had been in a very long time. "Okay, Lizzie!" He chuckled, "I give in. You win. You got me fair and square."

She was laughing too now, mainly at herself, at how stupidly pleased she was with herself. "I'm so sorry," she giggled, "I don't know what's come over me, I'm not usually such a competitive brat. But I did beat you didn't I?" She laughed again, her legs almost giving way under her as the pair of them howled, tears streaming down both their red, worn out faces.

Then, without thinking, as if it was the most natural thing in the world, Jake hugged her and kissed her on the cheek. She was so adorable that he just did it spontaneously but the second he did it, the moment changed. Not for the worse but for something that felt more meaningful. The laughter stopped and for a second there was nothing before Jake broke away, "So, guess I'm cooking breakfast?" He said somewhat awkwardly as he pulled open the french windows and stepped into the bungalow.

"Yep, guess so," she replied, smiling. "Maybe I should take a shower first though, huh? Cos I would bet I don't smell too good about now."

"Yeah," he smiled, "Me neither. You go first - the juice is in the fridge, help yourself, and the shower's at the back. There's fresh towels on the shelf. I'll put on the coffee and grab a shower after you."

"Sounds great," she said softly. "Back in a bit."

* * *

Lizzie appeared a short while later looking fresh and clean. Her hair was damp and loose and she was wearing one of Jake's old surfer T-shirts. "I found this in the bathroom - I hope you don't mind?"

She looked absolutely beautiful, even stripped of make-up and dressed in the oversized shirt. How on earth could he mind. "Course not," he said. "Be my guest. There's fresh coffee in the pot and today's papers are out on the table. Let me just get a quick shower myself then I'll make a start on that winner's breakfast of yours."

"Can't wait," she said, "I'm starved."

* * *

Lizzie sat on the veranda and blew her coffee. She was having a good time, enjoying herself. But it was not supposed to be this way, it was all wrong. Jake was supposed to be the mark, not a potential suitor. Yes, she was supposed to get close to him, to maybe even make him fall for her, as bad as that was, but it was all for the greater good, strictly part of the mission. Clean, detached, controlled. But she felt far from in control. In fact she felt out of control.

She was already smitten - just on the strength of these two dates and even after knowing what had happened with him in the past, maybe because of it. Even though Jake had tried to be a closed book, there was a vulnerability about him, a sadness, which she wished she could tell him she fully understood. But that was not part of the plan.

She knew if she had these feelings she should get out. All her instincts were screaming for her to do so before either he or she got hurt but she was being relied upon to do her part. It was her turn and she had to see it through but deceiving Jake just killed her. Lizzie knew she should perhaps back-off at least, give him a bit of breathing space and her some time to compose herself as things were moving way, way too fast. But she couldn't help herself, she wanted to be with him, to see more of him, to see if what she was feeling was real. It was as simple as that. The mission was important. The most important thing in her life but she was also a woman and this man had taken her breath away. And that was important too.

"Penny for them," Jake said as he came up behind her and sat down. He was now wearing a crisp white polo shirt and a pair of beige knee length needle cord shorts.

"Sorry?" Lizzie said, a little startled.

"A penny for your thoughts," he said. "You looked miles away just then."

Lizzie smiled at him, "Yes, I was, for a moment.

But I'm back now - and ravenous! Where's my breakfast? She snarled playfully.

"Ah, yes, my apologies. One champion's breakfast coming right up!"

* * *

The delicious aroma of sizzling bacon was irresistible as Lizzie wandered into the kitchen a short time later. Jake was working hard at the grill, a washcloth draped over one shoulder as he turned the fat, spitting sausages with a spatula.

"Anything I can do to help there, Chef?" She asked.

"No, thanks - I think it's all under control - sort of," he replied with a wry grin. "You like it crispy, right?"

She smiled. "Guess so."

"Good. Be ready in a few minutes. Oh, and by the way, I threw your clothes in the washer - hope you don't mind. They'll be ready after breakfast. Didn't think you'd wanna be heading back without them." Then he blushed, "Just wearing that old shirt of mine is what I meant."

"Yeah, yeah - sure you did, Mister Lime," Lizzie teased.

"Honest!" Jake held his hands up in surrender as he started laughing.

"Oh sure," replied Lizzie sarcastically. Then said, "So where are these paintings I've heard about?"

"Through there." Jake nodded to the bedroom.

"Help yourself. Don't expect too much."

Lizzie strolled through to the bedroom where she found the canvases, maybe twenty or thirty, all lined up in uneven stacks leaning against the wall. An empty easel was standing there too.

Immediately she was struck by how good they were. She was no expert but had grown up in a house that had been filled with expensive paintings so had a keen eye for talent. And it was clear that Jake had it in abundance.

She picked one up, a seascape painted during a tropical storm, and placed it on the easel to appreciate it fully. She stepped back a few paces to admire it more. It was sensational, the brushwork and use of colour absolutely staggering.

"Wow, Jake!" she called, "These are amazing. Really, really good. I had no idea —"

"Sorry?" I can't hear you. Did you say something?" Jake yelled back over the loud sizzle of bacon.

"I said, that you're paintings are really good. You're very talented, Jake." Lizzie said sincerely as she came back out of the bedroom.

"Thanks," he replied. "Breakfast's ready."

"Great. I mean it though, Jake. You're work is excellent - really something."

"Thanks," he said again, a little embarrassed, "That's nice of you to say. Come on, let's eat before it gets cold."

Again Lizzie noticed how deftly Jake changed the subject when it came around to him and was once again struck by how different he was to what she expected. She felt really conflicted about what she had read about him in the report, which she had studied again on the flight over. He was definitely something of a conundrum and had she not already known it for certain, there was no way she would have believed that this softly spoken, witty and self-deprecating gentle man was the very same person who had stolen those diamonds.

* * *

Jake and Lizzie fell into an easy rhythm as they chatted and laughed through breakfast, feeling more and more comfortable in each others company, then a little after eleven she made a move to leave. Jake retrieved her now clean, dry clothes from the dryer and turned his back whilst she put them on, trying hard not to think about what she looked like as she shrugged her tiny denims on over her firm, shapely bottom. Lizzie tied her Abercrombie T-shirt in a tight knot under her breasts exposing her lean brown midriff and impossibly flat stomach to make the most of the sun on the way back to her bungalow. "Okay, you can turn around now, I'm decent," she said. "Thanks for the loan of the shirt, I've left it on the chair."

"No problem. It looked much better on you than it ever did on me." He smiled.

"Thanks. And thanks for the breakfast" she said. "It was just as billed."

"You mean crispy, don't you?"

"Just a little. But it was great, though," she said, scooching her bare feet back into her expensive Nike's.

"Hey, no. A deal's a deal and you won fair and square, champ."

"That's right, I did, didn't I?" She giggled.

Jake wanted to kiss her and sensed that she was willing him to. But, with an effort, he restrained himself. Lizzie had got to him. She had somehow broken through the barrier, that huge wall he had put up which he thought would never be knocked down. Already his feelings, which had been dormant, almost completely absent for so long, had been awoken - shaken abruptly to life by this beautiful, funny, intelligent woman. He had to force himself to take it slowly, to be sure that what he was feeling was real. Because if it was then she deserved to know the truth about him and that was something he thought he would never be able to tell anyone.

"Will you have dinner with me again tonight?" Jake asked her. There was an intensity in his voice and the humour had gone.

Lizzie stopped giggling. Knowing that the moment had changed again, desperately wanting him to kiss her but berating herself for it. She knew she should say no to dinner. To keep him dangling would be the wise move, keep him waiting for a couple of days before seeing him again, but she couldn't help herself. "I'd love to," she said.

"Good. How about I pick you up just before sunset, then we can watch it together."

"That sounds lovely," she said. "But I'll meet you here." Then, unable to resist, she leant in and brushed his lips with hers, too quickly for Jake to respond. She didn't trust herself to linger there any longer, suspecting that if she did she would never be able to tear herself away. "See you tonight," she said, then instantly turned and left before Jake had a chance to stop her. By the time she was down the hill and out of sight he was already missing her and couldn't wait to feel her lips on his once more.

Chapter 29

That night, after watching the spectacular sunset together, Jake took Lizzie to an exclusive restaurant on the sea front. There was soft music, candlelight and a very romantic mood and the heat between the two of them was rising dramatically.

Jake couldn't help himself. He was intoxicated by her. He suddenly felt alive again, revitalised, vibrant even, like nothing he had felt in a very long time.

She was in a white, vintage Yves Saint Laurent dress with bare arms and a low neck that made the most of her tanned cleavage. Her shoes were simple white Louboutin sling backs with trademark red soles and killer heels. Jake had on a linen shirt, a lightweight beige suit and the same soft brown loafers that he had worn the previous evening. As a couple they looked exactly right, beautiful, stylish and wealthy as if they had stepped directly out of the pages of Vogue.

After a long intimate dinner, neither of them

were quite ready to go home, so they took a cab to the casino at Atlantis, where Jake lost badly at the roulette wheel and Lizzie won a small fortune at blackjack table. They had great fun and laughed a lot but by two in the morning they were both ready to head back to their own resort.

After tipping the taxi driver, Jake then walked Lizzie back to her bungalow.

When they reached her door, Lizzie said, "That was wonderful, Jake, thank you. I've had a lovely evening."

"Me, too, Lizzie. I've really enjoyed it."

"It's beautiful here, isn't it. Nassau, I mean." Lizzie said.

"It is. And so are you," replied Jake.

"Why thank you, kind sir," she mocked. "You ain't so bad yourself."

"Oh, stop it. You'll make me blush."

"I'd like to see that. I bet it'd be so cute." Her dark hair was plaited into a long thick pony tail. Very stylish, very classy. And very irresistible. The tiny scar on her temple gleaming white against her tan like a shiny star.

"I think you're the cute one," Jake said, and lent in to kiss her.

She lifted her chin in response and their lips touched. Just for a couple of beats. Then he pulled away, but their faces remained just inches apart.

"That was nice." Lizzie said.

"Yeah. I've wanted to do that since the moment I saw you."

"Really?" she said.

"Uh-huh."

"Wanna do it again?"

"Oh, yeah." This time when their lips touched, it was stronger, more passionate, electric. He lifted his hand and caressed her cheek, softly pulling her to him, feeling her tongue gently probing his. She placed a hand at the base of his neck, keeping him with her, not letting him go. The kiss lasted a long time, but eventually they broke away.

"How about I come in for a coffee?" Jake asked.

"That's a very good idea, although not tonight. I need my beauty sleep. But soon, Jake, very soon. I promise."

"Hey, no problem," Jake said, but his disappointment was clear to see, "I wasn't thirsty anyway."

"No," Lizzie said suggestively. "I know you weren't."

Jake grinned. "I'll have you know, I'm addicted to caffeine."

"I just bet you are," she laughed. She took her key from her purse, then leaned up and gave him another long kiss. "Another time. I promise," she whispered.

Then she turned and walked to her door. "Night, Limey." She said.

"Goodnight, Yank."

She opened her door, turned, blew him a kiss, then disappeared inside her bungalow.

Jake smiled wistfully. Then walked back to his own bungalow alone.

* * *

Lizzie shut the door behind her and with the bungalow still in darkness she went over to the window to check that Jake had gone. Then she shut the drapes and snapped on the light.

When she turned she saw the man sitting there in one of the white linen armchairs, looking directly at her and she very nearly jumped out of her skin.

The man's expression was intense even though he looked tired and drawn. The clothes he wore were functional rather than stylish in 'an Englishman abroad' sort of way and his bald head and sharp, pointed nose were both reddened with sunburn.

Aaron Sumpter smiled. "Hello Elizabeth," he said, "I never thought you were coming home?"

Lizzie let out a breath of relief, "Christ, Ronny, you startled me." She said. "I thought you'd be asleep by now. You shouldn't have waited up."

"Sorry. I know. I couldn't sleep - and to be honest, I was a bit worried about you. How did it go? Is everything alright - does he suspect anything?

Lizzie marched over and planted a kiss on his cheek. "Thanks for being worried, but you needn't have been. And of course he doesn't suspect anything, silly. Everything's fine." She said. "Everything is going just as we planned."

But even as she said it, Lizzie knew that it wasn't.

Chapter 30

Wendel Wallace was a big-hearted American, born and raised in San Francisco. But the majority of his business life was spent in the UK, where the head offices of Wallace Bearing were located, the company that his father, Langford Wallace, and Randolph Bearing had started many years before.

Wendel, like his father, was a natural businessman, but he was also a humanitarian. And proof of this was his benevolence to Aaron Sumpter.

It was Wendel who had given Aaron his first job cleaning the staff cars at Wallace Bearing and running errands for him and Teddy Bearing. Aaron was just fifteen and had been in and out of foster and care homes all his life. An orphan without a father to guide him. But Wendel had recognised his potential and had taken him on. Teddy, too, had played his part, both men mentoring the young Aaron and he was keen to learn.

Eventually Aaron moved into the Wallace mansion, where he befriended Wendel's young son, Jonathan. And even though Aaron was five years older, the two soon became close.

Wendel often took the two boys with him whenever he travelled to America where Wendel's wife, Ella, chose to live. But it was a happy marriage and life spent mostly apart seemed to suit them.

Ella was a loving mother to Jonathan, but she also had a very demanding career as a doctor so she allowed her son to live most the year with her husband in England, where he also went to school.

Teddy Bearing's son, Peter, was also around quite a bit. But he was a spoiled youth and very superior in his manner. He was extremely intelligent and liked to get his own way and Teddy would indulge him. Aaron got on well enough with Peter though, who was just a couple of years younger than him, but he never really took to him quite like he did to Jonathan.

Jonathan was eleven when Elizabeth came along, who he alone called 'Lizzie.' She called him 'Johnny' and Aaron 'Ronny' as she could not pronounce either of their names properly when she was tiny.

But somehow, the names had stuck and to her that is how they were forever known.

As for Aaron, he adored her from the moment she was born. To him, she was his little sister. However, for some reason, maybe because she was a girl, Ella chose to keep Elizabeth with her in the

States. But in the holidays she always came to stay with Wendel in England.

As time wore on, Aaron took on a more active role at Wallace Bearing. Ever eager for his mentor's approval, he had a knack for garnering information which often proved useful to Wendel and Teddy, earning their praise and encouragement. By his mid-twenties Aaron had a complete dossier on all Wallace Bearing clients, on every director, manager and department head. The good, the bad and the downright dirty. All their little secrets documented in black and white. It was vital intelligence which had proved to be useful leverage in many sticky negotiations.

Meanwhile, Jonathan was off at university, studying business. But it was Peter that shone in that department and he had earned himself a place at Oxford. Which was where he met Arthur and Charles Khan.

Aaron met the Khan's many times in those days as they and Peter were as thick as thieves, although Aaron and Arthur never really saw eye to eye.

Eventually, both Jonathan and Peter took up positions at Wallace Bearing. Wendel was exceptionally proud of Jonathan even though he was never the businessman he would have liked him to be.

Peter, however, made it plain that he was the boss, both at work and at leisure, but that was the way he had always been.

When Teddy Bearing succumbed to cancer, Peter, aged just twenty-eight, took up his seat on the board.

After that there was no stopping him. He would make decisions about the future of The Company, often taking it in a completely different direction without deferring to Wendel as the more senior partner. However, it could not be denied that Peter's ideas were effective and Wallace Bearing went from strength to strength.

Wendel was all but put out to pasture and Jonathan was viewed as little more than an irritant. Peter made it quite clear that he wished to be rid of them both.

Meanwhile, Ella Wallace, who had been diagnosed with dementia some years before was slowly losing her mind and the stress of it weighed heavily on all members of the family.

By way of escape, Elizabeth, now twenty-three and studying fashion in the States, had married a musician by the name of Roger Barnes. The pair had set up home together in California much to Jonathan and Aaron's dismay, but the marriage was in trouble almost as soon as it began.

That same year, Peter Bearing held a party at his Berkshire mansion, where he planned to rid himself of Jonathan Wallace.

Jonathan liked the ladies and they liked him

and on this night Peter made certain that he was surrounded by plenty of them. He also made certain that Jonathan's glass was never empty.

Late into the evening and drunk, Jonathan took one of the girl's into a bedroom where he supposedly raped her.

In reality, the whole thing had been choreographed by Bearing. Jonathan had been drugged and the girl forcibly had sex with him even though he had no memory of it. Afterwards, Peter went to work on the girl with his fists to make the claim of rape look more convincing. Lastly, he tore the girl's panties and smeared her dress with blood. The girl disappeared after she was paid off - although not before Peter got very explicit photographic evidence of what Jonathan had supposedly done.

In the morning, when Jonathan awoke with the hangover from hell, Peter told him that the girl had demanded fifty thousand pounds in return for her silence. Bearing said he had paid her out of his own pocket to protect Jonathan. Bearing then showed him the photos and said that he was a disgrace to the Wallace Bearing name but would help him on the condition that he resign from The Company immediately. The photos were to be retained by Peter as insurance that Jonathan keep his word.

Jonathan truly didn't know what to believe. Was he really capable of doing what the evidence suggested? He wasn't sure that he was but he was certainly different when he drank whiskey and he couldn't remember a thing except for seeing the girl in the bedroom wearing just her green satin underwear. It was his only memory and tragically a rather convincing one.

Ashamed, desperate and with no other choice Jonathan reluctantly agreed to Peter's demands and the very next day he duly resigned from The Company, convinced that he had brought shame down upon his whole family.

A week later he hanged himself.

Wendel collapsed when he heard the news. On route to the hospital he suffered a massive heart attack and was pronounced dead on arrival.

* * *

Aaron was utterly devastated by the double tragedy as was Elizabeth, who, grief stricken, looked thin and unwell at the funeral. Ella Wallace did not make the trip.

Elizabeth flew back to the States almost immediately afterwards, unable to deal with both her father and brother's affairs and begging Aaron to take care of things on her behalf. Which he proudly did. But he could not accept that Jonathan was capable of rape, so he decided to find out the facts for himself, without Bearing's knowledge.

It took him very little time to find the girl that had cried rape and only slightly longer to extract the truth from her; that the whole sordid affair had been orchestrated by Peter Bearing.

The seeds of revenge had been growing in Aaron's head ever since Jonathan's suicide but after finding the girl and hearing the truth the seeds had reached full bloom. He didn't know exactly how yet but one way or another he would make Bearing pay for what he had done. However, with no physical proof, Aaron could not reveal his findings to the police or even confront Bearing with them. His only hope, for the time being was to continue working for Wallace Bearing and remain in a trusted position in the hope that he would find something one day to ultimately bring Bearing down.

In order to do this effectively and to gain Peter's trust, he had to physically distance himself from Lizzie and the Wallace family, to publicly fall out with them in such a way that Peter Bearing would find utterly believable and when Lizzie asked Aaron to take care of things for her after the funerals it gave him an idea as to how such a rift could occur.

The answer was money, or more precisely, lack of it. Aaron was due to benefit massively from Wendel's death. Lizzie was to see to it that her foster brother had an equal share of the inheritance which would make him very rich indeed. Lizzie, of course, intended to honour her father's wishes. But, Aaron supposed, what would happen if she didn't?

Convincing Lizzie to cut him out of the inheritance was tricky and she was extremely reluctant to do so - Aaron was as much a brother to her as Jonathan was and fully entitled to every penny Wendel bequeathed him. But eventually Aaron made her see things his way. She too wanted to bring Bearing down and it made sense for Aaron to be close to him, to work on the inside so that he could find something to make that possible. Unfortunately, Aaron's plan also meant that he and Lizzie would not be able to see each other and would only be able to communicate secretly at specific times. This thought didn't appeal to either of them but in the end Aaron convinced her that it would be worth it.

So Aaron loudly made it known that Wendel had made no provision in his will for him and that Elizabeth had seen fit not to give him a cent. He made a huge show of being slighted by the Wallace family and spoke badly of them to anyone in The Company who had Peter's ear - and in particular Bearing himself. As if to underline his ill fortune, Aaron bought himself a small semi-detached in Hampstead which was a dramatic step down from the apartment suite he lived in at Wendel's mansion prior to his death.

From then on he always went that extra mile to ensure that Peter's faith in him was unquestionable. However, in truth, Aaron was secretly filing every bit of documentation, recording every conversation and noting every transaction, constantly trying to find that one snippet of information that would destroy

Bearing.

* * *

Six months after the death of her father and brother, Elizabeth's already rocky marriage ended in divorce and shortly after that, her mother died. Ella Wallace, once so beautiful, so intelligent and wise, passed away in her sleep, her mind so badly addled that she had not recognised her own daughter for some considerable time.

Elizabeth was heart broken and finding it difficult to move on. Aaron was her only comfort, even though he could only offer support by phone once a week. He was a godsend and she finally got through it but during those dark days, they often discussed their desire to avenge Jonathan and Wendel's deaths - the only question was how.

But after three years of searching they finally found a way.

Aaron had numerous recordings of Peter and Arthur Khan discussing a horde of conflict diamonds they were bringing into the UK and his plan was to actually film Peter taking delivery of them, thus providing actual concrete evidence and undeniable proof of his guilt.

However, the diamonds went missing. As did Aaron's evidence. But, as luck would have it, Bearing charged Aaron with the task of finding them, not suspecting that Sumpter's motive's were very different from his own.

After another two and a half years of searching, Aaron finally found the man who stole them and he immediately rang Elizabeth, now twenty-eight and calling herself Lizzie, in memory of Jonathan, to tell her the news. Together they formulated a plan.

The only thing now was to find out where the diamonds were, if indeed there were any left, and steal them away from the man who currently possessed them. Jake Sawyer.

Chapter 31

Arthur Khan had given up waiting for Aaron Sumpter a long time ago.

His patience had run out eight months before when Sumpter's latest report again turned up nothing new.

Arthur had done as Peter had said. He had laid low, he had bided his time and he had let the dust settle. There had been no repercussions following the murder of the Sawyers or Maddox, no arrest and now, from what he had gathered, the case had been stamped 'unsolved' and effectively filed. He was free and clear.

Now he was keen to get on with things, eager to get back the diamonds that he and his brother had so carefully collected. Their nest egg, their retirement fund. Their diamonds. But now Charles was dead and his share would go to Arthur who was desperate to claim it.

Arthur had never trusted Aaron Sumpter and

he had never made a secret of it, but Peter had always maintained that he was dependable. However after repeatedly being put off or told to be patient by Sumpter, even Peter was having his doubts. Sure, Sumpter had shown a modicum of success, tracing Sawyer to Amsterdam and from there back and forth across the globe, which was quite impressive even Arthur had to admit. But then the trail had grown cold. And had remained cold. In fact for the last year it had been positively freezing.

That was why eight months ago, Arthur, with Peter Bearing's reluctant approval, had taken matters into his own hands.

He had hired one of his own men, who he had fought alongside for many years. A man whose loyalty was unquestionable as it had been proven in battle time after time. A man who had the necessary skills to trail Sumpter, to find out exactly what he did know and exactly what he was up to. And, more importantly, whether he could be trusted. This man's name was Fabian Król.

Król, originally from Poland, was an ex-mercenary, just like Khan. He was tough, resilient and extremely capable. If Sumpter was holding something back or, as Arthur suspected, trying to keep the diamonds for himself, then Król would learn of it. And, if necessary, deal with it. Permanently.

* * *

From a distant hill, Fabian Król watched

267

Sumpter through an extremely powerful zoom lens, the whir and click of the camera's shutter the only sound in the tranquil Caribbean afternoon, as numerous photos were snapped and saved onto the memory card.

Król was embedded in the long grass, his tightly cropped hair and black stubble a natural camouflage in the dense scrub, his blue eyes and bushy, dark eyebrows hidden behind the camera.

Lying down, it was difficult to tell how tall he was, but he was six two and broad across the shoulders with thick arms that were covered with tattoos.

After being in Africa in full kit, in well over hundred degrees heat, the tropical sunshine of Nassau was very nearly like being on a vacation for Król, lying there in a T-shirt and cargo shorts, he could well have been sunbathing. But it was all about the work for Król. With him there was no such thing as leisure. Fabian Król had no family, no one to go home to and that's just the way he liked it. He was a loner with no conscience and ice running through his veins. To him, emotion was a weakness, as was family, love or friendship. The men he worked with in the war-torn countries of the world, Arthur Khan amongst them, they were comrades, brothers in arms but nothing more. Khan paid for his services and for that he got loyalty as did any of his paymasters. Król had a code of honour which allowed indiscriminate killing and mutilation but never disloyalty or betrayal as to him they were the ultimate sin. In Król's chosen profession, there was no place for squeamishness or humanitarianism, whereas a keen sense of loyalty was high on a client's requirement list and whilst he was in their employ, Fabian Król guaranteed it.

* * *

Sumpter had come ashore three days ago, and was using a bungalow at the Crystal Waters Resort, having been ensconced offshore, in a sailing boat for a week prior to that.

Król had since witnessed Sumpter with a woman at the bungalow - a young, beautiful woman, who he seemed to be extremely familiar with. But Król could not believe it was a girlfriend as she was way out of Sumpter's league.

Król had then followed the woman. She appeared to be just a tourist at first; she sunbathed and swam, did some shopping. Then Król witnessed a man talking to her, who was maybe just a few years older. Good looking, tanned, fit, much more her type, and it soon became clear they were an item. But who were they?

Król found out their names; Lizzie Barnes and Jake Sloane. He didn't know the name Lizzie Barnes at all. But he did know of a Jake Sawyer.

Could they be one and the same?

He studied the photograph he had of Sawyer; long hair, glasses, shaggy beard, overweight. Then he put it next to the shot he had taken of Jake Sloane earlier that day; lean, well-groomed, attractive. At first glance they appeared to be very different, yet, under closer inspection, there were undoubtedly similarities; the bone structure, the nose - both extremely alike.

Król could not prove it with one hundred percent certainty but instinct told him that Jake Sloane was Jake Sawyer. He would stake his life on it. But who was Lizzie Barnes?

Król downloaded the shots onto his laptop and emailed them to Arthur Khan. Maybe he would know.

* * *

Peter Bearing was studying colour swatches with Anya, the ex Miss Bulgaria who was now his live-in mistress. His pet project, The Bearing Building - the fabulous glass tower which had been under construction for the past eighteen months - was at last close to completion and Peter was now thinking about decor for his magnificent office which would sit right at the very top and represent the pinnacle of his business achievements. The building itself was a masterpiece of contemporary architecture, built from the very latest materials and constructed in the shape of a giant spiral which the media had already nicknamed 'The Twirl.' When complete, the building would dominate the London skyline and give Peter incredible three-hundred and sixty degree views of the capital. From the massive floor to ceiling windows that surrounded the vast circular floorspace he would be able to survey the whole city. In just a few short months it was destined to become the brand new, hi-spec, hi-tech, base of his business empire and he couldn't wait to move in.

Anya was sitting on his lap, behind his desk in his present office, wearing a silk leopard print blouse and a tiny black skirt. Her long, shapely legs, crossed in front of her, were accentuated by a pair of leopard print Manolo Blahnik's with towering heels. Around her neck was a diamond necklace and on her wrist a matching bracelet. The set was completed by a pair of exquisitely cut diamond earrings. She looked stunning; her light blonde hair loose and long and expertly coiffed by her personal stylist, her fingernails polished and buffed like glossy red talons. Everything about her was immaculate - another prize in Peter's collection to be lusted after, yet never possessed, by other men.

However, underneath the perfect exterior, her nipples were lacerated, her buttocks were cross-hatched with welts and her inner thighs were riddled with bite marks. Sex with Peter was rough, which was just the way she liked it and it turned out that they were a perfect match.

Anya had proved to be an excellent investment for Peter. He had installed her in his penthouse apartment and furnished her with a purse full of credit cards, a limitless allowance and a Bentley Coupé. She had provided him with an outlet for his sexual fantasies and an appetite for roughness which very nearly eclipsed his own. Her only stipulation in their very unique relationship was that he must never mark her face or leave any permanent scarring on her body as her vanity would not allow it. Anya also worked as a model occasionally for various S&M magazines, although only when the mood took her and scars were not widely sought after. Once she could have made a fortune as a super model but she had proved far too difficult and demanding for most agencies. She also had a tempestuous streak and a propensity for violence which had sent several assistants and at least two photographers to A&E after shoots with her. The fallout from these incidents had soured her standing within the business and ultimately ended her prospects of making the big time. But it didn't worry her, she knew that a beautiful woman with a high sex drive and a knowledge of how to please rich men would never go hungry.

Nevertheless, Anya and Peter were happily debating the colour scheme of the enormous semi-circular seating area which would dominate the centre section of the office, and the merits of matching or contrasting cushions when the intercom on Peter's desk buzzed. "Yes?" Bearing said sharply to his PA, "What is it, Susan? You know I didn't want to be disturbed this afternoon."

"Sorry to interrupt Mister Bearing, but Mister Khan's here. He says he needs to speak with you rather urgently.

Anya, instinctively taking this as her cue to leave, gave Peter a kiss on the cheek and slipped off his lap. Ever the enigma, Anya whilst beautiful and soft on the outside had cold steel within and her feelings were locked tightly away in the keyless vault of her heart. Power was her God and money was her religion and for the faintest whiff of both she would gladly sell her own mother. Fortunately for her, Peter was a kindred spirit. He knew what made her tick and how shallow the thin vein of emotion was that ran through her. He knew because he was the same. Anya understood him when so many other women had not. She knew when to attend him, when to indulge him and when to leave him well alone.

And the golden rule was never to keep Peter away from business, especially when it was with Arthur Khan.

As she slipped off his lap, Peter patted her perfectly formed behind affectionately and mouthed "See you later". She nodded her understanding then picked up her fur coat which was draped carelessly over a stylish leather armchair and headed for the private elevator. "See you," she whispered as she gracefully entered the lift.

When she was gone Bearing turned his attention back to the intercom. "Very well, Susan. Show Arthur in, would you?"

* * *

"Well, well, well," Peter Bearing chuckled as he studied the photos. "Little Elizabeth. My, how you've blossomed."

Arthur Khan was sitting opposite him. Spread out on the desk, scattered over the swatch books he was previously looking at with Anya, were a selection of high quality eight by ten printouts that Khan had taken off his laptop that morning.

"It's definitely her then?" Khan asked. "This Lizzie Barnes is Elizabeth Wallace?"

"Oh, yes. Well, Elizabeth Barnes as she is now. Married some American, I seem to recall. But it's definitely her."

"So you think Sumpter has betrayed us?"

"I think that is undoubtedly the case, Arthur. It seems you were correct, Aaron was not to be trusted after all. And your Mister Król is just as reliable as you claimed."

"So Lizzie Barnes and Sumpter are working together. But what about Sawyer, do you think he's with them too or are they just using him to get to our diamonds?"

"That is, indeed, the question, Arthur. My money would be on Sawyer not being part of it, but who knows. Whatever the answer, Aaron Sumpter has long out lived his usefulness. Do you think Mister Król can deal with that for us?"

"I'm sure he can, Peter, for the right incentive." Replied Khan.

"Make it so then, Arthur, would you? Once Sumpter is out of the picture Król then needs to use his charms on Elizabeth and Sawyer, to find out once and for all where our merchandise is."

"Fine, Peter, I'll arrange it. What happens to Barnes and Sawyer afterwards?"

"I think they've had enough fun at our expense, don't you, Arthur? Make sure Król finds out everything we need then tell him to get rid of them. I've had more than enough of these insects wasting my time."

Arthur Khan smiled, then picked up the phone and called Król.

Chapter 32

Lizzie and Jake had been almost inseparable for nearly the whole time she had been in Nassau, their blossoming romance becoming more intense with each day that passed. Exactly as Aaron had planned it.

But, after yet another long day in Jake's company, which ended with a romantic dinner watching the sun sink down into the beautiful Caribbean, Lizzie was having a major crisis of conscience.

The plan had seemed so easy when Aaron laid it out to her over the phone in Malibu.

But since she had joined Aaron in Nassau and actually gotten to know Jake, she was having serious reservations about what they were doing.

In actual fact, Lizzie now doubted she could go through with it at all.

The original plan was to get close to Jake Sawyer, find out where the diamonds were, then take them. But the reality was another matter altogether.

For a start she had not expected to even like Jake, let alone be attracted to him but she was, and if she was being honest with herself she was falling in love with him. It scared her that she had known him for only a short time, literally just a few days, yet already it felt like she had known him a lifetime.

Not only was he kind, gentle and funny but he was thoughtful and sensitive too, despite trying hard to disguise it. And even though he had made no mention of it, Lizzie knew about Jake's past, as Aaron had compiled a full dossier which she had read and re-read several times. But rather than being shocked or outraged or even just partisan about what had happened and what he had done, she found that her overwhelming emotion was empathy. He had lost his family, his children, and she could tell that he blamed himself. There was a sadness in his eyes that she found deeply affecting. He was clearly still grieving and it upset Lizzie that she was being so dishonest with him when all she wanted to do was take him in her arms and make the pain go away.

She had not told him of her own pain, of how she had lost her brother and her father on the same day - buried them both on the same day. But she wanted to. She wanted him to know that she understood his grief.

Furthermore, Lizzie genuinely believed that Jake was a good guy, which seemed strange when knowing he had stolen a case full of priceless diamonds. But wasn't she there in The Bahamas trying to do the exact same thing?

If he was a crook then so was she, in fact she was worse. Jake's crime, from what she had read, was spontaneous, an act borne of shear desperation, but hers was premeditated and had been in the planning for years, even though her motives were not for personal gain but to find justice for her father and brother.

Why then could she not find justice for Jake's family too? Why could they not work together to achieve the same goal?

She suspected that given the opportunity, Jake would jump at the chance to bring the real killers of his family to justice.

Lying in her bed that night, trying to stop herself wishing that Jake was there beside her, she resolved to tell him the truth.

But first she had to convince Aaron.

* * *

Jake was feeling guilty, too. For over two years it was the only emotion he had felt, because of what had happened to his family. But now, he was feeling guilty for another reason. Because he was happy and he did not deserve to be. But Lizzie Barnes had got to him. For the first time in a very long time, Jake was actually looking forward to the next day, and the day after that and for how many other days Lizzie decided to stay.

The other women he had been with - where he was trying desperately to feel something - he just simply did not.

But with her, it seemed like he was trying not to feel something, for fear of where it might lead. Purposely he had been putting off sleeping with her, almost to the point where she was probably starting to notice. But he knew that after making love to her he would no longer be able to resist her at all as she was already occupying almost every thought.

He was smitten that was for sure. More so than he dare admit. And even though being with her felt so right, he still couldn't help thinking he was betraying his family. But he couldn't stop seeing her either.

He decided that it was time to tell her the truth about him. It was a risk but it was one he had to take. If she still wanted to be with him after hearing everything he had to say then, perhaps, maybe it was right. If, on the other hand, she ran a mile, then maybe it wasn't meant to be. However, telling her was a scary prospect. He had told no one the truth about himself in all the time he had been on the run. But he resolved to do it. Tomorrow, one way or another, Lizzie Barnes would know the truth about him.

Chapter 33

Aaron Sumpter was deeply concerned when Lizzie told him what she intended to do. It had taken so long to find Sawyer that they couldn't afford for him to run again. Bearing and Khan's patience had long since evaporated and Aaron knew he was working on borrowed time.

For the last eight months he had been deliberately fobbing them off, telling them that the trail had gone cold when in actuality it was boiling hot and he was getting ever closer to Sawyer.

Then, he finally hit pay dirt.

When he was absolutely one hundred percent certain that Jake Sloane was Jake Sawyer, he called Lizzie. She caught the next plane out, her desire to nail Bearing and Khan every bit as strong as Aaron's.

But he had not anticipated this turn of events. Nor, in fairness, had she.

Lizzie was sitting on the couch in her bungalow, tears in her eyes, adamant about what she intended to do and Aaron, sitting next to her, knew he had no choice but to agree.

She was a bright, intuitive woman, if she trusted this man, then so must he. It was not the way he had planned it but, even though she was crying now, Aaron was glad she had found happiness once more.

"Very well, Elizabeth," he said. "Go tell him if you feel you must, but please be careful."

"Really Ronny? You really want me to?"

Sumpter nodded.

Lizzie beamed at him, wiping the tears from her eyes. "Oh thank you," she said, planting a kiss on his cheek, "It'll be fine, you'll see. I promise."

Aaron nodded again and smiled resignedly. "Of course it will," he said, as she bounded from the room.

* * *

Sumpter had noticed the man yesterday, as he walked back to Lizzie's bungalow with an armful of groceries. The heavily tattooed man looked somehow out of place in the exclusive resort, more like a night club bouncer than a wealthy holiday-maker. But then Aaron considered that he, himself, was not exactly the archetypical guest, so thought little more of it. Then, as he left to get a newspaper this morning, he noticed the man again, sitting on a bench several yards away and for some reason Aaron's suspicions started to prickle.

After Lizzie left, Aaron was about to pack away

his ever present laptop when something instinctively told him to be cautious. All the evidence that Aaron had gathered to prove Peter Bearing and Arthur Khan's guilt was on the laptop and the back-up files were all at his home in Hampstead. A fact that suddenly bothered him.

On the spur of the moment, Aaron grabbed up his laptop, shoved it into its battered, well-travelled bag and jumped into his hired, bright orange Mini Moke. He sped out of the resort and headed the short distance into town with the intention of finding a computer store.

Once in Nassau city centre, Aaron cruised around until he found a likely looking mall close to the port. He squeezed the Mini Moke into the tiniest of parking spaces and as he turned off the ignition saw a Volkswagen Jetta out the corner of his eye slip into a space on the opposite side of the road. The driver was the tattooed man from the resort. Aaron was now officially worried.

He jumped out onto the busy, cobbled street that was thick with tourists - the majority of whom being daytrippers who had alighted from the variety of huge cruise ships docked not too far away, and wove himself into the crowd, trying to make himself as invisible as possible.

Darting into one dreary souvenir shop after another, Aaron eventually found what he was looking for in a little shop called 'The Computer

Cove' which was located up a narrow side street. It, too, sold the obligatory souvenirs but the majority of these were computer themed, such as mousemats featuring various Caribbean scenes, CD racks shaped like palm trees and T-shirts with pixelated images of Bob Marley on the front saying '*My Computer Keeps Jammin'!*'

However, Aaron wasn't looking for any of these but after rummaging around the store for what seemed like ages he did, indeed, find just what he wanted.

An hour after parking it, Aaron returned to the Mini Moke, he was sweating profusely under the glare of the noon day sun and the white beanie hat he was wearing to protect his bald head against the powerful rays was damp with perspiration. He was not at all comfortable in holiday attire and looked decidedly ill at ease in the floral shirt and baggy shorts Lizzie had bought for him. He was much more a shirt and tie sort of person but knew that kind of dress was wholly inappropriate for a 'tourist' such as him. As for the footwear, he could not understand how people managed to walk anywhere in flip-flops, let alone drive in them, as his feet were now aching badly and there were large blisters on the balls of his feet. He slipped off his sandals with enormous relief and headed back to the resort driving barefoot - still not an easy thing but far better than attempting it in flip-flops. But Aaron knew he had far greater things to worry about than the state of his feet and before setting off saw that the Jetta was still parked across the street with the driver having just returned.

All the way back, the Volkswagen Jetta stayed at least two car lengths behind him, staying discreetly out of sight. If Aaron hadn't have been of an acutely suspicious nature he would never have noticed that he was being tailed at all. But Aaron's years of working for Peter Bearing had taught him to suspect everything and that there was no such thing as coincidence.

A short time later, the little orange Moke screeched to a halt back at the resort and Aaron hopped swiftly out.

Hobbling as quickly as he could along the little winding path on his badly blistered feet, he finally arrived back at Lizzie's villa with the laptop bag slung casually over one shoulder.

He let himself in, took the laptop out of the bag, placed it on the table and booted it up. As it sparked into life, Aaron sneaked a look out of the window. The Jetta had just pulled into one of the parking bays which were reserved for guests staying in the adjacent bungalows.

Quickly, Sumpter snapped open his phone and punched in Lizzie's number, he had to warn her that they were no longer safe.

Chapter 34

Lizzie's initial enthusiasm soon evaporated after leaving Aaron back at her bungalow and for the last two hours she had been wandering around the resort trying to think of what on earth to say to Jake. However, with still no idea, she finally arrived at his door and full of apprehension, tentatively knocked.

Jake opened it. "Hey, Yank - I was just thinking about you."

"Hi," she said, watching him walk back inside, expecting her to follow him.

He turned to see her still on the doorstep. "You coming in?"

"Yeah, I guess." She stepped over the threshold but she seemed subdued, far from her normal self.

"Are you okay, Lizzie? You seem kind of–" He searched for a word, "Nervous."

"I'm fine. Well, sort of."

"Anything I can help you with?"

"Er, yeah. I dunno. I mean, maybe. Say, could I

get a drink, I'm parched?"

"Sure," Jake said, a little perplexed. "Coffee, orange juice, water? Something a little stronger perhaps?"

"Water's good, thanks."

"No problem. One water coming right up. Make yourself comfortable, I'll be back in just a second."

Lizzie sat down on the plush linen sofa in Jake's stylish living room as he went to fetch her a bottle of water from the fridge in the kitchen.

When he got back, he, too, looked a little nervous and said, "Look, now that you're here, there's something I've been meaning to tell you–"

"No, please Jake," Lizzie jumped in, getting to her feet once more. "If I don't tell you this now I might never get around to it. So please, me first, okay?"

"Hey, sure, Lizzie, no problem." Jake was growing increasingly more concerned. Was she leaving? Was she having second thoughts?

Was she married?

"Okay," she said, "This is probably gonna come out all wrong, so I'm just gonna blurt it all out and explain later, okay?"

"Sure, Lizzie. Whatever you want."

"Right, here goes," Lizzie took a deep breath, then said, "I know your real name is Jake Sawyer and that you are living here because you stole a case of extremely valuable diamonds–"

"Whoa! What?" Jake was stunned. "Now hold on–"

"Please, just let me finish, I promise I'll explain," Lizzie continued. "I've been following you. I mean we have, me and the man I'm here with. We know you stole the diamonds and–"

"Lizzie, please," Jake broke in again, but she put up her hand to silence him, she had to continue or she would never get it out.

"I know about your family, Jake - about your wife and kids–"

"That's enough!" Jake snapped. "That's enough, okay."

Lizzie stopped. Suddenly aware of how callous she had sounded. "No, Jake, I'm sorry. I didn't mean–"

"Enough, Lizzie. You've said more than enough."

Suddenly Lizzie's phone began to ring, breaking through the tension. She looked at it, saw the call was from Aaron and sent it to voicemail.

"I'm sorry, Jake," she said again.

They were silent for a long moment, then her phone rang again. Again it was Aaron. Quickly she flipped it open and spoke into it, "Hi, yeah, look, it's not a good time right now, I'm–"

Aaron, on the other end of the line, interrupted. "No, Elizabeth, you must listen, it's important. Very important. I'm being followed. I think they're onto us. You could be in great danger."

"In danger? What?" Her mind was still racing from speaking with Jake. "What are you talking about?"

"Elizabeth," Aaron replied. "We have been found out. I believe Peter Bearing knows what we are up to. I am being followed, I am certain of it and I think that we both may be in grave danger. Do you understand?"

"I'm in danger. Yes, I understand," Lizzie was still reeling from her previous conversation. "I'll be careful, I will. But look, right now I've got to go. I'm right in the middle of something."

"Okay," said Sumpter, "But promise me you'll be careful."

"I will."

"Promise me, Elizabeth."

"I promise, Ronny. Now please, I must go."

"Okay. I'll see you back at the bungalow."

"Fine. See you then." Lizzie said and snapped the phone shut. She looked at Jake who was still standing there, angry, shocked. Disappointed.

"Listen, Jake–" she began.

"No, you listen." He said. "I don't know who you are or what your game is here but I'd like you to stop."

"It's not a game, I promise–"

Now it was Jake's turn to hold his hand up to silence her. "I'd like it to stop and I'd like you to leave. Now."

"But Jake, please."

"Now, Lizzie, or whatever your name is. I don't want to hear any more."

"My name is Lizzie, I swear it. But–"

"Please." Jake walked to the door and opened it. "Just leave me alone."

Lizzie looked at him, imploringly, but it did no good. He would not even look at her. She hesitated for a second, before realising that it was hopeless. "Fine. I'll leave you," she said, marching past him. "But there's more you need to know. Much more."

He couldn't look at her.

"You also need to know that I love you." She said softly.

For a moment, Jake's blue eyes met the chocolate brown of hers, which were now brimming with tears. Then he looked away and Lizzie left. He closed the door behind her.

* * *

Aaron ended the call with Lizzie and shut down his laptop having finished what he had so urgently been doing.

As he made to stand, he heard the faintest of noises behind him and knew that he was already too late. As he attempted to turn, a thick arm grabbed him around throat and the point of something very sharp was jabbed into his ribs.

"Make even the slightest sound and you're dead," growled Fabian Król.

* * *

Lizzie ran from Jake's bungalow, tears streaming down her face. What was she thinking? How could he understand? Of course he would think that she had betrayed him. And then, stupidly, she had mentioned his children. How unbelievably insensitive.

She needed to cool off, find somewhere to think. She couldn't go back to her bungalow just yet as Aaron would be there waiting for her, eager to find out how things had gone and she just couldn't bear to tell him just yet. For the moment she just wanted to be alone. All thoughts of Aaron's warning about her being in danger had left her as she fretted about what had just happened.

She decided to go to the pool bar, to have a drink or two to calm herself down, then maybe afterwards she would feel like going back and telling Aaron all about it.

* * *

After parking the rented Volkswagen Jetta, Król circled around to the back of the small nest of bungalows in which Lizzie's was situated, knowing that Aaron Sumpter was inside. The bungalows were set out in small hamlets around the complex - all very private and all very exclusive with cleverly designed aspects so that none of them were visible through the windows of another which was perfect for Król. However, there were always people wandering about such as guests and resort staff so he had to be certain that he was not casually observed as he found the back of Lizzie's property and slipped over the quaint stone wall that surrounded it. Within seconds Król was squeezing himself through the open bathroom window and once in, he stood still on the tiled floor and listened intently. He could hear

Sumpter speaking loudly in one of the main rooms so stealthily moved forward, eased the bathroom door open and silently crept through the bungalow following the sound of Sumpter's voice as he spoke on the phone with Lizzie. As Król entered the living area unseen, he immediately spied his target. Aaron had his back to him and was busy closing his laptop as he ended the conversation with Lizzie, snapping his phone shut with a soft click. His back was still turned as Fabian Król approached him. The rest was all too easy.

* * *

Aaron was slumped backwards, tied to a bamboo dining chair. His nose was broken and his front teeth had been knocked out. After a severe beating his face had been left bloodied and bruised and at least two of his ribs cracked.

"Where are diamonds?" Król asked in a heavily accented but conversational tone. "You are not hero, my friend. No one care if you live or die, so why not tell me. Make it easy on yourself?"

"I've told you," Aaron groaned painfully, "I've no idea."

"You want me to hurt you some more?" Król

said. "Because, let me tell you, you will tell me - either now or later - and later, well, you might not be so..." he hunted for a word and then found it with a smile, "Fortunate."

"I can't tell you because I don't know," Aaron gasped. "I've told you already."

"Very well, my friend. I see you are going to need little more persuasion, a bit more convincing. So sad, but, hey, you leave me no choice." Król looked anything but sad as he pulled an object from his pocket which Aaron immediately recognised as a butterfly knife, the kind of flashy weapon preferred by gangbangers and mobsters. It was a modern version of the switch blade which had two rotating handles that concealed a very scary blade inside. Król flipped it open and, sure enough, in an instant the murderous looking blade appeared.

Aaron blinked and instinctively recoiled. He knew now for certain, even if he hadn't already known it before, that he had seen his last afternoon. He thought of his tiny semi-detached home in

Hampstead and then of the impossibly blue sky of Nassau. At least it was a nice place to die.

He shut his eyes and tried to focus on something else as Król selected one of his fingers. Aaron didn't try to fight him as he knew it would do no good.

"Last chance," said Król. But Sumpter couldn't reply he just shook his head defiantly, his eyes squeezed tightly shut.

The pain was immense as Król sliced off Aaron's right pinkie, worse than he could have ever thought possible and he screamed in agony.

"Now, where are diamonds?" Król asked again.

Aaron couldn't reply properly as the pain was too much. He just managed to blurt out the word "No!" In between sobs.

"A shame. All this could be easily avoided but still..." Król said as he selected the next finger in. This time Sumpter did fight against it as he couldn't face that sort of pain again but his interrogator was far too strong and easily wrestled his hand free. Then, with an expert technique, sliced off another finger with a blood curdling crunch as the knife cut deftly through the bone.

Aaron squealed and emitted a dreadful gurgling sound as tears streamed down his face, "Go to hell!" He growled through gritted teeth.

* * *

Ten minutes later, Sumpter's right hand resembled a roughly pruned shrub. All the fingers and the thumb were gone and the ugly stump was covered in blood. A large pool of blood had also spread across the floor as if a full bottle of Chianti had been knocked over and the contents spilled on the cold tiles.

Król had been trying to make him talk, trying to make him reveal what he knew. But Aaron would not say. He would never say. He would rather die. And suspected that he would do very soon.

Fabian Król had tortured many men and had developed a sense for how strong somebody's willpower was. He could tell if someone was going to talk or not and with Aaron Sumpter he knew it was the latter.

Sumpter was resilient, with a solid strength of mind and an iron resolve. No one could resist that kind of torture unless they were prepared to die and Sumpter clearly was.

Król knew now, without doubt, that he would get nothing out of him. But there was still the girl and Sawyer. And one of them would definitely give him the answers he needed.

Król looked at Sumpter, his head lolling to one side, his eyes puffy and swollen, blood dripping from his nose and mouth. "You've had enough, my friend, eh?" Król asked in his gruff Polish accent.

Aaron lifted his head wearily and smiled, his teeth coloured crimson. "Never," he replied.

* * *

Jake sat out on his veranda looking at the wide expanse of ocean that he loved so much. But today his mind was elsewhere.

He was thinking of Lizzie and all that she had meant to him. He was thinking about what she had said about knowing who he really was and about knowing that he stole the diamonds.

And he was thinking about her last words to

him, when she said that she loved him. She had said that she could explain everything and now that was playing on Jake's mind. Surely if she meant him harm, then why tell him anything at all?

Her words had affected him. She loved him, she said. He realised now that he loved her too. But was it too late?

Whoever she spoke with on the phone told her she was in danger and now that was concerning Jake, too.

He decided that he had to hear her explanation after all. She had caught him unawares and he had reacted instinctively. But now he wanted to hear what she had to say - and if she truly was in danger then he had to protect her. He got up and rushed from his bungalow, determined to get to Lizzie as soon as possible.

*　*　*

Jake ran to Lizzie's bungalow as fast as he could, following the network of white rock lined pathways that criss-crossed the resort. When he arrived, he paused to catch his breath, then knocked on the door. It swung open, unlatched.

"Lizzie?" Jake called, but there was no response. "Lizzie - it's me, are you here?" Still nothing. Jake stepped inside, into the living room and saw a thoroughly macabre scene. A laptop computer lay smashed in pieces on the tile floor, a dining chair was over-turned. But what horrified him was the large pool of blood surrounding them and, scattered within it were what looked like chopped-off fingers. Five of them in total. An image of Jake's murdered family flashed through his mind and he cried out, "Oh God, not again - please not again!"

Suddenly he was frantic, "Lizzie! Where are you?" He yelled. "I'm here. Just please tell me you're alright!"

He was scared for her safety, but now wary also as it occurred to him that whoever harmed her may still be in the bungalow. He noticed a wide dragline of blood that led from the living room and down the hallway - clearly leading the way to whoever lay at the end of it and Jake's heart sank.

Then he heard a noise, coming from the bedroom, very faint but definitely something - a groan Jake thought. "Lizzie?"

Regardless of his own welfare he darted across the living room and headed down the hall following the gruesome dragline which disappeared under the bedroom door. Dreading what he might find, he threw open the door and was immediately appalled by what he saw.

A middle-aged man lay on the bed with blood pumping from a wound in his neck. He had been stabbed in the throat but judging from the marks on the floor and on the bedclothes it looked as if someone had dragged him there.

The man had the stumpy fist of his right hand

pushed hard down onto the wound trying to staunch the bleeding but it was clearly futile. He was ghostly white and obviously close to death. Jake ran to him, to try and help, but he knew he couldn't.

"I'm so sorry," Jake said to the man, feeling entirely helpless, "I don't know what to do to help you." The man suddenly grabbed Jake's arm with his good hand, his grip surprisingly strong. He glared at Jake intently, willing him to take notice of what he was about to do.

As Jake watched, the man, released the grip on his arm then reached into the pocket of his blood drenched shorts. With immense effort and willpower, he pulled out a bunch of keys that hung on a yellow, rubber fob that was shaped like a foot, with the words *'Beach Life'* printed on it. He forced the keys into Jake's hand and jabbed his finger on them, pointing to them, leaving a bloody fingerprint on the key fob. He was trying to speak but it was just a gurgle.

Jake leaned in, "What do you want me to do with the keys?" he said. "I can't hear you. Please, try again."

Jake put his ear to the man's mouth and clearly heard the name "Elizabeth."

Jake looked at him, "Where's Elizabeth? Where is she? Is Lizzie safe?" But it was too late. Aaron Sumpter was already dead.

* * *

Lizzie was halfway back to the bungalow when the man found her.

"Miss Barnes?" He asked in thickly accented English

"Yes?" She said.

"I'm with the management. I'm afraid there's been an accident."

"An accident?" Lizzie said, looking the man up and down. He certainly did not look like he was with the management - T-shirt, cargo shorts and tattoos. And he was clearly not Caribbean, Russian maybe, or Czech. Possibly Polish.

"Yes, your friend. Mister Sumpter. I'm afraid he's had a nasty fall."

"Oh, God. Aaron. Where is he - is he okay?"

"He's fine. He's at our medical centre. If you would just follow me, I'll take you to him."

"Of course, thanks," said Lizzie, immediately concerned. All reservations about the man's appearance dismissed from her mind.

The man led the way along the narrow path that was prettily lined with painted white rocks. They passed a signpost; Pool, Gymnasium, Medical Centre, Car Park, it read, with arrows going off in all different directions, the one to the pool pointing in the direction from where Lizzie had just come.

However, rather than take the pathway that led to the Medical Centre, the man took the one that led to the car park.

"We're going to the car park?" Lizzie asked.

"That's correct," he said.

"But I thought you said Aaron was at the Medical Centre?"

"That's right, we're going by car to the Medical Centre."

"But the Medical Centre is back that way," Lizzie said. It was at that moment that she noticed the red speckles on the man's sleeve and the large blood stain on his shorts. Aaron's warning suddenly rang out in her head, "I think that we both may be in grave danger," he had said.

Lizzie immediately realised what was happening and turned to run but it was too late, Fabian Król grabbed her and pulled her back. She tried to scream but he clamped a large hand over her mouth and held it shut.

Król then picked Lizzie up, she kicked and punched but he held her tightly and her efforts had little impact.

Quickly, so as not to be seen in the bright sunshine of the Bahamian afternoon, Król ran with her to the small car park, just a short distance away, where the Jetta was parked.

As he put her down to open the car, Król's hand briefly slipped from Lizzie's mouth and she let out a loud scream. In return, Król slapped her hard and she fell limply over his shoulder, allowing him to bundle her unceremoniously into the boot of the Jetta.

Chapter 35

Jake was in shock. The man's death had been so bloody, so appalling, like something out of a slasher movie. Jake, himself, was plastered in blood. His hands, his shirt, his cheek and ear where he had listened to the man's final word, *'Elizabeth.'*

But where was Elizabeth? Where was Lizzie?

Jake wandered into the living room and studied the shattered laptop. Obviously it had been destroyed for a reason.

The front door of Lizzie's bungalow was still open and Jake thought he heard someone scream outside.

He strode to the door and scanned the area, for a second not seeing anything of concern, but then he looked over at the car park and was horrified to see a man bundling Lizzie into the boot of a Volkswagen Jetta. She looked lifeless.

"Hey!" Jake shouted. But the man did not hear him and slid quickly into the driving seat. "Hey, stop!" Jake yelled again, But the Volkswagen was already reversing out of the parking space.

Jake started running towards the car park but by the time he got there he was too far behind to stop the Volkswagen was driving out. Indeed, the Jetta was already on the exit road and heading swiftly towards the resort's gates. What is more, it would be on the highway and gone in a matter of moments.

Still clutching the keys that Aaron Sumpter had thrust into his hand, it occurred to Jake that there maybe a car key amongst them and he was right.

It was a rental car key with a hand-written label stating the vehicle's model and registration.

Jake scanned the car park and immediately saw the little 'Mini Moke' the key belonged to and running quickly over to it he jumped in.

He sped out of the car park, in pursuit of the Volkswagen, the tyres screeching as he raced down the exit road, much faster than the 10mph permitted. Sparks flew as he launched the bright orange Moke over the speed bumps and out to the exit gates of the resort compound.

By now the Jetta had a good lead on Jake, but he pulled out onto the highway and pressed the accelerator pedal to the floor. He would not let Lizzie get away.

* * *

It was only at that moment, as he sped along the highway in pursuit of the Jetta, that Jake had pause for thought.

What was he going to do when he caught up with it? Was he going to run it off the road? Force it in to a ditch? Surely that would only put Lizzie's life in further jeopardy - if, indeed, she was still alive. Perhaps, also, the man who had taken her was armed. He could shoot her. He could shoot Jake, ending his rescue bid before it had begun and leaving Lizzie still in great danger.

Jake eased off the accelerator, dropping back to a safe distance but keeping the Jetta easily within sight. He would follow it, see where it led him, then when it stopped, Jake could formulate a plan on just how to rescue Lizzie.

* * *

They headed out of Nassau, along the beach road, passed the powdery white sand of Cable Beach, passed all the grand resorts and hotels that lined the beautifully tranquil bay and then, as the afternoon sun began making its slow decent toward the clear aquamarine ocean, they turned inland.

Jake followed still several cars behind as the road took them into the interior of New Providence. They drove through several small villages, the houses little more than corrugated shacks, the people who lived in them trying to eke out a living by whatever means they could. Jake couldn't help but compare his previous life in England with what these people had. All his debts and worries back then suddenly paling into insignificance as he realised that his life, in contrast, had been one of riches and luxury.

The guilt swept over him again like a wave. Had he not acted so selfishly back then, had he stayed, tried to work things out, his family would not have been murdered. Had he not stolen the diamonds then the man back at the resort would still be alive too and Lizzie would not be in danger. Jake refused to believe she might already be dead and focussed instead on getting her back safely. No matter what it took.

After several more miles, the Jetta turned off again. This time onto a dirt road that weaved through heavy woodland.

Cautiously, Jake pulled onto the road. There were no other cars now between his and the Jetta and if he did not keep a sensible distance then he would be easily seen. He let the Jetta round a corner up ahead before slowly proceeding. However, when he, himself, turned that corner, the Volkswagen was gone.

The road ahead was dead straight yet there was no sign of the other car. Jake pressed his foot down on the accelerator, his heart pounding harder, as the Mini Moke sped up, bouncing along the rough dirt road.

Where were they?

He very nearly missed the turn, which angled off sharply to the right and was concealed by dense foliage. Jake saw it out the corner of his eye and braked hard, the car skidding on the loose surface.

The Jetta was maybe two hundred yards up this narrow track, slowing to a halt in front of a run down farm house and Jake had to quickly reverse to avoid being seen.

Knowing now that the Jetta had reached its destination, Jake parked the Moke in some loose scrub and returned to the narrow track on foot. Keeping low and using the abundant foliage to conceal himself, he eyed the farm house warily. Lizzie's abductor had already carried her inside.

* * *

Lizzie had awoken in the dark confines of the Jetta's trunk. It was hot, humid and claustrophobic. She screamed again and again to be released but her captor had Iron Maiden blaring out of the speakers and was purposely ignoring her pleas.

When, at last, Król opened the trunk, Lizzie was ready for a fight. But Król was strong and trained in hand to hand combat and quickly he overpowered her. He slapped her hard across the face and Lizzie's world went black once more.

Presenting no more of a problem to him than a child's rag doll, Król carried Lizzie into the dilapidated farm house and tied her to a chair using the rope and chair he had left there, for that purpose, the night before.

* * *

For the second time in the last hour, Lizzie awoke in a daze, her head now throbbing badly. She found herself in a sort of disused shack, with stripped wood slatted walls and bare wooden floorboards. It had obviously been used as a house at sometime because there were still remnants of broken furniture strewn around the place and ragged curtains hanging shabbily at the two dust filled windows. There was also an old stone fireplace to the left of her with some rusted pots and pans stacked haphazardly beside it.

Her captor, Król, stood in front of her, smiling.

"Hello, girlie," he said in heavily accented English. "You be good now, yes? You stop struggling otherwise I have to hurt you. Understand?"

"Who are you, what do you want from me?" Lizzie said groggily.

"Who I am is not important. Who I work for and what they want is."

"Who do you work for?" She asked, already knowing it was Bearing.

"Someone who wants what you have got. Or at least what your boyfriend has got." Król said. "What he took from them."

"I don't know what you mean." Lizzie said defiantly.

Król grinned, his voice calm, friendly even. "I knew you say that. I expect it. It's what your partner say."

"Partner?" Lizzie said. "What partner?"

"Come now, girlie. I'm not a fool. The bald man in your bungalow in Nassau. Him. He was your partner. I see you with him. But he not your partner anymore I think." Król grinned again, wickedly.

Lizzie went cold. "You mean Ronny? What have you done to him?"

"Me?" Król feigned innocence and shrugged his shoulders, "I just ask him a few questions that is all. But he decide he do not want to tell me so I have to kill him. It is what I do. It is my job. If people do not tell me what I need to know, then is that my fault?"

Lizzie could not believe what she was hearing. This monster had killed Aaron and he didn't even show the slightest bit of remorse. Her lip began to quiver and the tears began to fall down her face. Ronny was dead. But her resolve strengthened. "I won't tell you anything, you bastard. Kill me if you want, but I won't tell. I won't.

Król sighed. "Of course, you say that now. I like it actually. You show strength, that's good. But you will tell me. This I promise. The only question is how long it will take. Personally, it makes no difference to me. Like I say, it is my job, I get paid either way. But you, I think, will not want too much pain. You are a beautiful woman. Very beautiful - I would like it better if you stay that way. But, if that is not possible, then, like I say, it makes no difference to me."

Lizzie remained silent, horrified by what she was hearing, scared beyond anything she had felt before. Certain that she would die whether she told the man what he wanted to know or not.

Król spoke again, his voice calm, conciliatory, "I make a deal with you. You tell me where to find the diamonds, I promise I make it quick. You not feel a thing. No pain. I guarantee it."

"But I don't know about any diamonds. I told you–"

"Do not lie to me!" Król suddenly roared violently. "I know you know, now where are they?"

"Please," Lizzie was shocked by the man's sudden change of temper, "I don't know. I really don't. I promise."

"Fine," Król said. "You want the hard way? Then we do it the hard way."

* * *

By now, Jake had sneaked all the way up the narrow track and had silently approached the farm house. As he lightly stepped up onto the ramshackle stoop, fearing discovery with every carefully placed foot, he heard Lizzie's captor shouting in an East European accent.

Jake peered in through the dust stained window, barely able to see through the thick layer of caked on dirt.

His heart quickened as he spied Lizzie, alive, but tied to a chair. The man standing in front of her was big, muscular and menacing with closely cropped hair and a beard. He looked tough and formidable.

He was also brandishing a knife. The same knife, Jake guessed, that had killed the man back at Lizzie's bungalow.

This was not going to be easy. Not by a long way, but Jake had the element of surprise on his side. He also suspected that he was about to find out if his boxing and karate lessons had paid off.

The door was just to Jake's left and he prayed that it was not locked. Very gently he placed his fingers on the handle and took a couple of deep breaths, trying to calm his racing heart beat. Then, all of a sudden, he saw himself turn the handle and throw open the door.

* * *

Król pulled out the butterfly knife and flicked it open in a fancy, yet very practiced way, like a professional gun slinger at a wild west show impressing the crowd with his deadly skills.

Lizzie saw the shiny blade spin round mesmerisingly and as it finally came to a halt, pointing directly at her, she saw that it was still stained with Aaron Sumpter's dried-on blood and gasped with fright as she glimpsed her own fate.

"This will hurt you, girlie," he said. "But feel free to scream all you want. No one will hear you. I choose place specially. It is only one for miles. So go ahead. I don't mind."

Lizzie whimpered involuntarily as Król picked up her hand and selected her little finger. "This one first, I think. Unless, of course, you tell me where the diamonds are." He said.

"I don't know," cried Lizzie, "I don't - I swear, please–"

At that moment, the door flung open and Jake burst into the room.

If Lizzie had doubted it before, she knew now, with absolute certainty, that she loved him. But her initial elation was quickly replaced by horror as Król turned to face him.

"Jake, no!" she yelled, "He's got a knife." But it was too late, Król had a murderous grin on his face and Jake had entered willingly into his lair.

"Leave her alone!" Jake snarled.

"Ah, Mister Sawyer," Król said, barely registering his surprise. "You follow me, yes? Very clever."

"Yeah, I followed you, alright. Now do as I said, leave her alone."

"And why would I do that? You were to be my next guest. You save me trip. Now I have both of you. All I need to know now is where the diamonds are and my job is done."

"The diamonds? Why, who are you working for?"

"Alas, that is not for me to say," Król replied. "But it is I who have been asked to find them. Now, if you would just tell me, it will save much trouble for you later."

"I'll tell you who he's working for, Jake," Lizzie

said. "Peter Bearing and Arthur Khan - the ones who are responsible for killing your–"

Król turned and slapped her across the jaw with the back of his hand to silence her and in that instant, Jake charged.

With his attention distracted momentarily, Król turned a fraction too late to raise the knife and prevent Jake from bowling into him.

The pair of them flew backwards, knocking Lizzie's chair aside as they went. The chair smashed as it went down and suddenly Lizzie was free.

Jake landed on top of Król, the force of the impact causing him to release his grip on the knife and it skidded across the floor towards the old fireplace. However, Król recovered quickly as he grabbed Jake by the ears and head butted him. Jake rocked backwards, dazed by the blow, which allowed Król to push him aside and regain his feet.

Jake scampered away out of reach and got to his feet just in time to block a kick from Król that was aimed at his head. He blocked another and countered with one of his own but it missed its mark and set him off balance, giving Król the opportunity to smash a hard right hook into the side of Jake's face.

Again he was stunned, but shook it off. He raised his fists and faced up to Król, whose smile was wide, already sensing victory and clearly enjoying the fight.

Jake sent in a jab, missing again, but then he

threw a hard left into Król's gut and a crunching right uppercut which caught the Pole squarely under the chin, visibly rocking him. Król's smile was now gone.

"Go on, Jake. Hit the son of a bitch!" Lizzie encouraged from the sidelines as she threw off the ropes that had bound her.

"So, Mister Sawyer," Król said, "You fighter now, yes? You boxer, you martial artist? You think you Bruce Lee?"

"No." Jake said, with cold steel in his eyes. "But I am pissed off."

With that he launched an attack on Król, using all the tricks and techniques he had learned over the last couple of years, plus a few that he had not - and he did genuinely hurt Król, landing several punishing blows to both the body and head.

But Król was hardened in hand to hand combat, a highly trained soldier and even though Jake's attack was ferocious, he was no real match for Król and soon the difference began to show.

After exchanging punch after brutal punch and kick after punishing kick, Jake was starting to flag and even though his fitness levels were high, they were nothing like that of Król's and soon the Pole started to gain the upper hand. First, a punch got through, catching Jake hard on the cheek, then a kick to the stomach and then another to the centre of his chest which sent him sprawling to the ground with the wind driven from his lungs.

Jake lay there, helplessly, battered, bruised and bloodied as Król went for the knife. Suddenly Lizzie leapt onto his back and began clubbing him as hard as she could with her bunched fists. But Król merely reached over his shoulder and with enormous strength, plucked her from his back and threw her across the room. She landed hard, near the broken chair and Jake thought that she was finished but all he could do was watch, his powerless body aching and unresponsive.

Król reached down and retrieved the knife, then walked back to where Jake lay and stood over him victoriously.

"A good show, Mister Sawyer. Very impressive. But enough is enough. Now, where are those diamonds?"

"Nowhere you're gonna find them, asshole!" Lizzie spat, and as Król turned to face her, she smashed him as hard as she could around the head with a broken chair leg.

Miraculously, she had climbed to her feet and crept up behind him whilst his focus was fully on Jake.

Momentarily, Król glared at her. Then his legs buckled and he fell, face forward, onto the dusty wooden floor.

Chapter 36

Whilst he was out cold, Lizzie rifled through Król's pockets and found a car key and a mobile phone. She took both.

Then she rushed across to Jake and helped him to his feet, he looked dreadful. But then so did she, her lip was split and her nose was bleeding but she was alive. At least for the moment. If they did not get moving before Król woke up then it could be a different story.

Lizzie dragged Jake to his feet. "Couldn't stay away, huh?" She said.

"Something like that," he replied. "Not too keen on your bodyguard though."

"Me neither. Come on, let's get out of here before he wakes up."

"Good idea. Hey, grab that knife - I've got an idea."

Lizzie ran to fetch it. As she picked it up Król was already starting to rouse. "Quickly, Jake. He's coming round."

Jake's strength was swiftly returning as he took Lizzie's hand and led her out of the house, in the failing light of dusk, and across to the Jetta. "Get in," he said.

As they shut the doors of the little Volkswagen in unison, Król appeared at the doorway of the farm house and staggered out onto the stoop, still clearly dazed.

"Quick, Lizzie - the keys," Jake said as he made eye contact with Król.

"What?" She asked.

"The keys, Lizzie - you've got the keys."

"Oh, right, sure. Here." She replied and passed them swiftly to Jake who immediately slid them into the ignition.

"Hurry, Jake. Hurry. He's coming." Lizzie said, her voice suddenly shrill.

Król's head had now cleared and he realised what was happening. He started towards the car just as Jake found reverse gear and the Jetta sped backwards up the narrow track.

Król began to run.

"He's still coming, Jake. He's still coming," Lizzie shouted.

Jake had his foot to the floor as he pulled on the handbrake and span the wheel round hard. The car skidded round so the back was now facing the farm house, but as Jake hit the accelerator it stalled.

"What! No, come on, come on." He shouted at it.

Król was looming large now in the back window as Jake turned the key again. Thankfully the engine revved and he jammed it into first gear - but Król's outstretched fingers were on the boot as they slowly pulled away.

"Quick, Jake - he's on us!" Lizzie squealed.

Jake found second and gained some ground, then third as he began to pull away. As he hit fourth Król was getting smaller in the rear view mirror and by the time Jake skidded onto the dirt track they were a good hundred and fifty yards clear. But then Jake did something that made Lizzie's heart stop.

He pulled the car up next to the Mini Moke that he had left parked in the scrub, took the knife from Lizzie's hand and jumped out of the car.

"What are you doing?" She shouted fearfully.

"Can't risk him following us," Jake replied.

Quickly, he stabbed a front tyre on the Moke, then a rear one. Then he jumped back into the driver's seat of the Volkswagen as Król came bursting out of the dense foliage, that disguised the farm track, onto the dirt road.

But this time Jake had it covered as the Jetta sped off yet again, finally leaving Król far behind in the gathering darkness.

* * *

They drove in silence for some miles, both

315

exhausted and still coming down from their adrenaline fuelled escape, until Lizzie finally spoke. "Thanks for coming to get me, Jake. You saved my life," she said earnestly.

"Hey, no problem. You saved mine too, remember?"

"But you were only there because of me. And that means a lot. Really."

"Like I said," Jake replied. "No problem."

Jake thought for a moment longer, then said, "Hey, Lizzie, about your friend. You know, the guy you were working with, back in Nassau?"

"You mean Ronny?"

"I don't know, but yeah, I guess so. Well, this is not easy but–"

"He's dead." Lizzie interrupted. "I know. That bastard back there told me he'd killed him. That son of a bitch."

"I'm sorry," Jake said. "Were you close?"

"Yeah. He was sort of like my big brother."

"My God. I had no idea–"

"Hey, listen, you didn't know. In fact there are a lot of things you don't know and it's about time you did."

"Well," Jake said, "If you feel up to it, there's no time like the present - and I'm not going anywhere. So, lay it on me - I promise I won't jump down your throat this time."

"You won't, huh?"

"Promise."

"Well don't be too sure. There's plenty to tell and I'm not too proud of my part in it. But here goes nothing..."

* * *

Lizzie told Jake everything. Starting with who killed his family and why. She then told him about how she became involved, searching for vengeance for the deaths of her brother and father. And now for Aaron, too. She told Jake about the diamonds, where they had come from, how they had been illegally obtained by the Khans and what they were intended for. Lizzie explained about Aaron's recordings, about the proof that he had gathered and how, with the aid of the diamonds they had planned to bring Peter Bearing and Arthur Khan to justice. She then, shamefully told how she and Aaron had planned to trick Jake into revealing where the diamonds were and their intentions to take them from him once he had. And finally, how she had intended for him to fall in love with her. Never expecting, for one moment, that she would fall in love with him.

By the time she had finished relating the whole saga, it was well after dark and they were very nearly back at the Crystal Waters Resort.

"So that's it," Lizzie said. "That's my whole sorry tale."

Jake remained silent, deep in thought.

"Jake?" Lizzie said. "Please, say something.

Anything. I know it's bad, I know it is - but please–"

"I will say something." Jake said. "In fact, I'll say three things."

Lizzie braced herself for what was coming, not sure whether she wanted to hear it or not."

"Firstly," Jake said. "The diamonds are in Zurich, and you and I will go and fetch them, together. Secondly, yes, I want to bring those bastards, Bearing and Khan, down too. I want to see them rot in jail for the rest of their lives and I want to use the diamonds to do it. And thirdly–" Jake paused, for a moment, to gather himself.

"Thirdly," he said. "I love you too."

Lizzie smiled and placed her hand over his on the steering wheel, the simple gesture conveying more than she could say.

* * *

As they drove through the gates of the resort, Jake spoke again. "There's one more thing you ought to know, Lizzie. About Aaron."

"What is it?" She asked, sensing his trepidation.

"He's in your bungalow, Lizzie. That's where it happened."

Lizzie put her hand up to her mouth, "Oh, God. Poor Ronny–"

"I'm afraid that's not the worst of it." Jake said. "If we are to get away, to Zurich, we need to move his body - otherwise the authorities will be searching for you, wanting to know what he was doing in your bungalow and how he came to be murdered."

"Oh my God," Lizzie said again. "But how, what are we–"

"I think I've got a solution of sorts - it's not great but it should hopefully work. Although I should warn you, you're not going to like it."

* * *

Jake's idea was to move Aaron's body, under the cover of darkness, to his bungalow, which was rented under the name of Jake Sloane. The same Jake Sloane who the police would want to interview when the body was found.

Jake had changed his identity so many times in the past that it would be easy for him to simply adopt another one and slip out of the country undetected. He still had passports that identified him as several other people. All Lizzie would need to do would be to check out of the resort before Aaron's body was detected.

Aaron, himself, was not a registered guest at the resort. Indeed, he was not even legally in the country, having arrived by yacht in the middle of the night. If Jake and Lizzie removed all his identification, it would at least buy them some time and prevent his relationship to Lizzie from being discovered too soon.

If and when Jake and Lizzie managed to fulfil their plans for Bearing and Khan, they would then come clean to the police and give Aaron the send off he truly deserved - and face up to any charges that may be levelled at them.

Reluctantly, Lizzie agreed.

Jake had chosen to do it this way so that Aaron's body would be discovered and properly laid to rest. They could have opted to dump his body deep in the woods, or out at sea but that would give Lizzie no comfort nor Aaron the end he deserved. Jake would again be a wanted man, at least until he could hopefully clear his name but he considered that a small price to pay compared to what Lizzie had suffered.

* * *

It was dreadful. Jake had tried to prepare her but as Lizzie entered her bungalow the scene that presented itself was more horrific than she could have imagined. There was a mass of blood, a big pool of it and then the wide smear along the floor which led down the hallway to where her foster brother lay mutilated in the bedroom.

Jake sat Lizzie down who was shaking with grief and shock and quickly fetched her a glass of water. He then asked her to look away as he picked up each of Aaron's chopped off fingers and popped them into an opaque plastic bag where they could no longer be seen. Then, after checking on her once more, he went down the hallway and entered the bedroom again. If anything, the sight of Aaron's body was even more horrific now and Jake had to fight the urge to vomit.

He needed to act quickly and efficiently and above all he had to be strong for Lizzie who was going to need every ounce of his strength if she was to make it safely through this night with her sanity in tact.

Jake was not a religious man, but he said quick a prayer over Aaron before adding in a whisper, "I'm sorry. I will make this right and I'll protect Lizzie. You have my word."

Then he gathered the bloodied bedclothes and wrapped them as tightly as he could around the body so that no part of it was visible.

A moment later, Jake was back with Lizzie.

"I know this is hard for you," he said, "And I'm so sorry for your loss, I truly am. But if we are to make it to the airport without being discovered then I'm afraid I must ask you for your help now."

"I know, Jake." Lizzie said simply. "I'm ready. I won't let you down I promise."

"Hey, Jake said, squatting down by her side and placing a comforting hand on her knee. "I know you won't. You never could. But do me a favour, try not to look at me, try not to think about what I'm doing. Focus on what's around us, I need your eyes and ears Lizzie, that's all - I'll do the rest, I promise. You just keep watch, make sure no one sees what I'm doing."

"I will. But is he—?"

Jake sensed what she was about to say. "It's okay," he said. "He's completely covered, you won't see anything. Just remember him as he was. That's the best way. Believe me, I know."

"I know you do, Jake. Thank you." She placed a hand over his and squeezed lightly.

"Ready?" Jake said.

Lizzie took a deep breath and slowly exhaled. "Ready," she replied.

* * *

Lizzie did exactly as Jake asked. She kept watch whilst he carried the body over his shoulder the short distance to his bungalow.

Even though the resort was deserted, with most of the guests attending an entertainment evening at the club house, it was too dangerous for Jake and Lizzie to use the network of pathways which connected one block of bungalows to another. So they had to stay in the shadows and cut across the grass, using the abundant palm trees as cover. But, at last, they made it without being discovered. They had not seen another soul and the only sound other than theirs was the distant noise from the club house and the steel band that was playing there.

Lizzie waited outside Jake's bungalow as he placed Aaron on his own bed and arranged the scene as it had been at Lizzie's. It would not fool the police for long, if at all, but at least they wouldn't immediately know where Sumpter had actually died.

After the body had been transported, Jake then set about swapping pillows, sheets, chairs and anything else that had traces of blood on them between the two bungalows, again being extremely careful not to be seen.

The only thing that then remained was the blood on the floor.

By this time, however, Jake was covered in blood himself - some of it his, from his fight with Król but most of it Aaron's which had unavoidably transferred with all the fetching and carrying.

As they stood in Lizzie's living room, she looked at Jake and said, "You need a shower and a change of clothes."

He regarded himself briefly. "Yeah, I know. Let's get this done and then I'll grab one."

"No," Lizzie said. "Get one now. I'll clean up this."

"It's okay, I can—" Jake began.

"Sweetie, you've done enough. You're bushed and you need to clean up. I can take care of this, I promise. It's Ronny's blood - my brother's blood and I should be the one to clean it. It was spilt because of me, so it's the least I can do."

"You're sure?" Jake asked.

"Go," Lizzie smiled. "I'll be fine, honest."

* * *

When Jake came back twenty minutes later, showered and refreshed and in a clean set of clothes there was not a trace of blood anywhere. Lizzie had done wonders but now looked completely spent.

"Your turn," Jake said. "Go freshen up and then

323

we'd better get going. Lizzie gave him a kiss on the cheek and then did as she was told.

She returned a short while later, looking beautiful, even if a bit battered from her encounter with Król, in a loose shift dress and a pair of white pumps. But her eyes were red and Jake knew she had been crying. The fact that she couldn't stay with Aaron and give him a proper funeral filled her with guilt and regret. However, she knew that Aaron, more than anyone else, would understand what she was doing and that gave her some degree of comfort.

It had been a tough night and the coming days would not be any easier as Jake knew from bitter experience. But Lizzie was a strong girl and she would come through it, he felt certain.

There was, however, one additional thing that troubled Lizzie which occurred to her when cleaning up the wreckage of Aaron's laptop, when she realised that all the intelligence he had on Bearing and Khan was saved onto it and that it was now completely useless.

"Did he have a back-up copy?" Jake asked, when she told him of her concerns.

"Sure, she said, back in England, at his home, but I don't have a key.

Jake suddenly remembered the keys that Sumpter had forced into his hand, that he'd had in his pocket since parking the Mini Moke back on the dirt road. "Give me a moment," he said, then as quick as he could, ran back to his bungalow once more to rummage through the pockets of his discarded bloody clothes. He found the keys immediately and ran back triumphantly to Lizzie.

He held them up to her, holding them by the big, foot-shaped key fob. "Aaron left these for you," he smiled. "It was the last thing he did. He handed them to me and said, "Elizabeth", he knew you would need them."

Lizzie smiled wistfully. "Typical Ronny. Resourceful right to the end. He really was very clever."

* * *

After using the remote check-out facility on the resort's TV channel, Lizzie finally left with Jake in the Jetta and headed for the airport.

From leaving Król to arriving at the airport it took five hours. Two hours after that they were on a plane bound for Miami and by the following day they would be in Zurich.

* * *

Fabian Król arrived back at the Crystal Waters Resort just as the sun was coming up. He had walked most of the way back from the farm house and had only been picked up by a truck once he hit the highway. His first port of call was Lizzie Barnes' bungalow which he was impressed to find completely clean. Next he walked up towards Jake Sawyer's bungalow but stopped halfway when from the brow of the hill he saw what seemed to be a police cordon around the property. From that distance, Król could see squad cars, an ambulance and several police officers swarming around the place. A large black woman dressed in the pale green uniform of the resort cleaning staff was sitting on the front step of the bungalow being quizzed by what Król assumed to be a couple of detectives.

He now guessed what Sawyer and Barnes had done with the body. Stupid, he thought, when there was so much undergrowth on the island where a body could be hidden and never be discovered - or a perfectly good ocean in which to discard it. What sentimental fools.

But Król dare not go further and knew, for the time being at least, that his pursuit was over. He felt certain, however, that he, Sawyer and Barnes would meet up again very soon and when they did there would be no more escape for them.

For now though, he considered it best to make a hasty departure from Nassau and catch the first available flight back to the UK.

He had much to report, although little that would lead his employers to the diamonds and they would not be pleased.

Failure was not something Fabian Król was used to or would accept lightly.

Chapter 37

Zurich, Switzerland. The Park Hyatt Hotel.

Lizzie was lying on her king-sized bed in the plush surroundings of her five-star hotel suite. She had just enjoyed a lovely long bubble bath in the huge marble tub, washing away all the grime of the last forty-eight hours. Fortunately, the bruising on her face was not severe and the split lip was healing nicely. It turned out she was made of strong stuff.

Lizzie's heart ached though for the loss of Aaron, her beloved foster brother and since arriving in Zurich the awful circumstances of his death had truly sunk in. Jake had given her some space to grieve and she had used it well. She had cried a whole lot and then cried some more. She now felt better - not about Aaron's passing as that was still extremely raw, but about how she was going to go on from here. Jake was a good man and together they would avenge Aaron and Jonathan and her father as well as Jake's wife and children. Knowing that fuelled her resolve and that helped heal her grieving heart.

As Lizzie lay on the bed, she was going through the cell phone she took off Fabian Król, checking through the caller log and the name that came up repeatedly was Arthur Khan's. The Wallace Bearing number came up several times too - either Khan or Bearing calling Król from the very building Lizzie's grandfather had built, trying to arrange her death.

Lizzie picked up the complimentary phone next to the bed and buzzed Jake's suite, down the hall.

"Hello?" He said, warily, trying to remember the name he'd booked the suite under just in case he was asked.

"Hey, there, Limey." Lizzie said.

Jake smiled with relief. Pleased to hear Lizzie's voice. They had not had much time together since arriving in Zurich the night before as they had both been feeling bruised, jet-lagged and in need of sleep. They had talked a little on the flight but Lizzie had been somewhat withdrawn. Jake fully understood though and was content to give her as much time as she needed. She had been through a horrifying ordeal - her brother had been brutally murdered and she certainly had his sympathy. He understood her emotions better than most having suffered a similar loss himself.

Jake had slept intermittently on the flight and had watched several movies, but his mind was awash with this new information about who killed his family and about how he, with Lizzie at his side, was going to make them pay.

Now, here in his hotel suite in Zurich, he could think of little else.

"Hey, yourself. You okay?" He said.

"Yeah. I am," she said. "Thanks for giving me some space - I just needed to, you know–"

"Hey, it's okay, I understand, no problem."

"And the two room thing, that was very impressive. Very gallant," she teased. "You're a good guy, Mister Sawyer, you know that?"

"What can I say," Jake said. "I try, that's all - and I think my name's 'Saunders' at the moment, isn't it?"

"Beats me. I was half asleep when we arrived so it could be Mickey Mouse for all I know."

Jake laughed. "You might be right, that does sound familiar now you mention it."

Lizzie smiled, then changed the subject. "I've just been looking through the cell phone that I took off that guy back at the farm house."

"And?" Jake said, immediately interested.

"And it turns out he was definitely working for Bearing and Khan. That son of a bitch. There are dozens of calls logged."

"You were right then. But I guessed you were. Don't worry, we'll get them, I promise. Aaron won't have died in vain."

"I know. And I know we will."

"How about we talk about it later, at dinner?"

Jake asked.

"Dinner?"

"Yeah, why not. Go buy yourself something expensive to wear and we'll have dinner in the finest restaurant in Zurich - let's spend a bit more of the money I got for a few of Peter Bearing's precious diamonds."

"Sure, why not." Lizzie said. "Shopping on somebody else's money sounds like my idea of heaven."

"Good. Seven o'clock okay?"

"Sounds great. Can't wait."

* * *

The money was well spent as Lizzie looked sensational in a black, Vera Wang cocktail dress with patent Louboutin's and a string of pearls. Her bruises and split lip made invisible by make-up and lipstick.

Jake wore an Armani tux and looked every bit as dashing as James Bond.

The Von der Flüe restaurant had a fabulous reputation for both its cuisine and wine cellar and did not disappoint. Lizzie and Jake spent the evening eating and chatting, getting to know each other properly now their respective histories had been revealed. Even though Lizzie had come from a much more privileged background and was now wealthy in her own right as the only living heir of Wendel Wallace, she and Jake had much in common - their likes and dislikes, their sense of humour and their delight in being in the other's company.

However, at last the conversation came around to Peter Bearing and Arthur Khan and how best to implement Aaron's plan to incriminate them.

First, of course, was the retrieval of the evidence from Sumpter's house which Lizzie was certain was backed up on a main computer there, as Aaron had told her.

Secondly, was to get the police on their side, so when Lizzie and Jake met with Bearing and Khan to hand over the diamonds, the authorities would be there to arrest them. This could prove to be tricky, but Aaron had already told Lizzie about a detective at the Met called Roper Coyle who, he suspected, may be willing to help. Jake decided that he would phone him before arriving back in England, to gauge for himself whether Coyle would be amenable to working with them.

* * *

After a wonderful dinner and several glasses of excellent wine, Jake and Lizzie strolled hand in hand along the banks of the River Limmat, the lights of the old city sparkling prettily in the calm water, making for a very romantic backdrop. They strolled in contented silence, only chatting sporadically, but both very much aware of the other's presence and relishing the closeness. Jake's hand brushed briefly against Lizzie's thigh and the feeling was electric.

They paused for a while, taking a seat on a bench

in the moonlight, the evening warm and calm. They sat close together and Lizzie casually rested her head on Jake's shoulder.

Jake turned his head to look at her and saw her deep brown eyes staring longingly into his. Her lips parted invitingly and he needed no further encouragement. He covered her mouth with his and kissed her for a long time, her tongue hot and eager as their passion intensified.

But then Jake broke away, suddenly awash with guilt. Lizzie's foster brother was not yet cold and here he was trying to take advantage of her.

"Sorry," he said. "That was clumsy of me. I couldn't help it, you're so beautiful."

"Don't," she replied, putting a finger to his lips, knowing only too well the guilt he was now feeling as she felt it also. "It's not just you. I'm here too. I made it pretty clear that I wanted to be kissed and boy, I can't complain."

Jake smiled. "Guess we should take it slow, huh?"

"Yeah," she replied. "I guess we probably should."

They sat in silence for a few minutes longer, still close together with her head on his shoulder but the heat between them had subsided a little as each of them tried to compose themselves.

"Ready?" Jake asked.

"Sure, why not?" Lizzie replied as they both stood and resumed their stroll. But as they wandered,

Lizzie's thoughts kept returning to what had just happened. She loved Jake, she knew it. And she was certain that he loved her. So why should there be guilt? Aaron would not deny her love, in fact he would positively encourage it - and had done so just shortly before his death when he had told Lizzie to go to Jake. She wanted to be with Jake and he wanted to be with her and what could be more normal than two people in love finding solace in each other?

The cobbled streets led, eventually, back to the hotel and, inevitably, they arrived all too soon at the door to Lizzie's suite.

"Well, here we are again." Jake said, as her big brown eyes once again stared alluringly up into his. But Jake did not want to push. Lizzie had been through much over the last couple of days and he did not want to make matters worse by being selfish.

"Yep. Guess so." She replied softly.

"We're picking the diamonds up tomorrow morning." He said.

"Uh-huh." Lizzie replied, standing so close that he could feel her breath on his mouth, "Early start then, right?"

"Right." Jake answered as he bent to kiss her. Her lips were soft and sweet, delicious. But he pulled away, conscious of losing control again, conscious of her grief and not wanting to intrude upon it.

"I'll let you get to bed then." He said. "Goodnight, Lizzie. See you in the morning." He made to move away but she caught hold of his arm.

"Don't you dare go anywhere, Jake Sawyer," she breathed, "Don't you dare."

Unable to control himself any longer, Jake pulled her to him and their lips locked together with unrestrained passion.

Still locked together, Lizzie somehow found the card in her bag that opened the door to her suite. The door swung inwards and they spilled into the darkness, pulling madly at each other's clothes with unbridled passion. All his previous restraint was now gone and Jake kicked the door shut with his foot and lifted Lizzie into his arms.

"You sure about this?" He asked softly.

Lizzie stopped for a moment and looked directly into his eyes. "Honey, I've never been more sure of anything in my life - now shut up and take me to bed!"

Jake smiled. "Great. Understood. Me too!" Then, as ordered, he carried her hastily to the soft, king-sized bed where they made love for the very first time.

* * *

Later, when finally it was over, as they lay contented in each others arms, Lizzie kissed him tenderly. "I love you, Jake Sawyer, with all my heart," she said.

"And I love you, too, Lizzie Barnes," he replied.

Then her lips covered his once more and they

made love again long into the night.

Chapter 38

The next morning, they awoke in a blissful afterglow, the sun streaming in through the floor to ceiling windows, bathing them in the glory of a new day.

Jake felt fresh, alive, new. And it was great. Like the first day of the rest of his life, although, deep down, he knew that would not truly begin until Bearing and Khan had paid for their crimes. But it was close and he revelled in the pleasure of just being there, in that bed, with Lizzie beside him, for just a few moments longer.

Lizzie, felt the same, and she rolled over and kissed Jake on the cheek. "Hi there, Limey," she said, a contented smile on her face.

"Hi yourself. You want breakfast? I could eat a horse."

"Me, too. I'm starved. Must be all the exercise you gave me last night."

It was Jake's turn to smile, "Yeah, although you

didn't do too badly yourself there, Yank. I think I might have pulled something."

"I didn't hear you complaining." Lizzie said.

"Who says I'm complaining? In fact I think I could do with some more exercise right now - work up a bit more of an appetite."

"You could huh?"

"Mmm hmm."

"Well, I guess you're in luck then," she giggled and pulled the sheet over them once more.

* * *

They breakfasted like kings; croissants, fruit, orange juice - after a good old-fashioned English fry-up which was prepared especially for them at Jake's request. They sat and ate it all hungrily dressed only in the hotel's complimentary dressing gowns. They chatted and giggled and kissed like any young couple in love. Afterwards they shared a shower and made love yet again, they just could not get enough of each other and were eager not to be parted for one second. When they had finished and were just standing together under the hot stream of cleansing, revitalising, water, Lizzie said, "Would you mind very much if we didn't go the bank today?"

"Of course not," Jake replied. "Why, what have you got in mind?"

"Oh, nothing really. It would just be nice to spend the day together without thinking about diamonds or Peter Bearing or Arthur Khan, that's all.

Just you and me. We could take a walk, have some lunch, maybe a little afternoon delight," she added cheekily. "Then perhaps dinner and a stroll tonight. Last night was so lovely, so perfect, but it was all about anticipation - which I absolutely loved, don't get me wrong - but tonight we could just take it easy, relax. Enjoy the city and each other."

Jake smiled. "I couldn't think of anything better. I'll call Drescher at the bank and re-schedule for tomorrow. We've got plenty of time so let's live a little."

* * *

It was a beautiful day in Zurich, warm and cloudless with just a gentle breeze to cancel out the intense heat. Jake wore a light T-shirt and chinos and Lizzie had on a crisp cotton blouse, a pair of vintage jeans, turned up to her ankles and a pair of white lace-up pumps. Her hair was tied back in a long, glossy pony tail.

They casually strolled around the city, stopping for coffee in one of the many bars along the way for a lazy chat and to watch the passers-by. They took in a couple of museums and climbed the tower of the old Romanesque church to admire the view from the top. Later on they meandered by the lake hand-in-hand along the boardwalk, until they came to an open meadow where hundreds of other young couples had come to picnic and canoodle and play. Lizzie and Jake found a space apart from the others and made the most of the sunshine. They, too, kissed and cuddled and revelled in the closeness they had found. As the idyllic afternoon drew to a close they went back to the hotel and made love yet again. At dinner, they found a secluded table in a small, candlelit restaurant, tucked away from the vibrant centre of nightlife - which for a city with such an austere reputation was surprisingly young and carefree.

As midnight beckoned, they once more found themselves wandering along the banks of the River Limmat but the feeling was more relaxed now, less urgent and far more content. Everything about their relationship seemed absolutely right, as if they were meant to be together - to find each other on this long, hazardous and tragic road they had both been travelling.

Lizzie felt it and told Jake so. Never had she felt this way about another person, certainly not Roger, the man she had married when she was far too young to recognise the difference between love and lust. "I know it's only been a short time," she said, "But I know it in my heart to be true. I love you Jake."

Jake felt it as deeply as her, maybe more so if that were possible. She had changed his life, rescued him from an emotionless, hollow abyss and restored his faith in love. She had given him back the will to live, the will to fight and, above all, the will to carry on, not just purely to exist as he had been doing since that terrible day in New York when he had learned the horrific fate of his family.

"I love you, too, Lizzie and I never want to be apart from you. I agree, it has only been a short time and I know our emotions have probably been heightened by grief. But I am more certain than I have ever been of anything when I say I want you to be my wife."

Lizzie looked temporarily shocked. "You do?" She said.

"I do." He replied. Then looked directly at her, his face earnest and sincere. "Will you marry me Lizzie?"

Her eyes brimmed with tears as the shock vanished from her face and a wide smile appeared. "Yes! Yes, I'll marry you. I will." She spluttered with joy, before throwing her arms around his neck and kissing him hard on the lips. "Of course I'll marry you!" She said again.

They embraced for a long time before she pulled away and looked at him sternly with only the slightest hint of mischief, "I take it you've got a diamond to put in the ring, right, Limey?"

"Hey, Yank, don't laugh," he replied, only half-joking, "Because if our plans don't work out you could be spending our honeymoon visiting your husband in prison."

* * *

The following afternoon, Jake and Lizzie were

standing in the imposing foyer of the Zeiss Schiller bank looking every inch the affluent power couple; he in a dark, beautifully tailored business suit and her in a navy Chanel dress and high, black Louboutin's. Stylish, sleek, successful.

As Otto Drescher approached, marching upright in his very military way, Jake held out his hand, "Herr Drescher, thank you for meeting us, my apologies for yesterday but something unavoidably came up."

Lizzie very nearly added, "Several times from what I remember," but thought much better of it.

However, Drescher looked puzzled as he shook Jake's hand. "Mister Sloane? Forgive me, but you look so different from the last time we met." It was Drescher's business to remember faces and Jake's had changed a great deal in last two years as had his physique.

"Ah, yes," Jake said. "A change of lifestyle, a healthier regime. Hopefully it's paid off."

Drescher smiled, "It has indeed. But now I see it is you, your smile, your eyes - unmistakable. Good to see you so well and welcome, again, to our little bank."

'Little bank' was probably the understatement of the century but Jake didn't labour the point. "May I introduce my fiancé, Elizabeth Barnes." It felt good saying it out loud and Lizzie, too, felt a little rush of delight.

"Miss Barnes," Drescher said, letting go of Jake's hand and taking hold of Lizzie's. He then snapped his heels together like a soldier and bent to kiss it. "My pleasure and congratulations to you both. You make a wonderful couple."

"Thank you," Lizzie said, a little flustered, "Nice to meet you too."

"Now, to business," Drescher continued. "You wish to visit the vault I understand?"

"That's correct," Jake said.

"In that case, would you be so kind as to follow me," Drescher said, already beginning to stride across the wide, oak panelled foyer.

* * *

Three floors below ground, in the bright, clinically modern vault with all its hi-tec security, Drescher nodded curtly and left Jake and Lizzie alone beside box number 1301. Drescher, himself, would wait in an anti-room until they were ready to leave.

Jake punched his personal code into the keypad then hit *enter* and the deposit box door clicked open. From inside that, Jake withdrew the large plastic bin and took out the leather bound briefcase. He looked at Lizzie and smiled, "Wanna see?" he asked.

"You betcha," she said.

Jake took the case and led Lizzie to one of the curtained booths at the far end of the room, swishing the curtain closed behind them and placing the case flat on the small desk in front of him.

"Ready?" He said.

"Mmm hmm," she replied, peering eagerly over his shoulder as he snapped open the catches and opened the lid.

Lizzie saw immediately that the case had many compartments. "Pick one," Jake said. "Any one, it doesn't matter." She pointed randomly at a compartment that looked identical to all the rest. "Open it," Jake encouraged, "Take out what's inside." Lizzie already knew what was there but the anticipation was still intense after all she had been through to get to this point. Almost nervously, she clicked open the compartment and took out a little velvet bag. "Go on," Jake said, "Have a look."

Lizzie slid the drawstring fastening open and poured the contents of the bag into her upturned hand. The small pile of large, beautifully cut stones sparkled prettily at her under the bright, halogen lighting of the vault. Diamonds bigger than Lizzie had ever seen - even coming from an extremely wealthy family where seeing diamonds, whilst not commonplace, did occur reasonably regularly. Lizzie still bore the scar on her left temple from one such stone - from her wedding ring - but that was nothing as sizeable or as exquisite as these. "Wow!" she gasped.

"Wow, indeed," said Jake. "Every compartment, every bag, exactly the same thing, give or take. This

343

case is worth millions - more than enough to kill for."

"Those sons of bitches," Lizzie snarled.

"Yep." Said Jake. "Wanna see some more?"

"No," she said adamantly. "I'm done with these goddamn diamonds."

"Me too," he agreed. "Come on, let's get going."

* * *

A short time later, they said goodbye to Drescher and left the Zeiss Schiller bank with the briefcase. Its contents being the cause of more death and anguish than Jake could ever have imagined in his worst nightmares.

He had sold fourteen of the diamonds and after expenses; passports, air fares, hotels, eye surgery, payment of debts and just day to day living, he had a little over one hundred thousand euros left. But he did not want it. Not anymore. It was dirty money. Blood money. And he wanted no part of it or the diamonds either.

To rid himself of some of the cash, he took Lizzie to a high-end dealership that specialised in luxury cars for the wealthy and using a large chunk of what he now knew to be Peter Bearing's and Arthur Khan's money, extravagantly splashed out on a brand new Maserati Gran Turismo, which he drove straight out of the showroom.

The remainder of the cash would be enough to get him and Lizzie back to England in style and see them through the next few weeks. But aside from that, Jake would be returning to England much as he had left it - or at least before he found the diamonds. Which he considered to be only right and proper.

They drove back to the hotel and packed their bags. Then, with the case full of diamonds stashed safely in the boot of the brand new car, Jake and Lizzie readied themselves for the long trip home.

Lizzie made herself comfortable in the plush leather passenger seat of the gleaming white Maserati and smiled at Jake. "It feels right, doesn't it, you and me?" She said.

"Yes, Lizzie." He replied, returning her smile and placing his hand on her knee. "It feels exactly right." Then he pushed the gear stick into

"Drive" and sped out of the underground car park, the throaty roar of the Gran Turismo bouncing off the concrete walls.

* * *

Heading for Paris, but taking it easy, they decided to stop off in the city of Troyes overnight where they strolled hand in hand around the half-wooden houses of the historical old town before dining like kings in a fabulous restaurant on the banks of the Seine. Later, they went back to the hotel and made love long into the night.

Next morning, after breakfast, they took to the road again and arrived in Paris shortly before lunch, taking a suite at the Regina hotel, which Jake booked for five days under the name of Mr. and Mrs. Sloane.

They were not yet married but this trip, they decided, was going to be their honeymoon as neither knew what lay in wait for them in England - maybe even the possibility of prison for Jake - so they were determined to make the most of the time they had left together.

Indeed, once they had checked in and Jake had tipped the bellhop, they did not leave the room again for two whole days, preferring instead to order room service and stay in bed.

On the third day, which began with a glorious Parisian sunrise, Jake and Lizzie at last ventured out. Jake was particularly keen to visit Montmartre and the Sacré Coeur, but especially to see the artist's quarter, to watch the painters at work, huddled under their brightly coloured umbrellas, creating breathtaking works of art. Maybe in another life, Jake mused, that could have been him.

Another dream of his was to visit the Louvre which Lizzie was equally enthusiastic about and they spent the rest of the day just meandering contentedly around the remarkable museum.

The fourth and fifth days were filled with sight-seeing, fine dining and love-making. It was perfect. They had chosen the most romantic setting in the whole world to seal their ever deepening love for each other. But the holiday was drawing to a close and the harsh reality of what was yet to be done remained. They were deliriously happy yet both were certain that what they were about to do was, without question, the right thing, no matter the consequences to themselves personally. They had to bring down Bearing and Khan. Whatever the cost.

So, on the final day in Paris, from a pay phone near the Place de Concorde, Jake dialled New Scotland Yard and asked to speak with Detective Chief Inspector Roper Coyle.

Several minutes passed, then a weary voice on the other end of the line said, "Hello, this is Coyle, you wanted to speak to me?"

"Hello, Mister Coyle," Jake replied. "My name is Jake Sawyer and I have a proposition for you."

Chapter 39

Roper could not believe it. After over two years the case that had been filed away unsolved and all but pronounced dead in the absence of any leads or evidence, had suddenly sprung spectacularly to life.

For some curious reason, gut instinct maybe, this case had always niggled away at him and all his original suspicions, all his natural intuition that he had found so hard to ignore back then had, as a result of one phone call, been utterly vindicated.

Jake Sawyer was alive. Diamonds - a whole lot of diamonds - were the reason for his disappearance and Peter Bearing and Arthur Khan were complicit, both in the illegal importation of the diamonds and in the murders of the Sawyer family and Richard Maddox.

All Coyle's boxes were ticked, except the one marked 'hard evidence' and that, he had just been informed, was going to be supplied by Sawyer himself within the next few days. This, apparently included tape recordings of private conversations, facsimile's of shipping records and a signed affidavit from a prostitute who had been paid by Bearing to implicate Jonathan Wallace in an alleged rape. All of this would be in Roper Coyle's hands very shortly. Enough evidence to send Bearing and Khan down for a very long time. And if they could be arrested whilst taking delivery of the diamonds then that would be all to the good. The icing on the cake.

When the elated Coyle told his sergeant the good news, Dave Eckhart was excited and congratulatory. But when Roper was through telling him and had gone for a celebratory smoke on the fire escape, the smile slipped from Eckhart's face.

No longer was Dave the exuberant young copper he used to be, always tired yet always eager, the epitome of a good policeman with the makings of an even better detective. He was now a father, a husband and a provider. However, his two year old daughter was keeping him up all night, the wife that he had married when they were both too young was no longer happy and Dave had a mountain of growing debt. This had been compounded by a losing streak in the casino that showed no sign of breaking and an over reliance on whisky to help ease the strain.

In short, Dave Eckhart was desperate and in need of major financial help.

Eight months ago, Dave had been approached

in the toilets of the casino he frequented by a burly Polish guy. Dave had been drinking heavily, so what was said was somewhat fuzzy in his memory, but the gist of it was that someone very rich would be extremely grateful to know any information about the disappearance of Jake Sawyer. Dave pushed the man for more information about who this person was who was so curious about a case that had already been effectively closed but was simply told that he was a wealthy business man who had an avid interest in the case.

"You wouldn't be talking about Peter Bearing would you?" Eckhart had asked.

"Maybe, maybe not," The man replied. "But he would be very grateful for anything you could tell him. Very grateful, my friend, if you take my meaning." He then reached out and tucked something into the top pocket of Dave's jacket, which he took to be a contact number.

That was pretty much the extent of the conversation as Dave then turned to use the urinal. However, when he was finished the big Polish guy was gone.

The next morning, Dave could not be at all sure if he had imagined the whole thing, the events of the previous night somewhat hazy in his mind, but he was fairly certain that he had not. To be sure, Dave checked the top pocket of his jacket and did, indeed, find a contact number, as expected, written on a card with the name 'Fabian Król' scrawled next to it, but with it he also found ten neatly folded fifty pound notes.

Suddenly the words 'very grateful' pinged into his brain and Dave now understood exactly what that meant.

For some reason that Eckhart could not quite fathom, he had never told Coyle about this meeting or the gift of that five hundred pounds.

Now, eight months on, the words 'very grateful' pinged into Dave's brain again and suddenly he felt extremely ashamed for what he was thinking.

He was at his wit's end and needed money fast to pay his mounting debts and to prevent his pretty young wife from leaving him.

As if in a trance, Dave pushed out his chair and rose to his feet, then walked out of the office and along the corridor. A moment later he was standing in the stationery cupboard, the door closed, with the card Król had given him in his hand, which had been tucked in his wallet, almost forgotten, for eight months. Quickly he punched the number into his phone and waited for it to ring, but immediately he heard a recorded message saying 'The cell phone you are calling is switched off, please try again later." Eckhart ended the call. "Damn".

Dave returned to the office and poured himself a coffee from the stale pot at the far end of the incident room. It was more for something to do than for the need of the caffeine and realised this the moment he stared down at the tarry black liquid. He felt sick. Sick that he had made the call, sick at his betrayal of everything he stood for and sick for the fact that no one answered when he was so desperate for money. His life was falling apart, creditors hassling him day and night, his mobile endlessly buzzing with new messages demanding payment for old debts. At the weekends he had taken to leaving the home phone on answering machine so that he didn't have to pick up. Seven days a week the damn thing would do nothing but ring and it was driving Dave round the bend.

On top of that, his daughter was teething and he and his wife were suffering from sleep deprivation. Dave worked long hours, early mornings and late nights, but when he eventually got home it was often just to row with his wife or comfort his screaming daughter. Sleep would often only come after a significant amount of whiskey which, along with his forty a day cigarette habit, was just another thing he couldn't afford.

The phone call, and Fabian Król's words, played on Dave's mind for the rest of that day and pretty much through the whole of the following night between fitful bouts of sleep. But by the next morning he had made a decision - either the worst or best one of his life.

On the drive in to work, he pulled his battered old Fiesta over into a lay-by and picked up his phone.

He had decided to play out a hunch, which he knew was an act of sheer recklessness born from total despair, but his options had become increasingly more limited.

First, he called *Directory Assistance*, then, when they had given him the number he was after, he asked to be put through.

Ten seconds later he was speaking to a receptionist and he heard himself saying. "Hello, this is Detective Sergeant Dave Eckhart, could I speak to Peter Bearing please."

Chapter 40

Jake and Lizzie arrived back in England after their wonderfully romantic break in Paris. They caught the early morning ferry from Calais and experienced a brief moment of panic as they drove through Customs in Dover, fearing that if they were stopped and searched the diamonds would be discovered and their plans would be scuppered. But there was no need to worry as they were waved straight through.

They drove into Central London by midday and had checked into The Dorchester just in time for lunch, which they attended only after storing the briefcase containing the diamonds in the hotel's safe.

After a shower and a change of clothes, Lizzie and Jake then drove the sixteen miles out to Hampstead, to Aaron Sumpter's house, parking the white Maserati on the road outside.

They walked up the short driveway to his front door and let themselves in, selecting the Yale, the most obvious front door key, from the bunch that

Aaron had forced on Jake.

The moment Lizzie stepped over the threshold, she knew something was seriously wrong as all the photograph's that used to line Aaron's hallway were gone. Photos that he cherished so dearly. She rushed into the living room and found it empty, completely void of furniture, ornaments, a television, everything. Not even a carpet. The kitchen was the same. No kettle, toaster or microwave. The security monitor that was previously attached to the wall had been ripped out and all that remained was a severed wire that fed into the wall.

Panicking now, she ran upstairs, Jake following several steps behind. By the time he had reached the landing, Lizzie's hands were covering her mouth. "No, no, no!" She was saying despairingly. It's all gone Jake, everything's gone. There's nothing left."

Jake quickly scanned the bare rooms but she was merely stating the obvious. The house was just a shell. Someone had been in, stripped it and left nothing behind - no beds, no chairs, no tables and, much more importantly, no computers.

Lizzie began to cry. The last trace of Aaron had been extinguished and she had nothing left. She felt violated. Robbed.

Hopeless. Furthermore, the proof that she and Jake needed so badly, the hard evidence that would put Bearing and Khan behind bars, had also gone. Her plans - hers, Jake's and above all, Aaron's, which he had worked on for so long, had finally come to nought.

"It's over, Jake," she said, running her hand across his arm as she walked past him and slowly descended the stairs in defeat. She sat down on the bottom step, put her head in her hands and wept.

Jake walked down and sat beside her, wrapping a comforting arm around her shoulders.

"Everything's gone Jake. There's nothing of Ronny's left. Nothing to remember him by."

Jake thought for a moment, then took Aaron's keys out of his pocket. "I know it's not much," he said, "but there is these."

Lizzie smiled and wiped the tears from her eyes as she took them from him. A bunch of worthless keys and a big, stupid, foot-shaped, yellow key fob. But they were Aaron's and she appreciated the gesture. "Thanks," she said.

Lizzie studied the keys in her hand and winced as she saw a bloody fingerprint on the spongy yellow fob. Aaron's bloody fingerprint, placed there with his last dying breath.

The key fob was a peculiar item, totally unlike the kind of thing Aaron would own, much too silly, too off-the-wall. Aaron liked sensible things, serious things, things that made sense. A big, yellow, spongy foot with *'Beach Life'* stamped on it did not seem to fit with him at all. It had obviously been bought in The Bahamas, but for Aaron it seemed too touristy, too frivolous. But it clearly had been his and so she would treasure it.

They sat for a while, long enough for Lizzie to compose herself, then left the house, locking the door behind them.

As they got back into the Maserati, Lizzie said, "It seems so unlike Ronny."

"What do you mean?" Jake asked.

"I don't know, it just seems so unlikely that he would only have one back-up."

"You mean the laptop, that was smashed?"

"Yeah. Ronny was so careful, so security conscious that it seems kind of odd that the laptop and his set up here were the only back-ups he had."

"What are you saying, Lizzie, that you think there is another copy out there somewhere?"

"I dunno. I guess. Maybe." She said, looking at the bunch of keys in her lap and at the bloody fingerprint on the key fob.

"But where?" Jake said.

"Unfortunately, I don't have any–" Lizzie suddenly stopped in mid sentence as she noticed something she had not previously seen on the key fob. There was a thin line, a join, she thought, that separated the toes of the foot-shape from the instep and the heel. "You say Ronny forced these keys into your hand as he was dying?"

"Yeah, you know he did, why?"

"Tell me exactly. Exactly, Jake. What was it that

he did."

Jake was confused. "Er, okay. Well, he pushed the keys into my hand, tapped them with his finger and then said 'Elizabeth.'"

"Did he tap the keys or the key fob? Try to remember, Jake, please, I think it's important.

"I suppose it was more the fob - see, look, you can see the fingerprint right there. Why, Lizzie? What are you thinking?"

"What I'm thinking is that Aaron Sumpter was a very clever man indeed."

Suddenly, she grabbed up the key fob, held the heel end with one hand and the toe end with the other, and pulled. The two sections snapped apart to reveal a USB data stick attached to the toe end. It was a novelty. A cheap souvenir bought, Lizzie assumed, from a computer store in Nassau.

"My God, Lizzie - you're brilliant!" Jake exclaimed.

"Not me," she replied. "Ronny, he was the brilliant one. I knew he wouldn't leave things to chance."

"You mean, you hope not. Let's get back to the hotel and plug it into my laptop to see exactly what it is that Aaron has left us."

Jake started the car and pulled away from the curb, heading back to the The Dorchester to check their discovery.

They were so rapt up in their find that neither of

them noticed the black Range Rover that pulled out after them.

The man driving it was Fabian Król and the man in the passenger seat was Arthur Khan.

Chapter 41

It was when Jake called in for petrol that he first noticed the Range Rover, double parked across the road with its hazard lights on. Jake thought nothing much of it until he caught a glimpse of the shaven-headed driver. The man was wearing sunglasses and was attempting to hide his face with his hand, but Jake would have known him anywhere. It was the Polish man he had left in Nassau.

Jake turned away quickly, pretending not to have noticed as he re-fueled the Maserati. When back in the car he said to Lizzie, "Whatever you do, don't look, but we've got company."

"Company? What you mean?" Lizzie said, immediately looking wildly about her.

"Don't look, I said!" Jake insisted and she immediately stopped. "The guy who killed Aaron," he continued, "who took you to that farm house–"

"What about him?" Lizzie said with alarm, "Is he here?"

360

"He's across the road in a Range Rover– don't look!" Jake had to remind her again as she went to look round.

"Sorry." She said."Oh my God. You mean he's followed us?"

"Seems that way. My guess is that he's the one who cleared out Aaron's place and that he's been waiting there for us to show up."

"But how would he know when to expect us? How would he know that we would even go there?"

"I don't know. But they both seem like very good questions for our friend DCI Coyle."

"You think he's betrayed us?" Lizzie said, suddenly shocked.

"I really don't know. But he's the only one, other than you and me, that knows what we're planning."

"I can't believe it, Jake. Ronny was sure that Coyle was an honest cop and his instincts were usually pretty good."

"Like I said, I don't know, Lizzie. But that Polish guy is across the road and we've just come from the very place where all the evidence was supposed to be."

"Except I'll lay odds that they don't know about the data stick."

"I think you're right. But they do still want the diamonds." Jake said.

"And us." Said Lizzie.

"Yeah. And us." He agreed as he drove off the

forecourt and back out onto the road. When they were maybe thirty yards from the station, he saw the Range Rover, in his rear view mirror, pulling out into the flow of traffic. "He's following," Jake said. "There's someone else in the car too. Can't tell who it is though - they're too far away.

"If they catch us, God knows what they'll do–"

"Listen," Jake interrupted. "They've got to catch us first. They've got a Range Rover, we've got a Maserati - I know where I'd put my money."

"You're right," Lizzie agreed with forced optimism, "I knew this car wasn't a waste of money - let's see what this sucker can do. Let's lose those sons of bitches!"

"That's exactly what I was thinking," Jake grinned as he pressed his foot down on the accelerator.

The Gran Turismo responded instantly, the engine roaring to life as it rocketed from thirty to sixty miles an hour.

Lizzie turned in her seat to check the Range Rover's reaction and it had responded likewise. "They're following." She said, squinting to get a glimpse of who was sitting alongside Król, but unable to see as the Maserati manoeuvred aggressively through the traffic.

Fortunately the road was reasonably uncongested as Jake sped fearlessly across Finchley Road, weaving in and out with reckless abandon and zigzagging madly through St John's Wood as he raced onwards towards Regent's Park. The Range Rover doing the same thing several cars behind him, although the big 4x4 was making slightly harder work of it than the high performance sports car.

Jake overtook cars, two and three at a time then swerved dangerously in to avoid those that were heading straight for him, their horns blaring as he missed them by mere inches.

"We're losing them, Jake - we're losing them!" Lizzie cried, as Jake gunned it passed the Central Mosque on his right with Regent's

Park just a blur on his left. The sleek white Maserati travelling now at nearly eighty miles an hour, bombing through traffic and speeding relentlessly passed pedestrians, buses and black cabs.

But the Range Rover was still in pursuit. It had lost ground but it was still coming.

The Gran Turismo skidded noisily onto Baker Street, somehow managing to miss a parked Mini and an elderly man who was trying to cross the street. Lizzie screamed and squeezed her eyes closed with fear as the back end of the car snaked wildly and Jake miraculously swung it around and out of the path of an oncoming taxi, only narrowly missing it. The cabbie shaking his fist and leaning on his horn. "Bloody idiot!" he shouted.

Then, like Moses parting the Red Sea, the road up ahead was suddenly empty - a true miracle in Central London, and Jake pressed his foot to the floor. The Maserati shot like a guided missile up Baker Street, eighty, ninety, nearly a hundred miles an hour.

"That's it, Jake!" Lizzie yelled, "they can't catch us - we've got them, they can't keep up."

Jake smiled and briefly allowed himself a quick glance in the rear view mirror, seeing no sign of the Range Rover.

However, he did not see the brewery truck either, pulling out of Allsop Place up ahead. Not until it was too late.

Jake slammed on the brakes but he was going far too fast. "Hold on, Lizzie!" He shouted, as the car skidded for what seemed like an eternity, screeching loudly and leaving two long lines of black rubber in its wake. It slowed considerably but still ploughed into the side of the truck at a hell of a speed, the nose of the beautiful Gran Turismo crumpling like folded paper, instantly activating the driver and passenger airbags.

Lizzie and Jake were thrust violently forward into the voluminous white pillows, their chests crushed against the safety belts with the force of impact as the Maserati buried itself under the truck. The windscreen shattered as it hit the steel side of the brewery vehicle, releasing the previously restrained cargo of barrels. Several bounced over the roof of the ruined car and rolled back down Baker Street from where Jake had come

The car was now motionless. The engine no longer running. Smoke rose from the front end, which was now jammed tightly under the truck and there was a loud ·hiss, like steam escaping, accompanied by a steady drip of water.

Jake was dazed. Slowly he lifted his head from the air bag and put his hand to his temple. It was wet and when he looked, his fingertips were coated in blood, although he could feel no pain from the wound. His chest hurt like hell as he slowly sat back in his seat, his shoulders and arms ached too, but he did not think anything was broken.

"Lizzie," he groaned. "You okay?"

There was a moan from the passenger seat as Lizzie sat gingerly upright. Her head was bleeding also and, like Jake, she was aware of a terrible aching in her chest. There was a red burn line across her neck where the seat belt had snagged her, but otherwise she seemed unscathed. "Great driving there, Limey," she croaked.

"Hey, I'm an artist - what can I say," Jake replied with a pained grin.

He saw Aaron Sumpter's keys, with the bright yellow key fob, laying in the foot well and bent carefully to pick them up. "Come on, Yank, we better get out of here."

He forced open the dented door, which creaked metallically with the effort, and climbed out of the car. Lizzie slowly did the same.

At that moment, there was another loud screech of tyres and Jake turned to see the Range Rover skidding to a halt just behind the wrecked Maserati.

"Quick, Lizzie, run!" He yelled. "Run as fast as you can!"

Lizzie glanced behind her and saw the danger. "Get out of here, Jake - don't let them get you!" She cried as she began running in the opposite direction, away from Jake, passed the truck and down into Allsop Place, however, Arthur Khan was already out of the Range Rover and hot on her tail.

There was no way for Jake to help her, the Maserati, the truck, the Range Rover and several aluminium beer barrels were all blocking his way, so he began running in the only direction he could, straight down Baker Street away from Fabian Król, who had just flung himself out of the Range Rover and started sprinting after him.

Jake ran as fast as he could but the accident had disorientated him and his body was racked with pain. Król was only fifteen or twenty feet behind him and gaining ground with every pace.

Up ahead Jake saw a black cab, which had just dropped off a passenger and suddenly inspired he put on a spurt of speed. Ten more paces and he was at the cab. He snatched open the rear door and threw himself inside. "Quick, go, please. Anywhere."

"Crikey, guv, you're in a bit of an 'urry ain'tcha?"

"Yes, I am. Now please, just hurry."

"Okay, okay - keep your hair on," said the cabbie. "I'm going - but you'll have to give me an address sooner or later."

"I will, I promise. Now please, let's just get going."

The cab pulled away from the curb and onto Baker Street.

Jake turned to look out the rear window and saw Król less that three feet away from the bumper and still gaining.

"Quick!" Jake pleaded. "Please hurry."

The cabbie looked in his rear view mirror, "Someone you're trying to avoid?"

"Yeah," Jake said, thinking quickly, "My girlfriend's ex-husband."

"Say no more, guv," said the cabbie. "Been there, done that. I'll soon lose the bastard for you." And with that he put his foot down and Jake watched with relief as the image of Król quickly got smaller.

Jake kept watching as he pulled a handkerchief from his pocket and mopped the blood on his forehead but it was only light, the wound obviously not serious.

When he could no longer see Król, Jake's thoughts turned to Lizzie.

He prayed that she had escaped too.

Chapter 42

Lizzie could hear the sound of Arthur Khan's feet as the soles of his beautifully fashioned hand-tooled brogues slapped at the tarmac just a few paces behind her, relentlessly chasing her down and catching her fast.

Lizzie was normally fast too but the accident had made her head woozy and she felt like she was drunk with the road ahead of her blurring wildly in and out of focus and her legs refusing to co-ordinate properly. She knew she was going to be caught at any moment yet she just could not make her legs work and was helplessly staggering down the road like a drunk desperately racing towards his last ever drink.

Finally, inevitably, Lizzie tripped and went crashing to the ground, grazing her chin and ripping her tight jeans at the knee. The moment she hit the tarmac Khan was on her. He was impeccably dressed in a tailored, three-piece Prince of Wales cheque suit over a clean white shirt with a turquoise Windsor knotted tie. Every inch the successful business man but the look in his eye was evilly victorious as he grabbed tightly hold of Lizzie's arm and said "Gotcha!"

Lizzie turned to look at his triumphant moustached face but it was just a blur that quickly faded to black as the concussion from the accident overtook her and she passed out.

* * *

When Lizzie awoke, she could smell the scent of luxury leather in her nostrils and she slowly opened her eyes to find she was face down on the back seat of a car with her nose pressed against the soft, cream pigskin upholstery. She realised too, that her hands were tied and that the car was in motion. She could hear talking and quickly closed her eyes again, pretending to still be unconscious, whilst she listened intently to the conversation between the two men in the front seats.

One of the men spoke in heavily accented English, the Polish thug from Nassau who had killed Aaron, whom the other man, Khan, was addressing as 'Król'. They were discussing Jake and Król was being reprimanded for letting him get away. Upon hearing this, Lizzie felt a rush of joy, knowing that he was safe. But then, almost immediately afterwards a shiver of terror ran down her spine as Król, undaunted by Khan's anger, said, "No matter. I kill them both when we make exchange. Sawyer has only put off what is—" he searched for the right word, then once satisfied he had the correct one said, "—inevitable."

"Good," said Khan. "Make sure you do, Fabian. Now drop me off here, would you - Peter will pick me up shortly. And make sure no one sees you taking her into my house - Anya, Peter's mistress, will meet you there and help you keep Miss Barnes quiet."

"I need no help." Said Król firmly.

"I know. But Peter feel's it wise. Two sets of eyes better than one and all that. Besides, I'm sure I need not remind you about what happened in Nassau."

Król grunted a response, clearly unhappy that his abilities were being questioned but decided not to say anything more as he pulled the car to a sharp halt.

"See you later - and keep your wits about you." Khan said, as he opened the door and jumped out of the vehicle before it once more sped off.

Lizzie briefly thought about jumping up, opening the car door and leaping out but decided against it. She was still concussed, her hands were tied behind her and the car was moving at quite a pace - if she jumped out now, assuming the door was unlocked, then it could be into the path of an oncoming vehicle. So she decided her best chance would be when the car stopped. She would make her move then.

* * *

A short time later the big Range Rover pulled over and stopped again, but this time the engine was turned off. They had reached their destination. Lizzie was still playing possum on the back seat as Król got out and opened the door nearest her feet.

As he leant in Lizzie sprang up and kicked him hard in the face. Then, as he reared backwards, she slammed her other foot heavily into his crotch.

Król was stunned, taken completely unawares and as he bent double in blinding agony with blood pissing from his nose, Lizzie scotched forward in a bid for freedom. But as her head emerged into the daylight, a feminine fist struck her hard across the cheek and sent her tumbling to the ground at Król's feet.

Lizzie, dazed once more, looked up from where she lay to see a beautiful, leggy blonde standing over her, wearing a very short mini skirt and towering stilettos. "Not so fast, bitch," the woman said in an accent not too dissimilar to Król's.

Then the woman turned to Król, himself, and added with disgust, "And as for you, I thought you were supposed to be professional."

* * *

Arthur Khan's mews house was situated in a quiet corner of Chelsea where the neighbours kept themselves very much to themselves. Indeed, most of the other houses were empty a good deal of the time and used primarily as expensive 'crash pads' for their wealthy owners or as stylish love-nests for rich businessmen to take their mistresses. So no one noticed as Król threw Lizzie roughly over his shoulder and carried her inside - although Anya stood guard anyway, just in case.

In a moment's weakness, after a bout of particularly violent, yet massively rewarding sex, Peter had told Anya about the diamonds and very generously said that she could have her pick of any five of them if she allowed him to video some of their little sessions. Anya had haggled the deal up to eight diamonds before agreeing to what she would have probably done for free had he just asked. However, she was now involved and was not going to let the chance of eight massive jewels slip through her fingers - especially not due to the clumsiness of a tattooed brute like Fabian Król.

Once inside the house, Anya ordered Król to take Lizzie upstairs and tie her up in the back bedroom. Król did as instructed but disliked taking orders from the woman, especially a woman such as her who he believed to be nothing more than a high-class whore.

* * *

Lizzie was left alone in a white painted bedroom tied to the wooden headboard of a single, unmade bed. Aside from the bed there was no other furniture in the room. Just bare walls and a beige carpet. The only light came from a dorma window in the sloping ceiling that allowed her only a view of the grey London sky.

As he tied her, Król had been muttering under his breath in Polish, clearly unhappy at being the blonde-haired woman's whipping boy and as a result had not tied Lizzie very securely. Not only was the rope that bound her loose, but the headboard was also wobbling in its mounting and she thought, with a good hard pull, it might easily pop out. So as soon as she heard Król thump down the stairs, she decided to give her theory a try.

The headboard was fixed better than she had hoped but with a few heavy tugs, being careful not to make too much noise, it eventually broke free of its mounting. Lizzie slid her bound wrists down and over the end of the post she was tethered to, freeing herself from it but leaving her still tied with her arms behind her back. However, without the bedpost to hamper her efforts she now had much more freedom of movement with which to better work on the rope.

* * *

Król strode angrily into the kitchen where Anya, sitting at the polished oak breakfast table, was applying bright green nail varnish, her long, bare legs crossed elegantly in front of her. But Król hardly looked at her, his contempt for her barely contained, as he clicked on the kettle and reached for a glass mug from the tree on the windowsill.

"You supposed to be upstairs with girl." Anya

said without looking up from her nails. But Król ignored her.

"Hey, you - ugly brute!" She barked, now staring at his back. "You supposed to be guarding girl so that she not get away like she did in Bahamas!"

"What do you know about The Bahamas?" Król sneered in better English.

"I know plenty. I know you fuck up and I know you better not do it again." She said.

"Says who?" Snapped Król. "You?"

"Yes me," said Anya. "I not fuck up. I success. You do as I say and girl will not escape again."

"I don't take orders from you. You're not even shit on my shoe. You know nothing about giving or taking orders. All you know is how to lay on your back and sell your skinny arse to the highest bidder." Król spat, his hackles clearly raised as he poured the scolding water into his coffee cup, spilling half of it on the worktop before aggressively tipping in a teaspoon of coffee and stirring wildly.

"Pah!" Anya laughed. "You're pathetic, you know that? You might think I'm whore and sure, so what, I fuck rich men and they give me nice things - is it my fault I'm beautiful? But I'm also smart, not like you. When I do job I make sure it right. When I fuck a man I make sure they are satisfied, I make sure they are pleased and when they ask me to guard girl to make sure she not escape - I do that too."

"She's not escaped!" Król growled. "She's tied up

upstairs. Not going anywhere. I know how to do job. I do it all my life - and I don't need whore like you getting in my way!"

"Hah! Well we see what Peter say when I tell him that, 'cos he obviously not trust you enough to baby sit some helpless girl." Anya's face was victorious when she had finished speaking with a smug, self-satisfied smile upon her face which Król would have dearly loved to have punched off but at that moment both of them heard the sound of footsteps and then a desperate scrambling noise of the latch being lifted on the front door.

* * *

Lizzie worked furiously on the rope, which was poorly tied, and quickly freed herself from its bonds. Carefully she slipped off the bed and tip-toed over to the dorma window hoping that she might find a fire escape but the window was locked and beyond that there was just a sheer drop to the small enclosed courtyard below - offering no way out.

She crossed to the door and tested the handle, finding it open. Silently she slipped out along the thickly carpeted landing and then down a short flight of narrow stairs to the first floor. The house was impressive, very modern and quite spacious, the walls white and stark in the minimalist style. The landing here was fitted with the same thick beige carpet that seemed to cover both upper levels, including the room from which Lizzie had just escaped. The luxurious carpet helped disguise the sound of her foot falls as she rushed along towards the elegant curved stairway. This led to the ground floor and was much grander in design than the small set of stairs that led from attic rooms. It had spotlights embedded into the wall at foot level above every tread and rather than a balustrade there was a smoothly worked plaster wall, finishing at waist height, that had been painted white to give a sleek modern twist to the classic spiral staircase. Lizzie crouched down behind the plastered curve as she warily navigated her way down, being careful not to be seen by anyone who happened to be occupying the large open living space below.

She could hear loud, angry voices, somewhere off to the back of the house she thought - certainly in a different part of the house to the one she was entering into and a wave of courage surged through her body. As her plimsolled foot touched down on the expensive hardwood floor at the bottom of the staircase she raised her head above the parapet and risked a furtive look around. She could see no one, although the voices were louder, even more angry now and Lizzie sensed trouble was brewing but she didn't intend to hang around long enough to witness it.

Remembering her way from when Król carried her in, Lizzie rushed across the main room, her rubber soles squeaking rather too loudly on the polished wooden floor, and into the hallway where she saw, with relief, the wide front door. She dived towards it and, with shaking, flustered hands, released the safety chain. After that she reached for the latch but it was locked. There was a catch that slid up and down to release it and Lizzie fumbled with it, trying to work as quickly as possible, desperately trying to escape before being discovered.

But it was too late, just as she released the latch and the first strip of glorious daylight shone through the widening crack in the opening door a rough hand seized her by the hair and dragged her backwards.

Lizzie span round and slashed Król across the cheek with her nails leaving three bloody claw marks but he was impervious to the pain as he raised his fist and before Lizzie had time to even brace herself, brought it swiftly down painting her world black.

* * *

Król threw Lizzie to the ground like a discarded rag doll and her limp body slid to a halt on the shiny oak floor.

"Idiot!" Anya shouted. "You stupid fucking idiot! What did I tell you eh? You got no fucking brain you big, ugly brute!"

"Shut up, whore!" Król snarled. "Just shut up."

"No." Anya snapped, "I not shut up. I not keep quiet. You got one job to do and you don't even do that. Stupid, stupid, stupid!"

Król had well and truly had enough of this

skinny blonde gold-digger with the big mouth and small tits. She was making his head ache with her constant belittling and whining. The worst of it was, that he knew she was right. He had not done a good job, he had not been careful. He should have made certain that she was securely tied, that there was no way she could escape but instead of that he had let Anya get into his head. Orders from Bearing and Khan were one thing, they were his employers, men he respected but orders from a Bulgarian whore that was entirely another.

Król felt his rage rising, building uncontrollably, knowing that he was about to blow. He had to step away, get away from Anya before he did something even more stupid, but she just would not stop talking.

"You sloppy. Useless. You wait until I tell Peter - I make sure he not pay you for yet another fuck up job!" She yelled, her face contorted with triumphant gratification.

Król turned his back, desperately trying to block out her incessant jabbering. "Shut up!" He yelled before sucking in deep gulps of air in a useless bid to cool his temper. But it was no good, Anya refused to keep quiet, clearly enjoying Król's anguish. "No, I not shut up - you have to make me - if you man enough, which I seriously doubt!"

Anya felt excited somehow by the barely controlled violence of the man before her. With Peter, the violence, the beatings although real

378

enough, were all part of an agreed game in which each knew the rules and boundaries. But Król was raw strength, a big, angry mountain of rage, wild and untamed - about as far from Peter Bearing's little sex games as she could possibly go and she found the thought of that tantalising. Arousing even. As Anya berated Król, belittled him, she knew with growing anticipation and excitement that at any moment he was likely to explode.

Suddenly she knew that she wanted him urgently inside her, to feel his hard body as he forced himself brutally upon her, ripping at her flesh, clawing at her breasts, making her suffer, deservedly punishing her for all her demeaning barbs.

"Come on you big, hairy brute - show me what big, hard man you are!" She goaded, purposely trying to provoke him. "Prove to me how big and tough you are - shut me up if you dare!"

"Be quiet, bitch, I mean it!" Król shouted, his self control at its absolute limit. "Just shut up!"

"Make me." Anya taunted wantonly.

That was it. Król snapped. He span around and charged towards her, grabbing her tightly by the throat with his outstretched hand, the thick veins in his muscular, tattooed forearms pulsating with venomous rage. In that one swift movement he lifted her easily off the floor and slammed her forcefully up against the clean white wall behind her. But as the back of her head connected hard with the wall, Anya let out a small gasp of pleasure.

As Król held her firmly, he snatched a handful of one of her small perfect breasts and squeezed it viscously. Anya gasped again, a shudder of delight and eager anticipation rattling through her body as she wrapped her legs around his and drew him closer to her. "That's it, you big, ugly brute," she said, "You want to fuck me now don't you, yes?" As she said it she reached down and grabbed his crotch expecting to find him hard and eager. But instead he was soft and flacid and as she looked up into his murderous eyes, a sliver of cold fear crawled into her belly, knowing with dreadful certainty that she had badly misjudged the situation. Her legs dropped, freeing him from the circle she had entrapped him in, but she could not touch the floor and they dangled helplessly as he held her.

Meanwhile, Król had released his grip on her breast and whilst still pinning her by the throat had reached into his pocket and pulled out something Anya had not expected.

"You want to be fucked, whore?" He sneered, with spittle on his lips and white foaming saliva at the corners of his mouth, "Well now you are."

Anya's eyes flew wide apart as Król pushed the lovingly polished tip of his razor sharp butterfly knife between her top two ribs. The full length of its thin shiny blade slicing through flesh, muscle and sinew until it reached the base of her dying heart.

Anya only fought briefly as she felt the terrible pain, realising much too late what was actually happening, but the fight went out of her quickly, like the light in her eyes as she slumped dead in his vice-like grip.

* * *

Król knew instantly that he had made a huge error and as he lowered Anya's lifeless body gently to the ground he turned his head and saw Lizzie staring up at him from where she lay, terror struck by what she had just witnessed. She had roused just at the moment Król stabbed Anya and had been transfixed by horror, unable to tear her eyes away and fearing desperately for her own life at the hands of this murdering madman who was now staring back at her.

Król was motionless, almost in a trance, for a second as his mind clicked slowly into action, thinking about his next very important steps. When they were clear in his mind he once again moved into action, raising a finger to his lips he said to Lizzie, "Ssh, girlie. You see nothing here. It'll be our little secret. The only people to know will be you and me, yes?"

Lizzie made no reaction as Król continued. "You keep quiet, you stay alive, understand?"

Lizzie nodded slowly, her attention shifting from Król's bearded, rough face to the large pool of blood that was spreading out on the hard wooden floor beneath Anya's body.

"It's okay, girlie," Król said, almost kindly. "It's only blood, it not hurt you. And neither will I unless you give me reason - so do not give me reason, okay?"

Again Lizzie nodded.

"Good," said Król, "Now let's take you back upstairs where I tie you up tight, like I should have done before. The whore was right. I was sloppy, but not anymore."

With Lizzie once again secured, this time in such a way that she could not possibly hope to escape, Król came back downstairs and began clearing up the mess he had made.

He was grateful that he had killed Anya downstairs on the wooden flooring and not upstairs on the pale beige carpet as the blood could easily be mopped up without leaving a trace. Firstly though, he had to dispose of the body before Arthur Khan came home and saw it laying there.

Quickly, Król wrapped Anya's corpse in several large plastic bin bags then sealed the finished parcel securely with a whole roll of brown packing tape that he had found under Arthur's sink.

The sun was setting as Król then carried the wrapped body back out to the Range Rover and stowed it in the boot under the parcel shelf. No one would look there tonight. Tomorrow, Król would drive out to the countryside, find a large forest and bury the former Miss Bulgaria in a deep, dark hole where no one would ever find her.

Bearing would, of course, ask questions but Król would just maintain that he had never seen Anya and that she had never turned up at Arthur's house. No one would ever know and Peter Bearing would have no choice but to assume that his girlfriend had moved on to someone even richer.

For now though, Fabian Król intended to go back into Khan's beautiful mews house, find a mop and clean like he had never cleaned before. By the time Arthur arrived home there would be no trace of blood or Anya's very existence anywhere.

* * *

Lizzie was bruised, battered and scared. From the crash of the Maserati to where she was now, it had been one hell of an afternoon and she was still reeling from the effects, her head throbbed and her body ached but there was to be no respite as she was tightly bound at the wrists and ankles with a wide strip of packing tape stuck firmly over her mouth. This time, she was not going anywhere.

Her escape attempt had failed miserably, having ended with the horrendous murder of that beautiful young woman by the man Lizzie now knew as Fabian Król. The same man who had murdered her foster brother, Aaron.

The murder of the girl and the look of pure insanity in Król's eyes afterwards had shocked her to the very core and she knew she was lucky to still be alive.

However, Lizzie realised the futility of her situation, knowing that there was nothing she could do now but wait and hope to be rescued before Król decided to kill her too.

But above all else, she prayed that Jake was safe.

Chapter 43

Jake was frantic. After escaping from Król in the taxi he had asked to be dropped off at the bottom of Regent Street. From there, he had slowly made his way back on foot to Baker Street, constantly keeping his wits about him, ever aware that Król and his accomplice might still be loitering about. But he had to find Lizzie, desperately hoping that she had evaded capture. The last time he saw her she was heading down Allsop Place with Król's passenger in the Range Rover giving chase on foot.

Jake arrived back at Baker Street to find the scene of the crash swarming with police. The brewery truck had been parked at the side of the road and the crumpled Maserati was being hoisted on to a tow truck. The pavement was thick with onlookers - people, Jake realised, who may have witnessed the accident and who had possibly seen him running away from the scene.

Quickly, he darted into a souvenir shop and

purchased a baseball cap which had the 'Baker Street Underground' logo embroidered on it and a pair of cheap, black wrap around shades. He also bought a grey 'Carnaby Street' sweatshirt to complete the tourist ensemble which, as soon as he left the shop, he swiftly put on, hopefully disguising himself from anyone who may have seen him earlier.

Jake then worked his way into the thick of the gathered crowd and stood watch for a moment as policemen in hi-vis jackets diverted traffic and several detectives talked to possible witnesses - one of them being a very shocked looking brewery truck driver.

Jake pulled the peak of his cap down, disguising his face further, before asking a woman standing next to him, "What's going on?"

The woman barely glanced at him, her focus fixed on what was happening in front of her. "Dunno, for sure," she said in an Australian twang. "Some girl's been kidnapped, or so the cops are saying."

Jake's heart sank. "There was a big crash," the woman continued, "Seems that fancy white sports car over there hit that truck. They're saying the driver scarpered and left his girlfriend to be kidnapped by two blokes who were after them. Sounds like a pretty nice type of fella, don't he?" The woman said sarcastically, at last glancing round to see to whom it was she was addressing, but Jake was gone. Lizzie had been taken and the guilt he felt for leaving her was eating him alive.

* * *

An hour later, Jake was back at The Dorchester, the key fob that contained the data stick tucked safely in his pocket.

He had tried Lizzie repeatedly on her cell phone but she had not picked up and he was extremely worried about her, not knowing if she was alive or dead. The men they were up against had shown themselves to be ruthless in their pursuit of the diamonds as the murder of Jake's family and Aaron Sumpter had proved. Jake just prayed that Lizzie was not going to be another of their victims.

He paced the floor anxiously, trying to think of what he should do next, knowing that there was only one real option left open to him. He had to phone the police, they would surely be able to find Lizzie where he couldn't. It was the only way to save her life - if he wasn't too late already. Jake snatched up his phone but before dialling the police decided to give Lizzie one last try.

This time the phone was answered on the third ring but it was not Lizzie's voice on the line.

"Hello Mister Sawyer," the voice said. "My name is Arthur Khan and I believe you have some rather pretty things that belong to me."

"Where's Lizzie?" Jake growled.

Khan ignored him. "I have a rather pretty thing which I believe belongs to you. So I propose an exchange."

"You better not have hurt her you–" Jake began but was cut off abruptly.

"You're obviously feeling far too emotional at present," Khan said. "So I will call you later, when you've had time to consider my proposal. Until then, goodbye Mister Sawyer."

And with that the phone went dead.

* * *

"Well?" Said Peter Bearing, who had picked up Arthur Khan on the corner of Baker Street a few minutes after Król had dropped him off. Peter and Arthur were now sitting in the back of Bearing's sumptuous Bentley en-route to his apartment, the chauffeur separated from their conversation by a privacy screen.

"I'll give him an hour or so to cool down," Khan said. "To let the futility of his situation sink in. If he wants the girl back he'll cooperate I guarantee it. He's got nothing left except for the diamonds to bargain with - no tapes, no files, nothing. His whole plan has collapsed now we've destroyed all the evidence that Sumpter had. The diamonds are the only things he has left. And soon enough we'll have those, too."

"You seem very confident, Arthur." Said Bearing.

"I am Peter. Besides, Król says Sawyer's in love and love can be very persuasive."

"It can indeed." Bearing agreed, thinking of the arrangement he had made with Anya - eight highly valuable diamonds for a few rolls of video tape of him and her having violently, rough sex - hardly a smart business decision but Peter was infatuated with her, maybe even in love with her, which was surprising for a man with very few emotions, and love, as Król had said, could be very persuasive.

"And now you have a friend at Scotland Yard to keep you informed," Khan continued, "I really don't see how things can fail. You mark my words, Peter, by this time tomorrow we'll have the diamonds and Jake Sawyer and Elizabeth Wallace will be dead."

"I believe you, Arthur. I do." Said Bearing. "But I think it might be wise for me to give young Detective Sergeant Eckhart a call, to remind him of our arrangement. If Sawyer does decide to go to the police then we need to be aware of it and act accordingly."

Khan leaned forward in the Bentley's luxurious interior and helped himself to a drink from the walnut cabinet in front of him. "I couldn't agree more, Peter." He said.

* * *

Jake sat on his bed at The Dorchester feeling as if he had been punched in the gut. Memories of that hideous moment at the Waldorf Astoria flooding into his brain when he learned the horrific fate of his family. Now the same thing was threatening to happen again.

He hung his head in his hands, trying to force

his brain to move on from the past and into the present, to think of something to help Lizzie. Then it suddenly became clear. But first he had to know exactly what it was that he had to bargain with.

Jake grabbed the bag containing his laptop and sparked up his MacBook. He then took Aaron's keys from his pocket and separated the two halves of the big yellow foot to reveal the data stick. He plugged it into the USB slot on his laptop and hoped.

A couple of seconds later, the stick's icon mounted on the desktop and Jake, with his heart suddenly beating faster, double clicked. A window opened to reveal several folders that were all individually labelled; Recordings, Documentation, Photographs, Reports, Logs and so on.

The data stick held four gigabytes of information, ample storage space for all the evidence it contained. There were sound files, scans of transactions and business dealings, shipping notices and timetables, photographs of meetings between Peter Bearing and the Khan brothers, geology reports, estimates from diamond specialists on the value of certain stones and a detailed log of every diamond that the case contained; the cut, the clarity, the colour and the weight. And written in the margin, next to each one, was an expected value. Jake scanned the columns and could not see one valued at less than thirty-thousand pounds. Most were estimated at considerably more. It seemed he had sold his at a bargain price.

Jake clicked on one of the sound files, obviously recorded in Bearing's office, where he and Khan were discussing the importation of the diamonds. He clicked on another where they were discussing Jake, himself, and what to do about him. In another Khan made mention of Angie and the kids and how he could make them reveal what they knew. When it had finished Jake felt sick, but he knew what he had was incredibly important.

It was all there. Everything, Every little incriminating fact, hard irrefutable proof that, along with the diamonds, would guarantee Bearing and Khan's long-term incarceration. It was clear to see why they wanted to destroy it. And they thought they had.

However, Jake had to save Lizzie and if that meant trading the diamonds for her then he would. But Jake knew that without the actual stones, the information on the data stick would be almost worthless. It would certainly be enough to raise questions but to secure a conviction leading to actual prison time, Jake doubted it.

Also, after what had happened at Sumpter's house, could he still trust Roper Coyle?

* * *

An hour later, Jake's phone rang and he snatched it up. "Hello?"

"Hello, Mister Sawyer," said Khan. "I trust you have thought about my proposal?"

"Yes."

"Good. Then you are agreeable to an exchange?"

"Yes. The diamonds for Lizzie - let me speak to her. I want to make sure she's okay."

"Alas," Khan said. "I'm afraid that is not possible but I can assure you she is unharmed. You have my word."

"I doubt your word is worth very much at all."

Khan chuckled, "You'll just have to trust me then, Mister Sawyer. My only interest is in the diamonds, once I have those then you and Miss Wallace - my apologies, Miss Barnes, are of little use to me."

"I bet," Jake said under his breath. "When and where do we make this exchange?"

"You know the Olympic Village at Stratford East?"

"No, but I'll find it."

"Good. Well there's a new complex being constructed there - called the Bearing Building - there's a sign outside with a logo on, you can't miss it. The gates will be open. Be there at midnight, at the northern point of the main structure.

"North point. Midnight. Fine." Jake agreed.

"Oh, and Mister Sawyer - no police, there's a good fellow, otherwise I'm afraid your Miss Barnes will not look quite as fetching as she does now. Understand?"

"Yeah. I get it. But Khan, a word of warning. You touch one hair on her head and I'll kill you. Do you understand?"

Khan chuckled again. "Of course, Mister Sawyer. Of course. Until midnight then?"

"Yeah. Until midnight," Jake said but the line was already dead.

* * *

Detective Sergeant Dave Eckhart was sitting at his desk staring at a blank computer screen, his thoughts a million miles away, when his mobile phone buzzed in his pocket. He pulled it out to see the caller display saying 'Peter Bearing'.

He looked around him furtively but there was no one within immediate ear shot. He pressed *answer* and said, "Hello - look, I told you not to call me. I'm at work, someone could hear."

"Then you had better listen fast," said Bearing. "I'm conducting some business at midnight tonight at the Bearing Building near the Olympic Village in Stratford East, you know it?

"The Twirl," said Eckhart, "Yeah, I know it. But —"

"Good." Interrupted Bearing. "I do not want to be disturbed. If any one phones, or if you hear of anything even remotely connected to that area, then you let me know, understand?"

"Yeah, I understand, but–"

"No buts, detective, just do it. As you are already aware, I can make your life very much sweeter or I can make it considerably more sour. So if you want to keep your pretty young wife happy and a roof over the head of that lovely baby daughter of yours, you will do as I say. Yes?"

"Yes." Replied Eckhart, begrudgingly.

"Good," said Bearing, "Do not disappoint me, detective." Then he hung up.

Eckhart turned in his chair and was startled to see Coyle standing behind him. "Problems?" Coyle asked.

"Er, no Guv," Dave replied, "No problem. No problem at all."

Chapter 44

Król had his story ready when Arthur and Peter arrived at the Mews house at a little after 11pm that night.

Bearing's first question was "Where's Anya?" But Król bluffed it out expertly, claiming that he had not seen her all day and had assumed she had not been required after all.

Immediately Peter pulled out his Blackberry and dialled her number but it went straight to voice mail. He then called his assistant, unconcerned about the lateness of the hour and asked if she had seen her. The answer, as Król already knew, was clearly 'no" as Bearing was obviously not happy after ending the call abruptly. He phoned Anya's mobile again and was once more directed to voice mail.

Król was actually quite enjoying himself as he watched, knowing that the phone his employer was calling had been switched off, its SIM card smashed, and bagged up with Anya's corpse in the back of the

Range Rover.

"Maybe she just forgot," Khan offered. He, himself, had little faith in women, or little use for them, aside from fulfilling his sexual needs. "I'm sure she's just back at your apartment taking a long, hot bath after a hard days" shopping."

"Hmm," Bearing mused, far from convinced. "Maybe. Maybe not."

"Anyway, Peter, we've got rather more pressing matters to think about tonight, wouldn't you say? You can reprimand Anya tomorrow, when we have our diamonds."

"I'll thank you not to remind me of what I can and cannot do, Arthur, if you don't mind. But yes, you are correct, tonight we must retrieve the diamonds and rid ourselves of Sawyer and young Miss Barnes. And, just for the record, I will certainly be reprimanding Anya tomorrow." Bearing could think of many ways in which to do that, all of them rather deliciously nasty and the thought was already exciting him.

Król looked on contemptuously. What a smug, pompous fool Bearing was. It certainly wouldn't be Peter getting his hands dirty with the killing of Sawyer and Barnes. It would be left up to Khan and him to do that. Bearing would merely just give the order as people in his self-satisfied and oh, so superior position so often liked to do. But they knew nothing of killing, of how it felt or of how empowering it was. If Bearing knew the truth about Anya, he might also finally understand who it was who had the true superiority and power.

After this assignment was over, Król might just take the time to tell him. Now he had reflected upon it, he didn't regret killing the girl at all. She was a spoilt, vain whore and Bearing was a stuffy, arrogant, buffoon. They deserved each other.

For the first time Król allowed himself to think about the diamonds and how they could change his life. Up until now, his life had been all about order, discipline and loyalty. His word was his bond and his loyalty to a client guaranteed. But men like Peter Bearing were beneath him and in the last few days of this assignment, having been on the receiving end of Bearing's wrath for what had happened in Nassau and then ridiculed by Anya, the whore, who had clearly been privy to what had transpired, he was starting to believe it was time to make contingency plans. And a case full of diamonds, or half a case if shared with Arthur Khan - a man who Król did respect, would set him up very nicely indeed.

Firstly though, he had to deal with Sawyer and Barnes. Then, just maybe, he would deal with Peter Bearing too.

* * *

"Król! Did you hear me, man?" Bearing was asking, having just given the man an order and being completely ignored.

The sharp tone snapped Król back to the present. "Sorry, no. What did you say?" He said.

"My God," Peter said with disgust, "No wonder they slipped through your fingers in Nassau."

"Peter, please!" Khan interjected. "Let me deal with this."

Bearing did not look at all happy but conceded to his friend. "Fine," he said, clearly exasperated.

Khan looked imploringly at Król. "Fabian, if you wouldn't mind, would you please go and fetch Miss Barnes?"

"Of course," Król said, leaving the other two men alone, but remembering, and mentally logging, the way Bearing had spoken to him, making his decision that much easier.

* * *

The room was completely dark now and it seemed to Lizzie as if she had been there for hours. All the feeling had gone out of her legs as she had been unable to move them properly since Król had re-tied her earlier on. Now though, she could hear the sound of heavy footsteps coming up the stairs and suspected something was about to happen.

The door burst open and Król snapped on the light temporarily blinding Lizzie, her eyes unaccustomed to the brightness. By the time they had adjusted Król was by her side.

"Hello, girlie," he said, a wide grin on his face. "You remember what I said about keeping mouth shut, eh?"

Lizzie nodded.

"Good." Said Król, hauling her up and throwing her easily over his shoulder. "Now let's go meet your boyfriend and get my diamonds."

* * *

Król carried Lizzie downstairs and out to the car. Then he opened the boot and threw her in next to the bagged up body. Again he smiled and put a finger to his lips. "Remember," he whispered. "Ssh, not one word."

He slammed the boot lid down plunging Lizzie back into darkness. But this time she was not alone as now she had Anya's cold, dead, corpse for company.

Chapter 45

Jake arrived at the construction site of the Bearing Building a little before midnight. The site itself was enormous, with large sections already completed such as the huge shopping mall that cleverly echoed the design of the main building and the multi-levelled underground car park, which Jake could just make out the entrance to in the moonlight. However, the focal point was the magnificent glass spiral tower that rose up, nearly a thousand feet above it.

'The Twirl,' as Jake had learned it was nicknamed since speaking with Arthur Khan, was a breathtaking piece of modern architecture consisting of high-end office space and exclusive living accommodation.

Presently though, it was largely covered in acres of white plastic sheeting which disguised an intricately designed spiral skeleton of metal, concrete, wood and breeze block. Some of the glass had already been fitted on the lower floors alluding to the beauty of the finished building but, for now, the rest of it was still very much a work in progress.

As such, the vast area of ground immediately surrounding the building itself was a mass of mud and gravel which covered an area equivalent to that of at least ten full-sized football fields. The whole complex was surrounded by temporary, ten foot high, metal fencing that ran around the entire perimeter and the only way in or out was through a wide set of high iron gates. At midnight, these would normally be padlocked shut to keep out intruders but tonight, as Khan had promised, they were open.

The site was dark and desolate with only intermittent security lighting which offered precious little visibility over the uneven muddy ground.

Jake slipped inside and walked swiftly towards the main structure of the tower some distance away. He kept purposely to the shadows to give himself as much cover as possible, even though they were ominously black and eerie. He felt alone, conspicuous and vulnerable, the suitcase full of diamonds stuffed into the rucksack on his back.

Should Khan decide to take a shot at him now from some unseen vantage point then there was not a damn thing he could do about it, but the risk was worth it for Lizzie.

At last Jake reached the base of the main structure at the northern most point. He was exposed, a sitting target, but he waited.

He looked at his watch and was concerned to

see that it was already ten passed the hour. Where were they?

As Jake was contemplating the precariousness of his situation and praying that Lizzie was still alive, he at last saw headlights approaching the site. A moment later the shiny black Range Rover drove through the gates and was heading over the rough terrain towards him. The grounds around the building would eventually be wonderfully landscaped with walkways, outdoor seating areas, reflection pools and fountains but for the moment they were crisscrossed with a rudimentary network of roads for the construction vehicles that sliced through vast tracts of churned earth and mud.

As the Range Rover found its way onto the large, trodden down circle of uneven ground that immediately surrounded the building's northern point, Jake took a deep breath to calm his racing heartbeat.

Król, who he could now clearly see driving the car, swung it round in a wide arc and pulled it to a halt several yards from where Jake stood before turning off the engine and extinguishing the headlights.

For a moment, nothing happened. Then Arthur Khan, in a dark roll neck and a black crombie coat, opened the rear passenger door and climbed out. He walked perhaps ten or fifteen paces in front of the car and stopped around fifteen feet away from Jake. Then, unbelievably, Peter Bearing got out of the front passenger side and strolled casually up next to Khan. He was wearing a grey suit and looked impeccable, as if he was going on from there to a cocktail party. Jake stood facing them, in a jumper, jeans and hiking boots. This was the only party he would be attending tonight. He just hoped it wouldn't turn into a wake.

"I trust you have brought my diamonds, Mister Sawyer?" Bearing shouted.

"You've brought Lizzie?" Jake shouted back.

"We have."

"Let me see her."

Bearing nodded to Khan who then glanced back at the Range Rover and shouted, "Król, he wants to see the girl!"

Fabian Król opened the driver's door of the vehicle and stepped out, then he went round to the boot and pulled Lizzie out, leaving Anya's bagged-up corpse where it lay, concealed from Bearing's sight.

With his butterfly knife, Król cut Lizzie's ankles free but left her hands tied securely behind her back. She looked bruised and tired but otherwise alright and Jake breathed a huge sigh of relief.

Król pushed her roughly up to where Bearing and Khan stood midway between Jake and the Range Rover. "Hey, Limey," she said rather croakily, her eyes full of emotion.

"You okay, Lizzie?" Jake called. "Have they hurt you?"

"I'm fine, Jake. I am, really. I'm not hurt–"

403

"I'm sorry to break up the happy reunion," Bearing interjected. "But, please, Mister Sawyer, we've shown you ours, as they say, now let us see yours."

Jake hesitated a moment longer. "Now." Khan growled. We haven't got all night."

"Please, Arthur," Bearing said. "I'm sure Mister Sawyer grasps the gravity of the situation, don't you?" He looked at Jake. "So please, you've made us wait long enough and you've played a very good game. But now the time for games is over. Show me the diamonds, Mister Sawyer or, as they say in the movies, your girlfriend gets it."

Jake shrugged off the rucksack and put it on the floor in front of him. He then opened it and pulled out the case of diamonds which he placed on the muddy ground, next to the empty rucksack. He snapped open the clasps, lifted the lid and turned it round to face Bearing and Khan. However, the diamonds were still in their individual compartments, within their velvet bags.

"Show us properly, Sawyer," said Khan. "Stop stalling."

Jake pulled open a compartment and lifted out a small velvet pouch. He tugged open the drawstring fastening and emptied a small amount of stones into the palm of his hand. They glistened and sparkled enticingly and Khan physically had to stop himself from licking his lips. Even Król was briefly mesmerised by the enticing glitter of the stones as they twinkled hypnotically in the moonlight.

"Satisfied?" Jake asked.

"Almost," replied Bearing. "How many are missing?"

"Pardon?"

"Come now, Mister Sawyer. You've flown several times around the world, stayed in the best hotels, lived on a paradise island in an exclusive resort - even bought a Maserati, I understand. I take it none of that was free of charge. So I ask again, how many of my diamonds are missing, Mister Sawyer?"

"Fourteen," Jake replied. "Just fourteen small ones, that's all."

"Fourteen. That's all," Bearing repeated. "How very frugal of you. How very thoughtful of you."

Jake said nothing.

"Please - pass the case to Mister Król, would you?" Bearing said. Jake packed the diamonds back into the case and closed the lid, then said, "First, give me Lizzie."

"No. Mister Sawyer. First you give Mister Król the case so we can check the merchandise properly. Then and only then, if everything is in order, will I return Elizabeth to you."

"No," Jake said. "Lizzie first, then the diamonds."

"I'm sorry, Mister Sawyer, you seem to misunderstand. That was not a request." Bearing then turned again to Khan. "Arthur, if you would be so kind."

Khan then reached into his coat and pulled out his huge chrome Magnum, which he pointed at Jake. Król also pulled out a pistol and aimed it in the same direction.

"Now, Mister Sawyer," said Bearing, "If you would be so kind?"

Faced with no other choice, Jake held out the case. Król walked the short distance to him, leaving Lizzie with Khan. He smiled evilly at Jake as he took the case from him. "You not escape so easily now, I think." Król whispered. And Jake guessed that he could be right.

Król carried the case back and gave it to Bearing, who took it over to the Range Rover and placed it on the bonnet. He opened the lid and began checking random compartments and bags.

"They're all there. I swear it." Jake called.

"Wrong, Mister Sawyer!" Bearing flared, spinning to face Jake once more, his normally calm composure replaced by sudden anger. "They are not all here, are they. The case is fourteen diamonds short, you have admitted it yourself. Fourteen, Mister Sawyer! Fourteen pieces of my property which you stole from me, which I will never get back."

Jake was suddenly very fearful, sensing what was about to happen, he stared into Lizzie's frightened eyes as he spoke again to Bearing. "I'm sorry, I know there are some missing but please, you have killed my wife, my children - you have taken Lizzie's brother and father from her - we have both paid a terrible price for those diamonds. Please just take the case and let us go."

Arthur Khan was smiling as Bearing replied, "You think that was payment?"

Jake said nothing.

"Yes," Bearing continued, "Arthur here did kill your family. But it was not as payment. It was because you stole from us Mister Sawyer. And yes, I framed Jonathan Wallace but that had nothing to do with the diamonds - that was just business. He was a hindrance - an annoyance that had to be removed and I did what was needed to be done. For The Company. So do not tell me you have already paid Mister Sawyer, because I assure you that you have not." Bearing looked almost insane as he finished, drunk on his own power, high on his own importance.

"I have nothing more to give you," Jake said. "There is nothing more I own. Please, just take the diamonds and let us go."

"Oh, I will take the diamonds, thank you, Mister Sawyer. But you will not be let go. As I said, you owe me a debt and I fully intend to make you pay." For a final time he glanced over at Khan and said, "Arthur, kill them for me, would you? There's a good fellow."

Chapter 46

Six hours earlier, Dave Eckhart was standing in the toilets at New Scotland Yard, studying his worry worn face in the mirror. He was twenty-eight but felt much older. The last months had been a living hell with the guilt of betraying his mentor, Roper Coyle, weighing heavily on his mind. Coyle was a man Eckhart not only trusted above all others but also regarded as a good friend. However, the simple fact was that Dave was desperate for money and he thought that solving his financial problems would be the key to saving his crumbling marriage. So he stupidly reached out to Peter Bearing.

But he had been a misguided fool. Dave knew now that his marriage could not be saved no matter how much money he had and certainly not by betraying his friends, colleagues and his own highly prized principles.

His wife, Lucy, was leaving him and taking their daughter, Gemma with her. That was now, unfortunately, an inevitable fact and Dave had at last realised it was not the money that had been the problem, it was just him and Lucy. They had married far too young, before either of them had really done any living and now they had out grown each other.

Dave had tried to save the marriage by gambling what little money they did have in a last ditch attempt to generate more but it had been a hopelessly flawed strategy which had ultimately landed him in more debt. The drinking, too, which briefly eased the stress, left him further out of pocket and desperate to get out from under the immense pressure being put on him, he had made an even worse decision.

Dave realised what an idiot he had been in accepting Peter Bearing's money. He hated himself for phoning Bearing to tell him about the evidence that Aaron Sumpter had gathered on him and Arthur Khan which was kept at Sumpter's home in Hampstead. Dave had found this intelligence out from Roper who had received a confidential call from the elusive Jake Sawyer, telling Coyle all about it. Eckhart's information had been instrumental in the destruction of this vital evidence and now because of his selfishness, Bearing and Khan could quite literally get away with murder.

Dave had always been a good copper. Police work was in his veins, it was what he lived for, but he had thrown it all away just for a few hundred lousy pounds. It was over; his marriage and his career.

And now he was in much deeper than he had ever intended to be with the stakes rising with every passing hour.

* * *

Down the hall, Roper Coyle was sitting at his desk, wondering why he had not yet heard from Jake Sawyer. Jake had called him on his way back to England, and told him that he was going to retrieve some evidence from Sumpter's house as soon as he arrived back. He also said that he would call Roper when he had it in his possession.

That call was supposed to have come this afternoon, as agreed. But as yet, Coyle had heard nothing.

Roper looked up to see Eckhart arriving back at his desk and thought that his young sergeant looked pale and unwell. Like death warmed up.

"You okay, Dave?" Roper asked.

But as Eckhart opened his mouth to speak, Coyle's phone started ringing and he held up a hand to silence Dave as he lifted the handset. "Hello?" Roper said, still looking at Eckhart curiously. Something was clearly troubling him. But the older man's focus now shifted to the telephone. "This is Detective Chief Inspector Coyle, can I help you?"

"Coyle, it's me," Jake said, "And you'd better tell me what the bloody hell is going on."

Chapter 47

Arthur Khan still kept a tight hold on Lizzie, even though she struggled desperately to be free. He grinned widely as he took aim at Jake with the big shiny Desert Eagle. "You know, Sawyer," he said, "Your son had the same look in his eyes when I killed him."

Jake was about to respond, when suddenly, with dazzling white intensity, the building site was bathed in brilliant light as somebody switched on the huge halogen work lights which floodlit the immediate vicinity, making it seem like night had magically turned to day.

Khan, Król and Bearing were temporarily blinded as a mechanical voice spoke loudly to them through a megaphone. "This is the police." Coyle said. "Drop your weapons you are surrounded."

Then bedlam ensued as Król and Khan started shooting and the police marksmen, who had been hiding within the shadows of the complex, were forced to return fire. A multitude of police cars suddenly screamed into view with their blue lights flashing, from where they had been lurking just out of view in the underground parking facility.

Król was blasting wildly about him as he ran back towards the car for cover. Bearing, unarmed, followed suit, keeping low, trying to avoid being hit by Król.

"Lizzie, get down!" Jake shouted as he dived for cover behind an abandoned digger. But Khan held onto Lizzie tightly as he dragged her off towards a deserted part of the building. He was firing the Magnum in all directions as he rushed into the shadows behind a huge section of plastic sheeting that was secured to the scaffolding.

The crackle of gunfire continued as the police tactical unit, headed by Roper Coyle moved forward, from where they had been hiding out of sight, into the open muddy battle ground to take control of the situation. Coyle was wearing a kevlar vest as was Dave Eckhart who was behind him, keeping low.

"Coyle, quick!" Jake shouted. "Khan's getting away - he ran into the building with Lizzie!"

Coyle heard and was about to go after Khan when a bullet buzzed past his ear and he was forced to dive for cover behind a squad car that had just skidded to a halt in front of him.

The young policeman driving the vehicle was not so lucky as Król's next shot struck the officer directly between the eyes, killing him instantly.

Coyle, with Eckhart huddling beside him, returned fire, enraged by the terrible thing he had just witnessed but his anger had affected his aim and his first shot missed as Król continued to flee, shooting his semi-automatic wildly over his shoulder as he ran.

Slowly, Roper took aim and fired again. This time though he did not miss. He brought Król down just short of the Range Rover with a bullet to the leg.

Jake, still fearing for Lizzie, saw Król fall but was astounded as the Polish assassin continued firing, seemingly immune to the pain of the wound which was pissing blood, like oil from a pierced barrel.

A shot narrowly missed Coyle, keeping him pinned down, but Eckhart leapt free of the cover and rushed forward, growling like some insane beast, firing his police issue pistol at the injured, yet still extremely dangerous Pole, some distance away.

Król's attention was forced onto Eckhart as his charging figure sped towards him. As Król dragged himself backwards, his injured limb completely useless, Roper Coyle could see from his vantage point that the wounded man had the look about him of a trapped animal, still dangerous, still angry and clearly determined not to surrender. Król raised the semi-automatic as Dave Eckhart's rushing form loomed above him and was rewarded to hear the click of the sergeant's spent weapon as he desperately

413

tried to fire off another round, all his others having somehow missed. Król smiled. This was too easy.

But as his finger closed around the trigger, Fabian Król's fight finally ended as Coyle shot him dead. Blood pooled from the neat, round hole in the centre of Król's chest as he slumped lifelessly into the mud, the shock in his eyes still clear to see.

Coyle rushed over to Król and kicked his firearm away before making certain that he was dead. Eckhart stood panting above the body, suddenly aware of how close to dying he had come.

"You were very brave there, Dave," Roper said to him. "But not too bright."

"Yep." Eckhart said. He couldn't have agreed more.

* * *

Peter Bearing scrambled madly over the uneven ground, his hand made Italian loafers slipping in the mud and the trousers of his immaculately cut suit all smeared with dirt.

Somehow he made it back to the Range Rover, where he cowered behind the open boot, sheltering from the hail of bullets that were buzzing like flies between Coyle and Król. One struck the brake light just above his head and ricocheted off, narrowly missing his temple, as the glass exploded over him, forcing him to cower even lower.

As he crouched behind the car, he glanced up into the open boot and saw the long black package, bound with brown parcel tape, that had the distinct shape of a body lying on its side with its knees up and Bearing inexplicably knew that's what it was. With awakening fear, an instinctive feeling deep in the pit of his stomach also told him who it was and suddenly he was desperate to find out for sure.

Staying low, he reached up to the head of the package and tugged vigorously at the plastic which after some struggle, finally ripped open. Peter tore it wide apart to reveal a hole the size of a dinner plate and was horrified to be confronted by the gruesome image of Anya's grey, lifeless face; her cold, vacant eyes staring straight at him from the hole in the plastic cocoon.

The vomit rose quickly in Bearing's throat as he threw up behind the car, surprised by how much her death affected him or, indeed, at finally realising how much she had actually meant to him. They were kindred spirits, she and him, if Peter ever allowed himself to believe such overly emotional hogwash. However, at the back of his mind, he also felt strangely vindicated. He had never really accepted Król's story about Anya not turning up at the mews house in Chelsea as agreed, or, indeed, Arthur's theory that she had chosen to go shopping instead.

Anya was not prone to flights of fancy and when she set out to do something, she invariably did it.

As he contemplated Król's role in all of this, Bearing wiped his mouth with the back of his hand, removing any last remnants of puke along with the brief moment of sentimentality he felt as a result of her passing.

Composing himself once more, he stared into the girl's dead eyes. "Oh, Anya," he said flatly, "You really were a nasty little girl, weren't you? What did you do to make Król want to kill you?"

Only then did he become aware that the shooting had stopped and that several people were now surrounding him. He turned quickly hoping to make a run for it but immediately realised it would be futile as four armed policemen stood menacingly over him.

"Well, well, well," said one big, kevlar-vested constable, "What exactly have we got here?"

Peter Bearing was still cowering behind the open boot as that same member of Coyle's team slapped on the handcuffs.

* * *

Coyle searched about him, looking for Jake, but he was nowhere to be seen. "Gibson!" He shouted to the man cuffing Bearing, "Have you seen Sawyer?"

"Yes, Guv." Said the officer. "He ran into the building after Khan - I think Sergeant Eckhart's just gone in there too."

Chapter 48

Arthur Khan was very nearly carrying Lizzie as he hurried into the deserted building. Dragging her roughly through the maze of construction debris, passed stacks of wood and piles of breeze block, passed cement mixers and scaffolding. Lizzie resisted as much as she could but Khan was strong and determined and her efforts were useless.

It was dark inside the building but enough illumination was seeping in from the halogen work lights outside for Arthur to navigate a way through.

He found an open sided works elevator with a mesh cage door, there was a wheel barrow inside and several sacks of cement. Arthur dragged Lizzie into it and pulled the door closed. A makeshift control box hung from a cable with a red button and a green button. Arthur punched the green one, marked *start* and the elevator rattled and shook into life as it rose steadily upwards. Up through the ceiling of the ground floor and upwards through the centre spine of the unfinished structure.

Jake arrived just as the elevator was disappearing through the ceiling of the first floor. "Lizzie!" he shouted.

"Jake - I'm here, help me!" She called back, but then Khan pressed the muzzle of the Magnum hard up under her chin, "Not another word." He snarled.

Jake was frantic, he didn't know what to do. The building was enormous and if Khan rode the elevator all the way up then there was no way Jake could get to Lizzie in time. He watched helpless as the lift ascended up through the rudimentary shaft, dragging a thick rope in its wake that was obviously tied to it as a some sort of safety precaution. Jake then glanced down to the space below his feet. He was standing on the edge of the area immediately below the elevator and saw the long rope rapidly uncoiling like a big, thick snake. Without thinking about the consequences, Jake suddenly sprang onto the rope and lashed it around one of his wrists, then quickly linked it around one of his ankles, securing himself as safely as he could, although leaving an arm and a leg dangling freely as the elevator dragged him violently upwards behind it.

The elevator continued to rise sharply. Ten floors, twenty, Lizzie could not be sure. She only knew that Jake was now a long way below her and her chances of being rescued diminishing with every passing level.

In actuality, Jake was hanging no more than three floors below her, the rope already burning red grooves into his wrist and ankle, but he was clinging on for dear life, trying to stop himself from looking down at the ever increasing drop below him.

Thirty, forty, sixty more floors up they went, the scale of the building utterly staggering. Then, on the sixty-fifth floor, the elevator eventually stopped with a loud metallic clang. Khan slid open the mesh door and pushed Lizzie out onto the top level of the building which was clearly nowhere near completion. The majority of the metal skeleton was in place but it was still exposed to the elements aside from some plastic sheeting which was flapping like the sails of a galleon on the high seas. There were no windows fitted as yet, just huge empty frames that allowed in the fresh night air.

There were stacks of brick and timber littered all over the cement floor. The open sides had no hand rails just a wooden plank walkway beyond the edge of the building itself, laid down across the exterior scaffold which allowed workmen to move around carefully on the outer edge.

Meanwhile, three floors below, Jake was hanging precariously on the rope, his grip starting to slip.

* * *

It was much cooler up here and the wind stronger but all that concerned Lizzie was Arthur Khan and how she was going to get out of this predicament.

Now Khan was up here he did not seem to have any idea of what to do next. He forced Lizzie to the ground and told her not to move then, still keeping a close eye on her, he quickly explored the immediate area. But it did not take him long to realise what Lizzie already suspected; that they were trapped and she was his only way off this building. The only card he had left to play.

Khan returned to where Lizzie was laying and placed a foot firmly on her chest to keep her from escaping. He then ejected the clip from his Magnum and checked how many rounds he had left. This revealed more bad news. Two cartridges, that was all he had. He had to make them count.

* * *

Jake's arms were throbbing badly as he clung desperately to the rope but his hands were now sweaty and slippery and even though the rope was coiled around one of his wrists he was steadily sliding further down. The skin around the lashed wrist had blistered and burst and blood was dripping down his arm. His leg, which had previously been entwined around the rope, felt painful too although that had unlinked itself moments before the elevator halted and both legs now dangled freely. Jake knew that it was just a very short matter of time before he plummeted to the ground some sixty floors down.

His only option was to try to swing onto the nearest level which was maybe ten or twelve feet below him.

Cautiously, he began to swing, slowly building up the momentum, dreading the point when he would actually have to release because that would be it, the moment that would not only determine his life or death but also the one to either increase or permanently end Lizzie's chances of being rescued.

Gradually, as the momentum gained speed, Jake carefully uncoiled his hand from the rope. Swinging as close to the side wall of the shaft as the rope would allow and trying to accurately gauge the trajectory of his fall. Finally, with as much courage as he could muster, he took a deep breath and let go.

For a second it seemed like he was going to make it but the awful truth was that he was just a few inches too short. Desperately he reached out as his body slammed hard into the concrete wall of the shaft immediately below the ledge of the opening. His breath was knocked out of him as his hands scrambled to find something, anything, to stop himself from plunging into the dark abyss below.

Frantically his ever slipping fingers searched around as the shaft dragged him backwards. At last his right hand fastened on a thin, black cable but he clung to it madly as he dropped back into the shaft, falling unimpeded to his certain death hundreds of feet below. But then, miraculously, his fall was arrested as the cable became taught and firm allowing Jake to grab onto it with his left hand as well. Again he slammed into the concrete wall of the shaft, his elbows and knees taking the brunt of the impact, but this time he was in the middle of two levels. Nevertheless, he clung on precariously but determinedly, his body racked with pain, as he tried to work out his next move.

However, that was quickly made for him as the cable suddenly seemed to lose purchase on its anchor and Jake slowly started to slide down the wall to the level below. Two seconds later, he was hanging directly in the opening to the fifty-eighth floor and he felt sure if he could just cling on for another couple of seconds he could swing into safety. But at that very moment, whatever the cable was anchored to broke free completely and Jake dropped violently again. This time though, he landed on his stomach on the concrete floor of the level with his legs still dangling in the shaft. As the cable continued to fall, Jake desperately hauled himself in completely, just in time to avoid being hit by an enormous, very heavy, circular saw that the cable was attached to, which sped past the opening at a rapid rate of descent.

For a few moments, Jake lay there on the floor, breathing a huge sigh of relief. But then, almost immediately, his thoughts turned once again to Lizzie.

* * *

From six floors beneath where Lizzie was being held, Jake heard the sound of another elevator clang to a halt somewhere off in the dark, maybe a few floors down and as he began his ascent to the top, scampering up ladder after ladder, moving as quickly as he dare over the small scaffold platforms that supported them, he could also hear footsteps behind him. It was the definite sound of someone else climbing the ladders below, somewhere down on a lower level, and he prayed to God that it was Roper Coyle.

* * *

Earlier that evening, Jake had taken a huge gamble in calling Scotland Yard and speaking to Detective Chief Inspector Coyle, not really knowing whether he could trust him or not. But he needed help and did not know where else to turn. Aaron Sumpter clearly had faith in Coyle and from what Lizzie had told him, Sumpter's judgement was invariably sound.

Nonetheless, upon speaking with him over the phone, Coyle had convinced Jake that he could be trusted and after much discussion managed to allay all the doubts about his honesty.

Furthermore, Coyle suggested that he and Jake should to meet up quickly to discuss how best to save Lizzie and apprehend Bearing and Khan - preferably whilst they were taking possession of the diamonds, which had been Sumpter's plan all along.

So, an hour later, Roper and a small team of techies arrived via the rear entrance of The Dorchester and were shown directly to Jake's suite where they sat down to discuss a plan for the evening ahead.

* * *

Until ten minutes ago, everything had gone as planned - both with Jake's rendezvous and with Coyle's timely intervention at the crucial moment. However, matters had taken a terrible turn for the worse. Lizzie was now in even greater peril and Jake was pursuing her completely unarmed and almost blind in the dark, half finished building.

Jake was shattered and sweating profusely in the heavy woollen jumper, his legs and arms aching desperately as he climbed up the last few ladders to the top level of the building. He had slowed now, taking care to make as little sound as possible and trying to keep his exhausted breathing under control as he gradually ascended the final ladder, hoping not to alert Khan to his presence.

Very carefully he pushed his head up through the large square gap in the ceiling, which would eventually form a stairwell, his eyes barely over the parapet when a shot exploded just inches from his head, blasting away a huge chunk of the wooden framework and smashing loudly into a concrete support beyond. Quickly Jake ducked back down. He had obviously made more noise than he'd hoped - no doubt due to the dramatic events in the lift shaft. And as a result, Khan had clearly been expecting him.

"Come out here slowly, Sawyer!" Khan shouted. "With your hands up where I can see them."

"I'm not armed," Jake called back, "I just want Lizzie, that's all."

"How very romantic. Now come on out here, before I lose my patience."

Tentatively, Jake pushed his head back up over the parapet.

"Hands up. Quickly!" Khan shouted.

Jake did as instructed, climbing out onto the top floor with his hands held high. He could just see Lizzie and Khan, several feet away in the darkness, close to the edge of the building. Khan was using her as a shield.

"That's it, Sawyer. Very good. Now walk very slowly towards me." Khan said. And again, Jake did as instructed.

* * *

Twenty feet below, Eckhart heard the report from Khan's gun as if it had been fired right next to him, loud, explosive and deadly.

Dave had followed Jake into the building, knowing that he had to put an end to this situation one way or another. If Khan hadn't already ended it then he would have to, it was the only possible solution.

He had found an alternative works elevator, further into the lower level, that took him only up as far as the fiftieth floor. But now he was just two floors

425

below and realised that if he continued up the same way as Jake it could be suicidal. He did not want to accidentally catch a stray bullet from Khan. He'd had quite enough of that from Król just a few minutes earlier. Król had been the one that had recruited Dave in the first place, sucked him into this whole messy quagmire of guilt, greed and betrayal and for a moment, Dave had seen red. He had just wanted to kill the evil, tattooed Pole, to silence him once and for all. But he had failed and had nearly been killed in the process. But now he had cooled down and was resolved to do what he knew he must.

Quickly, he scanned the murky darkness around him and could see no other way up to the roof. But then he glimpsed what looked like another set of ladders on the exterior scaffolding, outside the building itself, which presented him with alternative route.

* * *

Two floors above, Jake was speaking. "It's useless Khan," he said. "The building is surrounded by armed police - Bearing has been arrested and the Polish guy, is dead. There's no escape. It's over."

"You're wrong, Sawyer. It's not over. Not by a long way. Me and your girlfriend are getting out of here."

"How? There's no way out, nowhere you can go."

"Wrong again. You're getting us out of here - you and your friends in the police."

"Please, I don't know what you mean - just let Lizzie go and we can talk about it."

"Listen, she's not going anywhere. Not until I get a helicopter and the diamonds."

"A what?" Jake exclaimed, "There's no way I can–"

"If you don't want her to die," Khan interjected, "you'll do as I say."

"But how? You want me to go back down and–"

"You're staying right here where I can see you, Sawyer."

"But how then? How can I–"

"Call them on the phone. Tell them what I want and tell them I want it now before one of you dies."

"Okay, okay," Jake said. "I'll do it. But please, let Lizzie go. I'll stay. Take me instead of her."

"What, and have only one hostage when I can have two? Why on earth would I want to do that? No, Sawyer, you'll both stay right here until I get my diamonds and a helicopter. So make the call."

"But I don't have my phone - it's down there, in my rucksack."

"Jesus Christ, Sawyer - you're really starting to try my patience," Khan said with exasperation. "Here, come and get mine. Slowly though, mind. Very slowly, keeping your hands exactly where I can see them."

With the muzzle of the gun pushed into Lizzie's cheek, Khan reached into his coat pocket with his free hand and pulled out his mobile phone.

He held it out to Jake, who, out of the corner of his eye, had just seen Detective Sergeant Dave Eckhart appear into view, on the outer edge of the building. However, Jake was surprised to see that Eckhart seemed to be pointing his gun not at Khan but directly at him.

* * *

Coyle was on the ground floor looking up when he heard the faint sound of the shot being fired and saw a tiny white flash briefly flicker from somewhere up on the sixty-fifth floor. He had sent an armed team in prior to that and they were now swarming up through the tall spine of the building in full body armour but it would be a long time before they reached the roof.

Now, several minutes later, Coyle desperately hoped he was not too late. He was worried about Eckhart and his eagerness to be involved in the operation. His young sergeant was quite obviously stressed and suffering from anxiety but he had been keen to be a part of it and Roper could not deny him. The lad clearly wanted to prove himself and Coyle understood that. Eckhart's near fatal suicide dash towards Król notwithstanding.

Coyle looked about him. So far, the operation had only been partially successful. Peter Bearing was sitting in the back of a squad car in handcuffs and Fabian Król, who was a known associate of Arthur

Khan was dead. He would not be missed. The body of a young girl had also been discovered in the back of the Range Rover and her murder would be added to those already committed in Bearing's single-minded pursuit of the diamonds.

But also a young police officer had lost his life and Roper felt a tremendous burden of responsibility for that. He would inform the lad's family personally.

Three ambulances had appeared at the scene moments earlier to collect the bodies and Coyle hoped, with the operation still far from over, and with the unexpected turn of events, that more would not be needed.

He looked up again, squinting into the darkness from the well lit ground, through a pair of binoculars trying to spot any movement.

It was then that he saw someone, very high up, shrouded in darkness, climbing precariously around the outside scaffolding at the lip of the roof. Someone that looked very much like Dave Eckhart.

* * *

Eckhart was pointing his gun directly at Jake as he loomed silently out of the darkness behind Khan and up onto the lip of the roof. For a moment Jake stiffened with fear.

However, the gun was only aimed at him briefly as Dave sought to get a better foothold. As soon as he had, he trained the gun onto Khan and signalled for Jake, who breathed a sigh of relief, to get ready.

Jake was almost in touching distance of the mobile phone that Khan was holding out to him, although he now had one eye on Eckhart waiting for him to make his move.

He did not have to wait long because as Jake was about to take the phone, Eckhart said, "Freeze, Khan. Move so much as a whisker and I'll shoot."

Khan visibly tightened, inadvertently dropping the mobile phone, doing as he was told as Eckhart climbed onto the roof and positioned himself a few feet to the side of him, the gun pointed out in front and clasped expertly with both hands.

"Put the gun down, Khan," Dave said. "There's no way out, you're completely surrounded. Just slowly put it down and let the girl go."

"So, the worm has turned," said Khan. "Did you know, Sawyer, that this young man was very nearly responsible for getting you killed today? That all that lovely evidence that Sumpter collected was destroyed as a direct result of this policeman's betrayal of you and of his superiors?"

"Shut up, Khan!" Barked Eckhart.

Jake looked directly at Eckhart, as did Lizzie.

"You?" Lizzie said to Eckhart. "You told them about the evidence?"

Eckhart looked ashamedly at her, not able to meet her eyes.

"But of course," Khan said. "Everything you had on us is gone, thanks to this fine upstanding officer."

"I told you to shut up!" Eckhart snapped again.

"What?" Khan said gleefully, "And spoil the surprise?"

"It's no surprise," said Jake. "I know all about it. I know everything. The sergeant here is working with me now. And as for the evidence, well let's just say it's safe. You're finished Khan and there's nowhere left to go."

"You're lying," Khan said.

"You know I'm not," replied Jake. "Do you really think I would be this calm if this was the first I'd heard of it? Eckhart made a mistake, that's all. He's now put it right. Now drop the gun like he said. It's over."

After a moment of contemplation, Khan suddenly roared with anger and spun round violently, his shiny chrome Desert Eagle aimed straight at Eckhart as he fired. At the very same moment, Dave fired too and Jake reached out, grabbed Lizzie's hand and pulled her free of Khan, pushing her to safety behind him.

Eckhart jerked sharply as the bullet smashed into him at such close range then, almost instantly, dropped like a stone, his legs buckling underneath him, no longer able to support the weight.

Khan was hit too and he staggered backwards, his heels right on the lip of the building, his arms windmilling as he tried desperately to maintain his balance and stop himself from falling. The Magnum flying from his grip and out into the night. But momentum was working against him as he began to topple over. Somehow, though he managed to snatch Jake's hand, who, taken by surprise, suddenly had to use all the strength in his legs and arms to prevent himself from being dragged over the edge by Khan.

Jake skidded on the dusty cement floor, stopping mere inches from the edge as Lizzie grabbed his free hand and pulled back with all her might, her body near horizontal as she fought to stop him going over.

"Jake!" She screamed.

Khan still had hold of Jake's other hand as he was suspended over the drop, sixty-five floors above the ground, nothing between him and the cold mud below except fresh air. The blood from the bullet wound in his side dripping down into the darkness.

"Help me!" Khan cried. "Help me, Sawyer please! Don't let me die, not like this. I'll go to prison, do whatever you want - confess to whatever you want, but please don't let me fall."

Jake could feel Arthur's grip slipping and there was nothing he could do. Nothing he wanted to do.

"Help me!" Khan shouted again, as his grip slipped to just Jake's fingertips.

Jake looked into Khan's terrified face and spoke coldly. "You said you remembered the look in my boy's eyes when you killed him. Well now I'm going to remember the look in yours." Jake then jerked his hand away sharply so Khan could no longer hold on and the man who murdered Jake's family fell back into the vacuum of night, his blood curdling scream heard all the way down to the ground.

Chapter 49

Back on the ground floor, paramedics were wheeling a stretcher across the uneven terrain towards their ambulance. On the stretcher Detective Sergeant Dave Eckhart had a blanket over him and was being provided with air from a plastic mask covering his nose and mouth.

He had lost a lot of blood from the gunshot wound in his shoulder. The .357 cartridge, shot at such close range, penetrating the kevlar vest and travelling straight through his shoulder and out the other side. Should proof have ever been needed against Arthur Khan, it was the same calibre of bullet, shot from the very same gun that had killed the Sawyer family and Richard Maddox. But Khan was now dead.

Dave had told Coyle everything after Jake called Scotland Yard earlier. He had admitted keeping the initial five hundred pounds given to him by Król and admitted phoning Peter Bearing about the evidence at

Sumpter's house. He knew that he had been a terrible fool and was truly sorry. Dave offered his resignation and said he would accept any punishment that was handed out as a result of his actions.

However, Coyle was a pragmatist. He had also been young once, with a young wife and understood the stress that came with juggling married life with police work. He also had a soft spot for Eckhart and knew, even though he had made a serious error and had shown extremely poor judgement in this matter, that he was actually a very good and bright detective. So he had decided to give him a second chance, particularly as the evidence that had been destroyed was backed-up elsewhere. Furthermore, the gift of the five hundred pounds could not be proved and Coyle could see no reason to take the matter further. Eckhart had learnt his lesson, he felt sure of it.

When Roper met up with Jake at The Dorchester he told him what had happened and gave Jake his word that the same thing would not happen again. Jake had shaken his hand, instinctively trusting Coyle and deferring to his judgement.

Now, several hours later, Roper saw his sergeant on the gurney and walked briskly over.

"You did good up there, Dave," he said.

Eckhart looked up at him, clearly in a lot of pain, unable to speak because of the mask over his mouth. Tears welling in his eyes.

"Get well soon, detective." Coyle added, patting

Dave's arm as he was loaded into the ambulance. Then, speaking to the paramedics, he said, "Take good care of him, lads. He's one of the good guys."

* * *

Jake and Lizzie were sitting on the back of another ambulance. Lizzie had a blanket over her shoulders and looked a little worse for wear but otherwise she was okay. Jake had his newly bandaged arm protectively around her as Coyle wandered over to them. "Want to have some fun?" He asked.

"Sure," Lizzie said, "I haven't had enough of that tonight yet."

Roper smiled at her sarcasm. "Follow me then." He replied.

The three of them walked over to the squad car in which Peter Bearing was still sitting, handcuffed in the back seat.

Coyle opened the door. "Tell them what you told me," he said to Bearing.

"What?" Bearing said with disgust. "I have not said anything and nor will I until I speak with my solicitor. You have nothing on me Inspector. Not a thing. Just a suitcase that I know nothing about. I had no knowledge of what was happening here tonight and you have no proof to the contrary. As for the dead girl, well that cannot be pinned on me either as I suspect young Miss Barnes here will be able to verify. So whilst you may be enjoying your moment in the sun now, I can assure you by tomorrow morning you will be singing an entirely different song. I will be free and you will be looking for a job in a security firm. I have influential friends, Inspector, and I fully intend to make use of them to ensure that you never work for the police again."

Coyle was smiling broadly as he said to Lizzie and Jake, "See, I told you it was going to be fun."

They were now grinning too as Bearing spoke again. "I don't know what you are all finding so funny, but I can assure you, you will not be so cheerful tomorrow."

"Tell him," Coyle said to Jake. "Let Mister Bearing in on the joke."

Jake cleared his throat for dramatic effect, "Tell him about the evidence, you mean?"

"What evidence?" Bearing asked pompously, "You have no evidence."

"Oh, but we do." Jake said. "Lot's of it. Tons. Enough to put you away for years."

"What? Rubbish!" Bearing said, now looking slightly concerned.

"No. All true." Jake said. "All that evidence that you thought Khan and Król destroyed well, guess what? There was another copy."

"I don't believe it. You're lying." Bearing spat.

"You think?" Jake said, reaching into the pocket of his jeans and pulling out the data stick. "It's all on here. Everything. Every fact, every detail. Proof of corruption, of funding illegal wars, of trading and smuggling black-market diamonds and of fraud."

Bearing was visibly shocked.

"Show him what else," smiled Coyle.

"What else?" Said Bearing, still trying to comprehend the enormity of what he was hearing.

"You mean this?" Jake said, pulling up his jumper to reveal a small black recorder taped to his chest. "Every self incriminating word you and Bearing have said tonight, all recorded on tape for posterity. Proof of murder and blackmail, by your own boastful confession."

Peter Bearing glared at him murderously.

"I think Aaron would be proud, don't you, Lizzie?" Jake said.

Lizzie beamed. "I think he would be very proud indeed," she said and kissed him on the cheek.

"I demand to speak to my solicitor," Bearing squawked, "I will not say another word until I have spoken with him."

"Speak no more," Coyle said. "We don't care. We've got everything we need right here. You're going away for a very, very long time Peter and there's not a damn thing you can do about it."

Bearing gritted his teeth but said nothing. He knew Coyle was right.

Roper shut the car door and tapped the roof. "Okay," he said to the officer behind the wheel, "Take him away, we've done with him now."

* * *

438

As Jake, Lizzie and Coyle wandered back to the ambulance, Jake said, "What about me, Inspector - will I be prosecuted now? Will I have to go to prison?"

"I'm fairly sure you won't, Jake." Replied Coyle. "You've done well here - brought down a really bad guy and helped bring in an enormous consignment of illegal diamonds - admittedly a bit belatedly. You've also secured me the biggest coup of my career. So I think we can sort it so you get off with just a rap on the knuckles. You and Miss Barnes here have suffered enough."

"Thank you Inspector," said Jake.

"Yes, thank you," Lizzie echoed. "But I do still have one question."

"You do?" Said Coyle.

"Yes. It's about Aaron. About how we left him in The Bahamas - how we're probably now wanted for his murder and how–" suddenly Lizzie choked with emotion. "How we had to leave him there, with no funeral and no kind words spoken about him. He saved us, Inspector. He's the reason why Peter Bearing is going to prison. The reason for the biggest coup of your career. It's all thanks to Aaron."

Jake put his arm round her as she broke down in tears, the grief of Aaron's loss hitting her in a fresh wave now everything was over.

"Don't worry," Coyle said. "I will speak with the Bahamian authorities and explain everything. I'm sure it will be fine. And as for a funeral - well what's

439

to stop you having one now?"

Lizzie smiled, then leaned over and kissed Roper on the cheek. "Thank you, Inspector. For everything."

Epilogue

Three years later. New Providence, The Bahamas.

Lizzie bent down and placed the flowers on the grave of the man who had saved her. Her brother, in everything other than birth.

It was another beautiful day. The sky a cloudless glorious blue as the sun beat down upon the aquamarine ocean below. The cemetary sat on a cliff overlooking the sea and offered a spectacular view of the Caribbean. The grave faced the ocean, positioned precisely to catch the first rays of the morning sun.

Lizzie walked up here at least once a month with her extremely active two year old who was always busy exploring and getting into mischief.

Soon there would be another little one, in just five short months - a girl this time, who they were going to call Ella, after her mother who had sadly passed away prior to Lizzie meeting Jake.

Lizzie placed a hand on her swollen tummy and was rewarded by a little kick and she smiled, delightedly.

She need not have worried three years ago about facing murder charges in The Bahamas. Roper Coyle had been as good as his word and had smoothed everything out. As it transpired, Lizzie and Jake would not have been held accountable for the murder anyway as a hair from Fabian Król's beard was found embedded in the wound in Sumpter's neck, which offered perfect DNA evidence and near conclusive proof that Król was the killer.

Lizzie had been allowed to give Aaron the funeral he deserved and she spoke eloquently at the service. Once again, the only representative of the Wallace family. Now she was the only one left. The only adult anyway. Her little boy and her unborn daughter would be Wallace's by birth and heirs to the enormous fortune that their mother had inherited but they would bear a different surname to their grandfather.

"Come on, Aaron!" Lizzie called to her little boy who came scampering out from behind a grave, a great big grin on his face. "Let's go and see Daddy. See how he's getting on."

* * *

Jake was busy finishing paintings for his second collection which was due to be shown in San Francisco in a few months time. Just about the time the baby was due in fact, but Jake would be at the birth, there was no way he was going to miss that.

The first exhibition of his work had been a tremendous success and Jake had sold every single painting. He had always enjoyed working with oil and canvas but years ago when he was struggling to make a living, the design side just somehow took over. But he had rediscovered it during his enforced exile and had continued with it since getting married to Lizzie who had encouraged him all the way.

Now he had commissions from all over the world and his work had very quickly become extremely sought after as Lizzie suspected it would from the very first time she saw it.

Jake was just putting the finishing touches to his latest work when he saw his wife and son coming across the lawn towards his studio.

He waved and Aaron came running to him. "Hello, boy!" He said, sweeping him up in his arms. "Have you been good for Mummy?"

Aaron nodded and Lizzie confirmed it with a kiss on his forehead then gave one to Jake too, on the lips, just for good measure."

"You ready for your nap now, honey?" Lizzie asked her son and again he nodded.

"Uh-huh. I'm tired, Mummy."

"I know, sweetie. Let's go and get you settled then Mummy and Daddy can have a rest too."

Jake gave his son a kiss then watched as Lizzie took him off to his bed for an afternoon nap. A quarter of an hour later, Lizzie and Jake met up in the light, spacious kitchen of their beautiful island home.

"He go off okay?" Jake asked.

"Yeah. He's fast asleep."

"Good. He's had a busy day."

"He sure has. Do you want some lunch, honey?" Lizzie asked.

"No, thanks."

"A swim then - I've got the monitor I can put it out by the pool?"

"No."

"What do you want to do then?" Lizzie looked at her husband and saw the wicked glint in his eye. "Oh, I see - that's what you wanna do. Well come on then, Limey, before that son of yours wakes up," she giggled.

Jake walked over, with fake machismo, and picked her up. "Right, Yank - let me show you again what us Englishmen can do!"

Lizzie laughed mischievously as Jake carried her off to their bedroom and placed her gently on their huge four-poster bed.

"Ravage me then, you beast - but make it quick, I've got to organise dinner in an hour or two!"

They made love, as they did on most afternoons, revelling in each others company, enjoying the simple pleasure of being together and of being blissfully happy.

* * *

In a wall safe, at the opposite end of the bedroom, hidden behind Lizzie's favourite painting that Jake had done of her, sat an enormous diamond, the size of a large acorn. It was flawless, perfect in clarity, cut and colour. The value priceless. But it would never be sold, never traded. It was a blood diamond and the term was completely apt. Much blood had been spilled because of this and others like it. But Lizzie and Jake kept it as a reminder of what was once owed.

The debt had now been paid.

THE END

About The Author

Kris Lillyman is based in Northamptonshire, England and has worked as a freelance graphic designer and illustrator for over twenty-five years. He is married with two grown up children.

In addition to adult thrillers, he also writes and illustrates children's books - to find out more about these, please visit:

www.krislillyman.com

Alternatively, search 'Kris Lillyman' in iTunes, Amazon, Barnes & Noble or most other online bookstores.